Satya's Truths

Iain Dryden.

DEDICATION.
I pledge Satya's Truths to Camilla, my wife and to all who walk El Camino..

ACKNOWLEDGEMENTS.
I would like to thank the respected documentary maker Harsh Varma and his wife Rekha for inspiring me to consider writing this novel set in their extraordinary land. Thank you Camilla, your penetrating advice, positive criticism and suffering multiple rereads as the manuscript evolved, has been invaluable. Thank you - Stephanie & Patrick Early for your piercing insights and encouragement; Dawn & Hugh for your edit; David Dawson for your flurries of brilliance. Joining the debate over which version of the first page was suitable, I thank - Robert Thompson, Alec Dawson-Shepherd, Sue Bowles, Colin Chambers and Nathalie & Matt van der Haven, as well as internet votes. Finally, I would like to thank Sophie Chambers and her friend Shazia for helping me with proof reading.

Accepting ourselves as we are, with all of our shadows and shine, we understand what it is to be human. Here begins the journey of properly relating to others with empathy - for this is how we truly come alive.

Ten thousand eyes bobbing along the pavements took in tourists, but ignored him. This ought to have made him feel at home after all he knew about the country, yet he felt alien. Several incomprehensible languages clanged his ears. Radios fought yelling vendors who sat cross-legged on the pavement, calculating profits on-screen after each transaction. Perspiration trickled down his cheeks, soaking his neck, tickling his chest. Undoing a shirt button, he took a deep breath, held it, let the polluted air out - an Aikido trick which normally worked, but his heart kept racing.

What a whirlpool - there a barefoot man in traditional clothes, here a brisk woman gabbling into a smartphone and that old couple in acres of flowing cotton strolling across a buzzing road whilst scrolling the news on a shared tablet! Coconut oil in women's hair momentarily replaced smells he couldn't define, some sweet, some which itched his throat, others making him retch. Two dogs fought in a cloud of dust. In the tree above screeching parakeets dislodged a purple flower which floated down and tickled his nose. Damn my protruding nose!

His head spun as he struggled to sync this invasive reality with the ancient land he had absorbed at a distance since childhood. He looked at his watch. Why? Time no longer matters. 'Routine is a thing of the past... I can do or become whatever I want, but, used to discipline, this freedom frightens me.' Leaning against a wall, he scanned the bustling streets, seeking a hotel, not that his leather courier-bag was heavy, he'd packed lightly, convinced life as a fugitive would keep him moving. Half an hour before his plane landed, waking from a troubled night, he had sketched a fellow passenger. It was nervy, yet satisfying - brown wriggles tumbling over slender shoulders, moody eyes searing his paper; beneath it he'd scribbled: *What a mess I'm in!* Closing his sketchpad, he'd looked through the oval portal. Sparkling teeth bit the dawn and ripples of elation flowed across his tight chest. Wow, The Himalayas!

A sharp voice, "Relaxing good!"

Ewan's eyes shot open, "Sorry? Beg your pardon."

"Ho! You looking rich local, but voice foreign! You liking here? Much to see. Many ruin. Too much choice. Come! Me show you many place."

Blast! but be polite. This is my first conversation here. "Err, thank you, but I only recently landed. Sorry."

"Sorry excellent if I sick mother having, or my car broken. This instance, no need sorrying. I muchly happy taking many place."

"Err, no thank you, I'm, err, rather occupied."

"You Britisher."

Ewan blinked, guilt ridden with ancestral crimes. "Unfortunately."

"No unfortune. Without your excellent type, this country bamboozled. Snowflake in sun."

"Hmm..." Trying to ignore the yapping, Ewan took another deep breath.

Noticing the stilling exercise, "You like drug? I having excellent drug."

"Gosh no! NO thank you." The guy's a pain, why be PC?

"Don't drug? So seeing special shop," the tout smiled at the alliteration and, inspired, continued. "Exceptional export expertise. Brilliant bargain bundles! Plenty present purchasing." The man laid his hand on Ewan's bare arm, "Come."

"Let go!"

The hustler jumped back. "No offencing! Simply making money - childs many. You childs?"

"Leave me alone!" Ewan stomped along the traffic-crazed avenue. Gosh, it's hot and still February. No wonder my ancestors made for the hills. Tying to gather his jet-lagged brain, he focused on a point ahead, took a deep breath, held it, let it out as he walked. Nothing. What to do when everything you have treasured and known has gone because you have fled to another continent? Your personal history has no relevance anymore. You stand alone, without purpose.

Drivers honking, yelling, waving fists from open windows as they entered or left a circular road. A man in a three-wheeler streaked across the mayhem, risking his flesh to gain attention. Shaking his head, Ewan turned from the man's half-mad stare and saw, held beyond the frenzy, a park. Knowing an unfortunate driver who had hit a holy cow could face mob rule, Ewan crossed with a grey beast which was oblivious to the deranged traffic.

Leaning against a stout tree, he unzipped his large leather weekend-bag. His sticky fingers lingered on a cool plastic folder containing photocopied sections from his ancestors' letters, diaries and artwork. During his depressing childhood, they'd become friends and had inspired him to work for international cooperation, they'd made him wish his life wasn't bound by his rigid family with its long and often disturbing history.

He removed a neat rosewood box, released a silver clasp, lifted the lid, withdrew a silk pouch. Out slipped a miniature Mughal painting. For the umpteenth time he removed a yellowing note tacked to the back-frame. His ancestor's ink hand was beautiful. *"Our ideals and the systems they create have done much damage throughout history. These arrogant walls have closed us off from life, preventing us from seeing what is."* Ewan gaped at people in exotic clothes as he puzzled over the next sentence: *"How much better to discover the intelligence behind measured emotion, for it puts us in the midst of things, enabling us to devise a natural morality based on empathy."*

The words troubled him. Father used to bark: "Emotion weakens resolve!" Yet what feeling churns in my chest now, HELP, stop thinking! Stepping over tired grass, he headed for a stall-on-wheels. Wondering what the term *Bhang* meant attached to *Lassi,* he bought a glassful. The cooling liquid soon made him light headed. Hmm, must be a sort of yoghurt-beer. Really refreshing. He had another.

6

"Whoohoo, life's great!" He did a skip. 'I feel bright, safe. Have I ever felt this free? Am I hypnotised by the country? Is it because I'm unavoidably released from everything which bound me? Ha! Maybe it's the Bhang-Lassi?'

The smell of food caught him, he moved to a man squatting by a pyramid of eggs. Using signs, he ordered an omelette and watched the man break four eggs into a bowl, mix in blended tomatoes and spices, pour them over an iron plate laid over live coals. Excited, Ewan leaned closer, absently fiddling with his signet-ring. Without warning the family stamp slipped from his perspiring fingers and fell into the white-hot fire. Damn! He'd worn it since slipping it off Father's cold fingers. Using tongs, the cook removed the crest generations of Ewan's family had used. Ewan gawped at the unimpressive lump of gold containing shards of charcoal. He shrugged, Ha, ha! Family tradition melted. Hmm, I'm not usually so carefree, must be drunk.

The flecks of black pepper, diced chives, onions and tomatoes made him want to paint the omelette with the water-soluble blocks in his bag, but hunger drove him to squat and feast. Wow it's good, moist, full of taste, perfect. In a whizz of excitement, he handed over his distorted gold as payment to the astounded man. Ooh! Why am I behaving uncharacteristically? He drifted along with the fizzing swell of people in the park. Startling a man in a safari suit, he sang loudly, "This land's so good they named you twice! Bharat so ancient prancing beside microchip India!" Delighted with himself, he skipped like a clown. Hmm, I'm normally quite serious. Bhang lassi! Bhang lassi, what a great drink!

The sun struck anything unprotected and Ewan scurried from one patch of shade to another as the light shivered off dusty bushes, bounced from tired heads and was gripped by the path. Stepping from the swarm, he passed a gardener walking behind two grey cows pulling a mower across a smooth lawn. Elated, Ewan did a little dance. Interesting? I'm so upbeat! Brushing aside scarlet flowers, he settled against a tree in bloom, relishing its shelter. But a moment of angst swamped him, Damn my accidental crime! I'm adrift. My frailty is bared.

Fearing the emptiness of his unplanned exile would make him crazy, before leaving England he had decided it was a chance to reinvent himself by drawing and painting his forebears' movements across the Indian subcontinent. Ewan took out his sketchbook, but the intense light and unfamiliar subjects made him cautious, Hmm, my eye's attuned to England's grey shades and demure topics, easier to start with detail. His hard HB pencil caught sweaty lips, lacquered lips; drooping moustaches, peaky moustaches; tight beards, burly beards; rapid studies of people drinking: drips falling from clay cups or bottles which didn't touch their mouths. Ah. Germ free, how clever.

More at ease, with a softer 2B pencil he outlined silhouettes of smart office workers lingering in the shade, simple contours of families nibbling snacks under the trees. He got used to the exotic conditions and topics; his sketches contrasted women's colourful saris, bare arms, low necklines and exposed bellies to their menfolk virtually covered in white cotton. With a pen, he caught people buying glasses of tea from children bearing aluminium kettles. Child labour! Oh yes, loaned from debt-bonded families to that man to whom they keep handing loose change. Wishing to ease their troubled lives, tearing pages from his pad, he gave cartoons to these urchins and they giggled at themselves collecting empty glasses or wiping the used vessels with dirty rags.

The heat sapped his energy, he felt lazy, rather peculiar.

"Sahib-looking-tired." The woman tendering head massage reached him before the foot massage man. Ewan could think of nothing better in the intense heat and he reclined against the tree watching the masseuse. Eyes drooped with fatigue, she dropped her wooden box on the grass, hitched her worn but clean sari-skirt at her waist, flicked the battered lid open, removed a small bottle of oil, extracted the cork with her teeth, let a few drops fall onto her right palm, twisted her head to reinsert the cork, set the oil down and rubbed her palms together. Ewan flipped off his linen shirt

8

and with his arm crooked protectively around his beloved bag, let her work his scalp and shoulders and her expert fingers soon had him lose sight of the park.

An arm encircled his neck. His eyes shot open, a fist expanded before his eyes, pain, a foot struck his lower back. Red mist flooded his perception and, free as a leopard, he sprung after three men.

"STOP!" bellowed an old monk sitting in the lotus position.

Ewan's heavy bag swung round his torso.

"Enough. Hee-hee-hee."

Ewan slumped to the grass shivering uncontrollably as adrenaline swept through him, his sweat glands were in overdrive and he was gasping. The sadhu retrieved Ewan's discarded shirt and sandals, an act of humility in a land where it was degrading to touch another's footwear. Perhaps monks are beyond such rules? Quivering, Ewan fumbled with his leather bag. What luck, it hadn't been cut into.

Wow, I cast off three men when all I could see was red! OK, Aikido and rugby help, but is there more to it? And how did the old man made me halt? Oh yes, it's like a sergeant's high-pitched tone cutting through battle.

Taking a rag parcel from his shoulder bag, the sadhu winked, "Bhang?"

"BANG?"

"Bhang relaxing you." The rag held a cone-pipe filled with dried grass.

"Bhang!" Bhang lassi! Help, I've drunk a drug!

"You shaky muchly. Bhang stopping… helping-mind slowing."

"NO! I'm not taking drugs." Ewan stood up.

The sadhu wrapped the moist rag around the chillum's thin mouth, held it to his forehead and chanted, "Om, Ma Kali."

"Kali? The Gurkha goddess!" Recalling Father's tales, Ewan lingered.

"Kali my god." The old man held a lit match over the cone, puffed and dense green spilled from his lips. "Bhang taking sadhu... beyond-earth-mind. Bhang... calming." A rush of words, a head wobble, wide eyes.

The sweet cloud ignited a confusing memory. Working late in his London office to have Fridays off, over the years Ewan chatted to a young cleaner who loved reading. One evening a week ago, watching her mop the parquet floor, he realised how attractive she was. Unusually, she took a pack from her hip pocket and, opening a sash window, began rolling green shreds between two cigarette papers which she licked together. Heck! Smoking's banned. Stopping work, he watched thick smoke trickle from her nose. Beguiled, though confused by her uncharacteristic irreverence, he went over to enjoy her company. The smell, reminiscent of an autumnal bonfire, not the irritating tang of tobacco, was strangely alluring. Unexpectedly, she stepped forwards, traced his mouth with her forefinger. He gaped. Unused to young women due to boys' boarding school and a predominantly male working environment, he'd never noticed her hints. Parting her lips, she blew the heavy smoke into his open mouth; thrown by the unfamiliar turn of events, he gasped several times as she kept blowing. Quickly light headed, flustered, his innocent lips pulsing, he leaned towards her. A cleaning trolley clanking along the corridor stopped. The young woman dropped her roll-up out the window, huffed out the smoke. The office door partly opened, peeking in, her superior asked her something. Damn! Denied my First Kiss at my age. How sad is that!

The old smell and hurt softened him to the sadhu's billowing menace and alarmed his body was still out of control, he weakened. "OK, one puff." It took several attempts to get the technique - cupping both hands round the cloth and stem, sucking through the gap between thumbs; a violent coughing fit. The sadhu giggled. Each time he ingested a little more the dope eased his nerves, enveloping him in a haze of happiness. When the chillum was offered a second time, delighted, he accepted. "Yiihaa, haa!" I'm escaping my SOS - Stiff Outer Self. He chuckled, "Boggling bhang's like being merry on bounteous beer."

10

"Beer? Sadhu drink NO!"

Ewan chuckled. With his mind cleared of adrenaline, he mulled over his astounding response to the attack: instant animal adrenaline instantly turned off by an old sadhu. "Imagine harnessing that with Aikido!"

"I-kid-no!" The old guy stammered, "Sadhu... telling truth."

"He, he. We'll get along fine." Ewan tried a high-five, but missed.

"Weli-com India," the old man joined Ewan's half mad giggle.

Waving his hands in the air, Ewan sang: "India's been in my girth, since before my very birth." Startled by his barmy behaviour, he stopped. "Well, well, SOS certainly is slipping!"

"What this sos?"

"Silly old Self," chuckling, Ewan removed the rosewood box from his bag and withdrew the Mughal miniature. What pleasure those strong colours, clean lines, and the image itself. His first memory was of floating in to this masterpiece which always hung above his bed, of drifting round the twin domed temple, settling on those rounded rocks parting swirling waters, and dreaming of those sparkling Himalayan peaks.

ß

The light was fading as the sadhu slipped from the crowded medieval alleys and squeezed through a slit between buildings. Ewan found himself in a triangular oasis. Rising from the centre, a banyan tree whose broad branches arched above the roof-gardens of three crumbling Mughal mansions, creating a ceiling of ten thousand flickering leaves. Centuries of roots and growth gripped a red sandstone temple with open sides.

"Whoa!" Ewan jumped when two dozen arms reached through swirls of incense to irritate brass bells dangling from the lowest branches, adding to the cacophony a man thrashed a brass gong. Such loud discordance had chased them through the tight pedestrian lanes as the sun faded. The priest scampered through his congregation, bobbed reverently before the altar. Lifting a brass lamp, his haunting voice began a hymn which was taken up by the small crowd: "Om, Ma-a Kali hari…"

The whiff of butter-ghee lamps mixing with sweet jasmine incense made Ewan sneeze. Peering across the flickering gloom, he choked. Blimey! The swaying women and men were worshipping a naked effigy. Lithe, but deadly: red eyes, tiger teeth, red tongue lashing over black chin, a necklace of skulls draped upon ebony breasts, feet prancing upon a reclined infant.

Devil worship! I should leave. But his English politeness won.

"She-Kali." Raised eyebrows, eyes swinging in satisfaction, the sadhu beamed, "Swami, jaia Jagadeesa Kali."

His ancestors had had various opinions of Hinduism, some took to it, one stern Christian thought it evil. Although several had been Gurkha officers whose troops worshipped Kali, none had described her - perhaps afraid of a backlash back home? What had Father thought of Her?

Above the deafening discordance floated the melodious hymn and despite himself, Ewan began humming. "Om, jai-a

Jagadees-a Kali." The song cooled his bhang-ears, evaporating fears of witchcraft. Only yesterday evening, back in Paris over a glass of champagne, Julian had said his favourite experience was this most Indian of moments - the Sunset Prayer. Recalling his friend's bright face, gaiety surged through Ewan's dopey brain and he mumbled along, "Bhakta janon-ke sankata."

Ewan felt there was more to this scene than his secular mind could grasp. Generation upon generation of belief gave them a conviction he had not seen before. To a man in an Armani suit who swayed and chanted, Kali, his protector, was alive in the stone image. No, Ewan thought, these people are not evil. "Kali, you powerful witch," he sang. "Ohhoo, I am so soooo stoned!"

"Deena janon-ke sankata. Kshana mae doora karee."

Something stirred Ewan. Might there be an entity beyond the physical, a God? Impossible. The feeling arose from the glorious bhang, the thrill of the exotic, being released from his past and the subsequent welling of hope amidst despair. Ha! Hope - another opiate. Religion is based on hope, it's a supplicant mindset dreaming-up a super-grandparent. He, his parents and his consumer-driven compatriots rarely wandered beyond a practical glance at life's flickering surface. Each Sunday evening Father used to polish a medal from the Battle of Almora, 1815, which sat upon the drawing room's imposing mantlepiece. Along with the dry sherry they ceremoniously sipped, idolisation of valour, rather than pondering something universal.

The hymn rose to a crescendo, "Om, jaia Jagadeesa Kali!" and the caterwauling clashing stopped abruptly. The swish of cotton, bare feet scraping flagstones, scuffling on of sandals, shadows drifting into the night. Muted sounds seeped from hidden households settling into the night.

"The silence, how beautiful!" Gosh, that was effusive - not me at all.

"Kali beautiful....," the sadhu cooed.

The guy's delightfully half nuts. And I'm going bonkers too, which is just fine by me.

"You… eating-here," the sadhu commanded.

Ewan settled between roots thicker than his strong thighs. Opening the shoulder bag, he removed his sketchpad and smudging his pencil-work to create moody shadows, he traced the sadhu who was performing an elegant wash-ballet in an unlit corner of the yard.

Humming "Ma Kali" non-stop, stepping into a piece of cloth whilst slipping off his dirty sarong, the sadhu wetted his grubby cotton. Opening and closing the waist-high tap, he kneeled, scrubbed a block of red soap back and forth, rose and stamped the foaming material. Under a fresh gush of water he wring-rinsed it. Cutting the tap he wrung it dry and flipped his sarong over a washing line. Squatting under the flow, he wet himself, snapped off the water, soaped and scrubbed his skin with a chock of coconut fibre. The sadhu rinsed himself and dried with a tiny towel, stepped neatly out of the wet bathing cloth, dried his midriff and wrapped himself in a clean sarong. He washed and wrung out the bathing cloth and hung it on the line. It was all done without revealing an indecent part of his body.

Moving back into the flickering light, the sadhu ordered, "You-washing."

Closing his sketch book, Ewan took an Aladdin lamp to the standpipe. He removed his clothes, ha, the thrill of washing naked outdoors! He bellowed a rugby song: "I saw Billy Bailey / Out with the ladies."

"Sssh! No-Naked!" but the sadhu was unheard.

"Under a starry sky." Why, when I dislike macho men, do rugby songs make me joyous? Tradition, association, comfort. He chuckled. "Then along came his wife!" Lingering beneath the constant flow of liquid, casually soaping his body, enjoying the lamplight playing upon the rushing water, "With a bloody great knife." He rinsed his chest, back and shoulders, "And she chopped off the end / Of his toora-lay, Hey!" He soaped his tooralay-hey.

The sadhu ran over waving his arms, "India…no-naked!"

"Kali's naked," Ewan was used to open showers in sports centres and boarding school, "HEY! Off with his tooral-ay, HEY!"

"NO naked! Kali-She-God!" The sadhu turned from the bare fleshed taboo.

"Yet bare-bellied women walk the streets," Ewan did a belly dance as he slowly completed his blasphemous act. Still starkers, he bent to wash his clothes, occasionally stopping to drum the tune on his muscled bottom. 'Tooraly' dripping, he hung his clothes on the line, bleating, "Off with his tooraly-ay, HEY!"

Oops, turn off the tap boyo. Taking the lamp, he left a trail of damp footprints across the square and starkers before Kali, rubbed himself with his travel towel. Removing clean clothes he dressed, bellowing a final flourish, "YES! Off with his tooral-Y-ay, HEY!"

The baffled old man shook his head and rose from sitting cross legged. Stooping under the low canopy covering Kali, he pulled a small metal suitcase from beneath the altar, unlocked it with a key tied to a long string falling from his shoulders. Opening the lid, he removed a new sarong. "For… you-washing."

Ewan noticed few items in the trunk. Fingering the starched cloth, ashamed of himself, "Thank you. I… I … am so sorry."

Taking a twinkling butter-lamp, the sadhu walked to the tap-side of the yard. Upon an open fire a blackened pot emitted steam, lifting the lid he stirred the contents with a spoon apparently fashioned from the banyan tree. Ewan drew the sadhu tearing several leaves off the tree, washing them and using their long stems to stitch them together. Placing the leaf plates on the pot, the sadhu lifted his sarong to protect his hands and carried the load across the triangular plot. Returning for the butter lamp and mumbling to Kali, he took three leaf-packages off Kali's altar and added the food left by worshippers to dollops of warm rice.

"Sit," the sadhu snapped, pointing at the plinth. Holding the palm of his right hand above the food, the man muttered a grace to Kali. In silence they used the fingers of their right hands to consume the delicious vegetable curries. Ewan was hungry, he'd eaten little.

The sadhu offered a chillum.

I'm not sure. One thing cooling my nerves, but I don't want to become addicted. Yet I've obviously upset the guy, maybe I should?

Ewan had known little joy. His relationships with his parents had been stoney; afraid of them, he was shy and lacked social skills so found mixing and making friends difficult. Father had made him worship sport, and the thrill of doing well to please the man defined Ewan's happiness. Forced into Judo aged seven, as a teenager he switched to Aikido, preferring its philosophy of not harming assailants. His moments of pleasure had been drawing in the garden with Uncle Jack, riding Flika, studying the family's Indian dairies and illustrations. He gained a vague acceptance amongst his male peers because he was strong and fearless, fit and skilled - traits instilled by Father's discipline. Phff! He shook his head. He looked at the strange Indian elder. "Do you take bhang often?"

"Everyday," the sadhu's head waggled, ears almost touching each shoulder. "Bhang releasing emotion!"

Surrendering to the unpredictable adventure, Ewan realised he needed to soften up, the occasional cloud of this mild bhang might unshackle his locked-up heart. Not too much, though. Anyway, nobody's looking. He took a deep drag, it was getting easier each time. Light and dizzy, he leaned into the warm folds of the ancient banyan, "Stoned or what!"

The sadhu snapped. "Kali spirit, not stone."

Ewan chuckled. Another drag, the vapour escaping from their mouths fascinated him. "Beautiful!"

"Kali beautiful. Hee-hee-hee," the sadhu's laugh was welcome.

Ewan admired the colours picked out by the butter lamps, he listened to the movement of birds shifting on their night perches in the enormous tree, his nostrils picked up tepid odours seeping in from the choked alleys where the metropolis slumbered. Wow whee, everything's sharper! For the first time in days he was unbothered by invisible threats.

"Sleeping-here," the sadhu patted a spot within the open-sided temple. "This... you bed."

"No." Ewan protested, the rough sisal sacks were the man's bedding spread beneath Kali. Anyway, I'd prefer a hotel. And why stay? Is tracing my forebears' Indian travels enacting my childhood dreams? Does that matter? Anyway, I've no other direction. Mind, I'm too stoned, can't imagine trying to book a room, hee, hee.

"Me...no-needing."

With trepidation, for it would be his first night in the open, Ewan settled down. There were no walls, simply pillars supporting the low temple roof, and the slit leading to the city's pedestrian alleyways had no gate. "Are we safe?"

"Kali fright all thief."

Yes, Kali's a good lock. His ancestors had noted Muslims and Christians were also wary of Kali's occult powers. Whoo, this country's ancient faith! He watched the old man cover his thin body in a thin woollen shawl, sit cross-legged and stare at Kali's black figure. Wearing boxer-shorts, Ewan laid his head on his bag with its sturdy strap securely around his chest.

Sore ribs woke him, he noticed he was cleared of bhang's influence. A shiver caught his eye, it slithered across the yard and slipped into a hole. HELP! Snakes! Madness to have stayed... I'm guileless... ought to leave.... No, it's too late to wander through a dark city.

A breeze played the soft lamplight over the sadhu's erect body. Is he asleep, in a narcotic trance or meditation? Meditation's a mindset, like zoning before Aikido or rugby. If so, I'm well equipped for it. He'd spent his childhood learning to block out anything but Father's attacking fists and barked phrases: "At the top, everyone's perfectly fit - like you. Mental control gives the edge. See yourself as the best!

If you don't win, your attitude failed, not you. Attitude can always be improved."

I've controlled too much. I'm a misfit, incapable of emotional intimacy, will I be able to develop it? Course I can, even 80 year olds can alter their mindsets. It seems bhang helps? His rapid decline from fine Englishman to nomadic hippie momentarily shocked him, yet he was having the adventure he had long dreamed of. And I'm happy! His mind darted to Julian, who had also lost everything. Has Julian found happiness? The sadhu appears happy. What *is* happiness? Having a part to play? No, I loved the part I played at Merricott and in London, but wasn't happy.

Dawn's arrival woke parakeets in the banyan above. Ewan rose and rubbed his sore body before shaking and hanging up the sacking. Creeping across the dim triangle, he attempted to wash more modestly in the chilly water but ended up as naked, with his starchy new sarong in a knot around his ankles. Drying himself, he dropped his towel in the puddle, so used his hands to rid his shivering skin of water. He donned a livid-purple shirt and green shorts from his bag, "A gay-disguise," Julian had laughed.

Lifting Mother's old weekend bag, Ewan tiptoed past the sadhu slumped snoring against a pillar. In the bearable temperature, he felt alive. Beyond the Kali-space, grey half-light trickled through tangled webs of electrical cables looped between tall facades. Lone ghosts in tatty shawls moved silently before the once elegant Haveli homes, cleaning human faeces from the open gutter. Heck, still slaves, bottom of the caste system. India abounds with wealth yet why this still? It's shocking.

Beneath a plastic tarpaulin suspended between a lamppost and ancient doorframe, a man mothered a kettle puffing sweet smells into the cool air. A kneeling woman, babe tied to her back, plastered fresh liquid-mud over the colder parts of the home-made clay oven, beside her an infant played with kindling. A girl, crisp in school uniform, wiped crumbs off a makeshift table. Stacked against the wall, rolled bedding on a dented tin trunk. Ewan realised the lean-to cafe was also their home. "Good morning," he greeted.

The girl aged perhaps nine, responded in English, "Namaste sahib. Wanting nourishment?"

Settling on a rickety plank laid over two rusty oil cans, he smiled. Namaste? Ah, yes, yes, 'I greet the light within you' - much more delicate than Good morning. "Umm. Nam...Namas...Namaste!, Tea and bread, please."

Sipping a glass of sweet tea laced with cardamon, dipping a stale bun in the welcome liquid, Ewan was glad of ordinary company. Tearing a page from his sketchbook, he drew cartoons for the school girl. The chai-family's giggles warmed his lonely heart; inspired, fuelled by more chai, he gave them a fine drawing of their little home.

He didn't at first recognise his reflection in a scratched mirror. My hooked nose! So prominent with this shaved-head Julian insisted on, dear Julian. He recalled his uncomfortable journey from England hidden in the trunk of Uncle Jack's classic Citroen. Deep within the Channel Tunnel Ewan hoped nothing would go wrong. Released in a Parisian hotel's underground carpark, sneaking out the emergency exit, they walked the dark streets to Hector's apartment. Delightful Hector, Uncle Jack's current boyfriend, later crafted the latest Bollywood look, shaving off Ewan's hair but artfully sculpturing his four-day chin-growth. Delighted, Julian and Uncle Jack pranced about like Queens of Sheba as Hector showed Ewan how to keep the bald-head, trim-beard and moustache snazzy with a tiny battery razor. The following afternoon Uncle Jack, who knew bohemian Paris well, returned from his hotel and flashing his purple silk scarf back over his shoulder, bowed. "Hello Ewan McNaughton, good-bye Charles Merricott."

"My new identity?" Ewan was unable to sync with what was happening. How quickly Uncle Jack, had arranged for a new passport and credit cards. Baffled by so many changes within three days, Charles/Ewan followed Hector, Jack and Julian to three posh stores where they helped him choose colourful clothes.

"Darling, you're Mumbai macho now," Julian laughed.

"Suits your Italianate skin," Hector sighed with unwelcome delight.

They dined in a fancy Champs Elysees restaurant that evening, with Ewan worrying he'd be taken as Julian's camp Indian boy friend. Uncle Jack took a photo from which to make a florid painting and announced, "It'll front my next exhibition, sweeties!" On his fourth yardbird-morning, Ewan had picked up his mother's heavy leather bag, waved a tearful goodbye and caught a taxi to an airport hotel. Alone, depressed, he paced his tiny room for an hour before settling. His phone alarm woke him for the night-flight to Delhi.

By the time Ewan found his way back to the Kali yard, the sadhu was busy cooking. Balancing three balls of dough, one-on-top-of-the-other, with a deft flick of a rolling pin the old man ironed-out three chapatis at once. Wow! Ewan clapped.

"Namaste," the sadhu called over his shoulder.

"Na, Namaste! What's your name?" Yesterday Ewan had been too stoned to care.

"Name is no-matter."

"No-Matter, I'm Ewan."

"Unwun, eat."

Ewan laughed at the contortion of his new name. Much more fun than Charles. As he and the sadhu ate, worshippers came and went. Performing private ceremonies, they stood whispering before Kali with their hands together, they revolved their bodies in tight circles and completed their prayers with a series of ritual hand movements and a swift bob. Before leaving, they orbited the broad tree softly chanting, 'Maa Kali'.

No-Matter lit a chillum. Ewan hesitated. Amazingly, he felt free and content. But how long till SOS returns? I've never felt this good! Fearful of SOS, he sucked hard and the chillum performed its magic. Haa! Wowee! Great and googly good. Hmm, I like this new emotional me, he hee!

20

They had hardly completed another pipe when the sadhu said, "Come."

Human voices dominant, too early for radios. Pacing the narrow alleys with the nervy man, Ewan was stirred by exotic women leaning over suspended wooden balconies. With their long black hair wafting in the faint breeze, their voices sang across the narrow gaps as they chatted gaily with neighbours and saucy children peered between their legs before scurrying back into mysterious interiors. In Old Delhi's Muslim quarters women called orders to small shops below, lowering wicker baskets on ropes for their goods; Ewan dodged dead goats dangling upside-down outside halal butchers. In Hindu zones he brushed past women in bright saris as they bought fruit, vegetables and flowers and he gawped as they entered florid temples tucked between the busy shops.

"No-Matter, help!" he shouted through the ripple of voices.

"Worrying...big problem. Calming...monkey no problem." The sadhu turned to face-off a macaque baring its teeth at Ewan. Raising his eyebrows, expanding his eyes, No-Matter mimicked the monkey whilst taking a small step forwards. The creature sprang, its spider arms grasped a tangle of electrical cables, clambering and swinging, it quickly arrived at the slash of sky between rooftops.

Ewan's head was spinning. Too much bhang or simply unable to find order in the apparent chaos? Yet in spite of his love of organisation and cleanliness, he enjoyed the disordered city. It buzzed with life and animals. Languid cows head-butted cunning goats off rubbish piles; flocks of cheeky sparrows darted about the tight lanes; solemn raptors soared across the slender sky strips. Creatures softened the built environment, reminding him nature was out there.

They emerged from the busy warren and Old Delhi's centuries of tight growth gave way to searing light streaming from the enormity of sky. Ewan blinked. Only the faintest threads of noise floated through the scorched air.

"Holy Yamuna," No-Matter waved at a smear of dark liquid lost within acres of cracked mud.

21

"Hmm?" Unimpressed, Ewan studied the flat horizon. What am I, an atheist, doing hanging out with a monk? They sat on coarse grassy banks absorbing the supposed holiness as the sadhu mumbled prayers.

Ewan's phone sounded. He saw Uncle Jack's name and hesitated, how good to talk to his only remaining relative, but it could be dangerous. Furthermore, it would be an intrusion, he had started an amazing journey and needed to sink into what was happening. He texted: 'ALL'S FINE. DANGEROUS TO THUS COMMUNICATE. WILL WRITE. XX, C.' He extracted the SIM card, crushed it with a stone and tossed it away.

Suddenly dislocated from his surroundings, Ewan took his plastic file from his bag and opened at the second plastic sleeve, a photocopied parchment dated 1585 from his ancestor Hubert Merricott's report: *"Myne eyes beheld ye grande palace that will be muche admyred at Hampton Courte. Ye greate Delhee ruler thought little of giftes sent by our blessed Majestie Queen Elizabeth thogh they be ye best England produceth."*

Ewan gazed absently at tall modern buildings rising in the distance. The earliest English ambassadors and merchants had been awed by the country, stating Europe was far behind. His eye fell upon the Yamuna and he skipped several lines. *"Fore ye Hindoo rivers be ye veins of Mother Earth. Holy Yamunnaa borne of ye God Himalayaa be sister of ye mighty Gangaa. Dragged across Hindoo land by a god who tryed to defile her, her struggle to escape defines her meandering course."*

These passages touched him. Tracing my ancestors' steps feels right. Prompted to begin his adventure with a symbolic gesture, he gave his smartphone to the old sadhu, who rose and handed it to a beggar, mumbling, "He sell it."

They moved along the raised banks to a small temple squatting defiantly on a crest of rock, another timeless relationship of red stone and entwined banyan bark. Ewan knew that long before the Acropolis rose over Athens, Hindu temples had stood on these very banks. Gosh India's amazing, but unlike Greece, her ancient culture is still central to people's lives.

No-Matter greeted the resident priest with an offering of fruit. Splattered by heart-shaped shadows from the leaves above, the two old men in faded robes settled upon worn grey slabs before the brown-red temple. No-Matter unwrapped his cone pipe and set about the holy task of making a chillum, into it he packed some of the shredded olive-green leaves the sadhu gave him. Ewan noticed hashish growing and drying beside the temple and laughed, "Ha, No-Matter! Your supplier!"

No-Matter stepped inside the temple and spread his cheesecloth before a rounded river stone. Onto it he laid his newly filled pipe and the two sadhus chanted to the effigy. A dozen singing women swept in from the nearby city lanes. Leaving the chillum where it lay, No-Matter's friend rose and muttered the relevant prayers as the brightly clad women moved gracefully around the small shrine mumbling prayers, pouring and massaging milk, yoghurt and honey over the stone. No-Matter whispered that they were wearing their best saris and offering up their most precious as they implored their chosen god to intervene in a major illness. He explained the rituals could also be for a barren womb; with men it was more often a business deal.

"Sometime big ceremony...whole family. Sometime secret...one person."

As the women left, they gave the priest a pile of glistening vegetables. Wobbling his head in admiration, No-Matter said, "True sadhu...taking food...winter blanket...never money."

His impoverished friend chuckled, "Many Brahmins grow rich from such easy pickings." Ewan looked at the priest more closely, he spoke perfect English with an educated accent. Hmm, what's his story?

Remembering their waiting bhang, the two priests sat down, lit the pipe and shouted, "Chillum bolee!"

Ewan preferred not to join in, he was still light headed. He took out his sketchbook. Inspired by the miniature Mughal,

23

drawing was his love, but private school hadn't encouraged art and Father would grunt, "Sport makes a man of you, art turns you into a fop. Look at my brother Jack!"

In defiance, Jack and Julian, the two fops in Ewan's life, encouraged Ewan to paint. During his evening in Paris, Ewan's pen had captured Uncle Jack whose ruddy features were teased by curls of effeminate grey hair. He'd also sketched Julian's smooth features excitably changing with each turn of the conversation. These sketches took first place in his folder, bits of paper within a plastic sleeve now his only friends....

No need for colour, the scene is sombre. Hmm, smudging 4B pencil with my finger recreates the bhang mist. I'll do the sadhus' angled forms in sharp F. Drawing calms me, I see things I might have missed: that scar underneath No-Matter's chin, the battered silver ring his friend wears.

No-Matter and his pal rose and wobbled down old stone steps set into the dun-green banks. Ewan followed, rapidly outlining them as they waddled across the crazy-paving of parched grey clay. At the water's edge they stripped off their faded sarongs and, with charcoal-grey water up to their white underpants, they paused, lifted the ceremonial creamy strings falling from their right shoulders and wound them around an ear to prevent them floating away. Dunking their light-umber bodies beneath the grimy surface three times, they lifted the gritty liquid in upturned palms and let it pour over their wrists and onto their foreheads. The ritual actions were repeated twice more as the old men chanted a hymn. Ewan smiled as a shard of pink garbage stuck to No-Matter's chin.

"Come Unwun," No-Matter called, "Yamuna holy."

Ugh! Hot as it is, sacred as they might be, the murky waters do not appeal! A suspicious brown object was floating from a smouldering funeral pyre three hundred metres up-river. A scrawny black dog swam out and took the par-cooked human thigh in its jaws. Revolted, taking deep breaths to stop himself retching, Ewan scampered across the gun-grey flats, scaled the bank of burnt grass; gasping, he lay against one of the lush temple trees.

After a while, the theatre playing upon the sands inspired Ewan to do a series of swift sketches with a fine ink pen. Using precise lines and neat crosshatch shading, his paper held men and women scrubbing piles of clothes. The rapid-fire thumping of cotton faintly drifted across the broad flats and flotillas of bubbles turned the river cappuccino. One page bagged shoulders lugging damp bundles up the mud incline; coloured crayons portrayed clothes drying on the baking banks. A double-A4 page seized women in pairs leaning back, pulling saris taut, flamboyant-flags ironed by the scorching sun;

A man in a pale-grey safari-suit walked over. Lifting his forefinger off the samosa he was holding, he poked Ewan's current sketch. "What purpose?"

"Pleasure."

"Pleasure one thing," the man looked annoyed, "but each act must be having some reason, otherwise life wasted," and he walked away with no further interaction.

India Oh India, I do love you. Ewan laughed as he scribbled the conversation around the oily fingerprint.

He bought a golden pineapple from a passing vendor. He withdrew a Gurkha khukuri from it's buffalo-hide scabbard - a family legacy he had to explain to customs after retrieving the package from the luggage carrousel. Its lethal blade sliced the crinkled skin, juice flowed over the curving metal to seep along the ivory handle, turning his fingers sticky. Thick chunks of prickly skin fell to the sand and within a minute ants were all over them. The pale lemon flesh, sweet and succulent, smeared his face as he relished the treat. Picking fruit from his forgotten beard growth, he took out his wash-bag. At a standpipe beside a chai stall, he washed his khukuri, hands and face.

With their flimsy robes wafting in the faint breeze, the sadhus walked back across the baking mud-flats looking as if they had done the most satisfying thing ever. Well, well, satisfaction from immersing themselves in their fouled goddess, I do envy their simple faith.

25

I suppose contentment comes with commitment to a belief system. Yet contentment isn't everything, Hitler was as he walked through Paris. Hmm, that's confusing because we need fulfilment, it makes our lives. How ever will I find it? Stop thinking! Thinking - my way out of the emotional desert of my childhood became my shield, my Stiff Outer Shield or SOS, but this logical approach took me from myself.

The bhang's power was fading and his heavy mental load was returning. A little bhang might help? He knew it took only three months of attentive determination to shift one's personality traits. A series of controlled flirtations with the strange sadhu-haze would help and he knew he could control it, he was a highly disciplined man. And so he accepted a fresh chillum.

No-Matter's friend began, "You-Wong, my dear Sir."

"Another great name! What fun."

"Err? You-Wong, did you know Brahman performed yogic austerities on this very spot to persuade the goddess Yamuna to help him regain his sacred knowledge."

Spluttering smoke, Ewan chuckled, "Brahman the Universal Spirit was forgetful?"

"Yes You-Wong, Brahman was tired after envisaging the universe and forgot everything. When pleased with Brahma's rituals, Yamuna tossed him the Vedic Texts and he quickly digested them on this spot."

The religion reminded Ewan of Norse and Greek legends, historical heroes became gods. It had the atmosphere of village storytelling, madly colourful, yet woven with eternal truths. How interesting - Rivers are valuable, even to The Most Powerful - sit beside them and your inner wisdom awakens.

The old sadhus sat chanting holy texts whilst pouring Yamuna water over the stone effigy. Ritual over, they sank into meditation. Perched with his knees raised to his chin, the morning heat dragged and toppling against the wall, Ewan slipped into a stoned sleep. His sore knees woke him and he stretched. No-Matter and his erudite pal hadn't moved. I'm bored, Ewan/Unwun/You-Wong and who in the heck is

26

Charles anyway? He stood, stretched, walked to a chai stall where he drank sweet tea. What fun being stoned, so, so relaxing, whoopie! No wonder the cleaner liked it. Shame, never got to say goodbye. Spotting No-Matter moving, he teetered over with offerings of tea and treats. "No-Matter, when you sit, what are you thinking about?"

"Kali," No-Matter winked and sipped the warm tea.

"Obviously, but…"

The other sadhu interrupted, "You-Wong, a sadhu only tells when he wishes to."

"Without words, how can I know your ways? Understanding comes about through deduction and reasoning."

"This is the Western way, You-Wong," the man showed tremendous patience. "You see the world through analytical thinking. In the East we believe understanding is a matter for the soul, not logical thinking."

"For me, soul's the emotional self. From birth your mind developed with Hinduism, your thoughts grew with its influences all around you. Without your background, I require questions and answers to lead me towards understanding. "

This was met by silence.

Ewan tried a new tack, "What's the holy stone?"

"The god Shiva's lingum, or phallus." The resident sadhu's thin voice lilted in the air.

"Blimey!" Ewan choked on one of the vegetable samosas he had bought from a passing vendor. Those women earlier had been massaging a penis with honey and yoghurt! These male sadhus worshipped it with filthy Yamuna water!

"You-Wong, with his lingum Shiva created everything, hence we wash his resourceful tool in admiration."

"But Brahman created…"

"Brahman envisaged the universe, leaving the creating to Shiva." The man touched the stone plate beneath the lingum, his fingers tracing worn groves which channelled the spilt Yamuna water. "To do this, Shiva needed the help of Parvati, his consort. This is her yoni, or vulva."

27

"Holy sex!" Ewan chuckled. This is fun. I know I'm high, but these guys are soaring. "No-Matter, I'm confused. You worship Kali, yet bathe in the Yamuna, and rub her water over Shiva's phallus and Parvati's vagina!"

The other sadhu explained. "The Goddess Devi takes many shapes - Kali is her warrior form. In the distant past the gods were worried that Shiva, who sat in deep meditation, had shunned his creative duty. It was a calamity, nothing existed but the void. At his wits end, Brahman turned to Devi. Assuming her beautiful incarnation, Parvati, The Goddess began a series of austerities to woo Shiva. Finally impressed, Shiva withdrew from the void and settled into the materialistic level of consciousness where He and Parvati enjoined, thus igniting the multiple processes of creativity."

How admirable a religion which acknowledges women as equal players. "But why all these weird images?"

"All is one," No-Matter smiled bewilderingly.

"If that's so, there are too many Hindu gods!" Has Bhang created them? Bhang certainly makes them fun.

The other sadhu hesitated. "Really, these things are not to be taken at face-value. My view is that in the distant past god-images emerged when holy men tried explaining complex philosophical issues to ordinary people. One prehistory sadhu used Yamuna's waters, another Shiva's phallus and a third Kali's skulls. Over time, these parables interlinked to become accepted as holy texts."

"Thank you, but why divide Devi into Parvati, Kali and all those other goddesses?"

"Being individuals, we each need a different path towards the Godhead. Take our holy rivers, for example. Yamuna is love manifest, whereas Ganga is austere purity; I personally prefer the softer path of love."

"You are intelligent enough to rise above myths, why don't you?"

"Because I'm an emotional man who needs company in this lonely role I've chosen, and Yamuna's example encourages me."

In his normal sober mindset, such thinking would have irritated Ewan, but now it was tantalising. "So each god is an illustration of a concept to follow."

"Precisely."

The city was all-a-clang twice a day as enthusiastic men and women smashed metal onto metal or irritated all manner of bells. In the evening these Arti-sounds drowned out voices, radios and angry scooter horns. Ewan felt it was a moment of emotional extravagance, a welcome vent in the country's rigid social laws. After Arti one evening No-Matter and Ewan were preparing their meal when an educated voice stated, "Sir, I noticing you staying night time. What reason please?"

"Err, well, I'm not quite sure...."

Before Ewan could find an explanation, the woman, black eyes peering through pink-framed spectacles, said, "My-name Mrs Saraswati Gupta. State Bank-of-India, Sindh-Road sub-branch, sub-manager. Your name again please? Oo-When? Strange name, origin please?" Before Ewan could correct her, the woman flowed on, "Oo-When, occupation seeking god no doubt. For this task, India best place."

"I'm not seeking. I'm just, umm, how to put it?" Ewan hesitated, "Unfolding."

"Unfolding," the woman adjusted her day-glo glasses, "please be explaining?"

"Leaving hang-ups behind."

"Bhang-eyes good."

"As a banker, you see nothing wrong with your priest indulging in mind altering substances?"

"Bhang good for sadhu, disaster for banker. Bhang lifting mind from earth-bound perception to peer toward divine inspiration. Oo-When, what occupation?"

Although accustomed to people rattling out their social position, He was fearful of being caught and avoided revealing his past. No-Matter called, "Telling Unwun! No telling..people thinking...outcast...even villain."

29

How near the truth they'd be! To hide his reviving panic, Ewan exclaimed, "That's rich No-Matter. You won't talk about yourself."

"We trusting sadhu," said Mrs Gupta. "When arriving new place, each person questioned to be slotted into caste system. People behaving accordingly - if haughty to higher-caste or familiar with untouchable, disastrous."

Heck, what's wrong with India! Ghandi campaigned to drop the debilitating caste system.

No-Matter ordered, "Telling, Unwun."

Surely by now the law would have caught up with me, Charles/Oo-When, Ewan McNaughton was registered on the flight records. "A government post."

"British Government!" her eyes shot open. "Leaving tiptop career for religion. Oo-When, such wise direction!" The smart lady wobbled her head from side to side, acknowledging the unimaginable sacrifice. As quickly as she'd arrived, she turned, saying, "Must off." With hands held up in prayer, Mrs Gupta, named after Saraswati, Devi's manifestation as The Goddess of Wealth, pivoted to face Kali, Devi's fierce form. She strode off clutching a pink tablet.

Hmm, so incongruous, walking an invisible ridge between two vastly different worlds. How odd this India. And how old. He read a passage from a slender homebound book he had bought earlier from a man claiming to be the author. He could see the eager lecturer saying: *'My dear readers, please imagine as you turn these pages that you are growing with a civilisation reaching back to our trek out of Africa to our penetration of space.'* The text went onto explain that certain current Hindu rituals were still used by the Aborigines of Australia. Blimey. Roughly fifty-five thousand years ago the Aborigines migrated along India's shores. What continuity. Wondering what some of his ancestors would have made of such recent discoveries, he continued reading: *'Ind.ia's northern civilisation began by the Rivers Ind.us and Saraswati. When the Indu.s shifted course, leaving the now arid banks, these cities shifted to the fertile Yamuna-Ganga plain. That same civilisation is alive today - in the ancient*

Sanskrit roots of our language H.ind.i, in our H.ind.u religion, in the design of our houses, even in our art and artefacts.'

There was a photo of an excavated seven-thousand year old toy with moving parts. Ewan gulped. It's identical to a toy Mother bought during her Indian honeymoon. The wobbly cow still sat on his chest-of-drawers back home.

Although unsure of No-Matter's bhang-imbued philosophy, Ewan stayed on. The sadhu was interesting. And I'm discovering India from the inside, I'm living whole passages from my family library. He didn't take to all the man's habits and didn't always follow the sadhu. Instead, he wandered the ancient alleyways, sitting in chai stalls drinking tea and sketching the world about him. Around his drawings he wrote of what he saw, noting useful Hindi phrases people gave out. He only enjoyed the feather-light effect of a chillum twice a day because it kept SOS at bay.

It astounded him marijuana was now normal fare, Father's stern figure shivered his heart...but then he saw SOS's influence diminishing. I'm feeling rather than thinking - how wonderful is that. The dope made him jovial and carefree, rendering his days restful and distracting. He'd tasted pleasure at last and felt himself gradually leaving his troubles behind, stressful memories of his unwitting crime and his previous life were fading. He delighted in the lack of external duties and ignored Father's commanding voice which kept rising from within. Yes, taking bhang for a limited period, three months at most, will shift my personality.

Ewan went to post his bundle of four A4 sketchbooks to Uncle Jack for safekeeping. He had queued for ten minutes when the man behind the counter said, "Sir, please getting tailor opposite sewing goods. Cardboard packaging not secure foreign parts." Ewan stepped out of the small Post Office and sat on a ledge before the tailor's shop. He didn't have to explain, the man automatically hand-sewed Ewan's parcel up tightly in white cotton cloth. Proud of his attractive package, Ewan returned to the Post Office and waited in line for nine minutes. At the counter, the official used hot red wax to seal the stitching. He handed Ewan a black marker pen with which to write the address and told him to join another queue at the counter which sold stamps. Fifteen minutes queuing, Ewan's turn; using cow-glue to stick on the stamps, the stamp-man ordered him back to the first counter and after eleven minutes Ewan handed the parcel to the first man, who sat one pace from the stamp-man. The beautiful parcel was registered in a heavy ledger, stamped officially and tossed into a hessian sack marked "OVERSEAS". Not counting the stitching process, the act of posting a single parcel had taken over forty-nine minutes.

After a chillum one morning, Ewan pulled out the slim rosewood box and withdrew the Mughal miniature. Tucked into the frame was Gerald Merricott's hand written note: "15th May, 1857. *After the dreadful battle I found this picture in the dust. I looked up and beheld the same temple upon the rock beside the great river. What shame to have defiled this place for nothing more than company profit.*"

For this reason alone, I must find the temple, but where to begin? Gerald had written that the image was a true representation, unlike the imaginary pictures typical of the style. Now that he was less his SOS, it was time to trace his ancestor's steps. The inspiration to leave No-Matter and Kali had come the day before whilst reading a Victorian ancestor's letter - Delhi was only a couple of hours' train ride from the place it described. That, surely, was somewhere to begin his peculiar painting venture. Ewan packed his things into his scratched bag. Lifting a package, he said, "No-Matter, I want you to have this."

No-Matter undid the brown paper parcel and nodded thanks. Carrying the gift, the sadhu walked to the alley and called out. A beggar appeared. Bowing with respect, the sadhu gave the man the thick woollen blanket and explained, "Beggar having greater need."

"No-Matter, I want to see more of India."

"Unwun, we taking self...everywhere. Our thinking making...each place...heaven/hell."

Ewan replied, "Our experiences too! A beggar on Delhi's winter streets must be in hell."

No-Matter laughed, "Real journey...in soul...not in world."

Ewan recalled a quote from somewhere: *'It is how you react to events, what you learn from them and how you move forwards, not the events themselves which sculpt you.'* He smiled, "No-Matter, thank you, you've taught me a lot." Wondering exactly what, but knowing a dramatic internal shift had happened, he lifted his hands and uttered, "Namaste!"

Bowing, No-Matter replied, "Namaste."

With a last glance at the old sadhu, Ewan/Unwun/You-Wong or even Charles, stepped from Kali's tiny triangle and wove his way back through Old Delhi's soothing pedestrian alleys.

Despite the smells, the mess and confusion, Ewan the sophisticate had been at home with the men in long shirts hanging over bulbous sarongs, amongst the elegant women and their wide-eyed children laughing in the anarchy of their barefoot play. Unchanged since his family's earliest writings, despite owning internet-TV's, most of these people's lives were played out from birth to death in Old Delhi's maze of medieval backstreets. And with my olive skin, many have taken me to be one of them.

ß

Dawn at the railway station, Ewan was told to follow a smart ex-pat European whose porters' red shirts flowed over white pyjama trousers. Balancing luggage on their scarlet-turbaned heads, they walked through halls echoing with activity. Wow. It's as if an entire region is in flight from some disaster!

Thwack! Wood hitting bone. Ewan spotted an old man striking an urchin whose hand crept into a heap of luggage; a teenager slapped the elder across the face, enabling the child to complete the theft. Ewan leapt across the hall, kicked the teenager to the ground, lunged, caught the urchin. The family rallied round and grasped the fallen vandals. Knocking into cooking pots, the old man sank onto bundles of bedding.

Checking platform changes on battered smart-phones, the porters wove through the crush, chasing illuminated signs. Climbing a metal bridge spanning multiple railway lines, Ewan wondered how many of his relatives had trod this way as he peered at long platforms where overfilled trains rattled to and from destinations across the enormous subcontinent. They descended behind a group of smart business men tugging big suitcases. Many travellers wore sarongs and tribal dress and the ex-pat explained, "Country folk changing trains."

A little chilly as he waited for their train, Ewan donned a jersey. Colouring with crayons over fine pen lines, he drew: a family wearing red snoozing on hessian parcels; people in green sat in a circle eating off stainless steel plates; women wearing flamboyant gypsy costumes with toy-like babies at their bared breasts. Hey! I recognise them from a Victorian aunt's water colour hanging in Merricott. They must be returning to their west-Himalayan valley. He carefully sketched barrel-chested Sikh men with royal-blue turbans, glaring eyes and curved swords; rapid pen marks caught sly city youths skulking at the fringes of these transitory encampments.

Closing his sketchbook, he wandered amongst food trolleys, picking at balls of this or that whilst sipping sweet tea from a sun-baked clay mug. Vendors rushed here and there shouting, selling, touting, it was organised chaos. I love this disarray and gaiety! He waved, asking a European to join him; the man turned away. That would have been me a short while ago, crumbs, I've changed!

A loud hoot turned the transient population into a shrieking scrum. Eager to gain a seat, everyone grabbed their possessions and struggled with the mass squeezing towards the slowing metal beast. Ewan drew young men clambering up their relatives' backs, stepping over strangers' shoulders, fighting through the log-jammed doors. Those attempting to get off the still moving train battled against this swarm, Ewan shivered. Hope none fall.

The platform cleared, the porters searched names pinned to the 'First Class' carriages and placed the expat's luggage in a compartment. Clutching his shoulder bag, Ewan sat on the metal steps sketching in squiggles those arriving for the following train. Stilled by the process, he was in rhapsody.

"What you drawing?" a fellow passenger leaned over his shoulders.

"Those wonderful tribal clothes."

"Time wasting drawing simple peasant. True beauty seen with poetry."

"Err...."

"Just as child wishing ownership of moon, which obviously can-not be, beauty shown through combined talents."

"Err?"

"You not understanding because you having no poetic base."

"Hmm." Curious now, "what is your work, Sir?"

"Internet salesman." The man walked away.

Chuckling, Ewan scribbled down the conversation. His pictures bordered with words reminded him of the pages he'd scanned from an illustrated Hindi dictionary one of his Edwardian relatives had created for her children. The pages

35

he chose gave the basics: 100 essential words; phrases asking directions, ordering food; the first steps of polite conversation. His progress pleased him, he had not warmed to languages at school - Latin and ancient Greek had none of the appeal of this living tongue with its timeless mix of Sanskrit and Persian. 'ApkA kaHan jatA-heY?' felt more lyrical to him than 'where're you going?' or Latin's functional, 'Ubi tu?'

A whistle blew. With creaks and groans, the grouching beast took a minute to haul its weight past the uniformed Platform Officer who walked beside it sipping tea from a china saucer he kept refilling from a china cup. As he drew this awkward method of drinking on-the-hoof, Ewan's coach chugged painfully towards the platform's end.

Passing a shantytown hugging the track, he rapidly sketched a couple of young thieves jumping down, clutching bundles. It was a desperate domain of lean-to's made of planks and discarded tin. In this thriving city, *this*! Yet inside these scant shelters people lived as if within a more solid settlement. The overloaded train gave Ewan time to fill a page with lightening-flash figures: men laying back in barber's chairs having their faces shaved; women hunched over stoves; children chasing hoops alongside vile open sewers; women praying before a waist high shrine.

The previous day, beside a shanty town upon the Yamuna's precarious flood plain, No-Matter had explained, "Most here fled their ancestral lands because of natural disasters, expecting to return when they'd gained sufficient money in the city." Unfortunately, to their horror, many sank deeper into the urban mire with each passing season, desperate to find food for their children, eventually certain morals had to crumble. Life's unfairness baffled Ewan. How can these once proud farmers bear their shattered lives? OK, I've lost everything, but money gives me stability and choice. What can I do? What can one person do? Yes! Use my stolen money! But how?

He flipped to an entry from Gerald Merricott's diary, written during India's worst famine which killed over six million. *"21st November, 1877. I am dreadfully ashamed to*

36

have to enforce the Salt Tax. In many sectors starving villagers unable to pay formed gangs of bandits, or Dacoits, whom it is my confounded duty to rout. In short, our dire tax is creating wretched criminals who we slaughter. Those too weak for this understandable revolt try to get to the cities. Rotting bodies line the Great Trunk Road. Mortified, I ride past weary frames, weeping internally as I perform one of my most abhorred duties, searching these withered creatures for salt. Oh! Damn the curse of the Salt Tax."

In a Delhi newspaper, Ewan had learned those bandit-families from the 1876-8 famine still continued their 'trade' - their offspring lived on the wild banks of the Yamuna and he was on his way to the spot where another relative, Albert Merricott, once fought Dacoits. The train gathered pace and Delhi's skyline became a smudge on the flat horizon.

The day was warming when Ewan opened a window. The countryside swelled with spring crops. Ewan drew furiously: village ponds where children leapt off the half submerged backs of buffaloes; colourful groups of sari-clad women pulling water from wide wells; neat settlements with clean lanes cutting through flat-topped mud houses. Timeless rurality, hardly changed since Ewan's Mughal miniature was painted. He told the expat of his strong urge to leap out and immerse himself in this pastoral idyll.

The man grunted, "India's a mess." Staying in plush hotels, he was visiting the northern sites and asked Ewan to join him. Ewan declined, knowing it would revive his SOS. They slid through swathes of progressively drier countryside. Dull, uninteresting. *Like SOS me.* He noted his stiff personality was regaining control without bhang's influence. *But now I've learnt how to relax, surely I can 'escape' my dismal SOS-shield without help.*

Heat shimmered the air above swathes of badland when the brakes screeched and the train's furious pace lessened. A strong river flowed into a scrap of dense jungle and re-emerge amongst parched fields where it kinked north to slice through a bluff. A mud village rode the western slope of this water-cleaved ridge and, upon the shallow summit, massive walls stood sentinel over the rampaging river. Ageless, medieval! This'll spin me into another adventure which'll undo SOS-me. After all, Albert Merricott, a Victorian snob, became an Indophile here.

It was hot by the time the train drew alongside a platform with a single-roomed building. On the stone slabs in the harsh sun, a chunky wooden cart drawn by two light grey oxen whose upward-curving horns were decorated with red pom-poms and blue tassels. Gosh! Identical to a 4,400 year old Indus Valley clay-seal Uncle Jack once showed me in The British Museum. Leaning against one of the huge wooden wheels, four bare-chested men wore soiled sarongs.

Ewan noticed a single man jump off the train at the same time he did. The pale skinned man's quick glance, the incongruity of the cream suit, made Ewan shiver. A detective? I saw a cream suited man at my Paris airport hotel. Oh come on, this is SOS paranoia. The man walked to the far end of the station where the driver of a smart 4x4 greeted him with ancient courtesy. Absorbing the traveller, the vehicle shot off, creating an-ever expanding dust-cloud that split the dry land stretching towards distant hills.

The place was bleak. Should I climb back on again, get off somewhere less deserted? No, I'm here to paint my ancestors' travels. Apart from the hissing train, silence dominated the near empty scene. Two of the four workers clanked open a goods carriage door and into it off-loaded boxes from the ox cart. At a neighbouring wagon two others threw out sisal sacks. Both sets of doors clanged shut. The guard whistled.

Pistons pumped, became a burr; the engine emitted clouds of energy, the metal brute shivered along its length, and shifted. Ewan walked down the platform, starring at the train rattling over an iron bridge, half of which was taken up by a thin road made of hardwood planks. Far below, beside the bulky stone pillars of this imposing structure, a ruined ford, its disarrayed blocks creating rapids in the fast flowing water. Phew, this'll be a challenge.

ß

The heat rising off the flagstones fanned the hairs on Ewan's arms and his bag felt heavy on his heat-pricked shoulders. Crikey, the sense of remoteness is overwhelming. I've landed in a world touched only by a halting train. The only sounds the churning river, the huffing men at work.

He watched them. Two shared a hundredweight sack, swinging it thrice by it's four ears, finally landing it on the cart. Jumping up, they shifted the sack and their rhythmic movements were mirrored by the tipping cart and the oxen's reflexes. Ewan reached into his bag and donned a scarlet bandana he had bought in Paris to protect his bald head. Julian said I look like a bandit! Overcome with despair, he took an Aikido breath; exhaling, he walked to the men, grabbed the nearest sack, hauled it to his chest. Humph. Solid grain packed in a sisal tube longer than his muscular torso was heavier than he'd bargained for. Stirred by Father's voice: 'Never give up', clenching his jaw, propping the bulk on his knees, he slid his hands down the awkward shape, heaved and flipped it onto the cart.

The men looked on in surprise, and not merely because of the show of strength. No-Matter had told him it was demeaning for non-working castes to participate in physical labour. Panting, Ewan smiled in camaraderie.

"Jai ho!" A slim man joined Ewan and between each muscle straining they'd relax, watch the others swing, jump up, shift the latest sack. How good to do honest work, gosh, I really miss the farm. Job done, the dripping men flopped against the oxen, absently stroking the soft grey hides and long drooping ears. Ewan's helper smiled, "Namaste, mè Krishna."

"Namaste, mè Ewan," now happy with basic Hindi.

"Chewing, what part of India? Your accent's funny."

Chewing… interesting version. "I'm British."

"*Goodness Gracious Me!*" Krishna chortled.

"BBC Radio's popular here?"

"In your dreams buddy."

"That's a good impersonation!"

"Hè, Chewing, I like your pale skin."

A dark man with a wily face said, "Salaam. Mè Ali." Ali slapped the oxen into action with the flat of his hand.

Following the lumbering cart, they strolled along the baked platform, down its end-slope and onto the dirt road. Not far from the station, where a lane cut from the road and up hill to the village, three interlocked neem trees shaded a shop-cum-tea stall. Appreciating the shade, the workers slumped onto sagging planks suspended over large boulders. Ewan leaned against one of the trees and sketched the chai-wallah pouring sweet milky tea from a blackened pan into a glass.

Pulling the full glass from an empty one being filled, the man aerated it, swinging the jet of steaming liquid from his shoulders to his knees, and not a drop spilt. Ewan clapped, "Brilliant!"

Bemused, Ali asked, "Chillum Chewing?"

Hesitant, but wanting to be accepted, Ewan decided to take just one drag of the popular soporific. The mild bhang swelled through his sweating body, slowing and relaxing him, making his ginger-flavoured tea all the more interesting. Glasses emptied, Ewan followed the laden cart up the paved village slope. The heaving oxen slowed. Leaning with their backs into the load, the four men panted to shift the weight. Adding his own brawn, Ewan felt the task impossible but gradually the head-high wooden wheels turned. Gaining level ground, the cobbles ended and they flopped against the gasping beasts.

Entering the loose settlement, Ewan had the impression of strolling back through history. Centuries before British engineers built their iron bridge, this settlement existed beside the old ford. A single electricity line strung on leaning poles avoided all houses. Kicking dust, he followed the cart past meandering stick fences which surrounded single-storey mud houses. The front yards were neat, water came from garden wells, trees shaded old men asleep on string-strung beds,

41

women threshing or chaffing grain, infants chasing clucking chickens. A woman washing clothes by a well peered at Ewan, laid her hands on her waist and arched her back with her bent elbows pointing behind her. A squatting girl on a veranda stopped dicing a flank of goat; a snotty nosed boy ran from the roadside, crying, "Dacoit!"

Krishna and Ali laughed.

The soft pat of hooves in the dust and the creaking wheels cut the still dry air. The lane turned to hug the inside of the fortified walls. Wow. Left, a sun-exposed expanse of sand, a no-man's land marking the village edge. Right, the electricity line crossed a stone-laid square shaded by trees, dead centre, a weather-beaten fountain whose mechanism had long given up. The plaza's far side was defined by a sandstone manor, reaching forwards from either end, matching stone barns and stables. Gosh, the symmetry, so poetic. Each pillar and brace was delicately carved, but centuries of harsh summers and freezing winters were undoing the craftsmanship. And damn that ugly electrical cable piercing that elegant carving of a deer!

"The oxen are owned by the Zaminder," Krishna explained.

"A zaminder!" From his familial jottings, Ewan surmised he had entered a feudal world controlled by this landlord. Letting the cart continue, he walked along the square's sun-bashed open edge, tracing a solid kerb holding back the sand. It was a graphic border between the mud and thatch village and the ruler's sandstone structures. Half way along, a banyan tree encircled by a worn plinth held a whitewashed shrine no higher than a goat, a faded red flag limped atop its beehive dome.

Ewan wriggled amongst villagers who sat on the shaded apron chatting or watching the rare spurts of activity. He smiled. People nodded, but did not intrude on a decidedly curious man who might be a Dacoit. In the 1890s, great, great grandfather Albert Merricott entered the nearby bad-lands to sniff out Dacoits. He'd written to his wife in Calcutta, congratulating her on their eighth birth, hoping the child

42

would live to join the four survivors. Ewan could see the man's copperplate writing describing the Dacoit's elaborate settlement hidden for a decade within the maze of deep ravines cut into the fine alluvial soils which stretched back from the Yamuna. Albert admired the bandits, concluding they were loyal to each other. After the unjust Salt Tax and a decade on the run, they had permanently turned against the mechanisms of colonial rule.

A young woman with a thin green shawl draped over her head came out of the mansion and crossed the plaza. Placing a silver plate of diced fruit before the temple's idol, she waved the resident butter-lamp and chanted in a delicate, doleful voice. Replacing the ever-lit lamp, the green figure picked up her plate and offered morsels of the blessed food. Ewan noticed people treat her with disregard. She offered him the fruit, he peered beneath the gossamer shawl, their eyes locked. Her gaze spoke of an impending explosion. Stunned, he took a morsel of mango. Throwing a more furtive glance before lowering her brown eyes, she quickly turned to offer the plate to an old hag who tutted. Indian women, Ewan knew, do not look strange men in the eye. Responding to several sniffs of disapproval, the young woman shrugged, twisted round and drifted back towards the manorial entrance.

Whoo, she made my heart thump. To distract himself, he began sketching Krishna, Ali and their friends unloading the cart into a barn. He made studies of a sweeper shifting leaves from the expanse of heavy stone flagstones with swirling heat-lines. His drawings reminded him of an eighteenth century sketch by a maternal relative and he wondered if he could see India through his own mind, rather than his relatives'. Tired, he curled into the welcoming tree and was soon asleep with Mother's leather bag tucked securely between his arms.

It was cooler when he woke to familiar voices as the men he'd helped engaged in gentle conversation with other villagers. Krishna invited Ewan to eat at his home. They walked back along the station lane and people, he noticed, smiled at him no longer the Dacoit. At the far edge of the village, where the slope to the shop dropped, they left their sandals on the small step of a low house whose two rooms were parted by a narrow hallway reaching to a rear veranda. Forming a courtyard whose far side was a stick fence, two slim rooms extended from one end of the humble home. In the dimming light, Ewan made out fields of dusty winter-wheat dropping to a line of trees that defined the meandering river's continuation past the bluff.

The dusty road stretching north reminded him of cream suit.... he can't be a detective - they done nothing. But oh my gosh, are they watching, assuming I'm part of a gang, hoping to discover the others? Will I always be on guard? How desperate this new life.

His disquiet was soothed by tinkling silver bells as several women and girls in one of the extending-rooms knelt before a kitchen shrine to chant the sunset Arti. The two men and three boys of the household who didn't join in, bade Ewan to join them on reed mats spread over the veranda's compacted-earth floor. The bells and singing came to a crescendo and stopped. Hmm, women keep religion going but men control it.

Krishna's wife, a lively young woman with a saucy laugh, came out, flirting with Ewan as she dripped water over his hands. She held out the towel for him whilst shyer women dolloped food onto stitched leaf plates. Without speaking, the men ate the tasty aubergine curry, dal and rice with their fingers. I find it uncomfortable women only watching, serving, in silence. He said as much.

"They'll eat when we're done," Krishna scowled.

"I'm eating their share."

"They can cook more!" Krishna admonished.

Blast, this makes things worse, Indian cooking takes hours.

Ali arrived. He went straight into the kitchen to wet his chillum cloth and peels of devilish giggles came from the confined room. Krishna looked upset. Bearing a paraffin lamp, Ali came out to light the chillum and Krishna's young wife sat tight at his side in their circle. Uncomfortable, Ewan bade farewell. Extracting his tiny torch, he walked along the unlit lane. He had never been this far from electrical lighting. Within Merricott's dark vale, distant town lights tinted the damp air, blurring the night sky. Regret swamped him. Why did I do it? Will I ever recover all I've lost? Hating these suffusing moods, he grumbled, Life is too short for SOS. Don't waste it.

Gazing through the branches on that warm night, he felt insignificant, a speck on a pebble within billions of glowing points in a dark universe. Slowly the stunning splay of stars inspired him. I've found Utopia. Reclining on the plinth with his head on his bag, he drifted into a deep and peaceful sleep.

The plink of a glass on stone. His eyes shot open. The woman in green, alone with him in the dim light. Engaging with her jet eyes, he melted, her open smile igniting his heart. Throat pounding, he watched her swing her hips casually back to the Zaminder's mansion. I have found paradise.

Sitting up and sipping the welcome tea, he turned to part of a letter penned by Thomas Merricott in 1842: *"It befell me to wake to a most wondrous sight of a woman placing a cup of milk by my side. The damsel performed this duty every day of the long months we happened to be billeted beside her village upon the North West Frontier. Mother-fortune kept my life to the end of the Afghan-support campaign, hence I not unnaturally asked the young woman's father for her hand in marriage. You can imagine my disappointment when he informed me I was of the wrong caste. Bother the caste system!"*

Ewan's guts were bursting and he wandered about looking for public loos, hoping they were less vile than those in Old Delhi. A dawn migration out of the village caught his attention; wondering what extraordinary sight had attracted them, he followed but was surprised when women shouted at him; their unusual anger made him turn back. Passing men squatting in wasteland, he understood. How can they manage their bowels so efficiently? His didn't work only when dawn transformed the night sky. The area stinks! People were

45

despoiling their beautiful landscape. Why in this country abounding with geniuses, did they not think to cover their vile faeces? Heck, even dogs do!

After breakfast at the chai-wallahs, Ewan pulled on his bandana and spent two hours ambling about with his sketch pad. In the low morning light he caught a child trimming thorns off fat sisal leaves and another splitting the flesh into fibres on a wooden spike set in the earth. He portrayed them arranging strands of sisal to dry in the sun. He didn't see it as child labour, but each person helping their penniless family survive. His pencil defined a man plaiting dried sisal into string and he completed his visual essay with a child on a sisal rope-swing.

At the chai stall, he watched agricultural workers share a chillum, which he refused. They told him they grew the hashish by the tall sisal plants at the edges of their smallholdings. His drawings caught their gnarled hands, furrowed faces, weary eyes, heads haloed in placid smoke.

Krishna arrived and admonished, "Chewing, it is impolite to refuse our bhang."

The drug worked quickly. Sweeping his hands about him, Ewan sighed, "Poetic pre-industrialism in internet India."

Krishna grumbled, "We are poor peasants struggling in a land which is not our own."

A very old man who mixed English with Hindi said the last Englishman to visit had overseen the repairs to the iron bridge. "That was over seventy years ago."

Ewan hung his head. "From the 1600 to 1947, my family helped Britain steal your country's wealth."

The old man grunted, "You British were harsh but we knew where we were. With today's corrupt politicians and civil servants we're lost." It surprised Ewan how many Indians romanticised the Raj.

Quite stoned now, the talk of outsiders turned Ewan's mind to his crime and vulnerability. Disliking the sensation of being the victim, he rose and strolled along a little used track within a deepening gully between the station and the raised village. It dropped to the river and he noted it had once crossed the abandoned ford. Impressed by the water roaring over the wrecked blocks, he sat, sketching the wild river sweep around the curving gorge it had taken millennia to cut through the bluff. Rising from the western cliff top, the massive stone wall, the perfect defensive position.

It was hot when Ewan went to help Krishna weed his plot of wheat north of the bluff, beside the meandering river. After a morning's hard labour in the baking fields, he ate lunch at the chai-wallah's. As he drank tea, Krishna, Ali and their male friends drifted in from their own completed lunches. Ali laughed, "Our women are glad to be left alone."

A chillum loosened the men and with utmost charm, Ewan refused to join in. They explained their lives were dominated by the Zaminder, whose family had owned the land before the Afghan invasions of the 1400s. Mixing simple Hindi with broken English, the old chai wallah explained the present zaminder demanded ever more from the impoverished villagers. As he sketched the men, Ewan scribbled fiercely around his images.

Krishna grumbled, "We are bonded part of each day, related to the size of the fields he rents us."

Ewan nodded, "Aristocrats traditionally kept their peasants poor to have a supply of cheap labour."

Krishna continued. "On top of this, I am bound for five years because six months ago my parents borrowed money for my marriage."

The chai wallah said, "During a recent drought, the Zaminder handed out grain, bonding the entire village for an hour daily for three months."

Back in Old Delhi, No-Matter had explained many children working in the shops were bonded, repaying parental debts. Ewan had begun to notice bondage was widespread. Those with cash or grain lent to those in need who paid back with their sweat.

"I've been bonded an hour a day for three years," said a muscular man. "Sending my five year old girl to hospital, I borrowed a sum I could have repaid a bank in a year. She died within the week." The brawny man quivered. "Upset, I was understandably late with the first instalment so the Zaminder raised the interest from four to six percent, that's monthly, not annually, which has made it difficult to meet the repayments in full and so the sum increases and the pay-back time expands."

"You ought to have gone to the bank," Ewan suggested.

"Banks don't look after peasants!" The man angrily thrust the chillum into Ewan's hands.

Forced to partake, Ewan's nervous intake was over enthusiastic and he was rapidly stoned. His bulging eyes couldn't focus, the men's voices echoed in his head. He heard Ali grumble, "This present Zaminder even takes our women."

"Take Sati, the woman in the green shawl. To repay a family debt she's become his harlot," Krishna snarled, emotion swelling the veins on his forehead. "Sati is beautiful, intelligent. Since childhood we dreamed of marriage."

Sati! The woman in green.... Ewan's eyes flared; something snapped. No-Matter was right, dope is cracking SOS me, it releases my emotions. It draws out the wild young man I was never allowed to be. OK, another chillum. Ha! what good stuff! Wishing to end the injustice these people suffered, he thought up ways of getting back at the tyrant. When the old man translated Ewan's ideas, the villagers gawked in fear. Ali informed Ewan that he had dropped in on their lives from nowhere and could leave any moment, they were stuck with the Zaminder, who could ruin them if they merely whispered the least of Ewan's mad thoughts.

"How will you stop this if you don't act? This is the twenty-first century!" Ewan was too involved with his own narcotic judgements to notice the men's fears.

"Chewing, please," Krishna pleaded, "our gods and ancestral spirits protect and help us."

"What rubbish! You have that power!" Disgusted with their medieval capitulation to authority and religion, not understanding their impotence, Ewan stomped along the lane. He kicked the burning dust all the way to the Zaminder's square. Apart from the sweeper, the place was deserted. No wonder. With all that stone it was baking. Why the heck is the sweeper still sweeping? After a while his mixed emotions cooled, and sitting in the banyan's shade, he began to draw, but being stoned, his work wasn't good, although he thought it was brilliant.

He sketched a man sharpening tools, another fashioning a stave to repair the oxen cart. The door opened. Gasping, using a double-page spread, he created a semi-abstract whir of the reluctant young harlot in green, Sati's refined features set against a backcloth of disapproving faces and a stone engraving of a zaminder hunting deer. He drew the sweeper before the chipped decorations of an arch and pillar - at its base a pile of leaves, cattle dung, a broken tool. God, it's hot! Why does the poor man continue? Paradise hey! Ewan slept.

It was cool when the Zaminder emerged to check on his bonded workers. In contrast to their worn factory cotton, the man wore an elegant homespun kurta which hung loosely over ironed pyjama trousers. No-Matter had said the rich thought these simple clothes made them look like men-of-the-people. Noticing Ewan, the man ended a mobile phone-call and made his way to the banyan tree. "I say! Good afternoon, Sir. I see we are fortunate to have an artist visit us."

Ewan dropped his pencil. The Zaminder's educated accent was an Indian version of his old boss's back in London. The association awakened the fear of his accidental crime. Cream suit had alighted here! Befuddled by the bhang, by what he'd heard and seen, his simmering anger exploded. Looking the minor aristocrat in the eyes - in India an unacceptable challenge, he growled, "Not a con-artist like you."

"What do you mean Sir?" Cool, controlled.

"Your wealth belongs to the poor."

"Oh," the Zaminder looked disturbed by this unexpected confrontation. "Every country has its 'haves and have-nots', even yours, for I gather you are English by your accent, if not by your Indian looks."

"Italianate colour! You enslave these people in bonded labour."

49

"Tens of centuries before Europeans developed private banks, we had this ancient banking and insurance system." The Zaminder straightened his back. "Look what harm your banks have done."

"They're fairer than you!"

"Balderdash! They've destabilised economic systems, ruining entire countries. It is bizarre a man who grew up in a land which enslaved half the world condemns a civilisation that was ancient when Stonehenge was built."

Ewan realised the man was right on several counts, but his bhanged-up mind seethed. "History is as nothing! You bleed these people, unforgivable even in Buddha's days."

Dropping his voice the minor aristocrat snarled, "Young Sir, mind your manners. I could have you removed."

"Try," Ewan rose unsteadily, ready to wobble for justice.

"In my own time." The Zaminder walked casually away with perfect poise. A move designed to rub salt into smarting wounds.

"Bastard," Ewan snapped. Wow! I am stoned! I never swear.

Ignoring the insult, the aristocrat sauntered over to a villager and asked how his children were. Ewan hurled his barb again. Total silence. Without looking back, the Zaminder snapped his fingers twice. Two guards with bamboo poles emerged from the old stone porch, crossed the square with the assured swagger power generates in simple minds, their poles clacking the stone slabs, indicating what they were capable of.

Although not the aggressive sort, the certainty of his own fighting skills... and the dope, tempted Ewan to respond. Fortunately, his Aikido training crept through his bhang-bumbled brain and he stormed off mumbling, "Aikido forbids attack, only defence." He stopped, What is defence? Ah yes, I'll defend pheasant, peasant? pleasant? rights. Hmm, quite a puzzle....

Dust spurted from his feet, smothering his pounding legs as he turned through a portal in the old wall. Taking a well used path, he dropped down the slope, crossed the disused sunken track to the rapids, rose, skipped over the scorching platform, traversed the railway line and followed the continuing path into the riverside jungle. The temperature dropped instantly. Gawd, it's dark, mysterious, frightening! He sped up. Ten minutes later he strode out the far side of the bottle-green forest and found himself amongst shimmering rocks, parched earth and thorny shrubs.

He noticed movement amongst the river reeds. Gulp, Ali and Krishna's wife embracing! The dire landscape was braved by those charged-up sufficiently to ignore the supposed dangers of evil spirits and the real one of poisonous snakes. Ewan was stirred to interfere but the woman's giggles told him their tale was not new. He recalled somebody saying Ali and Krishna's wife had intended to marry, but being of different religions they couldn't. Damn religion! On the surface this settlement appears magical, underneath, it's a nest of disappointment generating deceit. And it seethes with ancient, incontestable power.

His mood was growing darker. He sped back along the thin path cutting through the imposing cathedral of trees. Where the trail skirted the river's edge, troubled, he sat on a rock, watching the current rage along the far bank. Slow whirls of water nearby brought up fish which peered at him before swimming lazily down into the calm obscurity. Stripping to his boxer shorts, Ewan plunged deep and lingered with the curious fish, refreshing his heat-weary body. He exploded late to the surface in a burst of bubbles. Gasping, treading water, he recovered his breath. Revitalised, he raced the placid pool's length until his anger lessened. His chest heaving, he lay on the rock, admiring yellow butterflies as big as his hand. Those poor villagers! And Sati! He bellowed, "Damn you Zaminder!"

An Aikido breath. Nothing. Emotion, he saw, was more powerful than discipline. Father was right, blast the man. Taking out a small chillum No-Matter had slipped into his bag, he studied the pipe. Drugs had done their job, he ought not take any more. But SOS is back and I need help. OK, for the last time. He filled it and lit the bhang. A deep drag.

51

"Whoo, this IS powerful, blast No-Matter! Ha, ha, he's blasting me! He, he! A real blast! Bye bye blasted SOS!"

ß

Dawn on the rocks, eyes heavy. Oh, I howled with the stars! A swim revived him, but it was going to be a tough day. I need help again. He lit a fresh shot of bhang, sang, "For Dacoit courage!"

High as a kite he stumbled about seeking the path two metres from him. Unsheathing his Gurkha khukuri, he unnecessarily sliced a new track through the jungle. Emerging sweating, puffing, panting, from the dense undercover, wild-eyed, he moved across the dry farmland howling greetings at villagers, "Yiha! Howdi hi!" They ignored him.

His mind rambled as he loped towards the village. Empires had come and gone - Auyran, Ashokan, Mauyran, Guptan, Mughal, British… and India was again becoming a World player, but families such as the Zaminder's persisted, bending with the winds of change. Back in England, he had disliked the way aristocrats he knew assumed the game was theirs, that normal people were pawns. But at least the British populous had degrees of self determination, here in pockets of antediluvian India, landlords continued to be the silent constant. Ugh, more powerful than the silly gods these villagers blindly trust! As ceaseless as the tired soil they till.

Crossing the station, dropping to the sunken track, he made for the decrepit ford. The exciting rapids fuelled his mood, but to fully charge himself, for he was not an aggressive man, he lit another pipe. And another. Yelled, "Off-to battle, rattle, tattle, battle!"

Lifting his bag, he rushed the defensive slope, bellowing "Dacoits, attack! The rack, what, a sack?" Con-fuddled, he fell, tumbling to the bottom. "Yihaa! Again!" But he slipped and was at the bottom once more. Third attempt, steady, almost, but at the top. He scaled the battlement, using worn gaps between the sandstone blocks. Astride the wall he discovered he was near the plaza's westernmost barn. Why didn't I just walk through the entrance? He sat swinging his legs, mustering courage, listening to the roar of water behind.

Wow! No-Matter's bhang's powerful, especially in such quantities. I'm light headed, more a ghost than a Dacoit.

The silky sun had not yet started to burn the sweeper who worked endlessly. There's Ali and Krishna! He yelled, "Krishna! Yoohoo! Ali Hiya!" Both ignored Ewan as they waited for their names to be written in what Ewan knew was the bondage book. Curling round the square, a line of villagers, as empty as the sacks drooping from their limp arms. The Zaminder stood by one of the stores supervising the distribution of wheat from the load Ewan had helped heave onto the cart. Sati appeared, bearing a bone-china cup and saucer. Without acknowledgement, the Zaminder lifted and sipped the tea, absently handed it back.

Enraged by such casual treatment of a goddess, Ewan vaulted down steep steps and fell ignobly in the dust, jumping up still in motion, wheeling to a stumbling halt. He, their lurching Saviour General, yelled, "Dacoits rule! Villagers! Let's have justice today! TooDaay HaayHay!"

Everyone turned from him. How will my Dacoit plan work without their support? Stumped, his feet scooped sand down the lane. At the unusually deserted chai-stall he shared another of No-Matter's pipes with the chai wallah who was quickly as stoned as Ewan. "Englishman. This's stronger than our local bhang! Hee, hee, ho, heeho!"

Ewan asked why villagers were buying wheat when it was ripening in their fields.

Garrulous as an idiot, the old man blurted, "The gods, those fickle gods, are not pleased with us. Last spring's crop was shrivelled by an unusually brutal sun, them gods! The summer crop was rotted by long-flooding monsoons, ugh the gods! The autumnal one eaten by a million hungry insects, oh what gods! We prayed, we made sacrifices, we held long rituals. Still the silly, silly gods did nothing. In the fields we tried everything we had been taught, but with three of the silliest of the gods levelling their cruellest tricks at us, what we did came to little. We worried we had displeased them gods, silly as they are, so we sought to work out how by paying a specialised mendicant to tease out the truth from those unhelpful gods. We got no answer. Not even a silly answer. During a harsh frosty winter we ate only one meal a day, and also fasted to please the gods. Even then they did not respond and soon our stocks ran out."

"Is the Zaminder, Zaginder, Zadinger? He is the Big Z! Is Z charging a fair rate?"

"Very, very high," the man looked upset. "Today Krishna relinquished a fifth of his single field to pay for a year's wheat. Although I don't rely on farming, I will inevitably suffer."

"What's the sweeper's poorly gory story?" Ewan gulped his tea earnestly.

"He stirred up discontentment over the Zaminder's unfair deals and his punishment is to work non-stop from sunrise to sunset every day for a year."

Furious, chillum-fuelled, Ewan jumped up, shaking the flimsy table, spilling his remaining tea. Bellowing, "Dacoits, to battle!" he dashed from the neem trees, pelted up the cobbled slope, puffed dust clouds over startled villagers, kicked the defensive wall to gain courage, belted across the slabbed square, knocking through the surprised queue. Yo! I feel powerful! OK, with a wee bit of a bhang-wibble wobble, but Dacoit-Determined. This is not how I'd planned it, but I'm sure few Dacoits' plans must work with precision. The Zazy Zar Dinger, ha, ha, needs stopping and everyone else is too frightened, so it's up to me to act. "ZarLinder! ZarKinger! You've gone too far!"

"What?" the minor aristocrat looked up.

"Bleeding these villagers!" Noticing the stunning Sati gawp in fear, Ewan bellowed, "Big Mr Z, you B bastard! Zarstard, ho, ho that's funny."

"What limited language you have you northern darkie."

That last word touched a nerve. At school Charles/Ewan the Dacoit had been taunted as the 'Chichi' or 'darkie', it was why Father had encouraged him to take up martial arts aged seven. "You, y...," he teetered, teetered, found his balance, just.

"Get him," the Zaminder casually told his two thugs.

56

Swivelling, unbalancing, our Darkie Dacoit confidently faced them. Ha, ha, I'm also a B, but a double BB black belt who plays regular rugby, so that should be BBR, brrr, he he! Ho, ho!

Unused to anything but submissiveness, the brutes slowed, tapping their bamboo lathis on the stone paving. The Zaminder barked. The poles flashed through the air. Although totally stoned, an Aikido move somehow manifested from within and grasping one of the pouncing poles, he twisted the man to the ground. Gawsh! Goowd hey! This made the second thug hesitate. An audible gasp spread round the onlookers. It appeared that this far from electricity, TV and even mobile phones, resistance and martial arts were unheard of.

The Zaminder bawled and the other lathi struck Ewan's shoulder. The shock enraged our swarthy bandit and he kicked out, tripping the man. Being Aikido-fair, he waited, giving the assailant time to rise. Both men attacked as one and when Ewan swirled his arms they fell. Gowd! And I'm stoned, toned, honed, ha, ha hiddly hee!.

But I'm no bully and My A for Aikido, AA, hmm, he, he, A hey, oops, forbids aggro … anyway, I've gone too far. Hope I didn't hurt 'em? He loudly prattled an Aikido phrase: "Respect others and they'll respect yoou hoo, bhoo hoo, woo, wee!" Feeling noble, almost saintly, he rotated. Too far, nearly tipping over, and he toddled off babbling, "Hee, he, heee, A for A-good!"

Searing agony flipped off his mind.

Ow, my head hurts. Ooo, shoulders ache. Ugh, chest too, ooh, legs, arms. It hurts to move. Huh, must get up. Why the sound of rapids? "HELP!"

Bright light blinds him. Ouch! Damn lathi. A door slammed shut.

A lost day, pain dominating his awareness, dipping in and out of consciousness. He woke, clear headed. Damn drugs! I thought bhang would free me, but its dreams became more powerful than fact. OK, drugs loosened my SOS, but unshackling my mind lead to anarchy.

And thirst, at first normal, but growing into an obsession. Surfacing in the dark yelling for water. The lathi. A stormy night tossed by Dacoits wrapped in green shawls. British expeditions galloping into the badlands. Zaminders riding harlots into battle. Cries for water. The lathi. Pain throbbing throughout his body, sinking back into oblivion. Time, what is it? "Help! Water!" A shot of lathi pain, Ooo, aaw. Oblivion.

Awake, eyes swollen, unable to focus on patterns of blue mould on the red-stone wall, pelvic bones on the solid damp rock floor. Aw, everything aches. Faint light emerged from a fist-sized grill below the ceiling, which acted as a funnel, intensifying dawn's screaming parakeets, amplifying the rapids. Hands covering his ears, his fingers touched his thudding skull. Blood crumbling in my fingers! This jolted him fully conscious. Remembering what had happened, he rose, thumped the door. His hoarse voice vibrated too loudly behind his eyes. "Help!"

The opening door flung him to the floor. A lathi slashed, slashed. He drifted in and out of pain, listening to the ache of the rushing river, to the torrent of blood pounding in his head, to his dry throat. The temperature increased as heat waves radiated from a tin roof which baked his cell. "WATER."

The squeaking door. Blinding light. The lathi. Blackout.

Throughout his second day he sweated profusely, constantly shifting, leaning against the moist wall or laying flat on his back upon the hard stone. He tried to sit or squat but the beatings, and lacking water, his body hadn't the stamina and he'd crumple. He kept blanking out. Upon returning to consciousness time was measured by the dryness in his throat, the jabs of lathi pain and the thud in his skull. Scuffling to the door, he kicked with his heel. The effort wore him out.

Bright unbearable light and the lathi.

The blow made him sink into his unconscious, opening Gerald Merricott's 1877 letter: *"How pitiful these wretched*

58

folk gasping for water, their hands as cracked as the parched earth they lie upon."

He drifted in and out of his dreams. Heat fell from the tin roof sucking damp from the rock beneath. Pounding water outside, driving him crazy. "Water, wwwwtr."

Time slipped by. Twice more, or was it thrice the slashing lathi when he cried for water. With practiced precision it flayed the same slashes on his skin. Yet not each time. Sometimes the cane stopped inches above him, the implied pain another torture. The beatings had made him incontinent. Not given a bucket, his frightened body's involuntary waste soiled his floor. The vile stench, one more torture to his sanity. Taken by his own bacteria, the perfect murder. His disease ridden body would float downstream and would not be seen as British, though if it was the authorities would note another druggie's death. If a proper enquiry ensued, a rare event, the villagers would be too fearful to say a word.

It's dark again. "Water!" How long … survive … without water … every breath .. wanting …? Time in hell is eternal. Hell… help. "Water," his swollen throat made a weak muffled noise. Bloody river, STOP damn you!

"Yes, they're killing me." His voice loud all a sudden startled him. I sound like Father! Did Father ever make it to this water? Oops, region? Great, great grandfather Albert had in 1887. I can see his copperplate writing on yellowed water, oops, pages as he describes some Maharaja's estate he was watering, oops, assessing. A graphic drawing of a Buddha raised within a pond, a watery pond! Behind, an elegant palace two stories high with rounded pavilions and curved upper balconies floating above formal gardens. Not the Zaminder's "WATER!"

He merged with the river's rolling current, tumbled through dislocated blocks of red sandstone, drifted along its meandering course, seeking the open sea. An eternal stillness hummed beneath the echoing waters - Where is this whisper of whispers coming from? A trick of the mind, perhaps my blood coursing through my ears? Who cares, it is blissful.

A dry moaning, an all too familiar rattle echoing from wall to wall. Mother lies in a coma. Her eyes pop open, she looks surprised I am before her. Her eyes soften as if she has realised she has love to give me, whom she once bore in her belly. I weep silently. Life stands still as we read each other's faces. Her tired eyelids drop. A dry rattle and I cry uncontrollably.

The door. Dawn's light. "Get the Zaminder! QUICK!"

Euphoric, waiting, waiting. Waiting my end. Rattling my last.

Footsteps echo, voices roll one upon the other. Then, "Englishman, I see they are treating you well," a snigger, "but you are such a filthy devil, lying in your own excrement."

Trying to respond, but incapable, Ewan shook with grunts, rattles, his eyes swirling. The effort made him wet and soil himself, moaning uncontrollably, vomiting.

"Quick," the Zaminder snapped.

Aah, water! Sensing coarse hands which understood suffering, he fainted. Awake, a warm wet cloth tenderly removing caked blood from my aching flesh. He fainted. He came round, recognising the man who eternally swept the Zaminder's forecourt. This man cleaned my cell. Coming and going all morning he fed me water as I fainted, woke, sipped, swooned. Must drink. Aah, cool drops explode upon my tongue.

Not another boiling afternoon! Senselessness.

Late afternoon light. Warm, soothing liquid, coating my mouth. Milk! I'm a babe given milk. Mother? Gradually, the warm honeyed milk returns him to life. He slept soundly. More milk, sensuously tepid. He nibbled soft rice pudding. "Honeyed rice pudding was Lord Buddha's first food after fasting." The voice a chamber of clarinets wafting across a soothing lake. "It helped him attain his enlightenment."

I can't focus on the face. Female? Before total night, the healing Buddha-gruel. I'm reviving. Sati? Sati's effervescent eyes, yes! Her Buddha porridge stopped me dying in this backwater, but she's generated an un-Buddhist desire in me. I want to free her, yes, for herself, but also for me. She's utterly lovely. I can see us together! That bloody Zaminder! We must escape.

As a test, when she'd gone, with her perfect features in his mind, he did a half body press-up and his energy surprised him and courage returned. The body is amazing, incremental exercise lifts you from death to life. Your cells respond, recreating the power-house you need to survive. In the dark cell, as he worked, he made a plan. And he slept. A breakfast of honeyed maize pudding again bought by vivacious Sati. Oh I want to rescue her... but I hardly know her, yet you can tell a lot from a voice. Hers is soothing but strong, vivacious but intelligent. Hang on, she's Krishna's, but he's married, so she's free! Yippie! Between her visits, inspired by memories of her face and voice, behind his locked door, Ewan exercised progressively, building back his strength, yet still publicly pretending weakness, playing for time.

Buddha's Gruel for lunch. "Sati, escape with me."

"We don't know one another."

"In this case, that doesn't matter."

"In India, it always matters." Walks out.

Damn India.

See where drugs get you, Unwun/You-Wong/Oo-When/Chewing! He smiled at his many names. Drugs took me from habitual self-control to a land where the usual social rules struck me as irrelevant. Yet breaking out from my stiff exterior led me to explore the vastness of the unshackled mind, but this made me act rashly. I could be dead, only my original fitness and training will enable me to survive where most people would not. "Bloody Zaminder!"

His voice alerted the guard. The door opened. Ewan watched the pole descend. I can take no more. Time in that tortuous hell coagulated into the present instant and the animal inside over-ruled his thought-based mind. Yes! Pure Aikido! With ease his muscles uncoiled, a hand and foot powered his body to swing from the floor, fluid, primate. The

61

other hand grabbed the lathi, the free foot kicked the guard's shin, tumbling him. Springing erect, Ewan snarled, "Ha!"

"HELP!" the man bellowed.

Like a leopard, Ewan slid through the door, bolting his tormentor inside.

I'm wearing only boxer shorts! He found his leather bag on a shelf. Nothing, not even the khukuri, was missing. Great! They're not thieves. He quickly dressed, slung his bag securely round his shoulders, tucked the khukuri into his belt, drank deeply from a water jug.

"Help! Help!" Over the guard's muffled crying, Ewan heard the Zaminder's voice echoing down the corridor. Blast! He dashed through an outside door, crossed a small yard, struggled to open a gate. A lathi's bite, blood gushed over his cheek, round his chin, down his neck. Weak, fainting, he stumbled, nose flat against the hot gate, slipping down peeling blue paint scratching his chin. No! Not back inside. Never! He rose, spun round. Another lathi! He dropped to one side. The bamboo cracked against the gate. Ewan kicked the thug's groin, grasped the Zaminder. Krishna arrived, reached for the fallen weapon.

"Krishna, leave."

"Chewing," Krishna confused.

"Please," the Zaminder half rose, worried, "be sensible."

"I want fair treatment," Ewan pleaded, suddenly weary of the fight, his righteousness uneasy with where the inner-beast had landed it. The Zaminder instinctually felt this weakness and dashed as the second thug appeared at the door. Krishna grabbed the cracked lathi. Ewan's distaste for violence was replaced by the crazy black-belt who toppled advancing Krishna with a sidekick as his hand thwacked the second thug's arm. Lightening Aikido defensive moves. He seized the Zaminder, withdrew his razor sharp khukuri from its scabbard, held the blade to the nape of the man's neck, wheeling him about as a shield.

"Please," the Zaminder cried over the guard's cries echoing out of Ewan's old cell.

Krishna raised a lathi.

62

"Stop!" Ewan's khukuri flashed. Blood spread across the broad silver blade. No! Not what I wanted. The Zaminder's involuntary flinch and pathetic yelp turned Ewan's stomach. Ugh, how many throats this khukuri has slit! I'd have made a lousy Gurkha.

"Don't kill me!" The Zaminder cried, pathetic. "Be civil."

"Civil!" A primitive snarl.

Stunned by the sound, aware they faced a beast, Krishna and the thugs stumbled stop.

Ewan rested his back against the hot stone wall, wishing for a less violent solution. "Drop the lathis." They obeyed. Pressing the knife against the Zaminder's weeping throat, "Open up."

One of the thugs went inside, found a key, returned, opened the gate. Ewan remembered the station, "When's the next train?"

Krishna looked at the Zaminder's Swiss watch, "Twenty minutes."

The gate opened on to the lane side of the plaza, exactly where our pirate once flopped over the wall before getting into a muddle. Sati stood there. He opened his mouth to ask her to go with him. Turning rapidly, she strode away. His world caved in. How foolish - I don't even know the woman.

Ewan ordered the men to walk a few paces in front. They left the square with his curved khukuri's point on the Zaminder's weeping cut. Ewan staggered, worried his back was exposed. I'm really scared. Whee, seems no villager wants to openly witness the Zaminder's humiliation. Yet in India eyes watch from the shadows.

How exhausted he was. It was not easy keeping the khukuri at the man's throat as they walked. There were moments when he felt sure the thugs could dash back and get the better of him and this made him sweat and the knife's smooth ivory handle felt insecure in his slippery palm. Hope I'm not injuring the Zaminder further. Seven long minutes and the strange group passed the unusually empty chai-wallah's. Two slow minutes and they were on the platform.

Ewan told the goons to move to the platform's edge and lie face down. They refused. Rushing with the excitement of the chase, snarling like a cat, Ewan thumped his fist into his victim's jaw, an uncivil act. Hearing his mindless growling and the Zaminder's piglet squeals, the thugs and Krishna lay unmoving on the sizzling slabs. His back near the boiling bricks of the small office, Ewan twitched his Gurkha knife from time to time to remind the Zaminder of its malice. In this rather awkward situation he found he could rest a little, gradually easing his back into the hot wall.

Three minutes dragged past. I've been tricked. I'm so, so alone and vulnerable. Five eternal minutes to go. Will a train ever come?

A 4x4 did. In clouds of dust. Out stepped two assistants and the smart man in the cream suit.

"Scheizer, Cream Suit!" Ewan lamented.

"Jaia Maharaja, Maha-sahib," the Zaminder managed deference in such a peculiar moment.

The bustling group froze and the smart man asked in English, "Namaste Daksha, can I be of any help?"

Ewan shivered. Not another Indian-Oxford accent! Are they breeding in the bushes? Yup, the man has to be an English cop, the whole thing's a set-up.

"Maharaj-ji, Ganesha shara nam."

"Daksha, you appear to have got yourself into yet another pickle." The new men stepped forwards. The thugs started to rise.

"STOP!" Ewan's taught nerves reacted as fast as a cat's. Slapping his free hand across the Zaminder's eyes, he drew him back, jammed the knife into the man's smarting wound.

The Zaminder yelped. "Aaw! Maharaj-ji! Arrest this man. He is trying to kill me."

The Maharaja, "Young Sir, could you please explain?"

Ewan, faint, hardly bothered to speak. "My state's proof enough," convinced he'd soon lose his grip, be back in that vile cell.

The supposed Maharaja's eyes took in Ewan's haunted appearance. "May I know your name, Sir?"

"Ewan."

"Namaste Ewan," he bowed, pronouncing it perfectly. "I am the local Maharaja, Indra will do." Stepping forwards, he held out a hand.

"Get back," Ewan snapped. This is an elaborate hoax.

"Ho dear." Scratching his heavy moustache, his brow wrinkled beneath neat black hair. "By the way, Ewan, we were both at Oxford, the Zaminder's family always Trinity, us Pembroke."

"Err?" the rapid turn in conversation confused Ewan, Oxford was a mirage. "Pembroke? Me too."

"Wonderful," Indra smiled generously. "Where was your room?"

"Umm. Far quad, beyond the JCR." How bizarre, but this is India after all.

"Snap! At first I had a wonderful view of Tom Tower, but the traffic!"

Strange world. He's obviously playing for time, weighing me up. I must keep this khukuri still, don't want to cut the Zaminder's throat.

"Ewan, my dear chap, as fellows we must help each other. Come, travel with me, I am about to spend two weeks in a monastery."

"Monastery!" Gawd! This chaps floating along the Isis, dreaming of Alice in Wonderland. "Not interested."

The rails started to sing. Indra peered into the distance. "I understand. Hmm, it is my duty to solve this problem."

"How?" Ewan was intrigued.

"I'm not sure." Indra hesitated. "Daksha, let being the victim teach you. It seems Ewan is simply trying to save himself. Fair play is in order. I'll be contacting you soon."

The train drew in. When it stopped, the apparent Maharaja climbed aboard a First Class carriage. Having settled him in, his two men walked quickly back to the 4x4 and drove towards the forested hills in the distance.

Thank goodness no cargo to be loaded or taken off. Only Indra and a small family alighted. Shoving the Zaminder, Ewan moved to the edge of the platform, yelling at the two thugs and Krishna to remain flat on their stomachs. Countless curious faces peered out of the windows. He waited until the train started to puff slowly out of the station. Blast, it's taking forever, but I'm taking no chances. As the last carriage passed, the speed increased. Now! Ewan kicked the Zaminder who fell in a heap. Quick, it's accelerating! Drop the khukuri! Panic…. Running sweating palms over his shirt, he jumped like a scalded cat, grabbing the vertical handrail of the last door scooting past. His feet were whipped away. Gaw! His sandals flew off, his bag heavy with three A4 sketchbooks, the two-hundred page family file, Delhi history book, Mughal miniature and a few clothes, unbalanced him. Blinkin' heck! Almost fell. God, imagine. He hauled himself aboard.

The thugs sprinted down the platform, gaining, gaining, the fastest leaping at the train. Kick his arm! Oops, he toppled into Krishna. The two men struggled comically with each other, separated, belted forwards, but off balance they tripped over each other's legs. Entwined, they rolled like passionate lovers, slowly tipping off the platform and onto the unforgiving rails. Ouch! That must've hurt. Entangled, yelling, they tried to get free of the other's awkward embrace as the crowd laughed from the open windows.

The second thug helped the Zaminder stand. The landlord bent, lifted the khukuri stained with his own blood; for a second he held his neck, fingering the curved blade. Bellowing, he threw the heavy knife at the wagons clattering on to the iron bridge.

The antique weapon bounced on a gleaming rail and the khukuri, fashioned from the spring of a stagecoach, soared and the iron butt of its ivory handle clanged against the first support of the British-built bridge. The khukuri had been old and treasured when a Gurkha leader had respectfully presented it to Roland Merricott after the battle of Kalunga in 1814. And Albert Merricott wore this same khukuri each time he marched his Gurkhas over this very bridge during his 1892 campaign against the Dacoits.

The knife spun in an arc above the raging river, hesitating in midair with the deadly edge sparkling in the bright sun. It plunged point-first without a splash into a whirlpool. Let it lie there. It could've killed the Zaminder. It's sliced too many necks. Bloody weapon! Bloody violence! Bloody history.

ß

"Devi tells me the sweeper can't believe his fortune."

Devi? Sweeper? "How long've I been here?"

"Um, now let me see Ewan," muting his phone, "do excuse me a moment. Err, this is your third morning. Thanks to your suffering, the sweeper will be working with our horseman. I do hope he will be accepted."

His hands, I can feel them, "He's a good man."

"Sorry, I must go." Closing contact. "Regardless of not being of the sweeper-caste, in people's eyes he has been defiled. If a sweeper says something to somebody carrying food, many will throw it away, believing it has been polluted."

I can't get my head round this culture. Gawd, I'm alone, with no friend, network or role. The torture has broken me. "Vile Zaminder!" Hang-on, I needlessly thumped him, at base we are all capable of being brutes. The train journey, vague memories of waking here, eating, going back to sleep, soft hands... "a young woman?"

"My sister, Devi. She left yesterday."

Gosh, I've been mumbling. "We are nobodies in a meaningless world of inflated nonentities."

Indra looked concerned.

All day Ewan slouched in the light-filled room, ignoring the stunning view, reliving his escape, torture. Oh Sati! I left you there.

Blinking, looking concerned, Indra answered another call. Golly, the man and that blinking phone. They were taking lunch on Indra's rooftop terrace when the Maharaja took three more calls, one after the other. After the last, Ewan said, "Indra, with all of our education, culture and technology, humanity's hardly advanced psychologically since we overtook the Neanderthals. In fact we're worse, destroying the planet... I dislike humanity, not individuals, but our species. Advice from our best minds is ignored." He shuddered. "Oh! It's all so worrying and without my past beside me, I'm lost."

"Ewan my-my, dear ch-chap, you'll rise from this dark valley by building up your strength. Go for increasingly longer walks. Let's start this evening, old fellow."

Returning from their sortie, scuttling through the monastery's central buildings, Ewan was again the quivering child under Father's frozen gaze, self-conscious to the point of being awkward with anyone but Indra. Gone the happy-go-lucky mood he'd discovered with bhang and all that drawing. But drugs…ugh! Life in that cell's killed the quiet confidence Julian said appeared like arrogance, but which came from financial security, my ancestral role and duties, and my inner discipline. Interesting, Indra has it; the Zaminder and Father too, hmph, proves security isn't enough! Bhang showed me the mind is mountainous, not the flat fenced fields I've been trapped in all my life. But what foolishness! Look what I've done! And have I damaged my mind? Help! SOS, Stop it!

"You OK old chap?"

Damn, mumbling again.

Indra closed contact. "Ewan my fellow, good news! Having slept on it, Daksha has handed Devi a formal apology."

"I hope the monster pays for his crimes."

Lifting his troubled head, Indra looked across the ashram's fields. "I cannot go back on my word, our family's reputation would be ruined. I pointed out - either a full scale enquiry, which will put Daksha in prison for years, or a compromise. Ewan, imprisoning Daksha, who is an unmarried single child, would destabilise the estate. His cousin would take over and Kaitabha is one of our most corrupt politicians, which is saying something in India. Such dastardly types bribe industrialists to do their bidding, they have thugs who bully villagers into voting for them, even kill opponents. Kaitabha's once bountiful estate where tigers roamed in his father's day is denuded of jungle because he mines talc, subsequently polluting his river with chemicals. At least the Zaminder, rotten as he can be, treasures what he has inherited. Where he mines red sandstone he is respectful of nature. If villagers do what he wishes, Daksha is a benign dictator. Furthermore, his letter illustrates he is open to change."

Ewan exploded, "He imprisons, tortures, rapes, extorts, ruins lives. He must pay somehow."

"Devi and I have worked out how."

"How?"

"We have instructed Daksha to plant potatoes."

"Potatoes!"

Indra stroked his heavy moustache. "With the shortage of rice and wheat, the poor are suffering. Potatoes here produce two annual crops. To his credit, Daksha absorbed Sati's ideas."

"Sati?" Potatoes became interesting.

"The woman in the green...."

"Yes, yes," his heart pounded.

"Daksha's going to plant his fertile riverside fields with potatoes. Half will be sun-dried and ground to powder which can be used like wheat flour. Sati suggested the rapids could drive a mill. She said the leaves make excellent compost after two years. She's a bright young woman. Thank you for inadvertently giving her to us."

"Giving?" Gulp.

"Oh dear Ewan, you have forgotten. On the train you revealed her situation. Appalled, I ordered my men to take her and the sweeper to my estate."

"The Zaminder will be mad!"

"Better than imprisonment, Daksha admitted."

Sati! I'm leaving on the next train. Yes! My new life has purpose.

"Devi insisted Daksha give the village five percent of every crop. He signed a contract to distribute half his harvest through her local charity. Mind you, this worries me... he is, umm, err, besotted with my sister."

"This is the Indian way of justice?"

"A pre-British way, yes dear chap. Punishment engenders resentment, but helping those we have harmed inspires empathy. To prove the point, the Zaminder's letter states I'll

70

have no reason to instruct my barrister to open his case. Like his name-sake in Indian mythology, at base Daksha is decent. Since his father's death he has simply been under his wicked cousin's spell, all he needed was to be shown Kaitabha's ways are counterproductive."

"Surely Kaitabha will seek revenge." Gosh! Is Sati safe?

"I have incriminating evidence against Kaitabha's cherished son. This is also set out in the letter my barrister holds. Oh I had fun writing it!"

It's all too much. I need to clear my mind with a walk. Stepping down the outside staircase to avoid meeting anyone, Ewan realised he had much to learn from this ancient culture. And Sati! Wow, what an inspiration. But I need to rest before meeting her. Moving from the buildings, passing through fields of roses, he ambled along the River Ganga, dreaming of a life with Sati. She's pale, Italianate like me… Sophia Loren, Yes! that's who she resembles. Hmm, a villa on the Italian coast, what life we'd have.

Indra closed his phone. "Having been made outcasts by the Zaminder, Sati and the sweeper need a place in society so I will arrange their marriage."

Ewan's chest deflated. Sati's ebullient eyes and strong, melodious voice danced through his mind. "But Indra, I'm interested in Sati."

"You!" Indra stood up. "My dear colleague, you two have nothing in common. In terms of experience and class, the sweeper and her are suited and his history shows he has guts. Marrying him, she'll stay in her culture, be near her family and friends, with you I'm afraid she'll become isolated."

Crestfallen, Ewan rose. He strolled along the Ganga's tree-lined bank. Sati! Dear Sati, surely…. But no, Indra's right. My concern for Sati surpasses my desire. Oh gosh, in a sense, I saw her as a way out of my predicament, so without her there's nowhere to go. Get a grip, I'm exhausted, can't think clearly. Realising he had left the ashram's confines for the first time, he sighed. This place is safe, it'll heal me and it's no big deal staying if I can escape whenever I want.

71

Heavy river mist enveloped the ashram on the morning the Maharaja said he was returning to his estate, "Ewan, please stay until I return. Go for walks, slowly get involved, not in the religious life, but by doing something. Err, on that point, umm, I have to admit to have found a gentle way for you to repay the ashram."

Ewan thanked Indra and watched the cycle-rickshaw melded with the mist. Now I am alone.

ß

Glinting in the lamplight, a dewdrop rolled off the unfurling rosebud. Ewan plucked the closed flower and put it in his shoulder sack. Two hours beside the misty Ganga, his last load spilled over the sheet piled high with opening buds. He helped a monk tie the corners and lift the harvest onto the cycle rickshaw.

At first disinterested in the task Indra set him, Ewan soon found pleasure in working silently alongside the nuns, monks and temporary visitors who regularly gave up time to concentrate on the 'indefinable'. They came from a cross-section of society, a few like the aristocratic Indra were wealthy, but the majority were ordinary townsfolk. Villagers couldn't afford the luxury of retreats, however, if the calling was strong they gave up everything to stay forever.

It was an existence designed to slow you. When the evening generator died at eight-thirty, most people were already in bed. The alarm sprang the ashram awake at four, within half an hour there was yoga chased by mediation. Ewan was glad those preparing breakfast, milking cows or plucking roses were excused. After the sunrise Arti ceremony, a hearty breakfast sent everyone off to farming, repairing duties or cash earning craftwork such as carpet making or bee-keeping. An hour's free time before a tepid shower in tepid water was followed by the sunset Arti and meditation, early supper, repose, sleep. Lay people dipped in and out, relaxing, reading or in Ewan's case, going for walks.

The sexes slept apart in elegant, two storey blocks with central courtyards. These weather worn sandstone structures created the northern and southern sides of a handsome plaza paved in the same honey coloured stone. Filling the square's eastern edge stood a beauty one floor high containing the meditation hall, office, meeting rooms, stores, kitchen and dining-room. Airy cloisters three paces wide rimmed the plaza, providing an attractive shelter from harsh summers, violent monsoons and bitter winter storms. It's western wall was pierced by arched doors and from this flower-festooned portal a gravel drive shot through wheat and mustard fields to a distant smudge of trees defining the main road to Haridwar.

Ewan would shower and dream-walk across the dark plaza, passing the still shivering bronze gong hanging from the cast-iron pulley system of the central well. Upon the kitchen veranda, facing the eastern rose fields, he would swig a cup of sweet tea. Swinging a kerosene lamp, he strolled along the path towards the Ganga and joined lamp-lit figures plucking roses. As he worked, he'd sniff open flowers specifically left for the ashrams' honey bees and having helped tie up three bulging sheet loads, he'd watch the monk's cycle-lights head for Haridwar's dawn flower market. The same monk took another freshly harvested load for sale before the sunset Arti.

It was three weeks before Indra returned and arranged for Ewan to transport the dawn roses. Peddling the heavy rickshaw through the ashram's peaceful fields, close lorry lights flashing past, faint lamps glinting upon bullock carts over-piled with spring crops. He imagined his bike-light was flickering along the nearby Great Trunk Road. Kipling had written: "You don't take The GTR, it takes you." Ewan pined to explore the GTR. Constructed by the Mauyran Empire in 300 BC as a secure alternative to the high-altitude Silk Road, it linked ancient cities from the Burmese frontier to the edge of Afghanistan.

On his return trip, Ewan would challenge commercial rickshaw drivers without passengers: "Let's race!" Draped in morning mist, a rickshaw could emerge from nowhere, dash alongside, overtake and be swallowed up by a halo of vapour, leaving only the driver's mocking laughter shivering in the chilled air. When these impromptu races were over, Ewan bought his new friends a drink in one of the many chai stalls-cum-restaurants lining the busy road. His Hindi improved rapidly, however, the monks asked him to avoid certain words. Those tough cycling men encouraged Ewan to repair the tired ashram bikes and rickshaws, which reminded him of

75

years of mechanical activity back on his family's farm. He told the monks regular servicing would make their trips to town easier. "The universe takes care of everything, Earring."

Laughing at his ever-changing name, "Somebody must keep the bikes going so the ashram can earn money from its produce and also do errands."

"Life has sent us you, Yee-Wong! When the rickshaws die, Oowin, they're given to the needy who repair and use them. Somebody always buys us another."

Not such a bad system, Ewan admitted.

When his clippers broke one dawn, a young woman quickly repaired them as they sat cross legged between the lamplit bushes. She'd recently arrived from a village ravaged by drought. Unusually, instead of following her family to Delhi's hazardous shanty towns, she chose to become a nun and joined his team amongst the roses. "Anita, d'you know anything about bikes?"

"No. Our village was too far from tracks or roads."

"Would you like to learn how to repair the rickshaws?"

"Yes," her eyes brightened at the challenge, but quickly dulled. "Being young and unmarried, the Abbot won't let me out of these grounds."

"I'll teach you."

"Thank you!" Anita smiled, bowing respectfully with her hands elegantly raised in the Indian fashion.

"Jaia Ganga Ma!" the monk's breath hung above the oil lamp.

"Jay Gaga Mal!" Ewan sang.

The monk laughed. "Ganga is a living deity, not a pop star."

Ha, deified because she created fertile lands. Ganga, appreciated since the Indus civilisation abandoned the unreliable River Indus. Hmm, myths are oral histories. Ewan unloaded the cloth bundles and released hundreds of opening buds. Lit by his cycle-lamp, he quickly sketched the mound of soft petals, the shaven monk's keen face and pink robes.

Stroking his own ever-growing hair, he wondered how they could rise, wash, shave and meditate before going off to perform their various duties.

Thirsty from cycling and plucking roses, Ewan strolled across the marble paving, aiming for pools of light at the edge of the wide promenade. In the first restaurant he called out, "Namaste, spiced tea please, no sugar."

"Sugar-not, Sahib!" replied a waiter keen to improve his English.

"Ne, ne - no sugar." Ewan relished the teaching-game which enlivened his morning routine. "Not too strong, please

"Putting more weak, sahib."

Ewan lingered in these half-smart establishments before the sun tinted the night sky, enjoying light philosophical discussions with those who tarried before Arti. A learned priest smiled at Ewan, "Oolong, cleaning soul in Ganga Ma when sun first rising to blessing earth, peace happening."

Oh yes, No-Matter's friend explained this. Ganga flows from the crown of Shiva's head. Shiva of lingum-fame, who Big-Bang Brahman gave the task of creating the physical universe. Forgetful Brahman, inventor of all that is manifest and beyond, whose knowledge was restored in Delhi by Ganga's dark sister, Yamuna. Hmm, was her rape a reference to the darker Dravidians pushed out by invading Aryans? Holy Haridwar, where Ganga's clear waters, sent by Shiva and his consort Parvati, gush from the Himalayan foothills and nurture creation.

A lawyer brought his attention back to the discussion, "U-Thong, there is a constantly repeating cycle during which Life is created and destroyed. It turns endlessly for eternity. Each cycle is One Brahma Day, or roughly 8 to 9 billion Earth years."

Ewan exclaimed, "That matches scientific calculations since the Big Bang."

"Hinduism very scientific, Oolong," the priest waggled his head. "All happening four stages. First Yug - Brahamn void - material universe unmanifest; Shiva lost contemplating it."

"Amazing! That's the pre-Big-Bang state of 'Singularity'."

"Oolong, too many billion years passing *Singularity*. Brahma worry. He implore Parvati make Shiva stop meditate, start work."

The lawyer continued, "Impressed by Parvati's austerities, Shiva rises and dances His Creation Dance. U-Thong, this marks the second Yug."

The priest nodded, "Oolong, third Yug - Shiva-Parvati sitting, lingum-yoni locked, supporting countless evolution process."

"Holy sex!" Ewan chuckled, recalling the discussion at Yamuna temple.

The lawyer said, "Gradually life becomes far too dense and materialistic."

"Oolong, this fourth Yug, Kali Yug. Excess materialism mean purity lost - Shiva angry, rising from Parvati, performing Destruction Dance."

"U-Thong, creation thus crumbles and we slide back into the first Yug, or *Singularity*. It is a beautiful progress from blissful spirit to perfect creation, which becomes overly materialistic, which finally triggers a meltdown that reverts everything to the nothingness of pure spirit."

The priest sipped his tea, thoughtfully, "Today Kali Yug. Shiva-Parvati," he coughed, "united lingum-yoni. Kali Yug creativity pinnacle, matter ruling, things evolving rapidly, spirituality almost non existent."

Holding up the latest i-tablet, the lawyer nodded, "Today we have undreamed of technologies, but I sense that we have lost our souls."

Ewan didn't know what 'soul' meant. Nonetheless, he couldn't resist singing, *"This is the dawning of the Age of Aquarius...."*

Laughing, the lawyer said, "Our sages really were wise, U-Thong."

Ewan nodded. The first chapters of The Vedas are the world's oldest known religious texts. Wow! So thrilling that extraordinary ideas dreamt up before ancient Egypt existed still thrive in modern India and can be matched by scientific thinking. What a country! Why, though, are her people still

78

preoccupied with Parvatis and Shivas, rather than the profound explanations behind them?

With the lightening sky, Ewan's eyes followed his companions to the temples. I see the marble paving as an ethereal bridge holding the divine Ganga from the commercial town clawing her banks. Yup, humanising nature with godly tales encourages people to be reverential towards it; we in the analytical West, emotionally detached, exploit nature. Yet nowadays India is convinced GDP, rather than 'soul', whatever that is, measures life's quality. Hmm, certainly feels like Kali Yug. Everywhere, our Planet's extraordinary creatures are suffering. Oh yes, Dostoevsky wrote: *'We are responsible for everyone and everything....'*

Sipping his ginger flavoured tea, Ewan peered at pricks of light flickering in the ill-defined temples perched above the rushing waters - priests preparing for the sunrise ceremony. As predawn defined the surrounding ridges, the promenade filled with sleepy women and men wrapped in shawls. Enigmatic figures, some local, most devout villagers who had saved for years for this.

He flipped to a letter penned by Daphne Merricott: *"Haridwar, 9th of November, 1937. The throngs travel from all over the enormous space which is the Indian subcontinent, bouncing all day and night on the cheapest wooden seats of the carts, buses and trains they can ill afford. Each impecunious family might only have saved enough to witness a single holy sunrise and sunset before reassuming their rough night-transport homewards. However, their exhausting ten, thirty-six hour, even six day travelling adventures, keeps them spiritually charged for the rest of their tough days."*

Oh yes, Krishna pines to come here, must get family return tickets. Indra can deliver them. He looked up Sylvia Merricott's, letter dated 1881: *"Mine eyes were wetted and verily sore from much weeping as I watched the man I have loved these many years walk from me. His naked body, smeared in sacred ash from the fire of his perplexing initiation, moved towards the mysterious River Ganges. He, now a sadhu, gave not a backward glance at me and was*

79

swallowed up by Haridwar's devout pilgrims. Thus was my husband forever lost to me."

I've lived these texts since infancy, and here I am where they were penned! He sketched crowds performing ceremonial ablutions in the cold clear water; poor No-Matter has the filthy Yamuna. He walked to his rickshaw, the monk's flowers were almost gone; he nudged his wheels through Haridwar's now clogged streets.

Sat upon the flower planter, Ewan admired the driveway slicing the recently harvested winter wheat, a fat orange sun sank over the distant road to Haridwar, bird song soothed his mind. He was calmer than during his bhang-weeks and because of them, more open. His task was to find a spot between his mundane rationality and the emotional child it had always hidden. He cocked his ear. Spilling over the wall from the plaza, muffled chanting.

"Avoiding Arti again!" Indra strode through the gates.

"Indra! You're back!"

"I have to keep an eye on my wayward ward."

"Do forgive me, but I'm not religious."

"I understand," Indra smiled. "May I sit with you? My dear chap, I must talk of a serious matter. Much as women like Anita might interest you in a purely platonic fashion, you must avoid talking to her. It puts undue pressure on her. Did you realise people think you will soon propose?"

"Marriage! I've simply shown a person the mechanics of rickshaws and talked about village life."

Indra gave the hearty laugh Ewan had begun to love. "India resembles Spain in the 1930s. Outside of the cities, if we talk to women who are not relatives, we do so in the company of their elders. Thus, my dear colleague, talk to Anita in the company of her new family - the nuns."

"Oops! I thought nobody would imagine me trying to chat-up a novice!" Deflated, he thought of Sati. "Ugh! Arranged marriages."

"Hmm," Indra appeared to ponder the enormous difference between their cultures. "They generally last.

Perhaps our parents are good at choosing our partners. Mine were, although my wife prefers her version of Buddhism, which I keep telling her is not much different to the ancient Vedanta it arose from and which we still practice here. I must state, however, that many of your western love-marriages do tend to end in divorce, my dear chap."

"We often chase sex appeal and sparkling personality, rather than friendship and commitment." Images of Sati flickered through Ewan's head. Which one represented his attraction to her?

Indra stroked his moustache thoughtfully. "Your civilisation pursues the gods of desire, satisfaction, materialism and change, whereas ours upholds duty, society, magnification and continuity."

"We're opposites! Magnification equals religion?"

"Exactly."

The creaking gate made them look up. Swami Prem, the Abbot, boasting the ashram's pink robes and bald head, glowed beneath the striking scarlet sky. The man sat and spoke of financial matters with Indra and afterwards he turned to Ewan. "Earwing, best not mixing with low-caste rickshaw wallah."

"Swami, you ought to know caste doesn't matter!"

"They bad-mash, drinking liquor, smoking."

"My mother drank and smoked."

"Your mother!" the old monk spluttered.

Indra quickly stood up, "Forgive Ewan's English humour, he does not mean alcohol and cigarettes venerable monk, but tea and incense." He quickly steered Ewan through the arch on some pretext or other.

"Lier," Ewan taunted as they moved around the cloisters.

"Alcohol is regarded as sinful because many get blind drunk. And, err, women smoking, umm, how can I put it without offending you old fellow, well, err, huff. In non-modernised India, though not in my case I must hastily add, such women are seen as, umm, well, err,...tarts."

"My mother a tart!" Ewan spluttered at the notion of his stiff, aristocratic mother, fag in mouth, whisky bottle in hand, leaning against a city lamp post. His mind went to a letter complaining of a young relative who gained a reputation as a vamp in Calcutta because she preferred drinking whisky with Maharajas to gin and tonic in the stuffy company of British civil servants at The Club. Dear Sylvia, after her husband became a sadhu.

They lingered in the male block's wide entrance, gazing over the attractive square. "Ewan, old chap, I hope this place is not bothersome?"

Ewan followed his friend through the wide, windy hallway. Hmm, physically, I'm great. Plucking roses, cycling, running and walking along the Ganga, a vegetarian diet, they suit me. I'm recovering my sanity too. The fear of being helpless after the torture is diminishing, yet I dream of Sati.... "Indra, ashram life is better than commuting to London."

Indra led them up stairs rising from the inner courtyard. Upon the first floor's orbital balcony Indra touched Ewan's shoulder, "That's a relief old chap. I do have a wife and family and also an estate to run."

Arriving at the stone awning shading the stairwell, they stepped across the exposed rooftop. Leaning over the western edge, his olive face tinted peach against a neon sky, a city visitor enjoyed the sun's dying blaze. Through a gate in a stone wall demarcating Indra's family zone, they entered a secret, arty patio decorated with Indian statues, Chinese pots, Tibetan prayer stones and gnarled wood. Sheltered from public view by Indra's sandstone penthouse which glowed tangerine, they settled in canvas directors' chairs. "That scarlet arrow of geese is chasing the Ganga." They could fly me to Sati's side. Maybe she disliked my cumbersome nose?

"Ewan, I am glad we don't always attend Arti," Indra smiled slyly as if skipping school. "Before you came, I missed this sunset spectacle."

Ewan stared at the purple hills. "Its splendour makes us insignificant." I'm insignificant without Sati in my life. On her I piled my infant need of a mother, adolescent desire for a lover, adult wish for a soulmate and fugitive's desperation for a harbour.

"Yes, yes." Indra stroked his heavy moustache and took a slow, deep breath, signalling one of the old fashioned speeches Ewan had come to enjoy. "Here we fragile creatures sit, our fickle minds delighting in a drama our frangible orb and bounteous sun performed for the long extinct dinosaurs. Each human generation has witnessed this theatrical display." He swept his arms across the spectacle, "amongst the other spheres within the tiny portion of the universe which is our vast expanse of sky, this frail earth is a mere dot. In the face of all this, we are but puffs of air in the passage of time and matter."

"But what puffs! Our minute brains register every hue of colour in this complex show. More powerful than any computer, they compare the effect to other sunsets we've seen." I will never share a sunset with Sati. Aah, what presence, what intelligence, how independent; she encapsulates the ideal woman haunting my dreams. Hang on, I'm mesmerised by her beauty, imagining that I played a part in saving her I assume I deserve a chance.

"The magic of existence," Indra smiled warmly. "Our delicate beings dangle from a fine thread of life suspended between the cosmos' hostile void and the intimate pulse of each heartbeat." Indra chortled, "ha, ha, my dear friend, I love sharing my space with you."

It was late when Ewan completed a heartfelt letter by candle light. In it, he told Julian of his misadventures, of his feelings for Sati who was lost to a meaningless coupling for the sake of convention. He wrote of the cavity within. What, he asked, is life about? Gaining purpose? But what purpose for an isolated fugitive? He implored his friend to come to India and add some warmth to this cold journey.

His candlelight flickered life to a bonsai whose miniature branches stilled his mind. He was always busy reflecting, analysing, planning, even within the peace of his hereditary land his thoughts used to scan the terrain for jobs to be done. He had felt mental stillness in Aikido, yet Aikido's still mind focused on your adversary's actions; even when drawing the focus was to capture what you saw. This bonsai-moment was

83

entirely new. There was no agenda, just a still openness to what was. When it evaporated, Ewan gazed over the crown of his golden light and into the utter darkness. What was that extraordinary stillness? How did it happen? The fleeting experience has left a shimmering within my chest. Pushing French windows, he tiptoed across Indra's spacious sitting room and entered one of four bedrooms. Windows opened to soft night sounds and the soothing flow of the Ganga, he fell into a deep sleep.

The tender warmth made the morning magical. Refreshed like on no other dawn, Ewan enjoyed picking roses and his trip along the dark road to Haridwar. Instead of sitting with the priest and lawyer, he took a warm clay mug of chai to the Ganga's edge and watched until the flickering temple lights on the dancing waters melted into the rising sun. Gosh, this sitting and watching without motive is quite something.

Returning from the flower market, he greeted the gatehouse monk as his rickshaw bumped off the tarmac and onto the monastery's gravel driveway. Deep breathing rid his lungs of diesel fumes and halfway, by a lone neem tree, he lingered, enjoying the shift to natural sounds. He continued, and bolted the cycle shed which leaned against the outside of the plaza wall. Ah, what peace. Trying to squeeze past the pink bulk blocking the gateway, Ewan chimed one of his best Hindi lines, "Perfect morning Swami."

"Indeed Earwing. How's Ananda doing at market?" Swami Prem's fat forefinger scratched the top of his bald head.

"The marigolds and most roses were sold when I left."

"Good." The Swami slipped from pure Hindi into the mix of broken English-Hindi Ewan used for more complex ideas. "Earwing, you working with energy."

"Thank you."

"Better channelling vision internally."

"Why?"

"Helping make anger useful force."

"Anger?" Ewan felt he was leaving the Zaminder behind.

84

"Beneath polite English facade, buried childhood hurt." The Swami peered intensely at Ewan. "Protecting wall holding development back. Go in, heal hurt."

"Interesting," and apt. Until last night I'd thought the opposite - that I need to be more extrovert.

ß

The breakfast alarm sluggish, off-key, tapped by an old monk after he had rolled out two hundred stuffed parathas; not this day. Brilliant brass notes zinged around the enclosed plaza. Ewan spun round and his jaw dropped. An athletic figure snapped the metal baton, each strike exact, with precise pauses letting the chime resonate within the cast bronze. From years of Aikido, he recognised somebody present in the act.

"Namaste Ewan!"

"Indra!" Ewan rushed over to hug his friend.

"We came on the night train. Devi! Come, join us," Indra waved at the bell ringer as she laid down the steel rod. Devi drifted over, feline, at ease in her world. Cross legged on long lengths of ashram-made sisal matting, they sat on the kitchen veranda amid nuns and monks who were hungry after weeding the fields, milking the cows and other duties. Jet hair in a pageboy cut, Devi, a beacon amongst the severely shorn nuns. Her gaze flicked over Ewan and a charge buzzed his mind. Dizzy, he dimly recalled a faint shape offering him a bowl of cold avocado soup. He remembered sipping out of politeness, passing out, waking, sipping more, recalled the apparition ordering, "Don't try to please! Sleep if you need to." His embarrassed gaze flipped over to the rose gardens.

"I see you've recovered. In the Zaminder's village, Ewan, you're a hero, but not the sort they wish to see again."

"Not so clever." Turning from her bright black eyes, he squirmed.

Uncomfortable, Indra said, "Devi's staying, but I'm on my way up to our Himalayan house."

"Indra, I've missed you these past weeks and now you're off before we've had the chance to linger over another sunset."

"Oh, err, thank you, but I do have work I must attend to. In any case, Devi's worth several of me."

86

"Ssh!" Devi whispered as a silver bell tinkled. Everyone hummed Om. In silence, using their fingers they scooped up the food servers dolloped onto leaf plates. It had taken Ewan a while to enjoy a savoury breakfast, but the physical work made him hungry, despite his habitual dawn snacks in Haridwar. When all were done eating, talking began again. Devi said, "Ewan, it's time you tried meditating."

"How?"

"Close your eyes, watch your thoughts. Nothing more. Anyway, after breakfast there's a short session."

"It does sound easy."

"I must do my duty. Listen out for the bell." She started clearing up the leaf plates which were to become fodder for the cows and water buffaloes.

How sustainable these Indian habits. Your plate becomes food, no forks nor spoons needed. Tipping water from a brass jug, he washed his lips and hands and went to the men's building to perform the new task the Swami had given him. Opening a large cupboard set beneath the open staircase, he removed a reed broom. With easy sweeps he made his way round the cloisters surrounding the inner courtyard, his heart beating faster as a subtle tension made him work rapidly; he was proud to complete the task quickly.

Splutering, Swami Prem came to check progress. "Earwing, less haste, less coughing, more peace."

"Yoga is about slowing down, living gracefully?"

"Fine way putting," Swami Prem slapped Ewan's shoulder. The two men bowed with their hands raised respectfully in the prayer mudra.

Devi pealed the plaza bell. Ewan waited until she was done and they joined nuns and monks in the hall. Pointing at a badly painted picture of an old yogi with roses and marigolds spread loosely before it, Devi whispered, "The guru who inspired my ancestor to build this place."

Swami Prem arrived, faced the picture, joined his palms in prayer and they followed the abbot as he sang Arti. Oh how I love this hymn. Each time people inserted the name of their chosen deity - Kali, Shiva, Ganga Ma, but there in the Vedic Ashram they used the original 'Jagadeeswar'.

"This is not God," Indra had explained to Ewan's relief, "but The Inexplicable."

They sat upon strips of thick ashram-made wool carpeting. Ewan was astonished he couldn't keep still like the others. My knees hurt, my weight hurts my folded ankles! Furthermore, my mad mind! Thoughts speed in, they zipped out, they dart about where they want. He opened his eyes, they slipped over Devi's athletic shoulders, he snapped them closed and he flitted from the storm in Sati's eyes, lingered upon the London office cleaner's lips, hovered before Father's stern face, heard the Zaminder laugh, felt the lathi bite, sensed his blood turning his face sticky, knew the pain of wanting death. His eyes popped open. This passive nothingness is torture, its revived my Hades! It's better to do, do, do anything but this! Aikido's stillness is, like drawing, active, charged with attention. Hang on, what about that bonsai moment? It arose naturally. Had no agenda. Yet trying to invoke such stillness has created its opposite. What's going on?

At last the bell sounded. Everyone bent forwards, placing their foreheads on the floor. Refusing to bow to anything, Ewan stood, stretched his aching knees. Walking awkwardly, he followed Devi and Indra over the plaza and up the outer-steps women used when visiting the family's rooftop apartment.

They were drinking mint-tea beneath a cotton awning and the land warmed. "Do tell me about the man in the painting."

Indra took a deep breath, "My dear colleague, where to start, err, at the beginning, I suppose, yes, err, ump, that would be wisest. Um, one day, after witnessing his overpowering landlord treating a fellow labourer most cruelly, a bright young peasant went and sat under a dusty roadside tree, where he began to think profoundly about mankind. He obviously had a mind capable of concentrating on a single idea and knitting together its logical connections, for he explored the topic all day and night. When his distraught mother found him at dawn, he was glowing."

"In this land of exaggeration," Devi smiled indulgently at her elder brother, "such tales have glowing gods under dusty roadside trees and of course, adoring mothers. It's how our priests condition society...."

Indra coughed. As head of the household and being a Maharaja, until he had met Ewan, only Devi interrupted him. "Dear chap, I believe his eyes were alight with intelligent insight, his relaxed facial muscles made him look bright."

"Why?"

"Err, well, Swami Premananda, who this glorious youth was later to be called, had had a revelation. He told his mother life was meaningless unless he became a student of Yoga so as to sharpen his body and enable his mind to find a solution to mankind's eternal problems."

Devi explained, "We Hindus think the mind can't develop without our first treating the body well."

Ewan nodded, "Research shows health and mental stability are linked to exercise."

Indra cleared his throat. "Sifting through many false sadhus, Swami Premananda eventually spent several years with a sage in a mud hut in dense jungle. It stood beneath the stage in the hall. After many arduous years of mastering Hatha Yoga's postures, his guru introduced him to the first stages of Raj Yoga, or as you Westerners call it, meditation."

"Here's where we come in," Devi appeared to be speeding things up.

Another cough. "Years later, our illustrious ancestor was on a shooting expedition. Upon hearing guns, Swami Premananda emerged from the jungle to stand before the hunting elephants, forbidding the party to kill living creatures. You can imagine the uproar."

"Shooting was permitted so close to a holy, vegetarian city?"

"That arrogant guy hunted wherever he chose," Devi laughed.

Indra shot a warning glance. "My dear Ewan, they remained locked in discourse for a long time. At some point our relative got down from his high sedan and walked off with the yogi. It took his staff two days to locate the jungle hide-out and they found the Maharaja had exchanged his silk robes for a cotton sarong."

"It must have shocked." Ewan knew well the constraints of aristocratic circles.

Devi smiled, "The family went nuts. And now we're bananas about the Swami's Yoga system."

Indra interjected, "Swami Premananda taught Vedanta, the form of Hinduism uncluttered by gods."

"More philosophy than religion. Many Indian nuclear scientists and world famous microchip guys are Vedantic Hindus," Devi stated. She stood up, leaned over the balcony, "Ewan, Swami Prem's asking for you."

Joining her, Ewan peered down at the red-roofed veranda encircling the plaza. What a sublime place Indra and Devi's relatives created. "Swami!"

Swami Prem stepped into view, "Earwing, coming please."

Ewan jumped down the exterior steps. "Hello Swami!"

"Earwing, here one month. Making choice."

"Sorry?"

"Leaving tomorrow," the Swami stood tall, "or stay learning."

Ewan was floored. Where can I go? I'm safe and cared for. India's crazy unpredictability is held at bay, enabling me to revive my spirits. To leave so soon might regenerate my inner crisis.... That's frightening.

"Answer my room, ten minute."

Back up with Indra and Devi, Ewan said, "I must decide to stay or leave tomorrow."

"My goodness, that is a surprise. I wonder what got into the old Swami. I tell you, Ewan, I had absolutely no idea of this. Dear friend, stay, discipline your soul. Three months is pointless, better six," Indra retorted.

Whoo, Indra's unusual brevity says a lot! I'm too unstable... there's something to learn from these people. Curious but confused, Ewan opened the gate, walked to the back of Indra's penthouse, turned the corner and entered a separate but adjoined apartment. A spacious room, white walls, dark pink rug with two shocking pink cushions atop, a clay water pot with a glass; no furniture, pictures, posters or ornaments. An open door showed a simple washroom; another, a bedroom containing a thick-reed mattress with folded blankets, on a single shelf, the Rig Veda bound in pink silk, three pink shawls of various thickness and two pink robes.

"This is so bare."

"Not when mind peaceful."

Hmm, interesting, perhaps we clutter our homes with objects because we're too busy to see beauty in simple things? The Swami's voice drew him back.

"Earwing, answer please?"

"I'm staying. Three, maybe six months."

"Good." The teacher and pupil stood barefoot on the thick rug. "Earwing. Countless generation yogi go Himalaya find peace, explore life meaning."

The atmospheric dust had subsided with a heavy overnight mist, unveiling an inconceivable curtain of livid blue draped behind the parched plains. Fold upon fold faded into the clear sky with the promise of unseen worlds. Ewan felt an urge to explore those enigmatic ranges, to follow his ancestors who had climbed those massive ridges into Nepal, Sikkim, Bhutan and even deep into Tibet. Some had reached China, others trekked westwards through Kashmir and Ladakh, one or two fought or died in Afghanistan. Two became yogis. A couple had married Indians.

By now Ewan understood the importance of using people's titles. "Swami, why isolate yourself from humanity?"

"Fine question, Earwing," the Swami smiled warmly. "Leaving busy street we study science or history; yogi contemplating infinite in ashram-college."

"What use the infinite in this mess?" It no longer surprised Ewan he was becoming provocateur. The period of rest after torture was awakening his emotive strength, for the first time he felt less need to cow-tow to social order. This a glint of the inner beast which saved him in Delhi and at the Zaminder's - few experienced this creature, even after gaining an Aikido Black Belt in England his life had been too distracting for it to happen. More's needed, but what? A simpler life? Yes, and that definitely means staying longer.

"Infinite giving perspective to small life, encouraging us rise above selfish desire. Yogic stillness is lotus flower - root in mud, flower above water surface." Smiling at this overused cliché, the old Swami sat on the rug, inviting Ewan to copy.

Hmm, religions, like cultures, exchange ideas constantly, who knows where the lotus analogy was first used. The Swami's voice pulled him back to the room. He sat on one of the pink cushions.

"You wanting learning... or adventure?"

"Learning, Swami." The healing calmness, the stunning environment, Indra, they lured him towards India's mysteries. Talk of mysteries! Sati! her eyes showed she liked me. I must intervene.

"Earwing," the Swami bowed, hands folded at his chest. "Life without peace, life wasted. Path to inner-calm starting Yoga. Yoga exercises cooling mind, keeping body fit. Eventually generating single mindedness."

Dragging himself from Sati, "Concentration is the aim of Yoga?"

Unused to being interrupted, the Swami coughed. "One aim. When single-minded we calm, reacting better to world. Relaxed muscle meaning easy communication between body and mind."

"Psychopaths can be single-minded and calm whilst committing dreadful acts."

"Pye so-Kaths?" The old man stuttered. "Earwing, only truly calm when knowing who we are. This Yoga real aim. Begin by controlling senses."

A welcome breeze wafted through the wide windows, "Hmm, Hatha Yoga is similar to Aikido."

"Eye-key-Know?" Baffled, the Swami shifted. "Proper breathing essential."

"Hmm. Better than a doctrine which talks of sin."

The Swami looked up quickly, took a deep breath. "Hinduism No sin! Steady mind appreciating nature's intricacy. Life more complex than anything man making - even simple ant."

Visions of the Zaminder filled his mind, "Life is ruthless: ants kill other insects and in turn are eaten by birds."

"Ant? Bird?" The Swami fiddled with his robes. "Earwing, if compassionate, feeling better."

Ewan saw his onslaught was disturbing the Abbot. Indra had admitted rhetoric was not a Hindu skill. He went to the window and leaned on the sill looking across the river. "May I?" he tipped the clay water pot, filling the glass. He drank in the Indian fashion, holding the glass above his back-tilted head, pouring a water spurt carefully, so his lips wouldn't foul the glass. It had taken him days at No-Matter's to learn this neat trick without wetting his chin and shirt.

The Swami rose and laid an arm on Ewan's shoulder. "Emerging from Himalaya, sage attack by leopard. He feeling, *'Have live good life, now ready for premature demise. Feeding leopard - serving nature.'* He detached, knowing life unimportant in detail, big picture best." The monk took the refilled glass from Ewan and drank deeply.

"The sage's pain is important! And life's detail is amazing: proportionally, a flea jumps faster than a racing car." The Swami fidgeted nervously with his robe. Knowing the Swami's reputation for long monologues, Ewan continued his interruptions.

Half an hour later, "Earwing, starting Hatha Yoga tomorrow."

93

The old monk snapped his windows closed to stop monkeys from entering the apartment and ushered his troublesome guest outside. By Indra's gate, Ewan shook his head as Swami Prem rushed across the warming terrace. The guy's certainly lost his cool. Back inside his own room, he put a new sketchbook in his leather bag, walked over the terrace towards the stairs. If I'm beginning this Yoga malarkey tomorrow, I need to escape.

"Can I join you?" Devi called.

"I'll be away all day," he wiped the mild sweat off his brow. "People will talk."

"To heck," Devi laughed.

He erupted into the cloisters. Indra, who was writing a note, rose from a stone bench set within the cloister wall. "Ewan, you'll have to move out of our apartment, because Devi's here."

"Indra, how can I thank you," Ewan hugged his friend. "Where'd I be without you?"

"In deeper trouble with another Zaminder!" Devi, breathless from scampering down their outside stairs.

"Stop teasing him, Devi."

"Indra, you've really helped me."

"You saw the opportunity," Indra smiled warmly. "See you in six months."

"Possibly," Ewan shrugged. After the meeting with Swami Prem, he was uncertain.

"Please. Stay that long for me." It was a command.

Considering his debt to the man, Ewan felt he had to shake on it. The siblings hugged. Indra picked up his suitcase and cut across the blazing plaza.

Fishermen's lines sliced the Ganga's silver-green surface, herons' wing feathers fingered the still air. Flipping off his sandals, tearing off his shirt, Ewan dived in and splashed to the far bank. Racing back with mountain-iced liquid clawing his skin, he clambered out covered in goose pimples.

"Damn the Zaminder! When a nun and I washed the blood off you, we thought those wounds would disappear." Devi touched the welts running across his back and shoulders.

He shivered. No woman's touched my bared skin since infancy. Embarrassed, he put on an Indian accent, "Holy Ganga water curing all ills."

"Oh Ganga Ma!" Devi laughed, wobbling her head from side to side, exaggerating in the British-Indian sitcom style.

Watching her, Ewan felt a pang of homesickness for the self-mocking theatre of melting-pot Britain. Will I ever be able to return? Masking his feelings, he threw himself into copying Devi's slow, comic dance. Stepping with bent knees splayed sideways, they leaned towards the holy river, their elbows forced outwards, their hands above their heads in prayer. Unbalancing, they fell to the grass chortling. Rippling with uncontrollable emotion, Ewan realised he had never really laughed, so frightened had he been of disturbing the peace at home. What is it about Devi that teases the wounded child from me?

"Come on, you mad thing," giggling like a teenager, she tramped off.

They passed an encampment of villagers from some distant corner of India whose hired bus driver had found a dusty track to the river. At the water's edge women washed soapy children, scrubbed clothes, scoured cooking pots with ash-laden grass and rinsed them all in the sacred Ganga. High on the banks other women cooked on open fires, stirring huge quantities of dal and curry with shaved branches cut from the overhanging neem trees. Squatting in circles, men played cards in the shade, clouds of peasant cigarettes or chillums hanging over their rounded forms.

"Want to join your lazy gender?" Devi taunted.

Ugh, drugs! "Indian women are never on holiday."

"It's the same worldwide." They had arrived at a crossing point and Devi suggested, "Let's have an adventure."

They stepped into a flat bottomed punt off-loading a man and his dog. The thin boatman leaned on his long pole and worked his way from the western bank, midway the current swung their nose downstream and they were fanned by a welcome breeze falling from the looming foothills. Upon the far bank they perched on the wobbly bench of a chai wallah's and drank tea. Draining it, Ewan smashed his clay cup on a pile of shards.

"Done with satisfaction," Devi smiled.

Hmm, I love the completeness of things here. Beyond the mound of shattered cups a boy mixed clay with Ganga water and kneaded it. He took lumps of the dough to what looked like his greatest of greatest grandfathers - a squatting skeleton pumping a spinning wheel with his bare foot. The man flicked river water over fresh cups forming within his stick fingers and the boy took each completed shape, adding it to rows sun-drying on grass mats.

"Indian Railways use these, not plastic cups," Devi said absently.

Noticing the looks they got from people, Ewan asked, "Devi, don't you mind being alone with a strange male?"

"It's a balancing act between being true to yourself and not behaving disrespectfully." She shrugged, "One learns to accept other people's unjust criticism as their problem and not carry it on your shoulders. Anyway, they'll assume we're related. And from the way I dress they perceive I'm different and was educated abroad."

"Where?"

She laughed, "Roedean in England, a Swiss finishing school, finally Oxford. The rich have always been above the norm, I'm not proud of this, it is what is. At least it gives me freedom from subservience to antiquated social rules. Anyway, these days I'm little different to the new breed of Indian women in our more modernising cities."

Ewan looked at her. Such words sounded arrogant, but Devi was of the people. She had shared a joke with the chai wallah and had teased the potter's great-great grandson. They rose to continue along the wooded eastern banks. As they walked Ewan found that, unlike her formal brother, Devi had a skill at drawing out his pent up feelings. It's her soft voice, direct, and penetrative mind. At one moment, driven by

96

muffled anger, he hurled a stone across the river, "Devi, being tortured still haunts me. I wake, find myself sitting bolt upright, blankly staring ahead." He could see the lathi beating him. My weakness depressed me! He told Devi about the pain of being bullied at school because of his skin colour, of father's teaching him to fight which the school silently encouraged. Unlike many of his ancestors, he disliked fighting.

"Move on from your pain. Not by burying it, but by accepting it, will you learn from it."

"What on earth can anyone learn from Sati's story?"

Devi tossed her hair. "Unfortunately, India abounds with Satis."

He took in her delicate features: bright black eyes, thin nose, not overlarge lips, the upper one rising to a sharp dip, a fine jaw. Wow she's alluring, not arresting - subtle, uncomplicated, but fetching flashes of mischief, a tomboy? Secure. Poised elegance alight with intelligence, yet sensitive.

Noticing, Devi turned away blushing. To bridge the embarrassment, Ewan found something to do. He slumped against a tree and sketched a reed hut built on a raised bank and the resident sadhu, who had long dreadlocks. The man lifted his chillum, offered it. Ewan shook his head.

"What did you learn from your Delhi sadhu?" Shading her eyes from the bright sunlight, Devi looked tantalisingly alive.

"Although I knew it intellectually from family's writings and paintings, No-Matter let me sense what India has to offer."

"True understanding arises from experience, not knowledge."

"How empirical." He licked a bead of sweat off his upper lip.

She jumped up, "Let's go."

A stream forced them inland until they found a crossing. Devi appeared at ease in the jungle. She pointed out long haired langur monkeys whose ebony eyes appeared to mock. She pointed, "Look, elephant dung, and hey, leopard tracks, tiger even roam here."

"Golly Devi, let's go back."

"It's OK. Look at the number of people."

Adjoining paths swelled theirs and at the foot of a hill they entered a road lined with shacks filled with pilgrims. They sat in the best of these and ate an early lunch of succulent vegetable curry and for pudding they dripped wild honey over yoghurt spooned from a broad maturation bowl made of clay.

"I'm wondering if I ought to leave."

"Why?"

"Staying six months is the easy option." He waved at the bustle, "I once loved this, but India now frightens me. I was out of my depth, swept away."

Her gaze was far away, "You're not of this culture, you can't understand it - what safer place to learn about India than an ashram exploring the basis of our culture."

"The ashram confuses me."

"The place prompts us towards Liberation."

"Is 'Freedom' a myth, a desire to escape reality?"

"Liberation arises when we let go of our ego."

"I don't want mental obscurity, I want to dig beneath my outer shell and discover me, which is ego-me. I want to explore life's complexity. Enlightenment seems too detached. Perhaps the Buddha was lost in a mental cul-de-sac."

"That's outrageous!"

"That's the problem with religion, your icons can't be challenged. Knowledge requires dispute."

"That's VERY Western! Look where your half-baked thoughts got you!" Devi snapped with her mouth half full of a sweetmeat. "Do as Indra asks - six months is nothing."

"That's smells of conditioned thinking."

She wiped her mouth and looked up intently. "I can sense you're ready to dip beneath the surface. To deal with life's demands our minds create many little personae: for family, friends, acquaintances, work and so on. They're each ego-creatures. We're something larger, less self oriented. Leaving now could ruin this rare chance to explore how much more interesting than those little ego-games you think you are."

"Mmm." He let a milky sweet dissolve. Ego isn't me? Then what is? Yet after all, I'm getting away from that stifling little SOS guy - OK, an ego-shield. India's changing my language too, 'guys', a term I never use. Brilliant! That word too. Maybe this yoga-lark will help. See - lark as well!

Merging with the pilgrim throng, they climbed a path spiralling up an ever narrowing hill. Ewan ran past an old man in a hired sedan-chair, stopping on the steep incline to sketch the weary bearers. Gosh, the way some poor people make a living! Along an exposed hogback, he pretended he was flying; Devi made to push him off. At the summit he did a series of rapid sketches of pilgrims who called down the gods by ringing a bell hanging from an arched entrance. What views! "The plains look endless."

Devi waved her arms wide, "Not long ago this was seemingly inexhaustible swampland abounding in wildlife. Inspired by Western charities, along came our Green Revolution with its tractors and harvesters." She sighed, "so tragic."

"Something in the imperceptible undulation has caught me."

"Watch it, you'll become addicted."

"I always have been," he told her of his family library. Her gaze latched on him. Unsettled, he screwed his eyes, peered across a sunburnt plaza of blazing modern colours and into a sombre interior dimly lit by oil lamps. "What's that sanctuary?"

"The river stone inside represents The Goddess Devi. Thousands of years ago our sages reputedly came here to condense oral traditions into The Vedas."

"How old Hinduism is."

"Perhaps as old as humanity's move out of Africa, with Shamanistic roots reaching further back."

"Oh yes, the Aborigines...."

"Exactly." She sighed. "The gods we invent to feel at home in this unsympathetic universe."

"It's amazing Socrates wasn't turned into one. He believed 'Good' and 'Truth' stood apart, almost as gods."

"Ewan, it's argued that Indian thought influenced cultures from here to Greece."

Burma, Thailand, China too, wow, India is awesome. "Trade involved all cultures in symbiotic exchange."

Leaning over the retaining wall, she wrinkled her fine nose at the clutter of modern India which looked neat from this elevation. Her voice dreamy, "Before the Buddha, deductive logic and debate between Indian scientists, atheists, religious leaders and rulers was normal. It's argued Pythagorus learnt his basic geometry from The Vedas's Sulva Sutra, and his 'unique theorem' was a restatement of work done by an Indian mathematician."

"I thought he went to Egypt."

"Egypt traded with India. Why doesn't the West acknowledge our heritage? For you ancient India, Eastern Asian and China are mere footnotes."

He peered at her. The unfairness. Ancient Indus settlements were the World's most populous, yet they are still little known. Why are Vedic texts, written long before the Old Testament, unrecognised in the West, despite four hundred years of British presence in India, which began before the European 'Enlightenment' rediscovered Greek thinking? Why not Indian thinking? The Vedic texts and practices were long established when Buddha argued against their corruption and he lived before Socrates. Ewan blinked, "Maybe India was too far beyond the eastern Mediterranean."

Devi's eyes burned. "Rubbish! At Oxford I argued Europeans see everything through Mediterranean/Middle-Eastern culture and history. Galileo, for example, worked out the world was spherical, but a thousand years before, the Indian scientist Aryabhata, who also gave us the concept zero, had already calculated that."

"Are you sure?"

"Check it out," she handed over her smart-phone. "The French claim Napoleon's scientists were the first to calculate the Earth's circumference, it's why they wanted The Meridian to go through Paris. It ought to go through Delhi, not London!" Her excited voice drew a small crowd of nodding admirers.

"Memsahib," said a man claiming to be a lecturer of Mathematics, "Athens might be more appropriate, the Greek Eratosthenes had already done so in about 250BC."

Humbled, but only slightly, Devi reluctantly assented. "Each generation of thinkers stands on the shoulders of those before them. Ideas grew in many places and exploded in the ones most suited to carry them forwards."

"Precisely, Memsahib!" The lecturer acknowledged.

Ewan smiled at how skilfully she'd regained face. "The vastness of human thought." Why've I not let my mind expand beyond accepted truths? Too concerned with the apparent facts to let go, I attained a 2.1. The real gain was a First, reserved for students like Julian who cast away from the dockside... as Devi's inspiring me to do now. What a woman. Embarrassing himself with such a thought, he said, "Wow, the Ganga's maze of wooded sandbars and shallow rapids. This'd make a fantastic abstract!"

"The last remnants of those stolen swamps reaching into the now farmed plains."

He used soluble ink crayons and Devi stood by his side as if they were siblings. "Ewan, you are a master."

He wasn't used to praise, Father said it blunted your edge. An Aikido breath anchored him. The physical intimacy disturbed him. Indians need less personal space... and I'm an extreme Brit. Help! He distracted himself with memories of barefoot sadhus he'd watched crossing the swamp and walking into the Himalayan jungle, propelled like countless others since the start of Indian civilisation to discover the meaning of life. It was this which singled out eastern cultures - they were concerned with 'spiritual' development. "Ah, India!" Something's shifting, I've an entirely new desire welling within. The fluidity of his crayons quickened as they moved across the page and he noticed the image grow more subtle. "Devi, I feel I'm crossing a threshold."

"So I sense."

101

Shaded by a cotton awning, sipping chilled mint tea on Devi's rooftop terrace, they watched the light shift subtly across the acres of farmland. Removed from the rigorous ashram below, they luxuriated in each other's company. Fearful of parental rejection since infancy, Ewan usually spoke in guarded, reasoned phrases, but with Devi he spurted and she added her own tints of insight and humanity. He looked at the stranger who in a single day had become a friend. Is Sati capable of such lucidity? Whee. Sati's a beacon, but Devi's... am I falling for her? Today she's replaced Sati. How fickle I am....

"I'm glad this place exists," Devi said absently.

Ewan rose to peer over the enclosed plaza. The nuns' and monks' shaven heads shone in the late afternoon light. "Yet imagine spending your life in this open prison."

"People are imprisoned by offices, mortgages, family duties, social conventions. Ewan, during this day I've sensed the traditional life you have lived never suited you. Stay. Learn to discriminate, gain clarity about your direction."

"I have discriminated too much!"

"In a materialistic sense. What I mean is discover what is important for your inner growth."

He became defensive, "The inner-journey is India's Achilles heel."

"What! Corruption, not religion, ruins our country!"

Reacting to her outburst, unwilling to fight, he said, "I must go."

Collecting his few things from his bedroom, Ewan left her enclosed terrace and stepped down the inner steps. At ground level he moved round the cloistered courtyard to his new accommodation. He liked the cell's simplicity. A tiny window above the washing area only guest rooms had, a small recess for a candle; a thick reed mat. He added his blanket and leather bag, his sandals were with the others on a shelf in the wide hall.

Placing his Mughal miniature in the alcove, he realised he was spending more time looking at it. He loved the gleaming temple, wanted to stand upon its rocky outcrop. He must find the place. But how? The topography was distinctive: the broad river's curve, the line of snowy mountains, as was the bulk of castle. The yellowing note tucked behind it was written when the East Indian Army attacked the castle during the so called 'Indian Mutiny', killing people who wished to regain their ancient independence. Perhaps Devi could help me find it, I must ask.

He undressed. Behind a chest-high wall water from the tap drained over the shower zone and into a squatting 'Turkish' toilet flushed with a bucket. He filled the bucket and used a small jug to wet himself. Wearing only a sarong, he went out and leaned against a pillar, allowing the warm air to dry his body.

ß

The baked earth was cooling when Ewan cycled Devi to Haridwar. They ambled through the pilgrims thronging the Ganga's wide promenade. The relief of sitting on cool marble, dangling their feet in the chilling river was gratifying. A henna sun hovered above the imposing hills, casting long shadows over the rushing waters and worshippers crammed before the line of ancient temples dotting the western bank.

"It feels like half of India is here," Ewan whispered, not daring to disturb the reverence.

"During festivals it's impossible to move."

"This is one of millions of such congregations."

"Don't exaggerate," Devi poked him.

"OK, the Indus Valley civilisation flourished 5,500 years ago. Multiply that by...."

"Hang on, here at Haridwar." Waking her phone she calculated: "3,500x365x2. Wow! Equals 2,555,000 Artis."

"Right here."

"The ceremony itself is sacred," Devi confided. "It is unlucky to change a single detail. Senior priests ensure everything is identical from one day to the next. Old Brahmins returning from distant places decades after schooling here find Haridwar's Arti precisely the same as before. Imagine, a priest from a thousand years ago ought to recognise it as unmodified!"

Ewan had often watched young Brahmins chanting in the temples. They were scolded for the slightest deviance in syllable, tone or movement, because perfect reiteration and physical movement was a holy act.

Devi said, "Oral histories are reliable, even elaborate myths are based on facts: Shiva was an actual king who built an actual city - Varanasi."

"Hmm." When writing a book about village story tellers in 1883, one of his forebears argued communal oral repetition ensures precise continuity. "Devi, preliterate peoples have astounding memories. They store everything internally rather than on paper." However, Sylvia's enlightened thoughts were unpopular in an assertive British Empire which belittled anything non-European. Watching the priests preparing themselves for Arti, he whispered, "Maybe Arti stretches back to the dawn of human worship. The sun sets, night arrives with her wild beasts and so we seek comfort in the gods we invent; the sun rises dispelling the unease and we thank these creatures of our imagination."

The sun sank beneath the first foothills. "Auuummm." The Vedantic mantra born in a priest's mouth grew in the chests of the devout, became an ethereal swell floating above the Ganga, "Auuummm." Thousands of voices took up the hymn of Arti: "Om, Jaia Jagadeeswari." The lullaby thrilled Ewan each dawn after delivering his flower load, but with no religious inclination he saw it as another people's liturgy, yet standing beside Devi, he felt involved.

Arti consumed the Ganga's rushing roll, inundating Ewan. He pulled back, frightened he'd been caught by the crowd's fervour, but the joy was too seductive. Arti, an ache rising from people's hearts, an acknowledgement of our frailty, of our connection to universal life. I'm one individual among generations of gatherings who, on this spot, performed a rite older than the Pyramids. The flickering line of butter-lights increased the entrancing effect as the priests waved their lamps in circles and figures of eight, blessing the temples, the pilgrims' offerings and flowers. I picked some of those opening buds, my fingers are thus part of this scene. Our lives are connected to everything. On a cellular level our skins are porous, our emotions are touched by the emotions of others. We are not islands. Maybe that's Arti's power - you belong. But Hitler's mass ceremonies hypnotised people to follow the Nazi doctrine. That's the danger of crowd-emotion, it catches our guts, toys with our need to be included. But no, this isn't tribal, it's universal.

Arti rose to its crescendo and stopped. Silence underscored by the Ganga's swell.

The priests turned from their altars, offering the sacred flames. Arms waving like barley fields swept up the imagined benediction. One after another the priests stepped from their elevated temples to walk amongst the worshippers who crowded round, scooping the holy vibes over their heads.

Heck, I feel my insignificance. I'm one spark, incredible, but alone in the emptiness of space. This expansiveness, is it a glimpse of my soul, even the 'indefinable'? Have I been hypnotised? Who cares, it is bliss. This void was peculiar, contradictory, impersonal but incredibly personal, he felt he belonged, not simply there, but to India's spirit, to universal life. Devi smiled as he whispered this.

As if in a daze, the crowd drifted apart, each person carrying their take on the 'indefinable' to add meaning to their troubled lives. At the edge of the Ganga many cast afloat candles set in leaf or clay saucers - a flotilla of sparkles caught by the strong current. Wow, it's as if the stars have descended to Earth.

Swami Prem sat in meditation as his flock entered the teaching room. When all was quiet he opened his eyes and surveyed his inexperienced audience. "Hatha Yoga is the basis of the Vedic approach. Indus statues and clay pictograms over 5,000 years old show people in Yoga postures, and over the centuries those original positions have hardly altered."

Ewan was glad of his stern translator, for his Hindi couldn't yet keep up. Having digested his translator's words, he blurted out. "Last week's papers showed an unearthed Parvati yoni archeologists claim is over eight thousand years old. What is boggling is that the villagers recognised it."

"You-One, ssh!" his translator whispered harshly.

Coughing, the Swami resumed his discourse. "Aim making mind one-pointed, not helter-skelterish." Pleased with his English joke, he smiled at Ewan and flipped back to Hindi. "Treat your body as a temple, not a tool." The Swami was back in his stride. "Our long departed guru taught us life is a university not a battlefield. Learn from Hatha Yoga, the Yoga of physical exercises, which leads to inner Yoga or as it is known...." The Swami caressed his bald head and

106

continued uninterrupted for an agonising hour and fifty-two minutes before his pupils could learn a few postures.

When he escaped, Ewan's head hurt from overt religiosity. Seeing Devi, he suggested they walk to town.

She scoffed, "It's too hot."

"Rickshaw it is then," he steered her through the gates and to the bike shed.

"My, my, you're stressed-out."

"I've concluded there's no ultimate Good," Ewan blurted over his shoulder as he pedalled along the dirt track, puffing up clouds of dust which drifted towards nuns and monks working in the fields.

Devi's voice rose from the bench behind as they moved beneath the lone neem tree. "Pure Vedantism is the original agnosticism! How can we be sure if there is, or is not a basic state of Good or Truth underlying everything?"

"If such a state exists, it is hence God. God the Sod, thus named because it created suffering! Everything from insects to elephants suffer!" Ewan bellowed over the traffic as he turned onto the busy tarred road. Hmm, I'm enjoying this assertiveness, throwing off Father is liberating.

"Do you have to go this fast?" Devi's bewildered voice bounced off trucks tearing past.

Panting, furiously pedalling in the boiling air, his speed created a bearable breeze. He pointed at a shanty settlement beside the road. "LOOK - misery. Sod the gods!"

"You monster!" Devi yelled. "In the ashram there's no mention of God! What's your madness arising from?"

"My brain's aching with Swami-words!"

She hollered in sympathy, "I once sat through three and three quarter hours!"

"That's frightening!" Ewan greeted other rickshaw drivers they passed, "Jaia Shiva!"

Devi chuckled, "You're part of the scene."

By the time they sped past the garish Shiva statue on a roundabout in town, Ewan's mind was easing. "Devi, what IS life's purpose?"

"We can't talk like this. STOP! At THIS restaurant!"

107

Standing on the concrete step she said, "Our yogis speak of a subtle energy which permeates all. Finding that, we find purpose."

"Sounds like God."

Irritated, Devi strode inside. After a cup of spiced sweet tea in the smart establishment, Ewan's intensity cooled. Devi told him liberation was not leaving behind the ego and the world, but seeing them in their wider context. "All things are impermanent. You will die, these buildings, those mountains, all will crumble. Living and acting with such awareness will change all you do and see." She laughed, throwing her arms wide, "behold! Liberation!"

"Behold Escapism."

"Then flee from us dreamers and our insecure assurances."

The thought of leaving alarmed him. He sought compromise. "Devi, sorry, I can't accept what there's no evidence for."

"There are no certitudes. Vedanta is more a questioning philosophy than a fixed set of thoughts."

This calmed Ewan and they spent the morning walking through Haridwar's maze of narrow streets. Getting half lost in the crowds thronging the brightly coloured bazaar, they picked at sweetmeats and drank freshly squeezed fruit juice at makeshift stalls, it was like being children again. Devi smiled as they took lunch in a restaurant, "I never do this in Haridwar."

"You ought to skip school more often."

"But I do. Elsewhere."

"Devi, some things in the ashram drive me crazy."

"I know. I wish it'd become more cutting-edge, but for me it's in the blood. I love the pace of life, the pressure's off. I like the gentle people, the beautiful buildings, the calmness, the Ganga. The escape from my role and duties. " She looked serious, "but it is illusion."

"Sorry?"

"Be Vedantic!" Devi put on a mock Indian accent, wobbling her head from side to side. "Thought turns billions of atoms into what I see as you, this tea, those walls, so it's all illusion or the curtain of Maya which veils the infinite light."

Ewan chuckled, "Equals - I think, therefore I am. But your supposed light is Maya too! "

Devi countered, "I am not thinking, thus I'm not?"

"I'm glad you are, I don't want to be supposedly Enlightened and not see you." To hide this unexpected revelation, he sucked a slice of the mango they were sharing.

"Ewan!" Blushing, she stood up. "I'm off to the mountains this afternoon." She had decided right then.

They had begun to reach out to one another and now she was off. It was a pattern he recognised. From time to time in his childhood his mother had warmed to him, perhaps after a particularly interesting afternoon play on the radio. It usually happened in the lounge as she walked over with a silver tray of tea and slices of homemade cake. On those rare occasions, rather than sit, they would stand stiffly side by side, looking out the tall dress windows, china cups in hand, glancing awkwardly at each other from the corner of their nearest eye. Strange dogs weighing each other up. A light would shoot through her face, a hint of a smile dash across her lips, struggling with herself, she'd go taut, bark something like, "Did you enjoy your ride this morning?"

His responding voice drowned in emotion, "Thank you Mother. Flika was in fine fettle."

A flush of intimacy would colour her cheeks. Taken aback by her own emotion, she would straighten and bark, "That nose of yours!" then turn and march from the room. It would be several cool months before another such moment.

Damn my protruding nose!

As they washed their hands at the sink, he sensed Devi, unlike Swami Prem, No-Matter, Sati or Indra, was beyond him, enigmatic... yet she was also closer, he could feel her whereas Sati, to survive, had become too strong for intimacy. Several paces apart, they drifted awkwardly back to their rickshaw. Devi sank into the couch. Flustered, Ewan pounded the pedals through the frenetic traffic.

ß

A postcard taken at dusk made Ewan stop before a narrow shop in Haridwar's alleyways. It depicted a sadhu setting afloat a small leaf-boat, in the background dozens of candles bobbed upon the river's surface. He bought it. At an impromptu chai wallah's squashed between tight buildings, he began writing:

Hey Julian, How I would love to row down the Ganga with you. Recovering in an ashram, I've made two friends, Devi and her brother Indra. I go for long walks, do farm-work, eat wonderful food, study Vedanta and Yoga. With warmth, Ewan. Vedanta Ashram, Haridwar.

Dear Julian, the bond's strong. We went through so much together when bullied at school.

Back in the ashram, Ewan did a detailed drawing of a nun pulling a bucket from the well to quench thirsty flowers. His art was helping him stay because there were days when the routine urged him to flee. He looked at people going about their duties, had he drawn all the activities representing the ashram's self-containment and sustainability? There was the ashram potter exactly as he had been when sketched three weeks ago, the grey cows tethered under the trees behind the kitchen hotter than when he did a study of their shadows, as were those backs clothed in pink cotton weeding between rows of luminous yellow mustard.

He studied an old nun weaving refined reed mats for sale, comparing the empty shapes between the stack of river reeds, her figure bent over her sought-after work, the knife, broad needle, home-grown sisal string. When he felt he understood the composition, he outlined the movement and balance. Devi was right, drawing was his thing.

Physical Yoga became another anchor. Yoga's slow, purposeful movements, almost ritualistic, kept his mind on his body. It was a continuation of Aikido whose routines he maintained each evening. Swami Prem claimed the moves and postures prepared one's body to channel the soul's energy. Mumbo-jumbo! The lightness gained comes from the ligaments and muscles being stretched, which affect the brain.

These activities held him there. Well, also the fear of leaving. Before the liberating day with Devi, the ashram had been a safe harbour; afterwards it felt more a college, its main lesson, independent discipline, rather than an externally imposed one. Born to manage ancestral lands, everything in his life once balanced on constant discipline - his Aikido, rugby, career, they consolidated his purpose. This Indian adventure is reinventing me. It helps avoiding religious conversations and spending time with the tough rickshaw drivers.

Lost in thought, he began walking down the darkening path to the Ganga. Sixty centuries of preoccupation with the soul had shifted Indian attention from the social awareness tribal people instinctually need to survive. Religion dominated, consequently the country's problems were explained through religion rather than instinct and thus they expanded - poverty, booming population, sewage, rubbish, disease, the caste system, corruption. As these increased, had the soul become an escape from misery? He shivered. I'm back in my old work mindset which seeks root problems. I must discuss this with Devi. Devi! Leaving the ashram I'd lose touch with her. During her irregular visits they kept touching each other, whatever that might mean and he had grown closer to her than anyone, ever. Why am I a loner? Mother, Father, they made me.

"Earwing," a familiar voice, a flashing torch. "Night time many snake."

"I'm sure they're more afraid of us."

"Snake think moving feet rat," Swami Prem swept his light about and encouraged Ewan back towards the ashram. "Many thousand peasant killed in twilight. Bitten last year on this path, this time of day, monk die."

"You killed the snake?"

"No! Bad karma kill even mosquito."

"So you have a sort of sin: Karma."

The monk frowned.

Clouds higher than mountains had been marching across the blue skies for some days. Sweltering in the chai stalls, roasting in the ashram, parched as the cracked earth, people prayed for the monsoons to start.

Sitting where a slight breeze edged through the male-only courtyard, Ewan read part of Henry Merricott's letter from 28th July, 1877. *"For a third year the blasted monsoons are late, yet the tantalising clouds pass overhead, destined to drop their nourishing load on others. For three months farmers have struggled to save themselves from disaster. The soil has turned tinder-dry and the wind lifts it, what hope has any crop of taking hold? We continue to dig the hundreds of miles of canals to share out the waters of the Jumuna and Ganges, but what use is this to these wretched people today?"*

One volatile afternoon thunder shook the ground, lightening split the indigo sky, a wall of droplets obscured everything. Soaked to the skin, adults stood in the downpour, arms raised, dancing, kids rushed from the crowded town to swim in pools forming in the fields.

Cycling back from Haridwar, Ewan battled silver rain rods which hid anything more than three metres away. A trillion water-pellets erupted in the puddles his tyres sliced open. Having to dismount, he waded knee deep through the deluge, his whooping, "The most exciting rain ever!" almost inaudible. Cool and shivering, he parked the bike in the ashram shed. Opening the heavy gate, he stepped into the sheltered cloisters and laughed. Laughing nuns and monks leapt about the plaza, rain bouncing off their shaven heads.

Another squally day caught Ewan walking through the rose fields. The sky boomed. Sprinting from the scrubland beyond, the towering monsoon's onslaught swung across the swollen Ganga, ploughing into her swell; the storm smashed Ewan's head and shoulders, hissed over the ashram's flooded farmland; water-buffalo were in seventh heaven, their black backs steaming with jumping globules, their curved horns mini-waterspouts. Drenched, Ewan dashed under the kitchen veranda and made his way round the plaza's cloisters where the rain drummed the tiled roof and he understood why wandering sadhus stayed put during this violent season. Over the past few days several of these fierce eyed men and women had arrived in the ashram. Have any attained wisdom? It intrigued Ewan he now thought like this…. Hmm, shows how our immediate environment influences how we think.

Having showered and dried, he listened to the wind raging around the inner courtyard. A fist bashed his cell door. This was a first. He opened to see Swami Prem with flying robes. The venerable monk beckoned, Ewan closed his door, stood in the wild courtyard. The Swami spoke in English. "Earwing, having learn still body, you calmer…" the monk's voice fled in the tempest. "Yoga teaching appreciate harmony within. Next step, meditation…."

Ewan groaned. Since his disturbing session months before, he had avoided meditation. In a lull he blurted in his improved Hindi, "They assure me perfected, it is as good as bhang."

"Ha, ha, ha," the old monk had come to relax during these edgy chats which pushed him to rethink traditional attitudes. The Swami claimed Westerners saw things upside down. "Earwing, meditation helping rise above lower self. We result of past deed, accumulating Karma equal non-spiritual self."

The final point was as disturbing as the currents of air playing havoc with Ewan's hearing. "Won't ignoring the lower self produce self-ignorance?"

The Swami's chuckle was taken by a blast of air rounding the courtyard. "First filling self with purer influence."

"This I can accept. Create a new mindset from which to watch myself. Aikido does the same."

"Meditation making you feeling life."

"Does this mean Hindus aim to 'feel' where we Westerners attempt to analyse?"

"Maybe," Swami Prem mulled over this as a violent clap of thunder rattled the cell doors.

The monsoons were a dream from a distant age as Ewan stood watching the postman in khaki uniform pedal down the

113

gravel track. Midway, by the lone tree, a small whirlwind moved across the parched fields to cover the cyclist and Ewan hurriedly sketched the machine clanking through the dust devil. Leaning the bike against the planters filled with bright flowers, the postman said, "Postcard Sahib."

The vortex of fiery air gripped them, sand pricked their ankles, burnt grass drifted into their mouths. Blinking away the dust, the postman opened his bag, careful not to lose letters to the pixie wind, and removed the ashram's bundle. The top item was a postcard of a man in pink dancing on the roof of red London bus. Turning it over, Ewan saw his weren't the first fingers to have felt the well read card. Together, the two men read:

Dear Ewan, It's taken over a month to reply... too many distractions. I bought this card because I want him! Lovely London = @hoo$h ! Love Julian.

"What it meaning sahib?"

"He wants fun."

The wide eyed man quickly mounted his bike. Entering the cloisters, Ewan chuckled, The hypocrite.

From then onwards Ewan had regular cards from Julian and he placed them alongside his ancient Mughal miniature. In his replies he would tell of life in the ashram and how the theories Indra, Devi and Swami Prem expounded were influencing him. He explained the Swami had taught him a mantra - a base-sound. Unable to unravel the Abbot's complex explanation, Ewan asked Devi when she next returned, "Why roll an imaged sound around your mind?"

"Base sounds are the simplest noises humans make and are common to all languages. Ancient sages discovered and categorised them by listening, so invented Vedic mantras. Imagining a sound requires more attention than listening to yourself mutter it. This transmutes thought, cleaning the mind."

"That sounds mad."

"A good drum beat affects us, why not a silent mantra?"

"The drum's resonance is real."

"Cynic!" She play punched him.

On reflection, Ewan told her he'd read that attention to a positive or negative word influences the mind's mood. He also knew of medical research discovering that attentive chanting of simple sounds improved certain cell responses to attack or degradation. "But once more, that is real sound."

Devi said, "Stop theorising, try it!"

Each time Devi flitted in from Europe or her estate, he grew more interested in her. Straddling both his and her cultures, she understood where he was coming from and what he was unwittingly turning towards. What am I thinking - she's beyond me.

Within a couple of weeks the disturbed postman would hand over Julian's naughty responses to Ewan's letters. Dirty fingerprints made it clear the postcards were appreciated as they moved across northern India and since Ewan had told him of this, Julian's writing had become wickedly bigger and neater. A postcard of a naked sadhu read:

Hiya sexy, Look at this guy! Whoo @hoo!!! Pulsing through relationships, can't make up my mind if I prefer galz-or-guyz. Damn my ex-wife, I was a simple queen before loving her. Xxx, Julian.

The summer's intensity had faded and Ewan when been there almost six months. Sat with Devi upon her terrace, watching the sun's last rays tint the tinder dry hills, she teased, "Ewan, you've made great advances, but you should spend more time meditating. You're still speedy."

"I'm happy as I am," he quipped, enjoying the half-wild resurgence of his lost adolescence.

"Yes you are more fun being lively... but think of others. We have to fit in with your impulses." Speaking without malice, Devi's words reached into him. "Listen more, enter other people's thinking rather than imposing yours."

"That hurts."

"Sorry Ewan, but it has to, to reach you." She smiled, "you're dynamite nowadays, but have controlled outbursts. Hey, I like your hair - explosive!"

Running his hands through his shoulder length locks, he rose and went down the outside steps Devi used and made his way to the river. I need to think over her words. Strolling through the rose fields he hesitated. Hey, I left her without a word. Does she now mean less to me?

The sun was high in the sky when a monk handed over a well read postcard. "For you, Hewing."

Recognising the writing Ewan laughed happily at the image of a London phone booth crammed with men in drag. He flipped it over:

Hi U-wun/Chewing/You-Gong! Love them names. Keep sending them. U-Thong's naturally my fav. Glad you're content. Thanks for the money, so welcome - my unfaithful wife's screwed me for everything. (Never bow to parental pressure, unless you want to live in a straightjacket. Poor woman, she wanted a man-man, not queenie-boy, hence her running off with that macho Flamenco guitarist). Jack showed me your sketch books. Marvellous! How I miss Bharat! French kisses, Julian.

Devi, back from a European business trip, asked about his eight months in the ashram. He stood up, enjoying the late autumnal warmth striking her roof terrace. Pacing around in rapid steps, speaking quickly. "With all this navel gazing, I've become too self-critical. I no longer know who or what I am. I'm lost."

Devi nodded. "It's a painful process, but in reality we are all lost. We simply pretend we're not."

"Things which once gave me pleasure, such as racing rickshaws are now empty ego games. That's classic depression."

"In Western terms," Devi joined him at the balcony. The clear light illuminated the rows of roses and the scrubland beyond the river. "For Hindus it shows your mind has started to discriminate between the trivial and the profound."

"Why is sitting doing nothing more profound than racing a rickshaw?"

"Pure Vedanta advises: with meditation and Yoga we calm our mind and if you do decide to race you get more from it."

"I meditate yet unlike Aikido techniques, nothing happens. Aikido and physical Yoga are active, hence they work. With this sitting stuff, I've come to hate my reeling mind. Once I thought without thinking about it and life was OK. Now I think so much about thinking I hate thinking and feel uncomfortable with the ordinary processes of living!"

"You have changed a lot, but typically, you Westerners want quick results," she laughed. "Instant coffee, instant internet, instant insight!"

"I still don't get this Enlightenment thing. It seems wrong. We're animals, we're stuck deep in the throng of existence. Instead of escaping our basic selves, we need to enjoy and play to de-stress, whether it's racing rickshaws, strumming music or dancing." Lost in thought, Ewan walked along the roof top, trailing his hand on the stone rail. In a daze he continued down the internal stairs, passing the first floor veranda and down to the ground level courtyard. Again I've left Devi without thought. She's become less important due to this raj-yoga malarky. How sad is that!

He flopped against a pillar supporting the cloisters. OK, what I call 'depression' is a self-aware mindset, not negative but neutral: it's what you think about your thinking which is important. Detach yourself from this cyclic mess by meditating on the imagined base-sound suited to your character and eventually something stirs in the soup of the 'deeper' mind. Hmm, gibberish or profound?

He entered his cell, found his file and read Emma Merricott's thoughts of 1903: *"I am teased when I mention it at the club, but like some of my ancestors I am humbled by the emotional composure of these women of India. For generations their lives have remained unchanged, everything was mapped out thousands of years ago, they know what to*

117

expect, what to do, what to think. There are few surprises. Being thus uncomplicated, they live with each experience. When they chant to the 'indefinable' it seems no other thought is present, for total belief has existed since the dawn of their civilisation, thus their minds do not doubt. For them god is in everything from the peanut to the tip of their toe. As they massage their babes they are nowhere else, I have often asked them, they say they are thinking of the shapes, the texture, the wonder of their child's limbs. When they sweep they think of nothing but sweeping, because god is the dust and is in their actions, thus sweeping is a holy act. I, on the other hand who doubt there is a 'higher power', worry over the pros and cons of ethics as I wash-up, bother about sewing when reading and fret over financial matters when writing!"

Inspired, Ewan went out, opened the cupboard beneath the stairs, withdrew the reed broom and began to sweep. He couldn't contemplate a 'god', but made his movements slow, determined as he chased his base-sound mantra through his mind and watched the movement of his limbs. Sweeping is my meditation. I'm not the sort to go inwards, I needed action.

Like a general at war, he moved precisely over the stone slabs, covering the ground in arcs. The broom's fronds of yellow grass moved slowly, hence the film of dust didn't explode into dirty clouds. At the end of each arc he left a pile which he later shifted to increasing mounds at the top step encircling the sunken garden. Methodically lifting these onto an ashram-made dustpan, he gently sprinkled the detritus over the garden, giving back what nature kept lifting off. He replaced the broom for the hose and artfully squirted the garden, sticking the dust back down.

As the weeks went by he had increased the time these tasks took. Time, once a burden to rush through, was becoming his friend. Monks on their way to their cells avoided treading where he was working and they smiled, understanding the inner-work he was doing.

"How Zen," Devi whispered from the sky-hole.

"And out of bounds to female eyes," Ewan teased, blowing her a comic kiss. To his surprise she lingered and they watched each other without complication. A monk appeared, she melted away. Ewan halted a while, delighting in the courtyard garden Devi had helped him redo with cuttings from her home. He smiled at tardy bees buzzing around a splay of flowers, he looked at the driftwood, *objets-trouvés* and attractive Ganga boulders they had gathered together. Yes, how Zen.

He was drifting across the plaza when an old monk held out another well thumbed postcard, asking, "You-On, what naval gazing?"

"Meditating." Ha, they too were reading his mail. The card was of a male couple entwined on a bench, kissing.

Dear Ewan, It gets cold fondling on London's park-benches as winter approaches. Pangs of southern India rise in my heart, or is it my limbs complaining? Has your bellybutton grown with all your navel gazing? Watch it - a hernia is on the way! Love, Julian.

Ewan's reaction was to write to Uncle Jack, asking him to buy Julian a ticket to India and give him more money. He posted it at Haridwar Post Office and in an internet cafe moved cash to Uncle Jack's Liechtenstein account from one of two Swiss accounts his parents had left him. His other untouched Swiss account held the contaminated money swollen with interest. It looked as if he would not be caught, but his accidental crime bothered him and he consequently shunned all thought of the stolen sum which was larger than anybody would ever need. He shook himself, 'I wish I'd never....'

A couple of weeks later he was handed a card depicting a male pole dancer.

Dear Ewan, Thanks for the ticket! India, oh Bharat! Sorry but winter's approaching, so it's south to the Goan beach boys. I'll seek you in the north in February. Love you! Julian.

119

As the bright cold of early winter set in, Ewan realised the soporific effects of ashram life had slowed him. I enjoy my own company. Devi's unpredictable visits were less important for his survival and this appeared to please them both.

Sheltering by the male block, the shivering postman was waiting for a gap in the tempestuous winter weather to cycle onwards and deliver his letters. Ewan said, "Your postal system keeps going come storm, shine or snow."

"Yes Sahib, mainly using feet or bicycles."

"And in the mountains, mules?"

"Yes, Sahib. Here's another card," the wet man handed Ewan a postcard of a bare chested man wearing a red skirt and, incongruously, bovver boots and he was walking a poodle wrapped in a fluffy pink jacket. It was covered in finger prints, some inky, others muddy, some ashy, others oily. Ewan fingered the grubby card, imagining postmen passing it around the various sorting offices and men reading it in chai stalls as it made its way across the country.

Hey sexy, Goa's mad. Paradise too. Runny guts for six days = NO SEX. Imagine such hell! Wet kisses, Julian.

Ewan's explosive laughter made the postman walk briskly off into the foul weather. They pant over my private mail yet abhor me for accepting it!

Cold winds from Tibet ripped across the plaza, zipping into the hallways, swishing around the courtyards. Ewan rang Indra and proposed a solution. Within a day a carpenter was measuring for folding doors to be fitted to the entrance halls of the three blocks.

One crisp and frosty afternoon Devi returned and they strolled towards the Ganga. Perching upon one of the benches she had recently installed, she told him of her latest trading trip. Her charity was doing well in the West, shoppers loved the quality material her women wove. The once impoverished village women bordering her estate now had money and their first moves were not to buy the latest televisions their husbands demanded, but to club together and purchase practical items such as water pumps for the wells. "Ewan, I am amazed how improved their homes and communities are becoming."

"I'd like to help with a donation."

"I sell, not beg! The charity is based on honest work, not handouts." She told him of the social events she'd attended in Berlin, Paris, London, "I met your Uncle Jack, he invited me to weekend at Merricott!"

This is shocking. I gave Uncle Jack's number out of courtesy. His mind whirled with images of his lost farm, his perfectly proportioned Perpendicular Gothic manor, the lively dogs and faithful Flika.

She laughed, "All those things from India! That's why you feel integrated. My favourite room was Merricott's library with its views over Merricott Vale."

I feel exposed. What does she know of my crime?

Sensing his concern she laid a hand on his, "Charles, how awful - forced to leave the valley your family have inhabited for fifteen centuries."

The use of his actual name ripped through him. "Oh gosh Devi, I...."

Her hand pressed his, "I've kept it to myself, not even Indra...."

"Thank goodness."

She winked, scampered off, "Ewan, Ewan, Eeedly weedly Ewan! Bet you can't catch me!"

Emotionally jolted, he fluttered. Gathering his wits, he chased her along the banks, catching her by a clump of bared trees and hidden from the world, he threw his arms around her shoulders and tugged her about.

Squealing like a child, Devi fought back, but remembering who they were, Devi went stiff. "Let's take tea over there."

Emotionally dizzy, he followed her to a clutch of huts where they sat with stale buns and steaming drinks. As Devi spoke about Uncle Jack, Ewan realised how far he had come. My old life feels ethereal. Summers swimming in our lake beneath Merrie Hill, riding through our farm lands, doing the estate accounts, discussing problems with the workers;

121

Saturday rugby. Catching the 06.12 to London Mondays, returning Thursday on the 11.37. Week days in my Chelsea mews-house, the theatre, sitting in parks or cafes, evening Aikido. It's all a dream. Merricott had been integral to his identity, yet this foreign river, this far off land and this astonishing woman had become more magnetic. Was it because he dreamt his infancy and youth away with tales and images of India? Or is there something more profound going on? Is it Devi? Am I in love?

Devi peered at him, her eyes half closed. He knew this signalled a penetrative statement. She said, "Where one is, is real."

Uncanny! He blinked, "I used to live in my mind, planning, scheming, commenting, judging, reflecting. What was happening around me was a backdrop for my internal theatre."

"With responsibility comes planning and stress. Without it, as you're discovering, you can relax. That's one of the values of an ashram. It gives you space to be."

He waved his arms, "Here it's the opposite. India's chaos tugs you outside yourself, you have to pay attention. Here, I'm being. "

Her eyes bright, "We waste our days not being intimate with this continually moving moment."

"I agree. But all this," he prodded the frosty window blurring the winter-sun washed scene, "is still too much for me to absorb. Won't minute awareness of it swamp us?"

"The art is to glide through the mire, discriminating, deciding what to ingest."

They explored the topic for a while and fell into silence. The absence of talk lifted his mind from the cold river their table faced. Ewan looked at Devi. She smiled. Aah, a swell, soft as a ripple, powerful as the incoming tide! A gentle hum is shivering the champagne light. I'm soaring! He recoiled, "No!"

"Are you all right?"

"I felt...."

"Yes?" Her voice reassuring.

"The inexplicable." Boggled, he looked about him wide-eyed.

"Perhaps nothing more than the shock of hearing about your home. Extreme emotional moments enable us to peep beneath our quicksilver mindsets." She tapped his nose.

He flicked his nose away. Why always my blinkin' nose? "Nothing more?"

"Who knows, but I sense there's never been a mystery. Things can always be explained."

He teased, "Even the inexplicable?"

She punched him.

A woollen shawl held the bitter north winds off Ewan's back as he leapt up the inner steps. He knocked on Devi's door. Lounging before a fire in her sitting room, she looked up, "Ewan, this Japanese Zen book is fascinating. They say the best way to grow as a person is to simply sit for an hour a day. No mantras, no visualisations, nothing but sitting. Listen to this: *'The Only-Being mind transcends all words and actions. Lost in thought, you miss the empty space beyond conceptualisation whose subtle energy transforms you. Sit empty twice daily, or your busy mind will dominate your days'.*" The remaining text explained simple sitting allowed the disorganised clutter of mental activity to settle: 'Like dirt in a glass'. In time your deeper nature emerged, and its calmness influenced you in countless ways.

"Devi, silently repeating a mantra is like brainwashing, I'm sure it's not good for the mind. Drawing, on the other hand, stimulates and opens me."

Devi smiled, "Then draw, but with stillness."

"Can us peasant adherents become Rishi-Royalty like you?"

"Fat-chance for an English snob wrapped in Italianate skin!"

"OK wise woman!" How sanguine her expression; yet behind it, fire.

Noticing his look, she smiled coquettishly. "Ewan you're impossible," play punching him, she turned away blushing.

ß

There was no snow but the cold winds rushing from the icy mountains and the frozen Tibetan Plateau beyond kept temperatures at freezing in the shade. Thank goodness for the continual 'Mediterranean' sunshine which warmed sheltered spots. In the afternoons Ewan basked in its rays and even fell asleep with the others after difficult nights in cold cells under thin blankets. Why are there no duvets? Why no stoves in the principle rooms?

Before dawn he and the clutch of faithful flower pickers gathered a blue winter thistle for the sunrise market. Haridwar's temples attracted few pilgrims and only a handful bought the expensive flowers, but it was the ashram's self-imposed duty to daily provide something for those who wished to brighten the holy altars. When the flowers went limp, they were tossed into the Ganga. Appalled, Ewan ensured the unsold stock was given each evening to two poor families whom he taught to dry and sell it as floral decoration.

Cycling homewards was torture. The early morning Ganga fog was laden with ice particles which cut through his thick socks and heavy boots. When he arrived at the ashram, his frozen toes sometimes felt as if they had the initial touches of frostbite. How did those impoverished professional cyclists stand it? One day he led twenty men to town in an excited caravan of empty cycle rickshaws. Having treated them to a warming breakfast, he headed for Haridwar's best shoe shop and bought each man from the 'untouchable' caste a pair of sturdy boots. They continued onto a smart clothing shop where his gaggle of shy taxi-cyclists chose thick socks, heavy trousers and decent sweaters. Today's expenditure is three months UK travel to work; it's hardly scratched my account.

After he had parked his rickshaw, in his now fluent Hindi Ewan told the Swami, "On top of a feather gilet, I use two woollen shawls when reading in my cell! How do you all survive this biting cold?"

"Our work is to transform our thinking so we can accept the difficult."

"Swami, there are certain vital things - comfort being one."

On a misty morning, having delivered his thistle flowers and taken his habitual breakfast, Ewan phoned Indra with another idea. Encouraged by his friend's response, he went to a shop which made duvets filled with kapok. When ordering one hundred, he was told, "It will take six weeks."

"By then it'll be warm. Hire tailors unemployed during winter, I'll pay. We'll want two covers for each duvet."

"Covers are not needed, Sahib. Wash everything and leave to sun-dry."

"Where will we dry one hundred duvets?"

"Ah, yes. I'll make covers too."

Two trucks delivered the duvets to the ashram eight days later. Ewan used more of his own money to construct a summer store for the duvets on the flat roof of the communal block. For a week he worked with the skilled nuns and monks, cutting wood, hammering nails, fixing a window and door, fashioning shelves, creating the roof and laying roof tiles.

He ordered a firm to fit several wood stoves throughout the ashram. Seven hundred metres of unused land by the main road would be planted in spring with ash trees ten deep, ensuring that in eight years there would be a sustainable supply of wood. None of this would have been possible without Indra's blessing, and Swami Prem had to accept the maharaja's wishes. Ewan also ordered secondary glazing for all communal windows over the course of the forthcoming summer. It's astounding how my own Swiss account where the farm's continual profits go, simply keeps growing. He dared not look at the 'stolen' sum swelling in its own high-interest Swiss account.

"Earwing," Swami Prem chuckled, "here's a non-naughty postcard!"

Ewan smiled. So the Swami too had become one of Julian's secret readers. In the sun shining on the public area of the male rooftop, Ewan read this latest arrival whose picture was tame - bare-chested fishermen hauling nets through waves lapping a broad beach:

Dear Ewan, Thanks a trillion darling! Warm seas, cool cafes, chilled out-locals, exactly what I need - classical dancing class each dawn, swimming, cooking lunch for the homeless, walking all afternoon, swimming and in the evenings, I write poetry in a cafe facing the ocean swell. Perfection! Catch you soon...if you've moved on, leave traces so I can find you! Kisses, Julian. P.S. Camp beach boys, yoohoo!

Offering further proof of his postcard passion, the Swami asked, "Earwing, why is your friend pleased the beach boys camp?"

"Oh," digging deep. "Well, um, Julian used to be in the Boy Scouts." No lie there, we both were at school.

"Camping on a beach? Is this normal?"

"Yes," Ewan laughed. "In pink Brighton or San Francisco."

"Ha!" Fiddling with his pink robes, the Swami smiled, "Yes, pink tents would brighten the beach, but why Goa?"

"Ha, Goa." Ewan looked down at the plaza. "Perhaps Julian has started a Goan Pink Camp Group."

"Excellent!" The Swami nodded, "inform Julian he is welcome to camp here."

Ewan chuckled.... He was happy his old school pal was warm at last. Julian's charitable work revived a forgotten idea. I could give my tarnished money away. Although this was obvious, suffused with guilt, he still pushed the stolen sum from his mind, never daring to even look at it. What a dreadful crime! Ugh.

What concerns me is those miserable folk alongside the railways lines. Some of the rickshaw men lived there. When Indra returned in spring, Ewan asked him to buy a plot of land in Haridwar, using some of the stolen money.

126

Devi organised for a charity run by a trusted ashramite to manage the land. One warm spring day, after the communal ashram lunch, the main players occupied a meeting room beside the meditation hall. Devi and Indra outlined how they could use Ewan's (stolen) money to lay a grid of water and power cables to solar panels, and sewage draining to reed-beds. Paving over this would give a framework within which the homeless could construct a solid village. The people would get 0.5% interest loans from a local charity-bank to whose director Ewan promised money. The community could make clay bricks from the excavated ponds. The construction was to be supervised by the honest developer. Providing constant income for the project, they could rent a roadside corner to another developer who frequently stayed at the ashram, who promised to build a small block of shops there.

In October Uncle Jack emailed the Swiss bank statements and Ewan was embarrassed how the dirty capital persistently grew, despite the expenditure. Crime obviously paid. Though he disliked having it, returning the vast sum was too risky - I don't wish to be imprisoned. Having tasted it, jail's the last thing I want. Yet why have they not caught up with me?

Another oft-read card arrived, this time of a woman bathing in a sari:

Hi Ewan, I'm lodging with a weird couple. Such tough lives, such sweethearts! They work the streets till midnight and they've inspired me to use your money to set up a centre for prostitutes. We will offer an alternative direction by teaching them to make the arty-crafty stuff tourists buy. Love, Julian.

Ewan shook his head. What would the guy get up to next?

"Devi," he began as they strode their favourite frost covered path beside the Ganga. "I'm confused. Swami says liberation is impossible without celibacy. Why is sex considered to be evil?"

"Beware Ewan, there's a route to liberation using sex - Tantra Yoga!"

Abashed, delighted, yet befuddled, his heart leapt into his throat. "You aren't...."

"Ewan!" She flushed.

Lost in their own emotional twirl, they stopped and watched islands of ice flow down the Ganga. After a difficult minute, she continued, "In Tantra you learn to harness your emotional desire and use its urge to rise above your lower self."

"Sounds more fun than meditating."

Reddening, Devi strode along the bank, kicking snow. "Intimacy is something I'm keeping for the person I will settle down with for life."

"I too pine for such a relationship." Will she become my first kiss?

She looked cruel, outlandish, "You're not ready to settle down." She softened, "ignore this desire for a relationship for a while. It will free up energy and time, making the search for Truth easier."

"Truth is here... now... in our senses, our desires, not in disciplining our minds to shun life." He recalled debating Platonic idealism from this Epicurean vantage at college.

She fluttered, took a deep breath, her voice timid, "I've often wondered the same."

"Perhaps sensuality tempered with reason and empathy is the answer. It could be seen as what your Zen book is hinting at: being mindful of all we do."

Their eyes locked.

She broke the spell, continued. "Epicureanism, Hedonism, they arouse emotion. That can be dangerous."

"Hitched to empathy, compassion, love, whatever you call it, I'm sure they can be powerful."

"Compassion's broader than empathy. And LOVE!" She wheezed. "Perhaps if, if... oh blast... can live without getting distracted in the quagmire of selfish emotion and greed...." She waved her arms hopelessly, trying to find the words. "Ewan you make me so... OH! Neither of us is ready!"

Am I? Is anybody? "People learn to survive emotion's chaos as they grapple with life together."

"Maybe. If both wish to see if this thing called Liberation exists. Until they resolve this they will not be strong. People pull each other down and regret their mistake. There are celibate yogis out there beaming with joy and wisdom. Once people understand what they have gained they might be ready to...."

"To?"

"How do you expect me to think when you look at me like this?" She pirouetted, strode ahead, bent over and tossed a snowball. He formed his own and lobbed it. Their laughter echoed across the white fields as they fought for a mad half hour.

The following morning, he discovered she had unexpectedly left. This devastating pattern! Oh, damn, I'm being adolescent! Do I feel attraction or fondness? Heck! What, in any case is love? He thought he'd felt it for the office cleaner, who rightly corrected him; he'd also had that urge for Sati. Relationships, he had to admit, he had no idea about. What they call 'love' must begin with a meeting of minds followed by an emotional commitment to share life's troubled track. That first stage had happened today, would the rest follow?

He became aware of a constant kernel of hurt in his chest. Unlike the macho lads he had grown up with, he'd wished to keep himself for the woman he would marry, but why hadn't he had a relationship? The cleaner? A series of conversations. Am I too mentally collected to relate? Sati leaning above me with a bowl of Buddha gruel, such soft sensuality. How absurd, without knowing her, simply because she's beautiful, strong, intelligent, I wanted her. Heck, my Zaminder fury was about Sati! OK, the sight of Krishna and co lining up for expensive grain pushed me, but Sati's plight was the trigger. Such exquisite beauty. What if she'd been an ugly duckling? And now Devi, neither beautiful nor ugly but bright because of her personality. Oh, my head hurts. Why do we need the opposite sex? He threw a clod of earth at a marble carving of the holy word OM, a little act of savagery he had long thought of. He cackled with joy when his missile hit.

He began his sweeping duty. Once done, he looked at the patch of coarse tropical grass he had been ordered to water. He turned on the tap, gripped the hose pipe and began to spray. Indra and Devi were right, this work was good for his nerves. With a jet of water he cleaned the OM. Softening the spray, he fed the flowers and the bushes lining the courtyard's edge.

Sat in his cell wrapped in a thick shawl, Ewan read a letter which had been opened, read and resealed several times:

Darling Ewan, Do forgive my not having sought you out, but a year in Goa has been good for me. I'm freed from the emotional muck which trapped me in Europe. And I've fallen in love!!

Bhansri Ma's a temple dancer, one of a clan who worship Lord Krishna as Gopis, (milkmaids - no butch guys here, saris are all the rage). When I first saw Bhansri Ma dance a thrill surged from within and over the months we've spent magical hours talking under the palms. Bhansri Ma's Guru has agreed to release him from the sect, but we are not allowed to even hold hands until we are formally married. After the ceremony we will both be accepted back as sidekicks. Don't ask darling. I have to become a transvestite. Yoohoo!! I'm made for that!!!!

Take note, me celibate!!! I'm immersed in weeks of induction, learning dances, songs, rituals and their philosophy. It is VERY serious, not a delicious folly dreamed-up on Brighton beach. The Guru will initiate me into His ancient sect as a lay-Gopi (No! not that lay) when I'm accomplished. What a rigorous life they lead. These men see themselves as nuns! Yes, yes, I know, a bit bonkers, but this is India. Although the coarser groups give Gopis a bad name, this lot are sincere, intelligent, talented and devout. And, blast it, celibate!

I'll keep you posted,

Hugs, your lay-nun-to-be, Julian, or using my Guru name - Gopi Bhakta, which means 'The Devoted Dancing Milkmaid of Krishna'. Imagine! Oh sweetie I'm in my tenth heaven, although I've always hated milk.

P.S. This Guru feels truly wise and I'm glad I've met Him. He laughed when I asked why a free spirit like him needs to hide behind such a bizarre way of acknowledging the infinite. I recorded his explanation on my smart-phone, here're his words ad verbatim:

'Mine is a classic Gopi story. My impoverished parents couldn't afford to feed their fifth child and I was starving. Rather than sell me to the usual child-trader who'd sell me to the Arab states, with great sadness, they gave me to a revered Gopi-Guru. I was just three and his clan were singing and dancing to favour the gods at a local wedding. Although we Gopis are shunned by much of society, this dedicated clan are my world, my family. Unlike many transvestites, we do not beg, nor do we prostitute our bodies, but live by a strict religious code. We gain money by pure worship at temples, festivities and weddings; we also sell the Krishna dolls we make. I eventually became their guru, somebody has to lead. If we do no harm, it doesn't matter how we dance the dance of life. Forget conventions, dance with joy and compassion.'

Ewan darling, I can't resist writing my name a second time, dancing kisses and hugs and love, Gopi-Bhakta! Yippee!!!

Perplexed, Ewan put down the letter and went for a long walk beside the frosty fields of stunted winter wheat.

Months had passed since Julian's letter. He woke from a daydream in which Devi was teaching him Tantric sex. Shocked, he blinked and looked at her. The early sun ignited her jet hair and warmed her perfect nose. Innocent of his unbidden fantasy, she was leaning over the balcony, reading her Zen book.

How did that happen? Am I going insane? Is this wish to find Truth no more than a desire to get closer to her? Was the spiritual journey the construct of desperate minds who, like him, had been unable to maintain balanced and caring relationships? If so, was it why the religiously extreme

131

despised sexual intimacy, which requires empathy and challenges you to manifest it beyond the bed every day in countless ways as you properly relate to another? He mustered up courage. "Devi, listen to what my maternal grandmother wrote: *'Perhaps Plato's Truth was nothing more than being able to actually love?'*

Devi laid down her book, blushed and admitted the issue confused her too.

Ewan told her another of his ancestors had had this problem. He went to his cell and returned with his file. Before showing her the relevant photocopy, he said he last read it in his family library, sitting in a window-seat watching the sun set over his ancestral vale.

Carefully brushing a fly off her cheek so as not to injure it, Devi said she had loved the way the library's tall windows mirrored the drawing-room jutting from the other end of Merricott.

He opened his file and turned to Graham Merricott's note on being in love with the daughter of a Maharaja. Devi glared at him and he found it disturbing to read.

"Is love no more than one's selfish desire to be with someone who makes one feel good? Does a mother feel love for her child, or is it some emotion brewed up to protect each species? Do crocodiles feel love for the hatchlings protected within her dagger teeth? When her infant grows to adulthood, does the mother fight it for food or remember it is her offspring? Does she cling forever to the thought of lost intimacy?

"Is the human mother's continuing love after adolescence nothing more than clinging? As adults, do we seek love to regain what we lost when we strode from our mothers? Is there more to it? Is it possible to feel altruistic love, for example, towards a stranger in need? Or is this no more than a selfish pulse - doing something which makes you feel good? Yet I have to admit this pulse I feel is stronger than anything I have known. How I miss her, hence I want to believe there must be love. Or is it desire...?"

They lingered in awkward silence. After a while he told Devi he'd missed her. It had been ages since her winter visit and like Indra who turned up and left like a shooting star, she failed to write or call and simply appeared and fled on a whim. She said nothing. Feeling foolish, he left. Devi, it appeared from her silence, wasn't his future. Indian women are married-off to suitable men. She might have little choice. He was not suitable, ergo, forget it. Maybe she would find him suitable when he became as spiritually strong as her? But no! Despite his Indian tan, he was a foreigner in a traditional country and she was a desirable woman.

An hour passed. Plucking a wild red rose growing beside the rushing river, he dashed back and dashed upstairs. Devi's apartment was locked. She had fled. I feel worthless. Waiting for her visits is wearing me down. Lost in swirling emotion, he walked from the ashram's enclosing world. He had enjoyed being disciplined and cherished the peace the place had given him, but he needed to find his own take on life. I've climbed over my SOS shield, but what now? Was there something in all this talk of Truth? Without my old life, I've no other direction than this, chasing family history now seems irrelevant.

It was a long second winter and he longed for Devi's return. She wouldn't respond to his texts or emails, but she never had. Her unattainability hurt him and month by month this destroyed his will. He felt pathetic. He watched himself drifting like the snow, wafting back to the mire of self doubt which had dominated his childhood. As an escape, wishing to discard prior preconceptions, he imperceptibly shifted from seeing a person's 'spirit' as their character, to believing what we perceive as *'me'* is the tip of our 'Soul', an eternal entity beyond material existence. When you leave empirical thinking, anything can happen and 'Truth', with that capital T, became his new fetish. What would Uncle Jack think? Once, in their family library after reading family letters together, they had dismissed the notion of an objective truth determining everything. As for this 'soul' thing, they had laughed. Accidental evolution made more sense. No over-all, predetermined design existed, nature's multiple forces reacted to each other, creating the complex interconnections we now witness. That was all.

Yet in the ashram, Truth, a vacant notion, filled the hole created by Ewan's lost life and Devi's elusiveness. This slowly gave his insignificant life meaning, generating drive and a false sense of importance. Wrapped in cashmere shawls, meditation in a stove-lit space was cosy, but Swami Prem was right, working outside in the cold Himalayan winds played their part in testing him, toughening his 'soul' for the path to 'Truth.'

But as winter faded, he knew he had to leave the ashram before his introverted trait glued him to the comfortable place. Wounded, dejected by Devi, he made a vow of celibacy. It would cure his desire for the impossible woman. Replacing his want of her by a wish to meet somebody capable of pointing out where or what Truth was, made him itchy to get on the road. Delightful Swami Prem lingers in the foothills with the security of this ashram, it's systems and Vedanta's established texts. Devi's smelt the way up the mountain but is still tracking Truth's indefinite route through life's confusing jungles. Ignoring her warning: *'The problems with ideals is that we imagine others have understood them better than us,'* he convinced himself a sage was out there waiting to be found.

After his dawn flower delivery, on the moody spring morning which heralded the start of his second year in India, as if in answer to his yearning, an oversized postcard arrived. Although Julian's muscular male temple dancer in drag was a tame photo, it had taken three weeks to arrive and was badly mauled.

Dear sexy, This guy could be one of my dancing friends. So, so sexy hey! I've heard of a man called Bol Maharaj, a Great Yogi who knows what it's all about. Really! Go to Bolgaon, between Haridwar and Naradarnagar. He's leaving for the USA on the 20th Feb. Go check him out and give me the low-down Big hug, Julian.

The card made Ewan think, why go find another teacher? I'm happy here. Mind you, my default is to remain in my comfort-zone, maybe I've learned what I needed here, Swami Prem is a delight, but real truth, if it exists, must be challenging. Hmm, I ought to get out there, sift through a few gurus, see if any of them can show me the way forwards.

In his new mindset, this was no coincidence - alongside Truth, came a belief in 'Fate', and Fate had acted, providing an escape route from the ashram and the pain of Devi. Devi's given me the cold shoulder enough times. They must be lining her up for marriage to a suitable aristocrat. I'm so, so stupid. Damn! I'm hurt enough, I really must leave.

Ewan reread the date. 20th Feb! Flipping heck, that's soon! Damn Julian's fans delaying this card. He quickly packed his few belongings, leaving most things for the next cell dweller, bar one of his cashmere shawls. Cleaning his cell for the last time, he closed its door and walked across the now very Zen inner courtyard. Passing the steps which rose to the first storey and up to Indra and Devi's terrace, he hesitated. Leaving meant he might not see Devi again, but it was months since she'd left without a word. Nevertheless, he wrote her a brief note, collected his sandals from the wide entrance hall and stepped through the new folding doors.

A familiar voice rang through the arched gate over the far side of the plaza, "By Jove Ewan! You do look different!"

"Indra!" Hair swishing over his shoulders, Ewan skipped over the golden slabs and hugged his friend beneath the jasmine covered archway. "It's been so long!"

Indra chuckled, "Ewan, my dear colleague, you have purpose, I can see it in your face and stance."

"Finally." Devi stepped from the rickshaw which had brought them from the railway station.

Caught out by her oblique reference to him and without even a greeting after so long apart, Ewan struggled to answer. "Hello M.Maharani," Stepping through the archway, grappling with his emotions, Ewan mimicked a Mumbai accent. "I am very much needing your R-Royal Rickshaw. I am having delayed p-postcard inviting me to meeting great R-Rishi."

Unaware of the tension, Indra placed his hand on Ewan's shoulder, "No need to be in such a hurry, old chap."

"Really Indra," Ewan dropped Mother's leather bag on the rickshaw's bench.

Swami Prem strode over to greet Indra. Once more revealing his interest in Julian's postcards, he said, "Earwing received a postcard and is leaving."

Snatching the card from Ewan's grasp, Devi scorned, "Ha! Some teacher has made him Truth-mad and off he goes."

"Devi, you come from out of the blue..." His nose throbbed. His voice was harder than intended. Trying to calm himself, he turned to her brother, "Indra, have you heard of Bol Maharaj?"

Swami Prem ground his words through his clenched teeth. "In India the blind elevate charlatans to Maharaj status! Earwing, please be careful. Namaste." He strode off.

Devi growled, "Find out for yourself. An hour away by rickshaw lies Naradaraghar. Go!"

"You left in autumn without a word!" He gathered himself, "and now it's spring and this postcard...."

"Arrived from a sex-fiend and you're off to meet a false guru!"

"That's n-not f-fair," he stuttered. "D-Devi, I have to discover -what's out there."

She snapped. "Real sages are scarce!"

Not appearing to sense the emotional drama unfolding before him, Indra added, "These gurus of India are masters at playing tricks on the mind, old boy."

"Discriminate, Ewan." Scoffing, Devi pushed him.

In a heap in the swaying rickshaw, he bleated, "Devi!"

Stilling the rocking machine, Indra reached over and clasped Ewan's hand, "Dear young man, you will always be our beloved friend."

Nervous, "I have a lot to thank you for."

"Here." Eyes flaring, Devi scribbled several phone numbers. "The palace, our mobiles, the hill house. Dare lose touch!"

Confused, Ewan lowered his head and folded his hands in the prayer posture, "Namaste."

Grimacing, she did the same.

ß

With mudguards rattling, the panting rickshaw wallah trundled round deep potholes. Mist half-concealed thatched homes at the roadside. Ewan asked the exhausted man to stop and he drew the arched backs of hungry hounds mirrored by men sat in a chai stall, clutching steaming mugs to their sunken chests.

"Jaia Bol Maharaj Hey!" the chai wallah cried in jubilation.

"Jaia ho!" Ewan, unwilling to honour the local guru as yet. "It is a cold morning!"

The reply came back in English, "Welicome Mr Kumar at number 42!"

Inspired by reference to a British-Asian TV comedy, Ewan climbed from the rickshaw and ordered two hearty breakfasts. The emaciated driver sat at a tatty table watching Ewan draw and when the omelettes came, he tucked in with gusto. Ewan ordered him another.

"Bol Maharaj greatest God!" The chai wallah exclaimed, tapping the guru's picture hanging on the mud wall of the storage shed his sacking tent leaned against.

"Bol Maharaj born here," a customer pointed to the simple village.

The chai man patted his leg with enthusiasm. "Bol Maharaj picture making me better. Chai business improving." he waggled his head from side to side with great emphasis. "Many pilgrim visiting me."

Ewan peered at the garish print in a tacky mock-silver frame, a fat face, an angled chin, spikes of hair. Raising his hand in blessing, Bol Maharaj sat on a stuffed tiger in a lousy mimic of one of the gods. Ewan was disappointed his search for a man of Enlightenment should start with this.

"Oh Great God Bol Maharaj," somebody entering the shack sang to the picture. The canny chai wallah joined in the chant, bowing and adjusting a string of fresh flowers he had bought from a passing vendor.

Ewan turned to his rickshaw wallah, "What do you think of Bol Maharaj?"

"I have my own guru," the little man shrugged.

"Half of India has a guru," Ewan paid, said goodbye and walked up a shallow hill. Nearing the summit, the mist was replaced by bright sunshine which warmed his limbs. A paved road, soon lined with concrete shops, tea houses, hotels; yelling touts, screeching Bollywood tunes and tooting motorbikes with high-pitched exhausts. Ewan's ears ache. Tracing a yellow wall topped with raspberry ridge-tiles, he arrived at imposing gates painted gold. Knots of women and men wearing yellow shawls took turns to slip inside and, to make room for the throng, Ewan leaned against the heavy gates.

"Stop opening!" Speaking English, the unifying tongue in Babel India, two scouts with yellow neck-scarves moved quickly towards him. One of them insisted on checking his leather bag.

Ewan grumbled, "You're not the police."

"Bol Maharaj order," the man glared.

"Your clothes bad. Wearing yellow!" The other scout jabbed a forefinger into the bottle-green, knee length kurta-shirt Ewan wore over white pyjama trousers - Devi chose the outfit last autumn. Devi! Stop thinking of her, she's beyond you!

Leaving his cheap rubber sandals with thousands of others, Ewan found himself at the foot of a shallow bowl carpeted with ten thousand seated black heads and yellow-draped bodies. Apart from the endless scuffle of unshod feet, all he could hear was the odd bird singing. Impressed by the hush, Ewan tiptoed up the slight slope, keeping to a grid of swept-earth paths lined with yellow-painted stones. Every few metres he lingered to read messages painted in raspberry on yellow boards and signed, Bol Maharaja: *"Love is all."* or *"God is love."* Ewan was already familiar with these classic Hindu texts, but the last two made him balk: *"Call out with love and I, Bol, am here."* *"Call me Bol, Krishna, Buddha, Jesus or God."*

139

At the crest of the gradient, a yellow palace two storeys high with a veranda whose raspberry doors were festooned with a line of men in yellow. Above this hung an ornate balcony spanning the upper floor. Ewan squinted, dead centre gold double doors embossed with silver figures from Hindu mythology.

The scouts emerged from the veranda's shade to poke and prod their bamboo lathis, encouraging the horde to remain speechless. To his neighbour Ewan sniggered, "The guru of love needs dictatorial order." The hollow tap of a lathi upon his shoulder. He fell silent, surprised those weapons of control could still make him shiver.

There was an atmosphere of great expectation. One of the grand old ladies of his past had fallen for a guru and Ewan opened his file and read Amelia's diary extract: *"24th June, 1817. Each day I rise from slumber before the sun touches the dusty plains and having purified myself with a rose-water wash I walk to the old guru's tree. He is usually deep in meditation when I lay at his feet a white rose plucked from the bush I have reserved for this ritual. I sit on the ground gazing at his wizened features until he opens his effulgent eyes. To my delight but to the dismay of my children this may take an hour. Inevitably, Baba smiles and tells me to return to my familial duties. Heavy of heart, I touch his toes tenderly and saunter through the mud village to our stone bungalow."*

Devotees kept pouring through the gates, soon no earth was bare but for the red paths the lathi scouts paraded. Loudspeakers squeaked irritatingly into action and after a painful period of adjustment, commanded: "STAND. BOL MAHARAJ ARTI!"

Ewan shook his head, Yes, the guy thinks he's God.

The crowd stood as a wave of yellow cotton. Yellow speakers fixed to walls, pillars, posts and trees jangled, replacing 'Jagadeshwari' with 'Bol Maharaj.' The groundswell of chanting drowned the tortured speakers as India's sweet signature song took over and came to an end with a sonic "AUM".

Eight yellow-clad priests with long black beards and raspberry turbans pulled open the gold doors and stood in a fan. Classic Bollywood. Mesmerised, the countless devotees fell utterly silent, no shifting bottoms, no coughing.

Glistening white silk laced with flecks of silver thread stepped past the saluting priests. Raising his right hand, the guru blessed his flock. The imagined power from these magical mitts washed over the devout legion who scooped the vibes over their heads, faces and chests. They clasped their hands in prayer, muttering their thanks to their saviour. The apparition retreated and the priests shoved the heavy doors closed. A booming electric voice prickling with back-play: "SIT! STILL! SILENT!"

Everyone obeyed. Disappointed, Ewan began to leave.

"Leaving not permitting!" another lathi wielding man ordered from behind.

The focus of innumerable eyes, Ewan felt stupid. It was the dictatorial atmosphere which had triggered his anger, not these innocent pilgrims. Why spoil their day? Maybe the discipline is required, crowds quickly become dangerous in India. He dropped to a gap between the closely packed bodies. Two bearded priests thrashed a big brass gong on the balcony eight times. Manifesting from the widest raspberry doors below, the silky-god entered the material world and mysteriously floated along the ruby paths.

The creature (from a closer vantage Bol Maharaj didn't look human), drifted calmly through his drove. Ewan looked closely. The white, silver-streaked silk flowing easily with the guru's movement gave an illusion of mystical grace. The impression of levitation was created by hiding the man's feet. I think guy's taken moon-gliding classes. Being a dedicated sportsman, Ewan recognised a person in control, an Olympian saunterer freewheeling before the yellow-clad flock at his feet. How hypnotic. Bol's an Oscar winner playing Jesus Christ Super-Sham. The manipulating, operatic set, the restrained boil of mass-hysteria, these worried Ewan, could he trust his own mind? It reminds me of Nazi footage.

As Bol moved, he patted the air with his right hand. The men in the chai stall had told Ewan this was Bol easing people's suffering. Smiling quickly at certain people, Bol halted to touch somebody or to briefly stare at another. Those with path-side seats reached out to touch Bol's silver-lined hem. Sometimes Bol shoved out a foot, allowing fingers to linger on his bare toes, but mostly he glided through the throng. Occasionally the guru would say something to an individual, point towards his palace and the person would rise and walk to the veranda.

After roughly forty minutes the cabalistic figure sailed back to the shade of his veranda where his raspberry doors closed on him. The lathi men organised those few individuals Bol had singled out. Without a tatty villager or peasant amongst them, Ewan surmised Bol courted the elite. His eye lingered on a slender, athletic figure oozing self-assurance to the last curl of bouncing auburn hair spilling down a lemon silk robe which fell to her ankles. Even at this distance her gestures fizzed. She went inside.

Outside the compound, with Bol worship over urban India was back on - speakers ripped the air with rival songs to the guru, vibrant Punjabi drum-rolls fought romantic Bollywood flutes and sitars, a rocky tune off-balanced the tempo. Chasing yellow signs, Ewan cut between rapidly shoved-up two storey buildings to a raspberry hotel called 'Bol Maharaj Retreat'. A slender man who quietly chanted 'Bol Maharaj jai!' all the while, showed him a room on the top floor with a balcony over-looking farmland. After washing under a tap-shower in the bathing zone, Ewan did some yoga on his balcony then donned more of the Indian clothes he'd worn since giving his fine Western gear to beggars in Haridwar last year. How good to be away from the constraints of the ashram, to find himself in the real world. Whoopie!

Hunger drew him to The Bol restaurant, a glitzy yellow and raspberry vulgarity squashed between a plush jeweller's and an expensive tailor's. Its frontage was a waist-high cooking wall from where heat and tempting smells spilled out. Ewan entered through a gap between the cash-desk and the platform upon which two fat cooks sat cross-legged, stirring huge woks over blazing holes. The front tables were filled with yellow-clad Westerners laughing and speaking loudly; further back neon strips lit families of middle class Indians talking quietly.

He sketched people whilst drinking spiced tea and nibbling coconut sweetmeats. An hour later the woman in silk rippled in. Whooo! she's exceptional. It's as if she's been to sensual acting school - every movement is voluptuous. Wow, a surge of passion's swelling through me, I can't take my eyes off her. Stop! Devi means.... Devi's lost....

"Tara, what luck!" the praise rolled round the Westerners.

Tara's green eyes were alight, her voice silky, "To be with God IS bliss!" Lifting her slender arms into the air, her superb body sizzling beneath the thin silk, she sighed, "Aah, Bol Maharaj! In His presence you take off."

Hearing the middle class Indians snigger, Ewan snapped, "Like on drugs?" What? His first words to her out before he could stop them.

Eyes blazing, calm Californian accent calculating, dangerous. "Don't mock. He IS the Avatar of God."

"He's only a man," Ewan shot back, putting more irritation into his words than intended.

"Such tenderness." Tara ran her hands over her flawless figure and quivered.

"Bol made love to you?" His cruelty surprised him. A gasp slurred across the room.

"Blaspheming! Foo-You!" Tara's seductive lips suddenly thin.

"He's no god, hence I didn't." This close he saw her hair appeared groomed to look wild... but Wow. Stop it! Diverting himself he said, "I like the way you swear."

"The F-word's for goofs."

"So how come a Fraud's Fooled you?" Again, not meaning to be so challenging.

She stormed out without looking back.

"Tara, sorry....," he sped after her, almost forgetting his bag in the process.

"Your Funeral leather bag! So uncool!"

"As are your leather sandals."

She stopped striding, flipped them at a startled beggar. "Keep the Flapping things!"

"Tara, forgive me. Sorry." hand formally extended, "I'm Ewan."

"Ivan, don't follow me with your slain bag and leather soul." She shot off.

He leaned against a wall sweating as if he'd run a mile in the dry heat. "Wow! She's a Siren!" How come a woman I met minutes ago has stirred me to insanity? Because Devi has taunted my emotions? He looked at his bag. The camel died decades ago, probably of old age, it was the one thing to remind him of his cold mother who had bought it on honeymoon in India. A waiter tapped Ewan's shoulder, reminding him to pay his bill. Fed up with his inner ranting, he pulled himself from the wall and followed the man. Settling into his old seat, he ordered the meal he had wanted to eat over an hour before.

The white young adults' obsession with Bol Maharaj irritated him. In loud and excited voices they cut across one another, trying to prove their devotion as if their lives depended upon impressing each other in Globlish, English simplified for international use.

"Bol Maharaj put jewel my heart," exclaimed an ecstatic Italian. Her vision was interrupted by an overdressed German whose yellow turban floated above frizzy black hair. "HE give sweet smile."

"HE tell go with...."

"Man sat next me..." injected a Finnish cat with a heavy Swiss watch.

"Bol Maharaj, come me last night," buzzed a Frenchman with long hair. "HE me fly top Himalaya. Shiva I meet."

"Maha Maharaj was telling me yesterday we could build his temple in our Bombay grounds," announced a cultured voice whose traditional yellow clothes were of raw silk. Another prince supporting a guru to earn a comfy couch in heaven? Was this the basis of Indra's belief? How collected in

144

comparison, dear Swami Prem and his obedient flock. Bored, Ewan rose and paid. The cross-legged cashier sat upon the raised cash-counter, carefully placed the notes in an old wooden box between his toes. Ewan strode past the cancerous buildings to where the yellow wall curled back on itself and entered swathes of no-man's land between the powerful guru's concrete cornucopia and the thatched mud village in the vale below. The mists had lifted and Ewan drank in the pre-industrial calmness of the rolling scrubland.

"A river!" He skipped down a winding path weaving through a sea of grass with islands of thorny bushes. He reached a rocky knoll rising from the swash of a little waterfall and found a cosy nook beneath a tree bearing the sign: *'Bol Maharaja order: No resting.'* There was nobody around so he sat on a cool beach and tried his base-sound mantra, but rippling desire for Tara and self-irritation prevented even a hint of stillness. He did a sketch. Pen closed, drawing done, he closed his eyes, picturing what he had spent fifteen minutes capturing.

"Go!"

Ewan opened his eyes, laughed, "Ah... Bol Maharaj sent you."

"Bol Maharaj telling I coming?" Eyes wide, the scout pulled nervously at his yellow scarf.

Ewan tipped his head to one side, raised his eyebrows - the silent Indian affirmation.

The man agape, "Blessing you, Sir. Most sorry disturbing meeting with Bol Maharaj."

Ewan smiled: mention a mystical experience and India is yours. Perhaps he could set himself up as a guru. All you need do was say little and let people build you up. Smiling, he stood, stretched and headed upriver, enjoying the tread of wet sand between his bare toes and the intense heat on his shoulders. Turning from the sandy banks, he put on his rubber sandals and wandered over rough fields to the old village. A small square shaded by the ubiquitous banyan, the tranquil statement of rural India. An old man on the surrounding plinth greeted, "Namaste."

145

Ewan responded. "Namaste babaji. This village is poor and yet god is next door."

The old man grunted, "There you have it! We knew him as the naughtiest boy in generations."

"Is the prophet never accepted in his homeland?"

The old man guffawed, "Charlatan rather. Sit and hear his story."

Wiggling his back into the banyan's welcoming trunk, Ewan listened and soon other villagers settled beside them, tossing in their own comments. Bol hadn't been a popular child because he was arrogant, a liar, a bully. He dominated the local youth and thrashed any who spoke against him. Upon festival days he sneaked into people's huts and snatched sweetmeats they could only afford to make for special occasions and he'd sell them in nearby Haridwar. Aged twelve, he was jailed over-night for stealing cash offerings from a temple on the banks of the Ganga. When fourteen, he made three Haridwar girls pregnant, dashing their prospects of marriage, ruining their lives. When a group of travelling magicians passed by, villagers pressed Bol's distraught parents to sell him and rid them of the plague. However, nobody was happy when the young man returned from oblivion a decade later, calling himself a yogi.

"Fifteen years ago he sat under this tree," the old man retold the event as if it were yesterday. "We kicked him out and he chose another tree, up there where his palace stands illegally upon communal pasture, but which we don't have the power to reclaim. He had grown rich with disciples arriving from Haridwar where he had impressed the gullible with his clever words and magician's tricks."

The inhabitants were open and relaxed and this soothed Ewan. He watched the sinking sun tint the mud homes and radiate the returning cattle. He did a quick sketch of the beasts with fat bellies whose thin legs were lost in the ruddy dust they stirred up and whose curving horns glinted red above the brouhaha of moos, whistles and calls. Wow, a scene as old as agriculture!

Beneath The Bol's blazing lights, Tara was in animated conversation with other carefully dressed Americans and Europeans whose raspberry and yellow based designer jewellery and watches sparkled. His heart pounding, he squeezed beside her. Why?

She continued to speak with a Parisian wearing a yellow shirt delicately embroidered in raspberry. Hopeful of making contact, Ewan waited, but she turned to a hard faced Israeli with a tender voice and repeated her story and when this conversation was over she leaned forward, resting her bosom on the table as she retold her time with Bol Maharaj to a fellow American with a heavy beard.

Although Tara kept ignoring him, before her all else faded. She's irresistible because, because? Her expressive green eyes? Her lively mouth carefully pouting as she speaks? Her stunning figure? How she's rapidly turned me from a calm adult into a gibbering teenager! Because…? I pine for my first kiss, or have I been too long amongst modest women? Is it revenge against Devi? No, it's something primal. Look, Tara has this effect on all men present. Stop it. Devi's more my type. Imagine Tara repairing my hurt with caresses and kisses. That's it! She's touched my… in her presence my heart climbs from the infant pain which constructed my SOS, I stand emotionally naked in her pheromone glow.

Unchallenged, Ewan left in a twirl. Leaning against his hotel's wall, he drowned in the memory of Tara's scent, more real than the surrounding whiffs. Fresh, fruity, on a familiar low note stirring my insides, making me believe she can set me free. The sultry hint of… of? In an instant Tara churned me up. Whoa! She'll destroy me. It'd be sensible to leave.

Upon his balcony he gawped at the billions of stars. The constellations he had enjoyed as a child had been the brighter ones, but in the dry Indian air he could see glimmers of others beyond these, there was no blackness, simply diminishing dimness filled with more stars. He imagined he could hear the universe turning and let his ears drink in this faint no-noise. Serenity seeped in, expanding him beyond his seething emotion.

147

Smoke from dawn fires teased him awake. Passing squatting men, who generally woke later than women, Ewan reached the river. Retaining his boxer shorts, he slid off his clothes and bathed in the pool beneath the waterfall as a saffron sun peeped above the eternal plains. Performing his morning Yoga routine, he smiled. How clear I feel.

"Hi there Ivan."

Halfway through a posture, he spun round, unbalancing, toppling to the ground. Feeling foolish, he scrambled to his feet, stroking his nose. Brushing dust from his bared chest, he said, "Hello Tara. By the way, it's Ewan, not Ivan." Why am I annoyed about my faux-name? "How'd you know where to find me?"

"I wasn't looking for you! It's a small place, Ivan."

Unsure of the ground between them, he said, "You're on holiday from university?"

She threw a pebble into the pool. "Time's your own on a PhD."

"To you Bol is divine?" He sought to heal the rift between them.

Tara stroked her fine chin. "I became convinced in Varanasi when somebody was healed by touching His picture."

"You saw it?" He balanced on a rock by the pool.

"A lecturer I respect told me. I knew the person was ill, seeing him fit was proof enough and so I began attending their regular Lord Bol Maharaj services."

What idiocy, the person would have recovered on their own, but Ewan stopped himself, to uphold their beliefs believers believe the illogical, making it impossible to debate. "What do you want from him?"

"Hey man!" Tara pushed him into the pool. When he surfaced she yelled, "Lord Bol Maharaj is The Messiah! Only HE can lead us to Truth!"

"We gain Liberation through our own effort." What do I mean by Liberation?

148

"Granted, but a living master shows you Enlightenment a thousand times quicker."

"Like bhang?" Yes - that's it! Bhang's her base smell, it triggers something fundamental within, reminding me of the cleaner.... This new venture I'm on, the persona I've become since arriving in India, it all began with that bhang lassi and No-Matter's bhang chillum! The mere smell of the stuff after two years abstinence churns me up. OK, smelt it on sweaty sadhus.... This is different because she's, she's, well she's a woman. And what a woman!

"You rat!" She tossed a clod of earth.

"Violence will get you nowhere!" Ewan swam to the rock. Climbing out, he pretended to tug her in and she shrieked in mock horror, struggling, giggling. Shivering with mirth, she pushed him in again and when Ewan climbed out he shook himself over her and they fought, squealing like children. He dived back in. She laughed, teasing him, egging him on with her flashing eyes and sensual changes of stance which made him pant with desire. Desperately trying to find his inner calm, he stayed in.

"Come out sexy nose!"

Why my blasted nose? "Come in Tara." Confounded, he was playing for time.

Tara stepped cautiously into the pool, "Look, I'm sorry about yesterday. I'm all high on Lord Bol Maharaj."

"And the scene."

"They're OK, if a bit bonkers," she lifted one foot back to the bank. "I'm off. It's Bol Arti time. I only came for a quick chat."

"Ha! You knew I was here!"

She stuck out her tongue and Ewan's chest heaved as he lifted himself from the pool. She stepped forward, reached out, her arms engulfing him, her fingers thrilling his bare back. "Tara," he heard himself wail. It was basic - endorphins flooded his veins.

Gasping at his primitive response, she sank into his body, kissing him. My First Kiss! He groaned as her tongue ignited his nervous system from his tingling toes to his itching nose.

149

How? How could that happen? Help Devi! Disgusted with himself, he dived back in.

"Stop teasing," she yelled when his head surfaced.

"I'm not! I'm struggling with myself."

"Why?"

"I'm trying to be celibate."

"What!" She shook her head. "Celibacy's for those incapable of intimacy. Our senses put us in touch with the world. Relish them."

Ignoring a similar conversation with Devi, but remembering what his bhang charged emotions had done for him in Zaminder-land, he said, "Surely controlling the senses enables the better aspects of the mind to rise above selfish emotion and find The Way."

"Suppressing desire creates dams of tension which impede our vision and lead us astray. Look at religious fanatics - they'd be healed with cuddles! Come out and immerse yourself in sensuality."

"Tara, I can't!" he moaned.

"Fluster!" She stormed off through the long grass.

Ewan pounded the pool, beating his hands through the surface, bashing the water with his furious hands, gasping for breath like a drowning dolphin until he was too tired to continue. He climbed out, lay on a rock, let the sun dry his exhausted body, let Tara's powerful memory amplify the joy he felt. The morning haze cleared, he admired the familiar line of purple hills soaring from the spring-green line of the plains. At this distance he could see above them. Sparks of ice! The mysterious Himalaya! Yes-yes! He wasn't in India to flirt with the likes of Tara. He must get away. But in her magnetic presence nothing else existed. Was this love? He had watched others turn mad through love. He took a deep Aikido breath, and sat down to draw those magical mountains. As his pen worked, his mind lifted from his muddle to dwell on the possibilities which lay between those Himalayan folds - hidden towns and villages, remote caves where yogis were said to meditate. He yearned to explore.

Hungry for breakfast, he went to The Bol. Passing the men on the cooking-counter, he ordered a spicy omelette and several cups of tea. His mind couldn't let go of Tara. The touch of her tongue tingled in his mouth, her fingers soothed the flesh of his lower back, her firm, full figure pressed against his. Impatiently opening his sketchbook, in short strokes he caught the two squatting men, their skilled chopping on wooden blocks wedged between naked toes, their deft fingers flicking spices into the sunken woks, their fat arms stirring the food over the bright flames. The drawing calmed Ewan.

"Brilliant!"

He hadn't noticed Tara standing over him. His pencil jagged over the page.

"Oops Ivan, I've spoilt it. Rub that out," Tara reopened the sketchbook he'd quickly closed.

Ewan looked up, "The mark tells its own story."

"I'm bored Ivan." She leaned on his shoulder, touched his nose, whispered, "interested in sweating through a hot morning?"

He gulped, turned his nose from her. Devi jumped into his mind. Damn Devi, she doesn't want me. "Tara, I told you I'm on a celibacy thing."

"Don't you miss sex?" She sat down, her hand slyly tickling his inner thigh.

Gasping, unwilling to admit he'd never had it and now pined for it…. But this is wrong! Surely he ought to avoid lust, find love first? "No."

She whispered. "No's not what I see down there. I've some bhang in my room."

"Tara, please…." The faint tang of bhang in her hair…. Yes, that is it!

"Tantra will blow your mind, Ivan." Soft California accent speaking her intimate name for him thrilled, massaged his mind.

He panted, "Tantra?"

"Tantra's liberating."

151

The touch of her lips on his ear, the gush of warm air. He was unable to grasp solid ground. "Tantra."

"Tantra turns touching into meditation." Her gaze calm, independent.

Tantra, she trusts Tantra. It suits her because she's sybaritic. My body aches for her. He tried to get out, but she had him trapped in the corner and all thought of Yoga, Truth and Devi were as nothing compared to her sizzling presence. This urge he'd never felt flooded him. No! Devi was his archetypal companion, not this hotted up creature! He came to his senses. "I can't Tara," quickly wriggling over her irresistible form, he stood up. She jumped up, stuck to his bulge like glue. Embarrassed yet yearning for her, he paid the giggling owner. The cooks chuckled.

She pushed him outside. They walked along the paved street, she softly chanting, "You can get Enlightened if totally concentrated during Tantra."

Sweat pouring from his arm pits, "Bhang's bad for me." What's happening to my resolve? Like a lamb knowing it's going to the slaughter, I walk beside her, unable to part from her, my body pulsing for hers. Blinking heck! the power her sultriness has over me, but I don't care. The surface of Tara's skin shone with desire, her green eyes flared madly each time she shot him a look. Oh god! The pleasure! His heart pounded as they separated through the main gates, reconnected, strode through crowding disciples, paced towards one of the blocks of yellow flats reserved for the well off.

They were directly behind the palace. Bol was outside. Gawping at Tara's unbridled nipples erupting through her silk dress, the guru strode over, took her hand, "Tara, goddess of Tantra."

"Whoo," Tara gasped, mesmerised by her god.

The guru led her into a private garden and without thinking, Ewan followed. They went into a semi-circle of bamboo. The guru wheezed, "Tara, you're the archetypal woman."

Ewan cautiously stepped into the bamboo and saw Bol rip open Tara's skin-thin silk dress, exposing her breasts.

Tara slapped her guru. Lifting her torn dress to cover herself, she stammered, "You're Faking Fabergé!"

"Dear Tara, all is illusion," Bol's smile sickly.

Running to Ewan, Tara bellowed, "Ivan, let's git out'a here!"

With bags at their feet, they settled on a rickshaw's wide passenger seat and Tara leaned over to lick Ewan's lips. It was an act of defiance. In a land where publicly touching the hand of a non-relative of the opposite sex is risky, it was a rebellion against Bol the charlatan.

Ewan gulped, his hands clasping her. "Tara!"

"Ivan Oh!" She kissed him with genuine ardour.

Thrilled, but aware of the glaring crowd, he pulled away, annoyed that he was annoyed. The agitated cyclist strained at the pedals to get the vehicle moving before the horde turned nasty.

"Here we go!" Tara laughed.

"But where?"

"Anywhere but here!"

ß

The sweet scented flowers and echoing birdsong enthralled Ewan as they waited for their bus. Across the road, weary passengers emerged from the railhead built to help British Raj families flee the baking plains. He recalled family photos of memsahibs in bulging dresses beside piles of luggage, overdressed children and neat servants waiting for charabancs to take them high into the hills where night frosts coated trim hotel lawns.

Ewan smiled. Tara. Wow, still together! His awkwardness usually made girls quickly lose interest, it showed the ashram had been good for him... and Devi's company. Oh heck, Devi... but she's beyond me....

A battered bus belching cheaply mixed diesel fumes arrived. Without the usual Indian scrum, the passengers quietly made their way aboard and the tortured engine began its daily struggle up a river gorge slicing the titanic Himalaya. The grey-blue speck crawled up densely forested slopes which shot skywards in leaps and bounds, fold after fold, buckling with multiple ravines and corrugations, each containing clear streams vaulting towards the main river far below. Ewan noticed the verdant pleats joined, forming a ridge which climbed and climbed to abut another chine that sprung further still. He muttered, "The town map showed we'll be rising one-thousand five hundred metres."

"Hump."

Ewan pointed through the scratched windows at tiny villages poised on small green mesas left high by aeons of erosion. Each had a skirt of neatly terraced fields etched into the jungle. The engine growled round each hairpin bend as if it were about to give up, eventually it stopped deep within the forest. Climbing down, they shook their weary limbs. A rickety chai stall hung above a terraced vegetable plot where a woman cut cucumbers. Inspired, Ewan went inside and ordered raita of grated cucumber and yoghurt spiced with salted cumin.

The chai wallah said in English, "Must visiting Yat Tal Lake hotel. Anglo-Indian owner."

The name rang a bell. Mother had spent part of her honeymoon at a lake called Yat Tal. She revealed little about her past, hence the unusual name stuck.

Recalling old photos, he told Tara of lawns flowing to a lake, she liked the idea. The horn blasted, they climbed aboard and the bus continued upwards. Tara chatted eagerly about the ever increasing views opening over the great Indian plain and the engine was overheating by the time they alighted in a small market town nestled in an orchard-filled valley hanging above the plunging abyss. The air was cool, refreshing, Ewan felt alive, but Tara embarrassed him.

"I love mountains!" Tara danced in a circle, flirting with several muscular men wearing the shortest of shorts and tattered shirts. They chortled and despite their violent head movements, their colourful skullcaps remained stuck-on.

Trying to distract her, Ewan said, "They're Gurkhas." He told her these men whose fierce ancestors once temporarily invaded the area, walked many miles from desperate villages in western Nepal to lug the Indian spring harvest to market. "Since 1814 the fittest have joined the British and Indian Armies."

"Mercenaries," Tara snarled.

"Regulars."

They climbed aboard an even more dilapidated bus. It belched black fumes uphill through a cultivated haven in until it burped into dense jungle. Emerging upon an exposed lip, an entirely new valley system. To save fuel, the driver switched off his ignition and gravity twisted and turned the vehicle down a sheer drop, Ewan was convinced the rattling bus would fall apart as it groaned into each hairpin bend. All the bustling laughter and chatter aboard stopped. Yikes, I can see why. Far below three mangled cars atop a contorted bus.

"They're recent!" Tara yelped.

Busy changing religious CDs, the driver careered towards a rising pick-up overloaded with sacks of produce, each vehicle behaving as if it were alone on the narrow road.

Ewan yelled, "Slow down!"

One hand on the wheel, the driver looked over his shoulder, eye-balling Ewan. "No worrying Sahib, Lord Shiva here!" Wobbling his head, he took a hand off the wheel and patted the windscreen shrine where Shiva with lit-up eyes shook his head like a dashboard-dog.

"WATCH it!" Ewan bellowed. The 4x4 honked. But playing chicken, both vehicles held centre.

"STOP!" Tara screamed.

Their driver again swivelled his neck so both eyes faced Tara. "Lord Shiva great god!" He looked forwards, casually turned his wheel and half the clattering bus bounced on a narrow grass verge, inches from the sheer drop. Without the traction of an engine they slithered on the damp surface. At the last second the driver of the 4x4 mounted the inside verge and the two vehicles, wing mirrors clacking, shot past one another.

All the while he was performing this daring manoeuvre, the driver had one hand busy inserting a new CD into his sound-system. Turning up the volume, he revolved his torso and hollered, "OM NAMAH SHIVIA!"

"Phew, that was terrifying. Speed keeps these crazy guys awake." Tara laid her head on Ewan's shoulder.

Whoo, I'm lucky. She's, she's... stunning, she's... perfection.

Turning down the music, the driver braked sharply, wiggly black marks scarred the road. He pointed at a tiny circle of light dancing within expanses of emerald. "Yat Tal!", realigning his Nehru cap over his prominent nose. The announcement, and the bus being still, so temporarily out of danger, prompted the passengers to extoll Yat Tal's beauty.

Ewan gawped out the window, "Paradise or what!"

Tara stood up and, acting, teased, "D'ho! Yat Tal dha paradise?"

The bus rolled with laughter. I'm amazed 'The Simpsons' have reached this far. "Sorry, Tara."

When they hit level ground, the driver fired his engine through fertile fields of wheat and orchards dotted with working families. They came to the jungle's edge and the driver stopped and announced, "Yat Tal road!"

Dwarfed by fat cathedral trees, their footfall noiseless on damp leaves; drooping lianas covered in moss, yellow and white orchids nestled between splitting trunks. Black and cream langur monkeys, lengthy tails hanging straight as rope, watched from above. Breaking the silence, Ewan said, "It's virgin jungle. Thank god British axes didn't get this far."

"Stop lecturing!"

"Sorry." I'm again the child wishing to please. Her beauty and sensuality create a charisma which thwarts me.

Long after their eyes had grown used to the sombre tunnel, a gleaming dot ahead. Emerging by a sandy beach, transfixed by an orb bottomed with silver, edged with greens, domed by the flawless blue sky, they whispered, "Yat Tal."

"How did this place survive intact?" Tara sighed.

"Because of the hotel, I imagine."

"That was rhetorical."

"Sorry." She makes me feel small.

"Stop saying sorry!"

"Sorry." Oops. He bit his lip.

She pointed to a ripple by the far shore. It expanded in purposeful rings swelling and spreading wider. "A creature!"

Thrilled he could feel her racing heart as she pressed against him. Hmm, she's a city girl.

"It's making its way towards us," she gripped his waist.

Mesmerised, they watched the shape grow steadily. "The head's low in the water."

"A Himalayan monster?"

"Who knows," Ewan began sweating. A flat head followed by a long fat body slithered onto a rock platform ten strides from them. Open nostrils, wide mouth, forked tongue flickering. Loose coils of olive brown with a black zigzag.

"Whoa!" Her hand pinched his flesh.

"Indian rock python."

"Holy Cow, Ivan! Six metres."

"Maybe even seven. Slowly step backwards."

Utterly vulnerable, they edged back to the track which curved between the water's edge and the towering trees. Sweating, hearts racing. The python's cold eyes studied them. Far enough away, they turned and ran and when the python was a small stain in the distance, they stopped, gasping for air. Tara fell against him, puffing into his neck. "Phwee Ivan."

"Tara." His rushing muscles absorbed her quivering firmness, her energy reached his core. Woo, intimate, raw.

Stroking his back in long light movements, "Tonight I'll teach you Tantra Ivan-oh." She nibbled the underside of his chin. She licked his blasted nose and in nasal confusion, his resolve melted. Her figure resonated with the force within him, he felt compelled to be hers.

A sandy beach, white wooden pier and a red rowing boat. Curling from the jungle, bands of shrubs fronted by bright flowerbeds, trim lawns cut by paths spreading towards stone chalets dotting the grounds. A sprawling Victorian bungalow draped in flowering creepers, a wide terrace. Upright in a cane chair, his bald head speckled by the shade of a cherry tree, an old man in a linen jacket laid a heavy book on a card-table, stood up and called, "Visitors, eh!"

"Hi! I'm Tara," relieved to be back in civilisation.

"Tara - the unquenchable hunger of life! Afternoon my dear. Major Fisher," formal hand offered, stiff bow.

"Hello Major, I'm Ewan," hand held out.

"Obi-Wan Kenobi!" The Major guffawed at his own joke.

Blinking, Tara looked quizzically at Ewan. Perhaps the joke's enabled her to register my faux-name.

"Almost! Ewan McNaughton, not McGregor."

The Major ordered tea, "Picked from the garden, fresh as a baby's bottom, hmm, not such a good association, eh," and showed them round. He spoke in sharp, muffled phrases as if he'd had a mouthful of hot chillies: "Good milk, own cows! Chicken-wire keeps wild beasts off vegetables, eh."

"Regent's Park," Ewan waved at the array of plants.

The dapper man nodded, "Thank you, sir! My passion, this garden, eh."

"How long, lived here, hurumph?" Tara snapped, mimicking.

Ewan snuffled a giggle.

"Since birth. Great, great-grandfather, clever fox, built the bloody place. Popular during The Raj. Hunting parties, honeymooners, orchestral evenings, wonderful balls. Never a dull moment. After independence, writing on the wall, fewer customers. However, India's star rising, more finding us now, eh."

They were at the jungle's edge and Major Fisher pointed under various trees. "Mother, bless her. Father, doesn't snore anymore, ha, ha, ha! Grandparents. Great-grandparents. My spot - fine company, eh?" They moved towards the lake. "No children, too busy fighting! Handing place on to manager. Six kids, damn him!" Major Fisher chuckled happily. "Nephews 're bloody angry. Never saw the sycophantic fools before. Now on me last legs, devils won't leave me alone!" The Major guffawed.

"Not lonely?" Tara snapped.

Ewan smiled. She's great!

The Major winked, "Don't worry lass. Had my times, ha, ha, ha!" He steered them towards the terrace. "Tea's up!"

"Lovely cake, Major." Ewan settled his china cup on its saucer. "Which regiment were you in?"

"Gurkhas. None better!" The Major relaxed and smiled warmly for the first time. "You can trust every little blighter amongst them with your life. No matter the danger, they are there at your side, ready for anything, fighting as a band of devoted brothers. They turn fear into action and it doesn't rest long in them either, when the battle's over they dance and sing, happy as children. They are the finest chaps on earth, eh! Manager's my ex-sergeant. Staff all from my regiment. Obligatory. Since the start."

"Major. The start. When?" Tara barked, perfectly matching the man's tempo and pitch. She hid her smile behind a cucumber sandwich when Ewan's toes tapped her ankle.

"1829. Archibald, bless his soul."

The coincidental link evaporated Ewan's fears. At last I can speak openly. "My family were Gurkhas."

The Major shot Ewan a cautious glance, "Who? When?"

Ewan smiled, how familiar his manner. "Our first Gurkha was Roland."

"Roland McNaughton?" The Major barked.

"No." Ewan bit hard into a slice of fruit cake. Blast, I've unwittingly set myself a trap. Can't utter my family name, one exposure too far. What made me reveal myself? Feeling safe lost in the Himalayan jungle; fear of the python followed by that lusty moment with Tara; the Major reminding me of Father? The man certainly stirs up some sort of military obligation to speak out. Heck, the grip of one's childhood! "Roland was involved in organising the first Gurkha recruitment."

"After the battle of Almora?" The Major snapped.

With reluctance Ewan responded to the test, Father had drilled him since infancy. "Almora was April 25th 1815, but recruitment began the following year, after Mukwanpur."

The Major nodded thoughtfully and tapped his book, which Ewan noticed was a history of the Gurkhas. "A Roland was under Generals Gillespie and Wood, mmm, oh, um, Roland... something.... Yes, almost got it! Roland Mer-Merry...," the Major looked up quizzically. "MerryBott?"

"Merricott."

"Legend amongst the ranks! Mentioned here. Only rose to Major, often the case, best fighters kept amongst the men, eh. Honoured to meet you young Merricott." He stood up, snapped his heels and bowed from the neck.

Well programmed, Ewan rose in synchronicity, back straight, head bowing formally.

Tara hooted hysterically at the comic scene. "Well, well, Ivan! We do have a dark horse in our midst."

The Major looked at her. "Men of honour never discuss openly."

"You constipated Brits!" she laughed.

160

Ignoring her rudeness, the Major said, "By the way Merricott, Gillespie's my line, wrong side of sodding sheets though, ha, ha, ha! Bloody mixed blood, ha, ha, ha! Looks like you too, eh?"

"Think I've a bit of Italian blood."

"When the British left, us Anglo-Indians stayed on and ho we can be snobs, thinking we're better than the Indians, yet we're Chichis, ha, ha, ha! Sad lot calling the kettle black, yet we stick out like painted thumbs, eh! Ha, ha, ha! I call myself Indian. Bloody good country! Eh. The best!"

Tara, bored with military issues, "Saw a python. With a hotel, kill it."

"Over my dead body!" The Major looked astounded. "He's a good chap! Taught him to steer clear of humans years ago."

"Is it safe to swim?" Ewan saw a way to escape the drilling.

"Absolutely. From time to time we tap his nose with a paddle. Soft spot, the nose, eh."

Ewan touched his own incumbrance.

The Major coughed. "This time o'year, mornings a bit cold, afternoon better for a dip. We station guards in the rowing boat."

"That's still necessary?" Tara asked.

"No. Puts guests at ease! Ha, ha, ha."

They were the only guests and their stone chalet was twenty strides from the water's edge. The three roomed structure had been swept and prepared whilst they had taken tea. The large bathroom had an old bath and a shower falling onto stone slabs. There was a good sized bedroom. The sitting room had comfortable cane furniture and French windows opening onto a wide veranda with folding panels of insect-proof netting. Tara stood before the sparkling sitting room fire, which the Major explained spread its warmth through grills into the other rooms and heated the water.

161

"On leaving, ensure veranda panels closed, monkeys etc., eh," The Major tapped a cane chair and retorted, "Any requests?"

"I'd love to swim," Ewan admitted.

"Not me!" Tara shivered.

"Sepoy! Sahib tal jaatha hey!" The Major barked as he marched off to continue pondering Gurkha history.

Ewan reappeared in his boxer-shorts. A man tending the flower beds quickstepped to the shoreline, undid the boat and rowed out twenty strokes where he occasionally slapped the surface with the flat of an oar. As the first thwack echoed across the lake, Ewan saw the distant python slither into the water and swim back to the far side. He dashed into the cool water and swam until he was tired. He splashed the Gurkha in the rowing boat and giggling, the man splashed him back. Ewan ran back to the stone chalet where he took a warm shower.

Tara stopped reading and joined him for half an hour's Yoga on the trim lawn. As she formed the postures, he admired her - a yoga book with pictures of her would be a bestseller. He sighed. He had given himself to her and looked forward to years of this.

When it was dark, dinner was served in silver tureens upon their veranda. In the candlelight, there was a slight distance between them, a nervous tension. The food, reminiscent of English cuisine, lightly flavoured with pepper and basil: a mixed salad, roasted vegetables, grilled lake trout, creamed potatoes, fresh fruit salad with whipped cream.

After a walk around the starlit gardens they returned to their quarters. "Let's start Tantra Yoga." They did several Yoga postures. Tara directed him to sit on a cushion upon the rug spread before the fire. They meditated. She loaded a pipe, "Bhang is used only ritually in Tantra."

He was confused; the drug had liberated him from his emotional prison, yet it had sent him to prison to die.... but when she blew the smoke in his face joy exploded and years of dreaming of that London cleaner's heart danced through his veins. Laughing, Tara offered him the pipe. Ecstatic. A deep drag, hold it. Oooh, is this too long to hold your breath? Wheeee, it's going out, out, ooh, "Ohoa, whata wonderful wicked World!"

"Silence from now. Close your eyes. Feel your breath working through your body as the base sound mantra Ssssaaaa," her voice calm, cool, controlling.

The drug lead him from his darting attention to his ears and her long, slow breaths smoothed the channels of his ears, stroked his eardrums, tingled his mind, creamed his nerves and he felt himself expanding from tracks of analytical thought to ride the expansive waves of sound welling from her lovely lips. Life, a lolling ocean, time a surfboard, he, warming jelly.

"Whazzat?" His unbolting eyes sprung him from deep within Tara's voice as she rubbed his nose.

"Carefully undress me. Never stop your mantra - SILENTLY!"

He wanted to kiss the hands slipping off his clothes. Oh, how soft your.... those stiff nipples woWoaWhat-beauts! She slapped his lowering face, commanded they sit cross legged, knees faintly touching. But why? Help, growing penis! Awkward or what! Big enough? Does that matter? Where to look? Unable to touch, talk or react, I'm invading her privacy. He peered around the room but his gaze kept falling to the base of her neck... lower and... frightened by her pert fecundity, wanting her, he snapped up to her curly hair. "Help!"

"Sshh! Ssssaaaa," in his ear more a sigh than a mantra and he in a lagoon filled with warm ripples of her life-breath, "sssŚssshhhA!"

"SssŚssshhhA!"

"No! Silently."

Why, why so commanding? We're starting love, not regimen....

"Ssh! Look at one of my pupils," her voice slow.

Awkward. Wishing to lick her flesh, nervous of his overwhelming desire. Golly! No. Focus on her pupil, so

163

black, poignant within that green iris. I'm being gawked at, I'm mentally naked, turn from her piercing stare!

"Look at me!"

Ugh, my vision's split by my big nose. Can she detect my innocence? What's she see in me? Ooh this is weird…. I want her! No. Shrink you brute!

Her gentle voice shocked, "Each slow breath, repeat your anchor, sssŚssshhhA."

Concentration settled him. Everything but her eye faded and a strange journey began: her face changed - teenager, child of ten, old; a man, vibrant woman in strange clothes, lad with a cowboy hat.

"You're seeing my past lives," she whispered.

Rubbish, I'm watching my mind at play, Texan hat - she's American. It's fascinating. This kaleidoscopic drama eventually dimmed, he was in a tunnel, Tara's bright eyes at the distant end.

"Come," she pulled his thighs.

Aaah! We're united! How I've dreamed of this. This! Sensational."Tara, Tara."

"Don't move an inch!"

Blast! Too late. I'm so, so immature! She must regret choosing me.

She insisted they wash. Yoga. They sat. Meditation. "No dope, you're too emotional." Eyes. Slid together. "Sssaaa. Come in. Slow. SLOW. Still! sssŚssshhhA."

"Tara, ahh Tara, I love you."

Shoving him, "GET out! Sssaaa!"

Why! Why angry eyes? Whatam-I-doing wrong?

"No Tara, no Ivan, only Lingum in Yoni, sssaaa," without disturbing her breath rhythm, "we breath, sssŚssshhhA, minds merge. OK? Calm? SssŚssshhhA. Come inside. Slowly! DO NOT move! Tantra isn't sex. The only movement is breathing in time, harmonising our energies, restraining desire. CALM down! Tantra harnesses and rides us towards our merging souls."

He leaned closer to kiss her. Pushing him back, she demanded he sit straight, breath in tandem. Swirling in a strange drug-like world of dammed-up passion and heightened sensuality, he discovered the peculiar power of looking into your lover's eyes, physical urge hardly contained. "Let your consciousness flow in and out of your pupils as you breathe your soul out to me and suck mine into yours. Soul, not ego, Tantra, not desire. Mantra/breath, not passion. Feel your breath subtly moving your whole body."

"Tara!" How I love this first woman I've kissed.

"Focus on mantra/breath."

Their combined breath mesmeric, SSSAAA. "I can't...." puppy in love.

"No talking till dawn! Turn passion into spirit with sssaaa."

"Sorry Tara, but...." She was everything to him. With her, his life was fulfilled.

"Shut up!" She nipped his nose.

Damned nose. Pain. Control.

"We admire each other as glorious creations. We don't like each other more than any other person we choose to explore Tantra with. It is Tantra, not the individual, we are devoted to."

Blast that, I'm hers forever. "TaraaAaaAA! I love you Tara I love you...."

Blinking, erupting from her trance. "...LOVE? ....Love... is... desire to possess."

"Blow Mantra/Tantra, Tara, I want to be with you."

"We don't exist in Tantra. This urge for personal attachment is the natural need to procreate and care for children. The magnetism we call love is endorphins which last three years, the time-span an infant learns to scurry from danger, but we've made it chain us."

How can she? I can hardly think, let alone talk. "That's... pre-Human. We've evolved... into...aaah." He kissed her, wanting her companionship forever. She relaxed into his arms. I'm so, so happy! Tara, whow!

She pulls from him.

What! "Ugh!"

165

"Ssshhhaaa!" Tugged him to the bathroom. In silence they ritually showered, washing each other slowly, acknowledging they were sharing something special but were re-entering the worlds Tara and Ewan inhabited separately. Her teeth had cut his shoulder, he pressed paper to stop the flow of blood.

Tara stated it was time to start again. Not having rested, they performed Yoga, meditation. Another pipe, the effect more powerful. Eye-gazing, stroking and again they sat enjoined. She functional, he emotional. She scolding, he repenting. For him, it lasted too long. They sat quietly afterwards. She riding high in bliss. He wanting to sleep.

"Staying awake all night you ride the half-dream world of the unconscious. You gain self-control as Tantra fights off sleep, lust and so called love."

Baffled, he went out to drink water with the stars. I'm bored. Without commitment to the other person's character and life, no matter how perfect her body, the act, though sensational, is meat meets meat. I feel used. How sad my first lover shuns emotion.

She commanded, "Shiva, come!" He zombied yoga; zonked meditation; smoked; dulled on mantra; fell asleep eyeballing. WOW! woke to her stroking; bemused his body still wanted the 'Sexual Prayer' - he could think of no other phrase for these strange sessions.

"SssŚssshhhA." Two years of yogic concentration settled on the movement his breath created throughout his body. Sssaaa. His thoughts slowed, he walked beside them. Time fell away, nothing but their union existed. And it hung above the void which pulsed electrical charges which ignited his entire nervous system. Cantering, cantering. Cantering in bliss above the horse of Tantra. They galloped. Her body as his, his as hers. No difference. "SsshIvaaaAaaAaa!" "Taaaraaa!" "Ivaaaa!" They, a simian symphony.

Stirring the dawn forest alive, howler monkeys echoed their calls. They laughed, oh, how they laughed, they hollered, chuckled, giggled and it released Tara from her

166

Tantric trance. They smiled into each other's eyes, kissed, stroked, adoring the moment, loving each other, the fire, the world. A slow, soothing shower in the early light, gods in paradise, affection in every cleansing movement. I love her! Yippie, I LOVE her! I am hers! Before the rekindled fire they slipped in and out of sleep with the monkeys' whooping cries and the birds' reverberating ripples.

Late morning, sunbathing by the lake, Tara silent in a state of detached bliss, he respectfully keeping his mouth shut but wishing to talk about their night. How wonderful, life. Ho! I adore her. But he fled from her stare. Rising, Tara wandered off to smell the flowers as if high on drugs, yet they'd not had a pipe since Tantra.

"Tara," he began.

"Ssh!"

"But Tara, I...."

"Shut it. ALL day OK!"

No interest in who I am, galloping with self-obsession, she's had me. What's the night achieved but loneliness, with me now ever wanting her, ever watching her? He'd understood she was no good for him, so why had he succumbed? Because her fingers lulled his skin by that waterfall, she, the only touch to loiter on his flesh. Mother's fingers flicked over his skin's memory cells. My wish isn't for Tara, but for a lingering touch. Yet knowing this, he was still unable to withdraw, so intense was the infant need she had rekindled in his chest.

A bell announced lunch arriving at their veranda, they ate without speaking. He, pining to communicate, understand her, discover who she was, who she wanted to become. She in her own world. I can stand it no longer, "Tara, I understand Tantra's a discipline designed to take you from the little world of ego-desires, but the intimacy makes me want to relate to you as a person, not be separated in the dislocated manner Tantra demands."

She dropped her spoon, splattering aubergine curry over her white blouse. It took her a while to sink to the mundane.

167

When she did, he strained to catch this forceful woman's weak mew. "Tantra is neither you nor me." Eyes closed, blinking, "Tantra's the electricity generated by the combination of our bodily sensations, desires, emotions and mental constructs transmuted into spiritual power." Eyes wide open, "Ivan, let go of your want of me and my personality. Astride Tantra you will ride higher than you've gone before."

"I want to know you, Tara, not some abstract notion called Tantra."

"That, Ivan-the-arched-nose, *IS* impossible without my wanting it."

He withered.

They were leaning against a rock, warming themselves in the sun after a silent swim in the clear lake. On the distant shore, tiny beneath the Himalayan oaks, the python sunbathed in great curls. Ewan looked at Tara. How I pine for her, but do I want this cool disunity? "I saw love where there was only lust."

She snapped awake. "Tantra's not lust! We seek love to fill the empty hearts Tantra repletes." She kissed the air, slowly, licked her lips, tempting him as she rejected him.

Fluttering under her spell, "Am I not Tantric enough?"

She swung her gaze lazily across the shimmering lake, then spun round. "You're not happy-go-lucky."

"I never was and I've been through a lot." He looked at her through a mist of memories.

"Yea," she conceded, a finger reaching out, stroking the welts slashing his skin. She chuckled, "and my marks!" touching his shoulder.

"In the ashram, turning my anger around, getting from my stern background, I became less reactionary... less spontaneous."

"That's it! You're too serious."

"Why then did you want me when anyone's flesh would have done?"

"You turned me on."

168

"That's lust not Tantra! Take me as my mind, not just my sex appeal."

"Stop making demands."

"I'm merely asking...."

"Hook-nosed Ivan! Unlike your protrusion, this is getting too Flaccid." She tore a flower off a bush, shoved it up his nostril.

Screwing up his nose, he shredded the flower. "Tara, all I...."

"That *IS* all, Ivan!" She stood up, slowly wound her sarong over her impeccable breasts.

Her body hypnotised mine.... "Tara, let's...."

"Furlough-off." She eased her exquisite feet into her sandals and stormed along the shoreline, her hips swinging in time with her hair.

Wow, she's beautiful. Which means nothing. Painted ladies and all that....

The Major called, "Lovely Tara, would you like mid-afternoon tea?"

Tara hesitated, turned, said, "This place has lost its charm!"

Embarrassed by her rudeness, Ewan strolled along the paths with the Major. Stopping upon the pier to watch light shifting over the lake's surface, Ewan asked, "Don't your Gurkhas miss their villages in Nepal?"

"Absolutely!" The Major gaped at him. "Two two-month bouts of R&R, during monsoons and winter, on full pay. Damned good deal! They don't look a gift horse in the mouth. Ha, ha, ha."

"What's it like in their homeland?"

"Hand-to-mouth peasant farming. No work. Poor blighters. Poverty drives them abroad. Army unit in Singapore; Indian Army; over 20,000 men compete annually for 200 British Army posts."

"Can't something be done to help them stay at home?"

"Complex issue. Kind foreigners set up health clinics, less children die, more women survive giving birth. Excellent, don't get me wrong... though caused population explosion -

traditional to keep having lots of children. Land can't cope; denuded, semi-desert. When I was young soldier, wasn't much different to this." The Major waved at the lush hills.

"Hmm," Ewan recalled the bus's frightening descent. Amid verdant slopes rolling to the distance, they'd entered a zone where the odd skeletal tree rose from tired terraces stepping down through too many farmsteads for the soil to bear.

The Major barked, "No use crying over spilt milk, eh? Err, bad phrase, Gurkha lands can't support cows anymore! Ha, ha ha!"

"Are there replanting and revival schemes?"

"Some. Keep trying to get Indian government involved, after all, employ 40,000 Gurkhas; falls on deaf ears."

Lost in thought, Ewan walked around the paths, wondering how he could help the Gurkhas with his stolen money. He wanted to tell Tara of his ideas and found her zipping her bag closed. She snapped, "I'm leaving!"

"Oh. OK. I'll pack quickly," he stroked her shoulder.

Shaking him off, "Leave me alone you phantom of the upper-classes!" She stamped towards the main building.

He caught up with her, "Tara."

"Shove-off!"

"Sorry to lose you, gal." The Major told her a bus to the market town would pass in forty minutes.

"Tara," Ewan touched her hand.

"Fucus," she tore from him.

He had to admire her wit, "Damn you Tara, I'm no seaweed!"

"You cling like it," she snarled and stormed across the lawn.

Watching her tight hips swing from him, her curly hair bounce upon her slender shoulders, Ewan sensed her perfect body with his weeping heart. The Major ordered somebody to follow Tara. Packing his bag, Ewan noted he'd done no sketches by Yat Tal. He was settling the bill when the Major said, "See you do Yoga. Chota Baba's the only sadhu worth meeting."

170

"Oh," Ewan was taken aback by this unexpected side to the Major. "Are you interested in such things?"

"Part of the Indian territory. Mark my word, Chota Baba's the man. Leaves no leaf unturned, ha, ha, ha: he's a herbalist!"

"Thank you Major," Ewan shook the man's hand.

"Glad t'ave met a Merricott." The Major's voice was tighter than usual and he kept a hold of Ewan's hand. Ewan felt memories, conversations and faint histories flowing between them; he would far rather have had the Major as a parent than Father. With a series of blinks, the Major snapped his ankles, let go of Ewan's hand, arms fell tight to his side. "We're fellow Chichis, eh!" A wink. "By the way Merricott, your parents honeymooned here. Looked up old hotel records."

Ewan balked at being reminded of Chichi insults from childhood. I've dark Italian blood? Surely? Who the heck am I: Ivan, Chewing, Charles, Chichi Ewan?

The Major winked, "Don't worry old chap. Got you down as McNaughton. Secrets with me, eh. Ha, ha, ha!"

"Err, t-thank y-you, m-Major."

Sensing Ewan's exposure, the Major clapped Ewan's shoulder. "Whatever reason you've changed names, wasn't for Tara, eh. Mum's the word."

"I-I will tell you one d-day, p-promise Major, I will be b-back." Ewan waved goodbye to the hearty staff. All the way round the lake he didn't rush. As he passed the python rock, Ewan peered at the mass of coils resting in the sunshine over the far side of the lake. Blast Tara and the bus, I'm going to walk. I've dreamt of doing this for far too long. Turning up a path The Major had pointed out, he was quickly lost in the dense shades of green which felt as sombre as his heart.

ß

To escape his torn mind, each day Ewan left his rented
room and walked till evening. He dared not return to the
ashram... or to Devi. He did yoga, he drew, he tried to forget
Tara. The wretched night after his crime, he'd decided to
become Him-Self, but what the heck is oneself? Is Tara
herself? She seemed it. Or was she lost in a sensual cul-de-
sac? Did that matter so long as you didn't harm others? Isn't
yourself an illusive identity flitting between a muddle of
conflicting mindsets? Amongst all that mental noise did *You*
actually exist? Oh Help! Had Father been right in saying:
'Soul-searching is destabilising'?

The more he walked the easier he felt, walking, he saw,
soothed his mind. But in the night, thoughts of Tara disturbed
him and by the morning he'd have to walk himself calm.
Sometimes he followed tracks penetrating the jungle which
reached mysterious settlements where he'd sleep in temples
and eat in chai shops. He'd follow farmers and their mules
along webs of bridle paths and every so often a fallen tree
revealed boundless forested ridges rippling to the distant line
of ice peaks curving with the Earth.

Beside a chai shop, three naked sadhus squatted on their
haunches. Wow, Naga babas! Neolithic beings, the original
Rhastas, unchanged since before Buddha's time. He quickly
sketched their ash-smeared bodies, dreadlocks piled high;
cupped hands held against their mouths, they drank water
poured from the chai wallah's pear-shaped brass container, or
lota. Ash, the substance they washed in twice daily, washed
off by rivulets of escaping water, revealed golden skin. Each
man carried long fire-tongs; a battered lota; a trident - Shiva's
symbol which helped fend off leopards; a thick blanket tied to
a cloth shoulder bag. No more. Their leader carried a second
lota suspended on a string, whose wooden bung leaked wisps
of smoke from glowing cinders.

They fascinated Ewan. Confident yet unassuming, not the
average sadhu parasites I've met who seek to entrap others,

but evasive, silent. They live in the jungle, ascetics who avoid settlements, who refuse to step into any building other than a Shiva temple. Feared for their complete independence, yet revered for it, admired by genuine sadhus like No-Matter, yet mimicked by the hoard of begging pretenders.

Ewan asked if they wanted food. Dark eyes sparkled from ashen faces, bright teeth smiled, they nodded. Before the men ate, they uttered the only words permitted: "Om namah Shivia!"Knowing they would not eat off plates, the chai wallah served a continual flow of folded chapatis wrapped around un-spiced vegetable stew, for their mouths would not be used to anything stronger than salt.

As he watched, Ewan read part of a letter written by Daphne Merricott in April 1822: *"For these bravest of men who survive the savagery of impenetrable jungles, terrifying mountain storms and all manner of austerities, Shiva is no god but a man of flesh who lives high upon the Himalayan slopes with his consort Parvati and in the company of sages, ordinary folk who have gained eternal life because they have attained control over the flesh. True Naga Babas hope their austerities will enable them to one day also live with Shiva, their living guru."*

After the last naga baba finished eating, they exclaimed, "Om namah Shivia!". Washing their hands and faces, they stood in a strange yogic posture for ten minutes, one ankle hitched into the forest of crotch hair, praying to a knee-high shrine beside the path. Ewan peered at a Shiva lingum balanced upon Parvati's yoni, both worn by centuries of devout hands. Sketching a scene Buddha knew, Ewan thought, How timeless, India. When they had finished, their leader, whose eyes were bright, took Ewan's pen and beside the sketch, wrote: *Your life will ease once you find the true path.*

"How, where?"

The man scribbled: *You will see it when you are ready.* He rose, called, "Om namah Shivia!" The wild men picked up their gear and made their way along a narrow path which cut into the web of oaks.

"Where are they going?" Ewan asked the chai wallah.

"After wintering in southern jungles, they are walking to their caves upon Mount Trishul. The youngest used to be a lecturer of biology at some university."

Trishul, Shiva's mountain, one of the highest! My heart goes with them. They've shunned the simplest comforts, the most basic desires. Iconic figures. Dedicated to finding Truth, but are their minds cleared from ego-driven desires? Are they half crazy like Diogenes? Mind you Diog... STOP!

Looking at them, Ewan was all the more convinced their predecessors had influenced Greek thinking. Sat with a glass of tea, he let his mind wander. Was there such a quality as sagacious greatness? Devi emanates something like it. If so, is it attained by only a few? And what is it in any case? Could I gain it? Graft gets you results. Excellence, be it kicking footballs or writing computer programming, is attained by putting in over 10,000 hours of concentrated practice. Less leaves you lower down the skill-ladder. Simple arithmetic. Given the average brain, four hours meditation a day should give an understanding of Truth in seven years. Ewan laughed. That's university twice over, Truth *is* graspable! However, if you clambered up the wrong path your truth wouldn't be Truth. Was Tara right in thinking sensuality was Truth? Devi said.... Help! Stop.

Another early morning, passing another junction, another sadhu. This one whittling a three-forked twig with a pocket knife. Slim, long white beard, silver hair in a bun, a worn but clean robe which might once have been orange. Pulling fingers towards a down-turned palm, he called Ewan over. Ewan wasn't bothered but, noticing the man's open face, he stopped. Eyes, so gentle, unlike the penetrative stare I've come to mistrust.

"Nature's beauty is immensely satisfying," the man waved at a bubbling brook.

"Yes sadhu, but one has to be untroubled to know it," the turmoil inside him seething. "What is your name?"

"They call me Chota."

"Chota Baba?" Hey! The Major's guy.

Chota Baba nodded, stood, undid his knot of hair, letting the locks fall down to his flat belly. He used the twig-comb he'd been fashioning to comb his long white beard and hair. "Forget gurus, do your yoga, it will lead you forwards."

Chota Baba rose and took the track which lead to the market town where Ewan and Tara had met Gurkha porters. Ewan wanted to follow, but didn't wish to intrude. Nor did he wish to repeat accidentally meeting Tara there, as he had three day's previously. Instead, he headed for the lake. He arrived mid afternoon and the Major, fishing from the boat, called cheerfully across the waters. Ewan dropped his clothes and swum to the small wooden craft.

"Good, you're alone."

"Tara's with a man called Nachi." Ewan's memory turned with images of Tara and the guru she had implored him to see when they'd been surprised to come across one another in the market town. Nachi - slightly chiselled face, arched nose, long black hair falling over strong shoulders. Superbly awake even with his eyes closed, a haunting calmness, an impression of quivering strength. He looked as if he was freed from all which is base. Ewan was impressed. However, the way the man stared at Tara, the way she'd fallen in to a spell, the cunning way he'd enticed her to his room, had worried Ewan. Having waited alone for half an hour, he took a shortcut through the undergrowth at the back of Nachi's temple-house. A familiar primitive sound turned his head. Through an open window, Tara moaning uncontrollably. Blast her! Naked beneath Nachi unharnessed.

"Nachi!" The Major chortled, "clever rat. Relies on good looks. Says little - gives impression of wisdom. Ha, ha, ha. Built a posh hotel to house his rich followers, pretending t'was disciple's gift. Knows how to set a trap, give him that."

"Major, this afternoon I met Chota Baba."

"Better not linger, man's older than me! Ha, ha, ha!"

They enjoyed a lunch of char-grilled chicken on the veranda and chatted about the Gurkhas, but the Major was more interested in Ewan's journey through India. Trusting the man, Ewan spoke openly about No-Matter's world, the Zaminder and the torture cell, Indra, the ashram and Devi, Bol, and Tara.

"Forget Tara." At ease, the Major spoke in longer phrases. "Wait for your soul to be ready for Devi, my boy. I met her type many years ago but her family did not want either a Major nor any minor Chichis! Ha, ha, ha! Imagine this lakeside brim full of shrieking kids shouting in a mixture of Hindi and my funny Indian English! Engdi? No, Hinglish sounds better! Ha, ha, ha!"

"After Tara I feel despoiled!"

"Don't. Not easy, eh, first lover dropping you. Laugh it off, ha, ha, ha!"

Wishing he could, Ewan talked of his confusions. Was this search for meaning a waste of the best years of his life? The Major said Ewan should see for himself. "What's a year? If you're not hooked, give the damn thing up! I did. Ha, ha, ha!" The Major became silent. "Ewan, what *are* you hiding."

Apart from the brief interaction with the Major two weeks before, it had been a long time since he'd looked over his shoulder. Concerned, he gawped.

"Don't worry old chap," the old soldier smiled kindly. "Oh, by the way, I've remembered your parents. Fine people. He outstanding, the sort you'd follow into the worst of battles."

"Good in battle, cold at home."

"Err?" The Major looked directly at Ewan. "Trouble at mill, my lad?"

"Um, yes." The man's OK, he listened with sensitivity to my tales, asked penetrative questions, gave inspired answers. I feel secure with him. Ewan let out a gust of air. "Major, in a fit of anger I committed an accidental crime in London and I've been on the run for two years. I have no idea if they are after me or have given up." He regretted having spoken. What if the man took against him?

"Dreadful thing to live with. Don't worry Merricott, secret's safe with me. Tell me all one day. This isn't the time."

176

It was with relief that Ewan bade farewell to the Major, knowing the man was on his side. Convinced he would return, he walked through the jungle, taking the old short cut which had saved three hours walking.

ß

One afternoon Ewan left his lodgings at Uma's homestead to seek out Tara in the market town. Discovering she habitually slept at Nachi's temple, he lingered to enjoy the blazing sunset from the Nachi Hotel's rooftop. With tigers in the jungle, it was too dark to risk walking back to Uma's, so he ate at the 'Andhaka Cafe' along the street which was filled with Westerners raving on about Nachi being 'the real thing'. He took a room and before the frosts melted, woke in sheets wet from a thousand dreams. The last, Tara performing a Tantric dance over his drooling mouth as Uma made puja upon his aching lingum whilst Devi cut out his shrivelled soul. What had gone wrong with him? One minute a callous Californian, the next, wanting Uma.

To get from lust, after a hearty breakfast at the Andhaka, with his mother's weekend bag slung over his shoulder he walked aimlessly along a path which led into the soaring hills, afraid, because of the previous night's dreams, of returning to the delightful Uma's lodgings until her husband Andhaka arrived from working his cafe. However, he'd miscalculated and arrived mid afternoon.

The stupendous Uma, backlit upon the stone terrace. Raising the heavy pole, she thrust forwards, thumping it into the hole in the grinding slab. Her breasts bounced firmly as she crushed barley seed into flour and with each plunge her lithe back flexed beneath her whipping flash of black hair. Uma, open, peaceful, a face to launch a thousand pants! She smiled and he recalled the last time she smiled at him.

I'd scolded Andhaka. He'd slapped her face because she'd not sufficiently shined his work-shoes! Affixing discredit to damage, he'd used his left hand. I ask you - his loo hand!

Ewan could still make out swelling around her right eye as he stepped from the bridle path. Panting, he adjusted his mother's leather travel bag to hide his pounding desire.

"Ewlang!" She laid her pole upon the grey stone slabs.

Almost out of control. Gosh she's sensual, I want her. I can't, she married! Assuming her black eyes penetrated his confusion, he strode across the stone slabs, edged past her home and walked into the terraced orchards. A line of young women of the extended family stepped gingerly past carrying huge piles of fodder balanced on their heads, lean, strong, yet utterly feminine. Ho, I ache inside. Why! I've never looked at women this way. Bloody Tara, she'd stirred my senses. The brush of Gowri's hand ignited him. He stopped. Her head turned and her free smile made him want her. Now! My palms feel her skin, her raw taste lingers on my lips, I sniff tinges of coconut oil and wood smoke buried in her long hair. I feel her powerful body devouring mine. Help! A mini-second fantasy. What power a mind filled with desire.

Disgusted, feeling no better than a dirty dog, he muttered, "Celibacy!" Celibacy's the way to rid myself of this sexual monster. Or is it? Was his body protesting after years of imprisonment within his SOS which had prevented him from relating to women? Celibacy was the monster.

He stamped through apple and pear trees, his emotions rising and falling with muddled urges for Uma, Tara, Gowri. Using extended stones serving as steps, he rose from one walled terrace to another and upon an isolated level of walnut trees he sped past two young women. How sweet their voices, how tender those hands gathering fallen immature nuts to pickle. Ho! Terrified of himself, he leapt up, up, until he was beyond the terracing and in the surrounding oak forest. In a clearing he stopped, boggled to find himself before a lean woman cutting wood. Women were everywhere! Help. He coughed. Surprised, she spun round. Her eyes flickered.

As he gawked at the comely twenty-something, Ewan recalled a rickshaw man in Haridwar telling him some young women, tired of the withered husbands they had been married off to, desired to know bodies their own age. In his seventh month in Haridwar he'd come across two young women who worked fields near the ashram. Like this woman's, their gaze had not left his. Provocative! Three consecutive days he'd passed them and each time they'd laughed and teased him all

179

the more, asking on the last day if he preferred men to women. He avoided them after that.

She must see my swell. I, I…. Oh, she's lovely. A simper of fear or titter of interest? How can I know? The thought woke him. These women, he realised, were attractive because they were fit, they shone with the quiet wisdom of living with belief, with nature and they had the humility which farming without machinery imparts.

I seek Truth, not lust! Gasping, he ran. But even fifteen minutes weren't enough to rid him of the thought of streaking back down to where he could hear her lone chopping. Halting within a thicket, he leaned against a tree, his mind's eye filled with images of her luscious figure. His muscles ached and Gowri was kissing him as Uma's healthy body took his and the wood cutter's confident hands grasped his bottom as they all rolled about with the walnut gatherers. Devi's rebuking eyes popped his daydream and he felt sick.

Yelling blue murder, he thumped his pounding flesh. Aching, he ran higher, uncaring his legs were rasped by the undergrowth. The slope grew steeper until it was virtually vertical. He slipped, fell two, tumbled ten, slithered thirty metres. Exhausted, cut and bruised, he slumped on a rock, crying with the agony of contorted emotion.

He walked off to find a secret spring he'd once noticed and washed his body, scrubbing out his obnoxious desire until it hurt. Having washed them, he hung his fouled clothes to dry over bushes. Naked in the warming sun, he slept beside the stream issuing from the spring, hidden from view by a screen of reeds. He woke to Uma's hair stroking his lingum and gasped, hearing her actual singing wafting through the regular slice of her sickle as she slashed thick reeds. He'd drawn her sewing together such 'mattress' reeds laid out to dry on her stone-slab patio. Embarrassed, Ewan dressed as quietly as he could. He walked forwards, "Uma," he began, startling her. He panted, rising. Gosh, she's close enough to lick. Ho, her golden skin. Oh, to….

"Ewlang!"

He stuttered, trying to seek a way from his walloping growth. Anything. Any topic. Help. "I'm, I'm," and it came to him. "I'm looking for a man called Chota."

She lit up, "Chota Baba! I will ask if people have heard where he is."

Uma doesn't stop all day! But her pace was casually relaxed and she sang continually to Shiva. All afternoon she'd been grinding barley and wheat, prepared an evening meal for her family, arranged the dried washing, now she was cutting these mattress reeds. She'd soon return home, pluck a leaf off her holy tulsi bush for her prayers to Shiva, wash her cow's forehead with Parvati's yoni water, serve her men food, eat only what they left her and Gowri, help her daughter wash the dishes. Gowri, Uma and the other women worked the land, fed the cows, tended to the barley, wheat, vegetables, pulses, herbs, nuts and fruits, thus keeping them virtually self sufficient; together they cultivated specific reeds for mats, bedding and thatching; three cows provided both milk, yoghurt and the dung used for floor-cement and cooking-fuel. He knew - he'd drawn busy women many times. They even kept a few sheep for wool.

Andhaka, who managed his popular cafe-restaurant, did little at home. For some weeks after early summer shearing Andhaka and the other men got busy hand-spinning, their bobbins shooting from rapidly moving fingers, their fluffy wool growing into yarn from a woolly pile which Biju the son had combed the previous evening after school. Ewan had drawn this and he drew men knitting thick winter jumpers. In some houses, he'd drawn women weaving wool into tweed upon wood-framed looms. Returning home from work each evening, Anddhaka did thirty minutes accounting; he was important, he bought in money; women provided him sustenance.

Ho, Uma amuses him with sex, how lucky he is, ho Uma. On the narrow suspended wooden balcony fronting the stone house, Gowri squeezed past, her bottom smearing him awake. She hesitated, smiled. Gulping, he looked without looking, panting, trying to control himself, angry he'd again risen for her.

As the last sun ray lifted from the farm, flamed the sky, ignited the icy line of the world's tallest mountains, Uma's silver bell rang. He peered through the tiny window, she squatted before her kitchen shrine, her winsome chant to Shiva lilting. Gowri joined her and their enchanted voices, like those of other women's in the hamlet, in all Hindu homes, villages and towns across India's vastness, chimed and flew with the singing birds. Twice a day for thousands of years those soft notes had held up the Indian sky.

Uma and Gowri sang to Shiva who perched upon those gleaming glaciers suspended in the purple evening light. Uma's certainty is beyond me. Oooh, to lick her compact.... No! I flip from the profound to the profane, sex is driving me mad. He knew his emotions were not stable enough for him to be as wild as carefree Tara, sexual emotion would destroy him, he had no option but to contain it. He told 'it' it was now Shiva's lingum, no longer his and he shuddered, comprehending the internal torture which lay ahead. Hey, Gowri worships Shiva, ha, to have her wor.... NO! Tara and her Tantric theatrics have battered the fortress of spiritual security Devi and the ashram helped construct. The walls of Truth/Nirvana/Peace or whatever you called it, feel like Fool's Gold under sensuality's bright lights. I'm walking through the valley of the shadow of lust. Oh! for Uma's conviction. Ha! for Gowri's flesh.... NO, No, no. A month ago he'd not even kissed one of these wonderful beings and now his once clean thoughts were soiled... Or rightfully stirred? I just don't know! The answer's brutal: celibacy. Help, oh help, I ought to talk to Devi.

After breakfast he ran down, down, to the market town. In 'The Andhaka', he made a call to Devi, using the 'public' phone Andhaka was making good money from. He hesitated before dialling her home number, wondering what to say. He'd been disloyal to her and to all they once shared. Gathering his strength, he turned the old fashioned dial which clumsily spun back to zero after each number. Ewan waited for the crackly line to chug out its double-pulse, silence, double-pulse, silence. When would someone pick up? He tried another number. A man in an ill-fitting suit made of glistening brown nylon came over and leaned on Ewan's shoulder, nagging him to hurry. Eighteen rings later he was going to hang up when it connected. Recognising Devi's voice, his felt faint. "Namaste Devi, how's the mountain retreat?"

"Ewan!" Devi shrill with excitement. "We thought we'd lost you to the Bol business."

He sighed, "No." The suited man leaned against Ewan, heavily breathing garlic and curry. Annoyed, Ewan turned his back and shoved the man, "Get off! Not you, Devi." His annoyance revived him. "I've met two rubbish gurus."

"Told you so," Devi laughed. Her sanity so refreshing, she was good for him. "Ewan, I'm glad you rang. Julian has arrived at the ashram. Swami Prem rang this morning, I will drive down tomorrow."

"Me too."

"Ewan it is good to hear your voice."

The business man coughed too loudly, too closely. Ewan kicked the man's foot. The fellow moved away. "Yes," voice weak, "it's the same for me."

"Well...." Her voice hung in the air, fragile. "We'll catch up soon?"

Hot flush. Must rush to Haridwar. "Devi, I think I've met somebody special."

"Your Tantric temptress!" A crack in her gaiety.

"A sadhu."

"Remember...." Her voice went soft, he could hear she was struggling with herself, "your first duty is to yourself. Discriminate."

"Thanks Devi. Miss you too." A tear wet his cheek. The business man slapped his fat fingers on the terminal, closing contact before Ewan could say farewell.

"Damn you sir!" Ewan pushed and the man fell to the greasy floor. Andhaka, arriving from his homestead, laughed. Ewan sighed, "India, oh India!"   ß

"I recognise that self assured walk!" a high-pitched voice speeding over a crop of yellow mustard.

"Julian!" Ha, my mate, my old, old friend! Despite the heat, Ewan leapt off the rickshaw, paid the driver, ran along the ashram's dusty drive. Beneath the flowery arch, a bright hippie in floral prints. "You've changed guise!"

"Behold, Goa Gucci!" Julian pirouetted down the two broad steps, emphatically tossing his long golden locks over one shoulder.

"You gay fool," Ewan laughed as they danced together in a drunken hug. Here's the tonic for Tara's stirring force. "I thought you'd be draped in the saris of your cult."

"Imagine - a canary yellow sari! Sadly darling, not allowed 'til I'm initiated."

"You aren't done?"

"Guru ordered a walkabout, gain a deeper understanding of India, only then will I realise the enormity of what I'm about to undertake. Darling, Indian clothes suit you better than a pin-stripped suit."

Ewan laughed at the memory of his London self. "You're more camp than ever."

"And now I've fallen for another queen. Oh, it's so confusing sweety, I'm not certain if I'm queenie-ho or macho-dho! By the way, Devi's lovely. Gentle sophistication hiding a knockout fire-bolt."

Ewan awkwardly changed the subject, "Have you any cash left?"

"Gave most of it to that centre for prostitutes. Spent my last penny on a hotel room in Hanuman Jula."

Ewan laughed, "Hippie-ville!"

"Whoo! Full of macho Israeli dropouts drowning the guilt of unnecessary military violence in clouds of hashish."

"To the bank this afternoon."

"I can't keep taking your money."

"I'm only creaming off a bit of interest from my farm's invested profits. As for the illegal stuff, that's growing far too quickly."

"Poor little richman," Julian kissed Ewan's cheek, "however, I don't envy you your fugitive problem."

"Hardly think about it. This place has emptied me of my past."

Dismissing the ashram with a wave, Julian said, "Let's find Devi and then a fine chai wallahs where we'll dunk stale buns in boiling hot cardamon tea, put the World straight and discover who've we each become." Entering the plaza, they walked towards the kitchens, waving at greeting nuns and monks busy with their chores. "You've quite a fan club, Charles."

"Earwing!" The familiar voice of Swami Prem echoed across the cloistered plaza. "Julian, he's an acting type, I think?"

"Swami, ha, to see normal seekers after the buffoons I've met!"

"We warned you."

"Ewan!"

My heart's racing, throat's catching. "Devi!" How he wanted to shrink from her as she strode across the stone paving. I'm ashamed, bloody Tara. They stood apart gazing at each other, a timeless moment of catching up.

"I see you three have no need of me," the Swami chuckled. "Earwing, take one of the rickshaws and drive your friends to town."

Ewan was speeding down his imaginary Great Trunk Road, racing another loaded rickshaw whose driver had thrown out a challenge and they were being cheered along by two empty rickshaws. They wove in and out of bullock carts, missing villagers carrying goods on their heads, dodging marauding trucks which disrespected everything smaller. Julian and Devi giggled like school girls, screaming encouragement, shouting mock abuse at their rival and as they passed familiar haunts, chai wallhas yelled encouragement to the sweating cyclists. Utter madness at high

185

noon on the cusp of the great Indian summer and the applause was greater when they slid to a halt at the usual finishing line by Shiva's gaudy statue upon a roundabout. The two perspiring men slapped each other whilst their laughing passengers stepped giddy on to the welcome ground.

Bliss - cool marble slabs! Collecting samosas and clay mugs of chai, they sat, thrilled by the contrast between the freezing Ganga tingling their feet and the sun baking their backs. Silently, they absorbed the magic of the ancient spot. With Julian here, everything's more exciting. And Devi? Devi turned to him, her face lively. A pang in my chest! She shines my heart awake. She transmutes raw emotion into sparkling dew, quite unlike Tara's predatory animalism. Tara! I took raw experience for fondness, emotional excitement for relationship - because my life lacked them. He shook his head. Devi shot him a quizzical glance, he melted, confused, but beguiled. So, is this friendship or more? Damn it, I've no idea.

Julian's voice broke the spell, "You darlings ought to get hitched." Ewan and Devi stared at each other, quickly turning from what they saw in the other's eyes. Although aware of their muddled reactions, Julian continued, "You belong to one another."

A long hush, three friends watching the reflections of trees, temples, hills and people break up, merge and burst into colourful ringlets. The ever-changing ovals of light flex like our individual emotions. Ewan let the river launder his emotions, enabling his mind to clarify. Julian lay back and fell asleep. After some minutes Ewan broke the stillness, "Devi," he let a finger secretly rush over her hand. It electrified him. Here's proof, a fingertip more sensational than sex because behind it lies…? Love?

With an uncontrolled pant, she shook herself from her private musing, gasped, "Ewan?"

"Devi," he dithered, his resolve baffled by her intense gaze. Those black eyes deep, absorbing. Did she feel the same? But what did he feel? Pain at deceiving her, but no, it hadn't been deceit, Devi hadn't been around for months

186

before he'd left her. A sharp breath rushed through his chest, "Each of us is a secret being, unknowable to any others."

"Umm, yes, but we can explore one another by sharing our thoughts and emotions."

"I've never met anyone like you...."

She smiled awkwardly, withdrawing her hand, "What of your quest?"

"Exactly." He shook his head in disbelief. She was always a one step ahead.

They continued to watch the Ganga play with the shapes and colours. I love this country. England's merely where my infant body dropped, Bharat's where I come alive.

Julian woke, they rose. Without wheels because a monk in town had wanted the rickshaw, as if in a collective dream they wandered along the Ganga path, heading for the ashram, stopping to admire the herons, dippers, a cheeky Himalayan Robin, with no need for words. Ewan noticed Julian walked slowly and had to stop more than you'd expect, but the sun was intense. When they grew level with the ashram's fields, they cooled their boiling bodies with a cold dip.

Ewan was sitting between Devi and his snoring pal on her rooftop terrace, gazing at a moon split clean in half. I'm a little worried Julian is dropping off to sleep all the time, but maybe his walkabout worn him out. It gave Devi and he time to talk. She told him her small estate charity was making headway in the Zaminder's lands, thanks to Sati's work with potatoes. Devi was weary of travelling back and forth all over Europe promoting the charity's business and wanted to settle to projects on their estate, hence was grooming Sati to take over much of her work abroad.

He shivered. Admitted he was muddled about relationships, were they friends, was there more? Guarded, she vaguely hinted at confusion; when they had parted abruptly some weeks previously, cold as she'd been, it'd thrown her. "Ewan, more than friendship seems impossible." She laughed when he said how terrified he'd been of meeting

187

her again; she smiled when he said her positivity inspired him to continue his search. She worried desire for the company of another would pollute his quest. "But, Devi, eventually I'd like to settle in to a lifelong relationship." Devi felt the same, "But with a high profile it won't be easy to find somebody suitable I like. It's OK for Indian men to marry whom they wish, not us women."

"Surely as your surrogate father, Indra's more understanding than most?"

"Since dad's death five years ago, Indra becomes ever more conservative with each passing year. He has his eye on appropriates... but they're all so stuffy!"

Ewan soaked up her frustration. Everyone's muddled about love, lust, oh and celibacy..."Devi, I wonder if celibates are fanatics incapable of intimacy who fear their own natural needs?"

"Go, explore celibacy, aware of your doubts, as you did with tacky Tantra."

Damn. Must come clean, this *is* hard. Voice quavering, "Devi, um," Help! Her eyes bore into me. "Tantra was a one-night disaster. I felt used. It stirred me up. Celibacy might help settle me."

"Hump. Watch, see if that's right for you."

Julian woke and sat up. Ewan began, "Julian."

"Charles darling," Julian mocked.

"Devi understands I need time...."

Devi poked a finger at his nose, "Presume to know what I'm thinking!"

"Ow!" He rubbed his nostril.

"He does sweetie! You two are deeply linked," Julian chuckled.

She took a deep breath, "Ewan must go away tomorrow." How enchanting her animated face in the moonlight.

"So soon?" Julian looked shocked.

Ewan laid his arm around his pal. "To catch a wandering sadhu before I lose him."

"Means we've lost you," Julian teased.

"Exactly," Devi turned away.

"Only for a while…." Oh blast! I'm caught between three strong magnets. Life's so unjust!

The morning meditation bell woke them. They had fallen asleep on the communal roof terrace. Ewan hugged Julian farewell, "Julian, leave Devi your wedding date and I'll be there."

"Have fun with your Yogi Bear," Julian smiled and almost fell asleep on the spot.

Ewan wondered if his pal was ill, but the sadness of leaving them both and the excitement of seeking Chota Baba drew his attention away. Waving at nuns and monks in the dim light, Devi and he walked to the main road. Waiting for a bus, they sat in one of the thatched restaurants serving the lorries ploughing back and forth.

"Ewan," she sighed into her steaming tea, "never assume anyone is wiser than you, but avoid arrogance by learning from what everyone has to show you."

"Wow, that's profound."

"Follow your heart, listen to what it urges, but be careful."

"What does follow your heart mean?"

"You'll have urges to do this or that, like exploring Tantra with Tara. Acknowledge them and if they persist, perhaps it's your subconscious asking you to listen. Listen, don't always act, you saw where that can lead."

"Sharing Tantra with Tara showed me what I didn't need."

"Chasing experience is the Western way. Only fools jump off a cliff to discover what it's like."

"Ouch. Perhaps that's why our world is being screwed up - we neo-westerners, for Indians and even the Chinese, have become like us, are lemmings chasing pleasure and economic growth over an environmental cliff."

"Ewan, you have to discover what's happening deep inside you. You knew you weren't suited to Tara, but chased desire, pretending it was to explore Tantra. Retain your integrity by discriminating."

"Maybe the celibacy thing was stirring up my natural urges."

"There's a better side to us than the beast."

"What you call beast is our sensual and emotional self. We're not simply rational, we ought to explore and understand all aspects of ourselves. That's what Tantra taught me."

"How can a person, at the moment they are filled with anger, understand the subtlety of communication, or somebody intoxicated with lust know the tenderness of affection? Such things are grasped when we are calm."

"Before I took bhang I was calm, too calm for my own good - I was SOS, collected, disciplined! I had to explore the opposite."

She looked up quickly. "Here's your ride."

He stood, waved the bus down. Looked at her, "Oh Devi …."

"Ewan."

"You know how I feel …."

"Know what you are before you decided how to live your life. As for me, my future might not be my own."

"We'll meet again."

"I know," she smiled.

"Devi, despite everything I've done, I…."

"Yes! Go!" She pushed him towards the halting vehicle.'

ß

The bell tinkled, ending Uma and Gowri's evening Arti.

Ha, Bharat! No other country would've taken me on this strange inner journey. Until now his passage through India had been part escape, part accident. Devi's enthralling personality had held him at the ashram, where the calm stability rather than the mystery had changed him. Tara's hedonistic stance had revived his scepticism of the abstract. Now, on his own, he wasn't sure what he wanted. But Uma, upright, a pure beacon, was hard to ignore. Her spiritual conviction was underwritten by the notion of Truth. She shines with it, ergo, must it exist? But Hitler's inner-circle of women shone, convinced he was their saviour. Conviction can be a flaw, yet what else is there? A life without it could be flaccid.

Uma burst onto the suspended balcony, "They say Chota Baba is near by."

"Uma, I've met too many false sadhus."

"He is too wise to fall into the guru trap."

Her words made Ewan look at her. Uma hid behind the archetypical veil of the Indian wife: gentle, supportive, but she was more. The day's final dimness flickered over Trishul's icy ridge as she told him a little of Chota Baba's life style and where to find him, she prompted him to seek out the old man. "But be warned, not wanting followers, he turns people away."

Biju, the beloved male child who rarely did chores, having completed his homework, was amusing himself upon the stone patio with his puppy. In the fading twilight, a distant torch flashing about, nervous, Andhaka's voice ringing along the bridle-path, dangerously late, demanding Shiva protect him from tigers and leopards patrolling the surrounding jungle. Picking up a powerful torch, Biju, the puppy plunging at his heels, leapt down the broad steps, dashed along the bridle path to greet his father.

Uma rushed inside. Ewan knew all else must wait. At her wedding to Andhaka, a successful older man her parents had chosen and whom she'd not seen until, tied with seven strands of sacred thread, she'd walked seven times around Agni's fire with him, swearing dedication. The ceremony made Andhaka more important than Shiva; her religion, written by men, cast her role until his death.

Ewan balked, but knew most Hindu arranged-marriages evolved into dedicated partnerships. Indra loved his wife as an equal and wanted his sister to enjoy the same, which was why Devi's marriage kept being delayed.

Fussing over Biju, Andhaka climbed the external stone stairs, turned along the floating wooden balcony. Having undone Andhaka's laces and replaced his soiled shoes with slippers, Uma followed him inside the large upstairs living space. Nodding unspoken commands to Gowri in the kitchen-corner, she poured a glass of water from the urn she had not long filled at the cool spring behind the house, handed it to Andhaka. He drank deeply. Ewan growled.

As the three males ate supper upon a thick carpet spread before the living-zone fireplace, Ewan sent praising the women who were constantly rolling out chapatis in the kitchen-area. Desire swelled each time Uma smiled back; how he hated this mindless male-urge; he had to leave before his body, for it was not his mind, tried anything stupid.

"Chota Baba is close," the woman said. Ewan had waited for her to complete her evening Arti at a tiny wayside temple. She pointed towards Trishul's imposing bulk. Picking out the wave of ice, Ewan wondered how many days it would take to walk through these isolated valleys and ridges where people were startled to see a stranger. For days he'd been striding up huge slopes and down the other side to toy villages, he slept in tiny temples, more shelters for idols than buildings, and woke each dawn to walk along more remote valleys.

He sometimes drew houses clumped side by side behind slab terraces, each backing on to orchards and stepped fields; a dozen such clusters made for attractive villages. Ewan was amazed each knot of houses harboured twenty to seventy relatives living cheek by jowl in three to eight clones of the original house. Uma's four glued-together homes was lightly inhabited in comparison. She had explained males stayed at home so generations of men kept shuffling along the rows of homes when space was vacated by deceased male elders.

Brides were obliged to leave their families, which irked Ewan - women were seen as a resource. Take Gowri. She stayed home helping until one day she'd marry and join a sisterhood of young brides in another valley. Ewan loved these jolly gangs full of chatter, laughter and song who worked endlessly, but noticed most boys like Biju did less. Men had their roles, mainly tilling the soil, repairing the home, and market related activities, but they had far more free time, waking later, they inhabited the chai shops, they dined in peace, they were in bed earlier.

Within a year of marriage most girls had babies, much longer and they were suspected of harbouring evil spirits which prevented conception. Attaining puberty, Uma had been married aged thirteen when her mother was twenty-nine, her grandmother forty-four, her great granny fifty-eight and when her great, great grandmother was seventy-three. Unusually, she even had a g-g-g-grandmother aged ninety. Bearing children hardly diminished their duties. Over the years these women made their way up the female hierarchy, assuming easier tasks until too old to stir the pots. When their husbands died, some ungrateful sons turfed them out to fend for themselves as beggars, but generally the elderly were respected for their life-gained wisdom. As at Uma's, there was usually a great, or even greater grandparent or two reclining in a shady corner of each terrace.

Ewan opened his plastic folder: *"Our English nuclear family feels socially impoverished in comparison. It is a diabolical, isolated existence. In an Indian home everyone has their role to play. This interdependency makes it easier to build up relationships of trust which have not been possible in my own minute family."* His mother's surprising words made

194

him wish he'd not been a single child, a thorn between two dreadfully formal parents; if only he'd grown up in India.

Ewan's feet were sore when he arrived in a village upon the ridge far above Yat Tal, because he'd gone in the wrong direction. A wandering trader camped by the temple told him, "Chota Baba went north, over those ridges." Looking at the folds of land he would have to hunt through, Ewan sighed and joined the trader in gathering pine needles for an insulating mattress. He slung a tarpaulin between trees and wrapped in his sleeping bag, slept soundly.

Wearing one of the khaki robes Uma had made him, Ewan was travelling light, although his leather bag was bulky, sometimes awkwardly bumping into objects. Senseless at it was, he couldn't let go of his only memory of Mother. It contained two spare robes, underpants, boxer-shorts for washing in, two pairs of winter socks, jumper, feather gilet, small towel, torch, pocket-knife, lighter, four sketch books, pens, pencils and watercolour crayons, his plastic letters folder and the rosewood box, false passport, travellers' cheques and a wad of money. Tied to its bulging exterior, a waterproof army tarpaulin wrapped around a woollen shawl and feather sleeping bag, strapped to it, boots for rough terrain.

It took five days to get to the village where Chota Baba was said to be, but he wasn't complaining, walking was unwinding him. Walking over the final hillock in an ever unfolding ridge, he witnessed the sun cast its last light over a row of old stone houses. Somebody in an orchard said, "Chota Baba headed east." The sadhu, Ewan was told, had no routine other than walking in random directions between villages. He could be anywhere. A small chai shop, a mere encampment with an oven and a bench hiding within a cleft beside a footbridge crossing a mountain torrent. All Ewan had eaten was the bundle of chapatis and vegetables a villager had pressed into his hands that noon. The chai wallah quickly reheated mild curry and chapatis, Ewan bought boiled sweets for two shy children by the owner's old farmhouse ten paces away on higher ground.

He slept beside the temple and after a hearty breakfast, with a bundle of stuffed chapattis, walked east. All day his path cut through dark jungle. The isolation was absolute. Worried tigers were hiding in the undergrowth he employed tricks his relatives had used, singing in two voices, one high the other low as if he had company, and he clicked a pebble loudly on a grapefruit sized lota he'd bought at the chai wallah's. He was occasionally amused by intelligent amber eyes peering from black faces framed by spikes of creamy hair - langur monkeys. Mothers cradled babies with cheeky faces; old males watched with the apparent wisdom of sages, scratching their belly buttons with elegant black fingers.

A pool of sunlight pierced the imposing greenness, a single stone house and barn, sombre jewels in dense jungle. Two mastiffs ran forward, deep woofing alerted the family hunched over potato plants. The dogs circled him. Dead still, Ewan called out, "Namaste! Have you seen Chota Baba?"

Grasping the dogs almost as tall as her, a tiny woman said, "Namaste! He passed that way." With her chin she pointed the way Ewan was heading.

Another day up and down, but it wasn't boring, quite the contrary, it gave him a sense of himself, something primitive, something strong, something to get to know. Late afternoon the impenetrable jungle parted, revealing a long village nestling beneath farmed terraces rising from a roaring river. Chota Baba, he was told, had turned south-east. How the heck will I catch up! Altering direction, he increased his pace. A subtle yet strong conviction was growing with all this walking. It was as if the walking itself was sacred, as if humans were born to walk. In the early evening the canopy gave way, revealing a village crouching upon a terraced hogback with views of Trishul's gleaming bulk. The first person told him Chota Baba was indeed there, but busy.

"Whee!" Ewan hopped over a low wall. British planted golden Scots pines surrounded a white domed temple no higher than his shoulders, its open side was adorned with flowers presented to an ancient Shiva lingum covered in ochre paint daubed with red marks and erect within Parvati's crude, welcoming yoni. After performing his yoga routine, he sketched individual villagers who arrived from time to time to clang bells strung between two pines: they each bent down, placed a flower, muttered a prayer, left.

Sunset. Ewan curled upon a pile of pine needles beneath his canopy. There was a warm breeze, life was perfect, he felt happy to be near Chota Baba and alone with the starry sky. Even the thought of tigers and leopards didn't bother him. I'm starting my quest for 'Truth'

ß

"Namaste Satya." A soft chuckle.

Ewan's brain popped from beneath his sleeping bag, "Namaste. Chota Baba! Satya?"

"Satya equals Truth - your nickname in the market town because you say what you think."

Oh yes, I revealed Nachi's obsession with Tara. "Hmm, Satya sounds lovely."

Chota Baba smiled, "Easier for the Indian tongue than Uerm." The old man chanted, "Satya, jaia Satya, aum."

Ewan joined in and giggling, arms hung out as wings of Japanese dancing storks, fingers splayed, they stepped a slow, idiotic prance. It was a mad way to start a friendship and they made passing villagers stop and gawp. Anywhere else but India we'd be locked away! Here it's taken as divine craziness. How he had changed these past two years, stiff old Charles Merricott was fading.

The old man pointed up the hillside to a hollow, hardly visible in the half light. "Satya, go wash before they ban us! When presentable, join me in my hut."

Careful not to pollute the water, Ewan, oops, Satya, nice name, washed then filled his lota from a spout issuing from a granite cow's mouth - the sign it was drinkable. After dressing, he followed the spring's enclosed stone flow through orchards and into a compact terraced village with carved balconies and doors.

The birds were stirring as he namasted women and men whose instant smiles flashed his heart; he ignored those who scuttled off, heads down with lotas in their right hands. Satya recalled reading a translation of the Athara Veda, a text outlining the ritual cleaning before and after evacuation. For the ancient writers, running water was sacred, hence it astounded Satya Himalayan settlements used their once clear streams as an easy loo. Yuk! Seventy centuries ago their ancestors built stone drains. Why beautiful paved bridle paths to the edges of their terrain, but no toilets or septic tanks? My

198

ancestors imported reed-bed technology from China in the early 1700s. Stop! Ho, I'm obsessed by sewage!

Satya, was chilled by the time he found Chota Baba's shed. Following jungle-sadhu tradition, the man once slept wild, a cave here or a temple there, but as he grew older most settlements provided a small cowsheds transformed into cosy dwellings. Removing his sandals, he tapped on the door, "Jaia Shiva!"

"Jai ho!" Chota Baba was sat cross-legged, stirring a pan balanced between stones upon a welcoming fire. The old man poured warm milk into a tin mug, stirred in some local honey, they ate chapatis stuffed with mild vegetable curry and the seductively warm tastes comforted Satya after his frosty night. Beneath the crackling wood, silence. Acutely aware of every sense, facing a grey beard sparkling with flashes of orange, Satya wondered if he'd been hypnotised. He'd felt this expansiveness when first registering young Nachi's physical perfection. Hmmm, deep within our brains lurks the desire for the untainted leader: the Adonis, powerful as Hercules, wise as Socrates with the compassion of Pericles; someone who will save us from rampaging savages and dangerous beasts. The archetypal man, the Thor, the Shiva. It's why we are continually fooled by egotistical politicians. Satya recoiled. He wanted something deeper. "Chota Baba, those tales of sages, do they exist?"

"So they say," the old man tittered. "But our impression of others never contains the whole picture; it is tainted by our conditioning and muddled logic."

After a while Satya asked, "Is there an objective something, a Truth which stands apart from the material world?"

"Many have thought so; but they may have been wrong."

That's confusing. "Can another person lead us to Truth, if it exists?"

Chota Baba played with his long beard, "We are each on our own."

"Can another hint at techniques?"

"Even this can be fraught with danger." The baba threw a feather in the air, watched it curl slowly to the floor. "We are kept buoyant by our personality, and are pulled and buffeted by life's breezes. Watch, see your old traces at play, try to discover what feels true to you, but beware of self delusion."

"I often feel lost."

"In a sense, we all are. We invent lifestyles to hide it." Ending the conversation, the man turned and started his routine tasks.

Satya realised he had to sit and wait, this was no Western lecturer but an Eastern yogi. He watched the old man lay a sarong on the floor and tip onto it herbs from cloth parcels. Once this was done, Chota Baba closed his eyes. Ewan did the same.

All day the herbalist sat cross legged, welcoming villagers into the hut. Farming folk wearing clean but threadbare or repaired clothes, entered without touching the old man's feet; one or two newcomers who tried this traditional flattery were gently pushed away by Chota Baba. There was none of the adulation Satya had experienced at other haunts. People brought in small parcels of specially prepared food for the sadhu and Satya was in seventh heaven - much to people's amusement, he'd smack his lips dramatically, finishing what the yogi tasted out of politeness.

Before giving advice, Chota would ask about the individual's life and, fiddling with his long white beard, listened with complete attention. He frequently recalled things they had told him years before. Some saw this as evidence of greatness. Mmm, when your life is simple without the bombardment of radio, TV, books or newspapers, and you visit the same places regularly, you remember it all. I recall small things from a far more complex past-life.

Sketching and making notes all the while, Satya watched Chota Baba sprinkle specific herbs into his patients' right palms. The villagers would shake the dried herbs into a fold in their skirt or shirt and knot it securely for the journey home. Satya smiled, perfectly sustainable, no bags nor waste. Sometimes the sadhu gave the villagers dietary advice, telling individuals to drink milk or not, to avoid spicy dishes or to add a little chilli to their food. There was no formulaic rigidity, each case and situation called for fresh advice. Chota Baba told a keen young man to take yogurt with each meal, another not to; a weak woman was ordered to eat cooked nettles for the iron content; a frail old man was gently chided for being lazy and told to walk around his village each morning to get his blood moving; another was told to do less. A twenty-year old depressed woman with a husband nearing fifty was told a younger man could have demanded more than she might have wished to give.

Hmm, this guy's simple, straightforward, he emanates a subtle charisma, but am I projecting?

"Sit quietly after Arti," the sadhu told a woman with postnatal depression. Careful questioning revealed she had wished to further her education, but was forced into early marriage. "What you tell yourself is what you eventually believe. Know you are doing the most important job in the world. Make books on childcare your further education, giving your child security and moral rigour is your degree. A person growing up with love is at ease with life, imagine how much less consumptive and aggressive it would be if we were all like that!" He wagged his finger comically at those present. The villagers smiled, enjoying this sagacious grandfather who had visited their remote valley for decades.

It pleases me the man isn't aloof, nor does he philosophise much. Unlike Swami Prem who upheld a system and ensured the ashram followed it, Chota Baba gently prodded people to make the most of the lives they had already carved out. "How refreshing," Satya mumbled.

"Satya, only fools like me talk to themselves," Chota Baba chuckled. The villagers laughed.

As the sun set Chota Baba went to the remote spring and washed himself. Once the old man had moved away, Satya washed. Later, a woman left food at the hut: a simple vegetable curry, dal, rice, yoghurt and a milky cardamon and honey drink to finish. Having eaten, Chota Baba sat quietly before his fire and after a while they began to talk of the difficult lives of mountain villagers.

"Why have you chosen such a solitary life?"

Chota Baba stirred the fire, "I will probably bore you with the tale one day. Seriously, Indians turn anybody into a guru. This way nobody owns me. Wherever I go I make my home with these." He waved his hand at his herbs, lota, fire-tongs and bedding roll which contained a second robe and a towel. A few villagers entered the hut.

"It is time to praise Shiva," the sadhu picked up his broad fire-tongs and clacked them like castanets as he chanted. There in the fire light, for over an hour they sang with joy and softness. The more time he spent in these mountains, the more Satya realised people sincerely felt Shiva was peering down at them from his icy peak Trishul. OK, so that's why Chota Baba sings to Shiva.

"Talking to yourself again, Satya! Sleep inside tonight, there's leopard and tiger about." It was warm and they slept under shawls beside the low fire. At dawn they bathed, enjoyed a cup of tea with stuffed parathas and still the sky was half-dark. Chota Baba carefully lifted a few glowing embers and placed them in his lota which he sealed with a wooden bung containing air holes; around the lota's overturned lip a carrying string was secured.

"Why do that?" Satya asked.

"It gives me fire tonight and is also in homage to Agni, the fire god."

"Why not use matches?"

"Ha, ha, ha," Chota Baba laughed, "matches cost money, which I don't touch and they get damp. I vowed to keep a glowing ember given to me by my teacher. His fire came from his teacher and this link has passed down a long line for hundreds, even thousands of years, perhaps back to the original yogi."

"Wow!" Satya found it amazing the chain had stayed alight throughout the troubled British Raj, was aflame during the violent yet brilliant Mughal period, sparkled throughout India's two thousand year Aryan era and gave light when the

202

Buddha lived. Yet its origin could have been before Aryans pushed the Indus valley Dravidians south, to a period before world's first villages… at the birth of shamanistic Hinduism somewhere in central Asia. Gosh! I feel incredibly small.

The yogi packed up his things and said, "With nobody left to attend to, it's onto another settlement. Let's go." In the low light, the two men were watched by a silent group of villagers as they turned towards the forested track.

Treading the fine frost, Satya smiled. At last I'm walking the walk! When reading those mysterious family letters as a child, he'd dreamed of becoming a yogi; not a real yogi, mind, from his family's writings yogis emerged as enigmatic figures shining across the darkness, adventurers who braved the Himalayan weather to find the Golden Fleece: Himalayan Spidermen. Father had mocked him, not wanting him to be interested in anything esoteric: "Judo is as profound as any religion!" But Charles/Ewan/Satya found Judo too cold, in Aikido there was mystery. Soon more tangible problems occupied his mind. "Chota Baba, what if a big cat confronts us?"

"Then we'll be tested!"

Satya wished he was not walking the walk at dawn!

"Step from worry and gain strength of mind."

Tigers loomed in dark patches, leopards' tails curled off thick branches, bears roamed the somber slopes, pythons coiled in the dense undergrowth, King Cobras six metres long protected leaf-pile nests, but Chota Baba continued as if none of these real Himalayan dangers lurked near by. Knowing well they did, Satya was relieved when the sun rose. Overjoyed, he admired the pink Himalayas sailing over the waves of emerald jungle.

They moved in silence. From time to time the yogi would stop, lift his wooden bung and revive Agni with a blow. They stepped over swift streams with plunging waterfalls; they lingered by tranquil pools shimmering with clouds of brilliant blue butterflies as big as out-spanned hands, and echoing bird song tickled Satya's ears and his heart burst. Astonished at the

203

speed the old man moved up and down the steep inclines, Satya asked, "How old are you Chota Baba?"

"I've no idea, I am still walking, that's the point!" He chuckled.

"Is it Yoga which gives you such strength?"

"Life's a lottery. Some, like you and me have good bodies, others suffer with bad ones from birth, disease strike the fittest without warning. Yoga helps you make the most of what you've got." The old man stepped uphill as if his life depended on it.

Chasing the man, Satya asked, "What is religion saying, Baba?"

Chota Baba giggled, "Impossibly trying to explain the inexplicable. Oh Satya, how you want to define and refine!"

"Without defining and refining, patterns aren't seen and change doesn't happen quickly." His words came out muddled, but he continued, "perhaps the Indian way of acceptance is why there's poverty here. People don't fight, believing in what they call 'Fate'." 'Fate', he now doubted.

"You are too intense, we're too laid back!" The sadhu laughed. "Let's wallow in the middle."

Atop a thin ridge a couple of hours later, they arrived at a chai stall guarding one of the bigger junctions. Mountain folk on their way to and from trading rose to salute the respected man. Chota Baba accepted tea and administered to those present. A passing woman stopped and said she was worried her son had joined the Army. Chota Baba told her to give him love rather than try to change the direction he'd taken. A man was upset his wife had died the day before, the yogi silently stroked his hand. An old Vedantic monk argued a belief in God arose from mental weakness, religion was a distraction, it produced a mental rigidity which lured one from the search for Truth.

"Truth is illusive," Chota Baba smiled.

The Vedic monk nodded, "Belief accepts unquestioningly, thwarting inquisitiveness."

"How I love the inquisitive," Chota Baba agreed.

They went from settlement to settlement, leaving when Chota Baba's work was done. At each location the herbalist began in the same way and Satya realised this was how the man coped - routine made each place home. After briefly greeting the villagers, he would light his sacred fire, reciting a prayer to Agni as the flames brightened. He'd warm and drink the milk and honey provided before sitting quietly. Is the man meditating? All day long villagers sat with him, some had serious problems, but most were there to enjoy the old man's company or to ask questions without fuss. Ha, here's an old man playing out the game he's enjoyed much of his life. Come late afternoon, he was left to wash, do Yoga, meditate. Sunset heralded Arti after which food would be brought in by villagers who'd join in singing religious songs. Satya grew to understand these chanting sessions were as important to Chota Baba as they were to the villagers. They were TV, theatre and church rolled into one, giving these isolated communities without electricity the buzz they needed to face arduous lives, giving the sadhu the joy of human warmth. Occasionally, a woman or man would slink in and quietly engage in Chota Baba's private routines. Satya discovered these individuals had spent time travelling with the yogi.

One evening Satya told his new hero to accept only those with serious problems, arguing the old man needed time to recuperate. Chota Baba retorted, "Yoga postures and meditations are selfish without caring for your immediate world. Without fondness for others, including those outside your comfort zone, your endeavours will be of no use to anybody, not even for your own growth. Forgetting this, many think they are advancing but in truth they are shrinking into self-delusory mindsets they've created."

"What's the difference between reflection and meditation?"

"Meditation arises when your reflecting mind stills."

"And between thought and reflecting?"

Chota Baba laughed, "Setting me traps! In my warped logic, reflection is a calmer mode of thought."

With the morning still cool, Chota Baba stepped off the bridle path, disappeared over a rocky edge. Terrified, Satya scanned a vast bowl indented with a series of hanging valleys. He was on the sky's edge, he could fly… and die. An Aikido breath. He clambered over. Hands sweating across bare slabs, blindly seeking footholds, ants following no path, one slip and pip. Above, a leaf twisted in the still air, its ribs backlit by the intense sun; arriving aimlessly before his eyes with a red beetle hitching a ride, it fell, fell, became a speck. The haunting sound of reed flutes, assuming he was going mad he grasped the rock-face, "Music!"

"Boys scaring predators from their animals."

Screwing his eyes, peering downhill to where the rising jungle faded into alpine meadows, Satya recalled Uma speaking of a young herder recently eaten by a large cat. "We heard his cries. By the time we arrived the cows were scattered. Blood was everywhere." Stray clouds billowed across the rift's floor and rose up the slopes, edging over the escarpment at the end of the suspended valley they were scrambling into. They clutched their way down a cleft darkened by moisture-loving trees. Overcome with relief, Satya stood amid car-sized boulders beside a gushing river which split the emerald forest. Enchanted, they lingered beneath a tree with orchids wedged into drapes of moss. It feels like paradise. "Chota Baba, surely absorbing this is Truth enough."

The old yogi sat on a thick liana that looped down from the dense canopy. "This quest for Truth! Better look at what's happening inside your mind. See what you think of your life, of the people and things around you."

"What I see disappoints me."

"That's everyone's problem - don't judge, simply watch. Gradually you will find patterns, but only if you don't interfere."

"Thus anything we do before we understand ourselves is tarnished by the mess we are in?"

The herbalist nodded. "If we stopped rushing towards notions of perfection, towards ideals, we'd have time to correct our own as well as humanity's mistakes." He lifted the lota's cork, blew his embers. "Morally, humanity has advanced little since my fire's line began."

"What hope is there?" Satya realised even this remote haven could one day be tarnished by human greed.

"We must never give up."

They took a red gravel path plunging after the wild river. It burst from its green canyon to leap over alps where the flute players stood with their cattle. Spurting over boulders, the river went on to cleave terraces which juddered down, down. Their path twisted and turned, knee aching stuff.

What! A bear's call! There! Ah, only a horse, whee. But, up here beyond it all? Oh yes, that hill's unusual tip, that rocky knoll, I know where I am! Flicking away flies, they followed the packhorse's whipping tail. The path eased, became hemmed in by walls retaining flying farmland, it shot through fields of barley floating in the near vertical landscape, became cobbled with silver-grey river-stones. Voices spilled out of the fruit trees, "Namaste Chota Baba."

A spirit danced through the gathering workers. Stunning Uma bursting with excitement, ethereal before Chota Baba. I see who she loves. Uma bowed slightly, her hands raised to her chest. Chota Baba smiled, waved her on and they followed her and the locals down the bridle path. Chota Baba laid his things on the wall holding Uma's family terrace above the bridle path. Gowri lifted a broom, crossed the stone path, stepped over a meadow to a stone shed similar to those given over to the herbalist. With their legs dangling in thin air, they drank ginger-spiced tea. Satya took out his sketchbook and drew the range of mountains, with Trishul at their centre. A woman gasped, touched his hand. "You are a saint bringing Trishul to us!"

How weird. To her, drawing is magic.

For hours after lunch Chota Baba sat in the hut administering herbal medicine and chatting to people from scattered farms and the village so far below. As he watched the old man at work, Satya opened his folder and found Emma Merricott's letter from 1910: *"Ayurvedic medicine is worth exploring. I have seen it work. A soldier, weak after a battle, unable to walk, was taken to the local 'doctor'. Interested, I followed. The fellow measured the sepoy's pulse, asked all sorts of questions about his life and emotions, looked in his eyes, at his tongue and fingernails to help work out the type of person he was dealing with. To shorten a long diagnosis, an hour later the chap wrote a list of herbs and oils to be purchased from an Ayurvedic shop. These were mixed and left to steep for three days before being massaged into the soldier's skin and left to 'sink in' before being washed off after three hours. This was done for a week, followed by a week's rest, a cycle which continued for two months. There was a list of foods to be taken and others to be avoided as well as certain types of exercise. Had I been your regular English memsahib, I would have dismissed all this as mumbo-jumbo, but I have often seen Ayurveda work. The man was fighting fit at the end of the period. Perhaps he might have been in any case, who can ever know. Some say it is simply because they believe in Ayurveda. Well, I think I do."*

The old man was in no hurry, it was as if he were imparting something invisible to Uma, who glowed as she helped tend to his visitors. One day as Satya walked the hills, the air became heavy. Blinding lightening smashed into the jungle and the ground quivered as thunder shivered his eardrums. Rain rushed downhill, he dashed under the jungle canopy and watched a flash-flood cascade like a mad sea, cutting into places where the grass was thin or the soil bared, churning up the surface, undermining stones, tipping them, tumbling them, quickly creating a fierce slip liquified by wet mud which streamed downhill with a terrifying 'Whoosh'. Exposed, a boulder the size of a hut turned slowly like a drunken elephant and it lurched down the alp as if hellbent on doing maximum destruction. It finally dumped itself in the river, perfectly blocking the already swollen waters which carved another route out of the grassy hillside.

Nights of rain followed days of downpour. It looked like dawn at noon as sheets of impenetrable precipitation obscured the world. The bridle path was a rushing flow flooding the fields and orchards it passed. Satya thought of Tara as he removed leeches each time he went for a drenching walk. She had found them despicable. Sane people stayed indoors, the women weaving cloth, children doing schoolwork, men knitting. Andhaka did his books and stormed moodily about his home. They sat around Chota Baba's fire singing to Lord Shiva and Satya felt the joy of these simple melodies warming his soul. He caught himself - Soul? That part of the mind occupied with morality and aesthetics. No more?

Dispelling the darkness one morning, the sun split the damp air and warmed the soaked soil, creating vapour creatures which rose towards the bluing sky. The monstrous monsoons were over. For a week Chota Baba stayed in the suspended valley tending to new physical and psychological ailments. Satya listened to the old man chattering in Gurkhali to an injured porter. Some of the words were familiar because Father had insisted he learned the basics, assuming he would join the Gurkha Regiment.

One evening, with welling need, Satya asked, "Is there 'A Way'?"

Laughing, Chota Baba said, "Satya, what you call 'A Way' is doing ordinary things in an extraordinary way. Look at the unhurried perfection of Uma's work. Motherhood's wisdom arises from balancing devotion and practicality, there is no better moral training." Chota Baba reached out to gently lift Uma's chin. She wiped away a tear.

I'm not surprised. Uma knows Chota Baba's remedies, she often goes off to help women with their sick. There's elegance in all her actions. Is this because she gives equal weight to all she does? Oh, how confusing it all is.

ß

The summer's shimmering intensity was lessening when they looped back towards Uma's farmstead. The evening sunlight spotlighted Uma rushing up the bridle path. Satya saw her as the finest orchid, luminous, graceful, exotic. He was untouched by passion, it had been a long time since its heat had stirred his loins. The unsavoury Andhaka was a thistle, hard, dark, spiky. Gowri a brash chrysanthemum full of pleasure. Her brother Biju, a self-obsessed narcissus. Chota Baba, a mysteriously complex passionflower. How odd to see people in this way! Too much time with a herbalist, hey.

Halfway through the following morning, Uma ran across the field, "Visitors!"

Satya peered up her stepped terraces to the distant plateau. Tiny indigo silhouettes riding flaxen swathes of barley. How on earth did Uma spot them? How can she know they are strangers?

The mirage disappeared amongst foliage and fruit. Curious, Ewan walked across the meadow to sit on the bridle path's enclosing wall. The vision reappeared, burnt-umber-blue beneath ripening apples and pears. He found his limbs pelting upwards. A summer rose. He was about to call when his eyes settled on a body. No longer a neon tulip but a wilting lily, Julian head upon a cushion, arms and legs splayed across the powerful horse which Devi led.

Satya rushed forwards, laid his hand on his friend's shoulder.

Julian opened his eyes, "Charles."

His attention on his broken friend, neither Devi nor anything else existed. By the farmstead, Satya helped Julian dismount and climb Uma's steps.

Julian sighed, "Charles darling, oh you're so strong! If Devi wasn't here I'd jump you."

"You're light as a feather Julian!"

"I'm on the ultimate diet. Go on, greet and kiss your beloved Devi."

Embarrassed, thankful they were speaking English, Satya went limp, his eyes darted between them both, "D-Devi, w-what's wr-rong?" Tongue tumbling over teeth.

"Introduce us," Devi retorted.

Disappointed, floundering for names, blinking, in Hindi, "Uma, Gowri, meet Devi and Julian."

"Welcome to my home." Uma tapped Satya's shoulder playfully, "we no longer call him Ewlang but Satya."

"Ewlang? Oh yes...." Julian beamed.

"Satya, Satya," Devi rolled the name round her mouth as if it were exotic food. "Satya. I love it, Satya."

Uma giggled, "Devi, it suits his character. Now he's a baby yogi he's even more direct!" The two women laughed, teasing Satya with their eyes.

He felt stirrings in his guts. I want to touch Devi, but can't in front of these innocent villagers. What's happening to my resolve to be celibate? Dazed, he said, "It's been months, Devi."

"Our summer residence is by a tiny lake high above." Devi pointed along the ridge dominating their side of the vast canyon - the perilous slope he'd once climbed over with Chota Baba.

Satya couldn't recall anything up there.

"Further along." Devi looked shy, "the staff have looked after Julian all summer...."

Julian kissed the air, "As she came and went."

"Julian," Satya lowered his voice, "you look too ill to have travelled."

"He was insistent, boss." Devi shrugged dramatically, Jewish Broadway cum Punjabi Bollywood. Acknowledging the actress, Gowri chortled uncontrollably.

How Satya loved Devi!

Switching to English, Julian said, "Tell no one. I caught HIV from those lovely Goan prostitutes."

Goan? and Satya recalled. "Oh!" He hugged his mate. "What's the prognosis?"

"Bad boss," Devi now mock Mafioso. Not understanding, the women guffawed.

211

Julian shrugged. "No regrets. T'was shocking fun."

"Said the fool who jumped into a croc-infested river." Satya bit his lip, annoyed. Anger's made me insensitive. He supported Julian's meagre weight as they moved down the steps, along the bridle path and over the meadow. Uma held Devi's hand in companionship. Satya smiled. A fugitive, a gay guy, a jet-setting princess and a mountain peasant, yet there was no awkwardness as they chatted as gaily as blackbirds at dawn. Seeing Devi in a place which had become his own was revealing. She's at home in this mountain terrain: head high, back straight, legs swinging easily, content, a healthy body confident of itself and ready for anything. No hint of arrogance, rather a woman in the moment, glowing as if humility's a lotion rubbed into her. She melt's my heart. To hell with celibacy!

They helped Julian into the cowshed where Chota Baba was sitting by the fire. Chota Baba's thin face, solid behind that flighty white beard, showed unfathomable confidence, an assurance that everything was OK. His strong, slender hands belonged to somebody who could look after himself and his slim body gave off a quiet aura of self-possession. Satya had spent his life around fit men, here was an ancient man oozing life.

The old man, attention locked onto an old woman who told of her aches and pains, twiddled his beard, eyes to the floor, mouth slightly open. When she was done he lent forwards, gathered an assortment of dried herbs and sprinkled them into her open palm saying, "Grind these, eat them with honey each dawn and nightfall." Satya had asked why sunrise and sunset were frequently used in India. Chota Baba chose the times because they were memorable moments in a peasant's life, not because of the supposed magic of the rising or setting orb.

"Slim Santa!" Julian whispered in English. Devi choked back a giggle. Satya was annoyed his friends were debasing the moment.

Chota Baba retorted in perfect English, astounding Satya. "Santa's handing out presents! Satya's unruly friends I presume? The man's a liability, who will he bring next?" The mendicant peered at Julian. "Tell me why you're this weak."

"A wasting disease," Julian no longer the bullish queen.

Devi leaned forwards, her lips to Chota Baba's ear. Chota Baba took Julian's hand and again spoke in English, "My dear young man, everything we do has its consequences, we must measure the results we want before we act. Your friend tells me it's a dreadful disease. To make your future less traumatic, quickly learn to find peace of mind."

"I'm doing yoga." In the dim light with its vague shadows Julian's face looked even more harrowed.

"When you've polished the headstand, teach me. My beard falls over my face but I'm too lazy to shave." The yogi chuckled. "Then there's the plough, my feet won't touch the ground! Imagine such an undisciplined man telling you what to do!" His giggle infected the uncomprehending villagers. When silence returned, he looked at Julian. "Rarely is life easy, so we must do the best we can. Julian, if ever you need company, we are here." Reverting to Hindi, the old man waved, "Go outside and take a gentle walk."

"He's the real thing," Devi admitted as they strolled about the meadow.

"The grand-pappy you always wanted," Julian said, but broke off coughing.

"Julian, Satya and I need to be alone for a minute."

Settling on the bridle path wall, Julian waved dramatically. "Abandon me in my hour of need!"

Laughing, Devi and Satya strolled downhill. "Satya, you're lucky to have found Chota Baba."

Seeing her again had turned his head, "Yes, but I'm muddled."

"What else do you have to do?"

Unsure of where she was leading him, "That depends on what else is available."

"Which means?"

"You Devi." He regretted it the moment it was out.

"Why put it all on me?"

213

They lingered for a while, watching an eagle soar across the village far below. Unable to read her, he changed the subject. "Julian's state is upsetting."

"Terrible."

"What can we do?"

"Let him tell you," she rose and moved back uphill.

Regretting their time had ended, he watched her. The familiar cobbled path had become alien; he hesitated, wiped his moist eyes and in confusion moved towards the farmstead.

"Devi, it's lucky w-we m-met up." Satya nervous, "W-we only returned y-yesterday."

"I sent a note to Uma," her voice cool, "who sent a runner to find Chota Baba."

"He never t-told me."

"These yogi bears like to appear mysterious," Julian wobbled towards them.

"Julian...," Devi complained.

"Satya can carry me," Julian grinned.

Satya's fingers strong on Julian's arm, he lifted his friend onto his back. Crossing the barn meadow, they stepped down to a thin terrace and lingered, relishing the dramatic drop to the village. Resting his head on Satya's muscular shoulders, Julian whispered, "Curving ridges frolicking before savage spikes of ice." He gasped, "everything precisely placed," coughed. "Organic village beneath a maze of interlocking terraces." Another halt. "Arranged by Shiva's proverbial hand."

Devi said, "Since childhood I have thought of this area as Shiva's canvas."

"You don't believe in gods," Satya teased.

"Up here I might," she smiled.

They continued to the narrow terrace's end, drank from a cold spring gushing from a cleft in a rock face and moved over flat bedrock to an old chestnut tree. "Uma says a leopard often sits here at dusk," Satya remarked.

Basking in the autumnal sunshine, Satya stroked Julian's forehead, fiddling nervously with the thick shawl covering the reclining form. He told them of his summer's walk with

Chota Baba. Devi began singing Bollywood pop songs and Julian joined in, making frequent mistakes, laughing, gasping for air, moving onto other tunes. I wish I could be as carefree, Devi must see me as a dullard....

"Charles-Ewan, Ewlang-Satya," Julian chanted, "we've solved your problem."

"Which one?" Satya thought of the many negative things about himself he was becoming aware of. "My cool demeanour? My arrogance? The way I make assumptions about others?"

Julian's accent became heavily Bollywood, "No, tarnished Yogi."

Devi cut in with her mock Mumbai accent, "We mere mortals be talking of money you be stealing."

"What?" Forgotten fear flared in Satya's mind.

"You wacky fugitive!" Julian smiled, "Secretly stick it in my account and I'll leave it to you. That way it'll be legally yours forever!"

Satya countered, "I never wanted it, I have enough of my own. Anywise, you'll have my problem until you die."

"That'll not be long."

"What?"

Julian was serious. "AIDS is ruining my defences." He hesitated, breathing deeply. "Other infections are already attacking me. Look my skin's blistered, purple, weird." Julian lifted his shirt. "I left it too long before seeking medical help."

"That's awful. How can it be treated?"

"That's why I came here."

Satya said, "Herbs won't be sufficient. Let's fly to Switzerland, the US anywhere there's a cure. We'll inform your loved one."

"The troupe have wandered off, we'd arranged to meet at a Gopi festival in Mathura in mid December."

"Plenty of time."

"I've less than that." Julian wiped away a tear. "Look at me, I'm too weak to travel. I want to die in peace."

"Die? Oh come on!" Satya said sarcastically.

215

"He *is* dying, Satya."

"Julian, no." Satya put his head in his hands. Devi laid her hand on his arm. He hardly noticed.

"I want to go here... under this leopard's tree... if you'll let me." Julian's voice had an affable authority. His fleshless jaw and jutting cheekbones added poignancy to his words.

"Julian," Satya couldn't stop the tears. He leant over, tweaked his schoolmate's ear.

"I've watched others go in the Delhi unit. Terribly alone, surrounded by white coats they rot in pain and fear, kept vaguely alive by tubes and pills. I'm not going down such a frigid route." Julian looked saintly as he gazed into the distance. "I'll understand if you can't bear it."

Gulp, I must help. "I'm taking you to the best doctors in the world. Anyway, we'd need Uma's approval."

Devi announced, "She understands."

Julian faked a wobbly accent, "Satya sahib, this Shiva land suiting my exit."

"Julian, I can't bear losing you."

"I have a stark choice. An inevitably slow, dismal death facing tasteless white tiles, or taking my own route through these mountains." Julian's voice sweet as an ebony flute.

"What if there's a cure."

"I've talked extensively to Julian's consultants, the best in Delhi, as good as anywhere worldwide... he's in the final stages. Really, it *is* too late."

Satya stared at her blankly. He turned to Julian, shaking his head, tears streaming down his face. "Julian."

Julian touched Satya's cheek, "To make it easier for everyone, me included, I'm terminating myself."

"Suicide!" Satya exploded. And regretted it.

Julian waggled his finger, "Not suicide, sahib, Choice of Exit."

Devi nodded, "It takes a brave person."

"Or one who's lost," Satya thought of his own near-attempt in the Zaminder's dank cell.

"One who's no other route." Julian became serious, "The hospital gave me a month's worth of strong barbiturates. A

216

quarter of that'll send me to sleep before it does its work." He shuddered. "It is how one faces death which renders it terrifying... or graceful."

Satya grew uncomfortable, "Julian...."

"Stop! It's fitting I end it with you two after a fine meal as the sun sets." Julian turned mad as a March monkey. "Woof!"

"Woof!" Despite himself, Satya joined in their childhood salute.

"Woof!" Devi coy.

"Woof, woof, woof!" Chanting the improbable mantra, Julian waved them into action for a minute. "Woof, woof, woof!" Upon stopping, the three of them laughed until their sides hurt.

Once he'd regained his breath, Satya asked pensively, "When?"

"Sunset tomorrow. I want my last day to be with you two." He looked over the mountains and began to weep. Satya and Devi draped an arm each around his shivering shoulders.

When taking lunch in Chota Baba's hut, Julian asked, "Uma, can the small hump beside the leopard tree be my eternal spot?"

"It has to be," Uma smiled.

The idea inflamed Julian. "To lie with Shiva's Leopard!"

"It's actually Shiva's tiger," Gowri corrected.

"Tigers are too brash, darling," Julian winked. Everyone chuckled nervously.

Enjoying the clear early autumnal weather, they rested on the busy family patio for the rest of the afternoon. Julian composed poems in a scrapbook. For supper they ate a potato curry in Chota Baba's hut. Julian asked Chota Baba what he thought of suicide. To Satya's surprise, because he knew Hindu texts state taking life leads to bad karma, the old man smiled. "Julian, faced with your choice, I might do the same."

"Could I get you into trouble with the government?"

"Only we know," Gowri said with pride.

"Can I have a special Last Supper?"

217

Uma and Gowri asked, "What would you like?"

"Mountain dishes with their gentle spices and no chilli." Julian wobbled his head, "and, if possible, sticky sweet jalebis!"

Chota Baba boasted, "I once cooked enough for a hundred people."

Uma laughed, "Being only twenty, how sick we felt!"

"What a day!" Chota Baba began giggling.

The others joined in, their insane noise rippling into the Himalayan night. Chota Baba started tapping his fire tongs to insert rhythm to their laughter and their increasingly mad music drifted above the tidy orchards and Satya imagined it floating over to the leopard tree. Julian stood and started a wobbly dance around the fire with Satya supporting him. They all joined in and their laughter soared towards Mount Trishul where Satya imagined Shiva, now the snow leopard of the gods, danced for Julian with feline Parvati.

Satya kept waking and wondering how he could save Julian. There has to be a medical scientist somewhere working on a cure who would jump at a no-blame opportunity to save him. T-cell regeneration kills cancer, why not AIDS? The night fled, he set about his morning routine without enthusiasm. Usually the stunning scenery caught him, but not today. Life's substandard. Julian's dying. Why do the best go early when evil old sods continue with impunity?

After a breakfast of mushroom-stuffed parathas, Satya and Devi lifted Julian onto her horse and took him along the bridle path. Julian, Satya discovered, was set on his path, none of this morning's discussion about seeking a solution changed his mind. At the break of slope, the distant roar of the tumbling river rushing through fruit trees grated on Satya for the first time, reminding him of the Zaminder's cell. Ensuring Julian didn't slip, they negotiated two dozen hairpins plunging into the valley. The stone track levelled, the river slowed to meander through lazy fields where villagers of all ages removed cereal stems from earth being turned by ploughing oxen.

How unfair life. They have health and Julian's dying.

They entered the village with its short rows of terraced houses. Beyond, more riverside fields, now being levelled by more oxen and planted with seedlings of winter wheat. The river swung against an end moraine, creating a tarn. Beneath weather-twisted oaks, between moss covered boulders, by the pool's tranquil edge, they let the horse graze. Distant snow peaks laid themselves upon the untroubled pond. Julian sighed. "A Zen park with an infinity pool holding Trishul at our feet."

A muffled hiss drew their eyes to where the water breached the grassy hump to shoot over the cliff where their hanging valley died. Like Julian soon will. But he said, "This is one of Chota Baba's favourite spots." So meaningless to a near-dead man.

They chatted quietly, exploring their common pasts, philosophising, singing the odd Bollywood song, chanting to Shiva. Julian said, "I'm an unfaithful Gopi. Abandoning Krishna, I've come to die with Shiva."

Letting their emotions rise to the sky, they dozed on the vibrant grass. Satya woke with an understanding that his own mood was making it harder for Julian. I must brighten up. At noon Chota Baba, Gowri and Uma arrived with a picnic and they ate in reverence. Julian broke the spell, "Uma, this evening can we take my ultimate meal beside the leopard tree?"

"Of course," she smiled. "And I'll lead your horse."

Since Julian had arrived they had each taken turns filling the handmade pages of his scrapbook. In his wobbly scrawl, Julian wrote: *'This last day slips across mirror water, slides over waterfall; Trishul lifts us to gleaming ice, and then there's death.'*

Satya had sketched around each of Julian's stanzas - today Trishul reflected in the pond. Devi had jotted down reflective notes, today on parting. Uma had written about the earth, today the mountain. Gowri about young love, today an ending. After they had eaten, Chota Baba wrote in English: 'Chota Santa wishes you a Merry Christ-Pass.'

Julian laughed… and silently wept.

219

Their food bearers began packing up. They watched the three figures move through the imperceptibly upward-sloping fields and then climb through the orchards until they were lost in a hundred hues of green. Julian sighed, "I'm having one of the most wonderful days of my life, and it is my last." He stood up, staggered across the grass and slipped into the pool where he swam around like a child.

"Careful..." Satya called.

"What does it matter now."

Satya swam over to his fragile friend. Devi swam to meet them and helped support Julian to the water's edge.

"I'm almost a ghost!" Julian wheezed as they laid his frail body on the warm grass. Exhausted, he fell asleep in the benign sunshine. When he woke, he sat up, looked around, muttered, "My Evening approaches."

Silence surrounded them as they helped the stick figure onto the horse. Satya's eyes filled with tears and Devi wept silently as they guided the steed, the unshod cluck-plop rolling softly between the low dry-stone walls bounding the path and evaporated above the fields.

"Namaste friends," Julian said in Hindi to villagers smiling warmly upon carved balconies. "We'll meet again on Trishul."

Rising, rising, they eventually reached the edge of Uma's land and looked down the steep slope. "This truly is Shiva's valley," Julian said.

Sunk in sadness, Satya looked at his friend. Something had shifted. The previous day Julian had arrived with resolve, but also with a quivering shield of fear. Since meeting Chota Baba and gradually over their reflective hours, he had settled. At the pool a deep peace had begun to soften his face. Upon this ride he had stepped through a portal. Emerging from his hut, Chota Baba skipped across the field, "Julian! I salute a brave man."

"Chota Santa," Julian replied.

On the terrace they enjoyed spiced tea and an almond biscuit Gowri had baked that morning. Satya was dazed as they walked Julian round the immediate farm. His friend said he was looking with fresh eyes, everything sparkled. My eyes are occluded. Julian kept stopping to compose poems about hidden secrets. First a field mouse's nest; next, flattened grass where deer had slept; he moved onto the carved water-head at the spring and whispered, "Prior to my words, these things were already poetry."

"But you noticed them," Satya said in admiration. "You always have."

They helped Julian mount and Uma took the stallion and Chota Baba watched from his hut, which leaked the rich-sweet smell of frying jalebis. Under the leopard tree Julian was helped off and relaxed whilst Uma returned to her kitchen. Julian slowly cut long green grass with Gowri's sickle, purposefully piling it against the chestnut. Adding a final layer of early autumn leaves, "The year's last burst brightening my final bed."

The sadhu had told villagers of Julian's wish to be taken by Shiva's night rather than face a dire hospital death and all had agreed Julian was thus worthy of burial, a rare honour reserved for the righteous. That afternoon, as Julian swam, locals dug a grave. Satya shivered. I can't bear this. Four stones held a drooping saffron cloth across the void.

Fearful of the leopard, they lit a fire before the sun turned the mountains from fading white to peach. When Trishul's long ice ridge turned apricot, Chota Baba returned with Uma and the horse loaded with food, "Gowri's stayed behind to feed her brother and father."

They set the pots by the fire to keep them warm and admired the sky blazing vivid magenta. They sang Arti as Trishul glowed madder-pink against pale blues. Julian whispered, "Trishul, Shiva's Trident of creation, preservation and destruction."

They placed the food on a gay cloth Julian had bought in the market town. In a circle, woollen shawls draped over their shoulders, they served themselves. Satya smiled. How wonderful, Uma is sitting with us.

Uma and Gowri had harvested their best to please Julian the foodie. They sipped strawberry lassi, nibbled carrot samosas and paratha stuffed with spinach and paneer cheese. Julian gasped when Trishul became a slash of gold upon Oxford blue. They ate cucumber and turmeric raita; toasted barley, beetroot and walnut salad; mild tomato curry and okra with cumin, butter fried wild-rice, honey toasted parsnips. A million stars lit the inky sky when they enjoyed Chota Baba's warmed jalebis.

Holding a candle, Julian read aloud from the scrapbook which traced his last two days. Closing it, he said, "Devi, please post this book to my beloved. It is time."

Satya swallowed his pride. I'm a wanderer, she's more reliable. He sipped warm milk lightly scented with cardamon, ginger and Uma's honey. "To eternal life." Why when I don't believe it? To soften dear Julian's plight.

"To passing." Julian's face alight with flashing fire. He dallied, tasting his drink, lost in his final moments of sanity. "Thank you for my… Last Supper," tenor notes hanging in the cold air. "I'm frightened."

Satya hugged him, "You don't have to."

Julian looked at his friend. "I see that Delhi unit and know this is better. Here goes, CURTAINS!" Lifting his milk, hand shivering, Julian threw into his mouth barbiturates, lips quivering, he swallowed hard. His eyes expanded in fear. And he did it again and again.

There's no going back. Poor Julian.

Julian sat, looking at his friends, taking them in one at a time. After a while he stood and walked around the fire, his eyes wide. He paced the area around the tree, he stood admiring the stars. It was as if he was trying to imprint everything on his soul. He soon became groggy and sat down in the circle once more. "Devi, thanks. Thanks everyone. Charles, I've always loved you,"

"Me you too," Satya whispered. Oh gawd, this is awful.

Julian's eyes faltered. He slumped. Devi and Satya lifted his frail body, carried him to the chestnut tree, laid him tenderly upon his bed. "I'm an old rag," Julian looked down his thin body, "I'll give... the... worms little food."

"Your spirit will charge this Leopard Tree," Chota Baba whispered.

"Want... eyes open... till end... help... me," Julian wheezed.

Either side of him, lifting them apart with thumbs and fore fingers, Satya and Devi tenderly held Julian's eyelids open. This caused Julian to giggle. He clutched his chest, yelped, but continued talking once the pain had passed, "Bones'll... whisper poems... in soil."

"We'll listen with our ears to the ground," stroking his hand, Devi held back tears.

"Hara, hara, Mahadev," Chota Baba began a delicate Arti to Shiva.

Julian gawked at the yogi as if he'd seen a ghost. "Jai Shiva aum kha...," his every breath slowing.

Satya stroked Julian's brow, whispering, "I love you, Julian." Oh, this can't be happening.

Enormous distance was in Julian's eyes. Knowing his vision wasn't working properly, Satya and Devi let the lids go. He writhed. His thin arms banged into Satya and Devi. He shivered. Devi encircled Julian delicately. Satya stroked his friend's cheek. Julian's eyes shot open, but showed he was not there. Satya bent, kissed Julian's brow. Devi did the same. As did Uma and Chota Baba. Together they paced the final steps in this dance of death. Across his frail body Julian's thin hands clasped and undid. His face immobile, his mouth rhythmically grasping for air.

This isn't Julian. It's some unknown being undergoing a strange metamorphosis. It's a gradual winding down, a closing of the body's multiple functions. Timidly, Satya and Devi whispered love though Julian must be without understanding, only his primitive brain functioning, the hearing unable to make connections, the heart and lungs slowing.

A minute last breath.... hardly passing dry lips.

The pulse on Julian's neck gave a strong thump, followed by a flutter.

Stillness.

It was over.

My mind is blank.

Time stands still.

It hit them.

Shucks, a moment ago he was here chatting, now he's nothing. Vitality one minute, the next nothing. That inspiring character gone without trace. Julian, dear Julian, years of exciting life extinct, only a memory.

Satya and Devi blubbered on their dead friend's chest, letting go of all the tension they had tasted but hadn't shown. They felt every kind of emotion entwined in one whirlwind - profound loss, fathomless angst, yet a strange completeness. They looked into each other's eyes and recognised a moment of momentous depth.

"Reaching its finality, death becomes safe," Devi breathed.

"Devi," he touched her hand, remembering most Indians knew death; she had watched people die; she had been there for her parents. They gazed beyond the drooping leaves flickered by firelight and understood their private scene was going on in countless places around the world. Oh I love you Julian. Julian, where are you? Stupid question.

Uma, standing on the floating rock's lip, contemplating the chain of starlit mountains. An owl hooted. Chota Baba began softly chanting, his voice seeping across the valley's dark depths. "Shiva, parameshwa rahia, Shiva Shankararia, namah Aum."

In the flickering firelight, Satya realised this was religion's purpose - a comfort zone in a chaotic world. He plucked a blue flower growing at the cooling feet and placed it in the forever silent mouth. They picked up the empty body, wrapped it in Julian's gay tablecloth. Drawing back the villagers' yellow cloth, they carefully lowered the light bundle into the grave. They covered Julian with both cloths,

224

his cropped grass, bright leaves, heaps of soil, three large flagstones, more soil. They replaced the peeled-back grass clots.

Coursing through me weakness. Why Julian? Oh Julian.

Gowri arrived to help clear up, "Julian's karma caught him," and she wept.

Wow, she fancied Julian. OK, karma explains things for her. But bloody hell! Karma, what stupid rubbish! Julian brimmed with empathy, helped others, always sought common solutions, spread joy. OK, sexually different, but giving and harmless. Billion times better than the nasty wealthy, healthy Trumps and Blairs of this world. Ugh! Gawd, I'm so angry. ANGRY! Why Julian! WHY?

Uma and Gowri steered the horse away, Chota Baba sat in meditation. Satya and Devi paced aimlessly beyond the fire's potency, drinking in the cold air, gazing up at the eternal sky. Sometimes they wander further, crunching the heavy frost. Mindful of the leopard, they kept restocking the fire. Coddled in heavy blankets, in the orange light they read Julian's Death Book. His handwriting, I'll never get another postcard from Julian. Tears flooded out, Devi leaned into him weeping.

Julian's death has opened a current inside me, something deep. Oh, I can't work it out, it's too powerful to understand. Aah, allowing it to wash through me, I feel strong. Emotionally exhausted. Devi and Satya nestled together for warmth.

Faintest hint of lemon tinted Trishul, fading Shiva's frozen void. Far beyond, deep in Tibet lay Mount Kailash, worshipped by Hindus as the centre of the Earth, as Shiva's actual home. Waters from near Kailash's form the Indus, Brahmaputra, Ganga and other rivers. Satya sighed, Kailash too far away, Trishul, Shiva's trident, is visible and somewhere to place Julian.

Devi, she's so sweet asleep. My lips pulse with emotion. I'm urged like Shiva to create life after death. Devi, Devi, I want you.

ß

225

Stunned, deeply wounded, all day they wandered the hills, absently collecting a rainbow of autumnal leaves as if it were a link to Julian. They kept sinking, weeping, lifting each other by talking of Julian, of death and of what they wanted from life. Devi desired to continue charity work on her ancestral estate. I, I am so, so confused.

After swimming in the infinity pool, they stood by the waterfall's crest, gazing at minute fields surrounding the market town. Their eyes followed the chain of interlocked valleys, rose up ridges, traced the layered lines, flew to Trishul's three interlinked summits. Trishul! "Chota Baba loves Trishul."

"Do only fools go where angels wish to meditate?"

"Meaning?"

"You'll find out," she turned, strolled back along the pool's shallow edge.

How unfathomable she was. Watching her graceful limbs, desire to be with her flooded him. She gathered her things. Confused about his life's direction, he stepped beside her, electrified, his body unwilling to part from hers as they wandered inches apart along the level bridle path, through the friendly village, past people harvesting the fields. Climbing the steep slope to Uma's land, he pined to leave with her, not Chota Baba. Watching her easy movements, he recalled one of Rupert Merricott's diary pages from 1664 in which he'd regretted parting from an Indian woman he loved. Satya knew from the family tree they'd not had the luck to meet again. "Devi," he began as Uma's terraced houses appeared.

In their perturbed night, stirred occasionally by a fading chestnut leaf falling on their faces, Devi and Satya had dozed on and off, their limbs and bodies flushing with desire. Knowing they weren't ripe for a first kiss, they had desisted.

The intensity in her eyes! "Devi, I must be a fool walking from you."

She gulped, gathered herself. "By not going, you will spend the rest of your life wondering what you missed. I'm not sure how easy that would be to live with."

"For you or me?"

"Satya," she rolled his new name around her mouth, "Satya, Satya, I love the name, better than Charles, sweeter than Ewan. You must honour it's meaning, seek the Truth which haunts you."

"The universe has no ultimate purpose, everything evolves by reacting within the restless sea of changes."

"My Truth right now isn't yours."

"May never be?"

She tarried, eyes red, she exhaled. He wanted to hug her, but Uma's extended family were watching from the infinity wall. At last, her voice, small, "Satya, you'll never get this opportunity again." She wiped her eyes, "that is incredibly important."

"Or is it chasing clouds?"

"That you must find out." She mounted in one fluid movement. Neither could hold back tears. Silently lifting hands, they namasted. The horse pivoted.

Will we meet again? How much will our lives have changed if we did? Satya swallowed. She'll be married off. She's getting too old to be an Indian maiden. Oh god! I must declare my feelings. "Devi!"

Pulling the reigns, turning her head, "Satya?"

"Will you...."

She kicked the horse in to action.

Gawping at her cantering figure, Satya wept silently. Have I missed the most important moment in my life?

ß

In the immensity we are ants. Insects are eating Julian
now, mind, it's only flesh. Gosh, I miss him.

Golly, this is exposed. Grass dropped away either side of
their feet as they moved up a suspended watershed dividing
entire river systems. The steeply rising spur held apart
different worlds where ancient tribes had evolved different
languages, foods, dress and customs. Ahead, a soaring
mountainside over which ice peaks spike the clear sky. The
top of the world! Emptiness outside, emptiness inside me.
Julian who's always been here, now flashes of memory.

Their day waned with a sunset spanning a thousand miles.
A gnarled protrusion protecting five rows of long-barns
stepped thirty paces apart. Entering heavy doors, passing
animals settling down without fear, they climbed an internal
ladder which could be lifted in times of danger. In the
protected living quarters, the old sadhu tended to the small
population before being fed supper.

Unlike the others, they slept downstairs with the animals
and upon awaking, went upstairs for tea. Frosty footprints
crossed the terrace, lead to a stone bridlepath traversing the
sheltered slope, cut through terraced barley fields hanging
above dropping grassland, the tree-line, jungled ridges, fainter
and fainter; beyond the last of these the delicate smudge of
the Northern Plains where Arti bells had long stopped ringing.
Devi, down there somewhere doing yoga. What to make of
her?

Their floating ridge sunk into the sweeping flank of
mountain. They hit a wide trading track cutting east-west.
Three naked naga babas drank water at a spring. Satya waved
in recognition, they smiled, big innocent smiles. Respectfully,
each man stood and raised folded hands to Chota Baba. The
herbalist smiled, patted the air imploring them to sit.

Human voices murmured with the wind. Two rows of four
houses joined in a right-angle by a barn for animals, created a
plaza sheltered from gales, there was a warehouse, a shop,

228

three cafes, a hostel, two dormitories. The shop bursting with essential goods was run by a man with a kind, strong face, Chandra, who had led them from his rock-sheltered village. Satya noticed other familiar faces serving, cleaning, cooking, selling, bargaining, paying. Ha, so this is why the settlement is up here beyond it all.

Satya sketched thin men with weather-sculptured faces arriving with packhorses. They wore woollen trousers, thick wool waistcoats, worn-out tweed jackets and brightly embroidered felt caps - Gharwalis from the vast complex of valleys to the west. After taking tea the traders sold half their discharged packages to Chandra's shop, purchased grain from the warehouse and fed their sweating beasts tethered beneath a line of stunted beech trees. They traded goods with long haired men wearing black robes, bulky amber necklaces, long single earrings and peculiar hats - tough Tibetans. The Tibetans bartered with the Gharwalis and skull-capped Nepalis, exchanging Indian goods for antique jewels and bronze statues their yaks had carried over the Himalayas. Eating around a sun-splashed table, men with curved swords, blue robes and saffron turbans - Sikhs returning from a pilgrimage to Roopkund.

Chota Baba said, "Chandra's people have a tough life, imprisoned by high winter snow, with bears and snow leopard wanting to eat their dogs, sheep, cows, even their children. However, as you see, in summer this place has its rewards."

Satya found a sepia postcard of two British men wearing pith helmets standing proudly by a postbox they had set in to one of the houses. He turned his head, it was still in place on Chandra's front wall. How incredible the British: no matter how remote the location, they attempted to 'tame' it. Drinking spiced tea, eating sugary biscuits, he wrote upon the yellowing blank side:

Dear Devi,

A hundred and seventy years since my ancestor surveyed these mountains and I'll use that postbox to send this! Chota Baba says we are near his 'Home'. Julian's passing has turned my head, life now feels frozen.... Yet the invisible thing

which occurred between you and I has warmed my chilled
centre. You, though, seemed unsure.... I hope it is not too long
before we meet again....

Love, Satya.

Julian's last moments leap out at unexpected moments. I
can't imagine death. Is it frightening or are you dulled? It's
madness - this complex being we each are snuffs out,
becomes nothing, yes, nothing. What use then, our lives? To
find fulfilment. What's that when the cows come home?
Love? Hope? And Devi, tantalising as ever. All I have is this
peculiar search, search for what? At least I've met an
exceptional man. But Chota Baba might be up his own tree.
And the yogi-game - delusion attracting the desperate? Help!
Stop thinking.

Dodging loaded animals emerging from the barn, they left
Chandra's busy plaza and joined a caravan of yaks heading
along the track curving round the mountain. Chota Baba said
the route was also used by high altitude villagers far below
who lead their animals to alpine meadows above. "This
attracts leopard who move up and down with the flocks and
the weather."

"It must be dangerous."

"Smell a cat and together these Tibetan yaks are
unbeatable," Chota Baba let his hand run up a curving horn.

"Where are we going?" Satya noted only the Tibetans
went their way.

"There," the old yogi's finger pointed to a sparkle in the
sky.

An hour passed. By three towering rocks, they bid
farewell and the leathery Tibetans bowed respectfully,
touching the ground, wishing luck, imploring the gods protect
Chota Baba and Satya. Moving directly up towards the ice in
the sky, they passed scattered clumps of weather twisted
juniper. Bit by bit these hardy plants gave way to single trees,
eerie, ever-more stunted the further from the track they
walked. Satya wondered if amongst them might be a tree
older than the World's supposedly oldest, recently discovered

230

in Sweden, which Tara argued was in California's Sierra Nevada. Tara! How little I've thought of her. Is she still in Nachi's bed? Tossing a cold stone as far as he could, he symbolically rid his mind of her and replaced it with a smooth knot of juniper, letting it warm in his palm as a reminder of Devi.

They moved up the expanse of undulating grassland. In the far distance nomads grazed their beasts beneath rarely seen ice peaks cutting into the smooth sky. Water! I'm parched. He drank from a rocky spring. Silence echoing through space. Realising he rarely listened, only noticing intrusive sound, Satya consciously drank in its absence. The air grew fresher. Over the yellows, fawns and faded golds, the silver sun sparkled. Unlike the florid lustrousness of the boiling plains.

They moved upwards without rest. Heaving, low on oxygen, Satya stopped but Chota Baba did not slow and Satya was impelled to continue. To distract himself, he tried to work out why the terrain was the shape it was and after a while he was climbing more easily. Being mentally relaxed had helped the body to adapt. How interesting. A couple of hours later their part of the boundless beige buckled and thinned into a hummock. As they climbed, it became an incline so steep Satya's heart jumped into his mouth, but Chota Baba kept stepping up. Worried, he exchanged new trainers for walking boots, but even with a better grip, he dripped with fear as the flaxen slice narrowed. All I can see is this strip of grass climbing the sky. Blimey!

They rose to a crest. Ewan froze. A musty-blue strip of rock bowed into the air. The silence, now haunting. Terrified Satya grasped the crag, he took a deep breath. Unlike poor Julian, I'm not ready to die. To ground his madly racing mind, he looked down the yellow chine they had scaled, over the endless burnt grasslands, over the infinite green ranges and all the way to the vague pink of The Plains.

This did nothing to calm him. Yet Chota Baba appeared excited. They snacked on vegetable samosas. Seeking more distraction, Satya opened his family diaries and flipped until he found Harold Merricott's 1821 passage:

"Eternal steppes halted by the fierce Himalaya, reborn beyond the icy northern slopes at the top of the world continue across Tibet, broken every so often by enormous mountain ranges, across uncharted Mongolia, through wild Siberia, eastwards deep into lost China, and west over unknown Turkmenistan, Kurdistan and far in to Russia. A gleaming grassy sphere the various Tatar tribes once dominated on horseback, treading turmoil into communities from Peking to Jerusalem, the banks of the Danube to Spain. Yet above the grasslands, these peaceful Himalayas unchanged for millennia, only ever visited by yogis until William Webb came to survey them."

Hand sweating on the sun-warmed stone, Satya faced the narrow spine. Blimey, it's one pace wide! A meeting of two cliffs! Each falling to dark canyons. Lost worlds untouched by humanity's vain passage. Chota Baba laid an encouraging hand on Satya's shoulder and stepped purposefully onwards. Blinkin bongles, he's balancing on air. A rogue gust could whip you off! Where the rising backbone crested, the sadhu disappeared, leaving only spike and sky.

Satya shivered and stepped out, his trembling knees aloft nothing, his feeble feet insecure on the knife-edge. Terrified, he withdrew, clung to the rocky-knoll. I can't. He again looked back over the flexing grasslands. Returning to the trading post I'd miss Chota Baba's 'home'. Defeat. Yet I'd see Devi! If I fell, life will be lost. However, if I retreat I'd have lost this chance. Must I continue? Somehow.

How had Chota Baba walked the reedy incline as if it were a bridle path? And where the heck's the old yogi when I needed him? Shuffling on his belly, eyes fixed on rock, pushing his bag ahead, Satya made the crest. The vertebrae instantly widened to several paces, relieved, he closed his eyes. When ready, he looked up. The broadening tail dropped and merged with an emerald hillock dotted with colourful flowers of all shapes and sizes. He yelled, "Flower Hill!" His

232

voice bounced back and forth, fainter, fainter, eerie with only the spine behind, the hillock ahead, fragments of solidity within the vast emptiness.

"Welcome Home," aloft Flower Hill, Chota Baba, voice playing back several times. Ghostly.

Satya stepped through the floral carpet trying not to crush a single bloom. So, so beautiful! Wow. At the crest he looked up. Gulp. Way above, waves of shocking whites within whites.

"Trishul!" Chota Baba whispered. "Om namah Shivaiya."

Dwarfed by the icy mountain, awe, fear and delight soared through Satya's chest. Gawping, following Chota Baba's lead, his hands together, he bowed to the holy ridge and the ringing silence.

Leaving the contemplating yogi, Satya moved to the hilltop's edge. What! A bowl, long ago etched into the massif's southern facade by Trishul's retreating glacier. It's back wall, a cliff of yellow limestone topped and bottomed by blue slate. The cliff rose from Flower Hill's foot, crested at a waterfall issuing from the glacier's snout and it sank towards the sanctuary's far edge - a dark drop into one of the canyons the rocky spine separated. In this protected haven plants flourished, creating a natural garden. Flipping heck, azalea, rhododendron, juniper. It's a Zen garden.

After hours of nothing but faded grass, Satya streaked down amongst scattered giant juniper and laid his nose against their bark, sniffing the strong scent, admiring the dark green foliage perfectly etched against the golden cliff. He ran over the exposed blue-base rock, skipped through shed-sized boulders singing, "Boulders so Blue, Ooh hoo hoo!". Gosh, the cliff is honey solidified. Dead centre, the pencil-thin waterfall landed with an elegant splash, the predominant noise. Its centuries of spring melt had carved an oval pond into the rock base. Brrr, that's freezing. He removed his hand.

The overflow spilled across thirty metres of blue stone to warm an emerald pool. He heard a splash. Satya tore off his green robe and pitched his hot body into the cold clear water and followed Chota Baba to the pebble-filled bottom. How magical the light, the shapes. Surfacing in an explosion of bubbles, the old man puffed, "Your lucky lingum." Half sinking, he gripped a stone as long as his forearm. The dark slate's soft texture pleased Satya. It'll be my Julian stone. I'll imagine Julian on the ice above prancing amongst jungle yogis. They hauled themselves out, frozen to the core and lay on a hot expanse of blue rock to enjoy the warming afternoon sun.

Satya woke hungry and asked about food. The yogi rose, they made their way through the jumble of giant boulders to the base of the cliff and behind a Prussian blue lump as big as a bus, a further surprise. Leaning against the honey rock-face, a stone hut with a slate roof and veranda. Sliding back three crude wooden latches, Chota Baba opened a weathered door, revealing a room with a prepared fire within a circled of stones, opening a shuttered window Satya noticed the hut fronted an intimate cave. Tipping out his embers, the yogi blew, reviving Agni within dried moss and wood. Chota Baba opened a small iron door set at chest height into the silk-smooth yellow marble and removed glass jars of rice, lentils and wholemeal flour. "A shop in a cave!" Satya joked.

Chota Baba chuckled, "Chandra regularly brings up supplies. He and the villagers helped me build this hut frontage when the open cave got too draughty for a frail old fool like me."

Whilst Satya cooked rice and dal in pots balanced over the fire, rolled out and pan-fried chapatis which he piled on a brass platter, the sadhu walked outside and returned with a selection of wild legumes washed in the top-pond. They cut up and stir-fried the wild onions, parsnip and chard, using salt and herbs from the cupboard and ate outside where the last splash of sun hit a dark rock beneath an ancient juniper. Satya sighed, What a home.

ß

Damp grass is as slippery as snow and childhood images of shooting down slopes on a tin tray tormented Satya. Mind, in summer it was great when he'd shot in to Merricott Lake. Here he'd get a one-way ticket to eternity. The alp, frightening enough with its tilt, ended above the deep canyon. Here it's 85% sky, 15% land. Slip and you're a gonna. Satya avoided looking up to Trishul's interlinked glaciers or at the terrifying nothingness below.

Sweating fingers clutching frail roots, shivering boots gripping scant soil. Why risk your life for herbs, who cares what they do. Chota Baba had long given up trying to explain their characteristics, properties and specific environments, how each species was shaped to suit its specific niche. Cloth bag between his feet, dumbly catching stems the old man tossed down, fearing for his life, watching the ancient guy scurry up yellow marble cliffs with drops to hell and beyond, Satya stood his ground, if you could call shards of slippery blue slate security. Boggled, Satya watched the yogi casually drop from the cliff, slide on the tipping scree, skid past, come to a halt within ten paces. Looking at the top of the old man's head, Satya thought of death. Air! Too much of the blasted stuff. "Baba, we worry about the pain of dying," he could see Julian's face. "We worry we'll never see our loved ones again," he pined for Julian, Devi, Uncle Jack. "We know we'll fade like the mist without having completed what we want." What the heck did he want to do, certainly not this.

"Why worry about the inevitable?"

"Because humans can't believe their complex beings and life achievements will end as nothing."

"What is there to achieve but to make each hour important? Work with conviction. When fully attentive to each task, your brain grows connections...."

"You know some science, Baba."

"Ho, ho, I read back copies of 'The New Scientist' when I stay with Chandra."

"How inspiring," Satya looked at the old man in a new light.

The sadhu risked his life to make Chowan Prash, a mash of multiple rare herbs and honey given to the weak or severely ill. Chota Baba's version of this traditional Himalayan medicine had been handed down his long line of yogis, and Satya asked how many would continue the secret recipe.

"Chandra's unmarried sister lives permanently in a cave nearby." He pointed east over impenetrable terrain. "For two weeks each autumn we travel round the nearest villages. There's a caveman west of here," Chota Baba pointed beyond Flower Hill which guarded their haven's western edge. "Scattered about, there are a few such as Chandra and Uma who are tied to worldly duties."

Before the sun dipped beneath Flower Hill, Chota Baba dried his rare herbs upside on a line slung between the veranda and a sturdy juniper. "How did the first herbalist know what to harvest?"

"Animals instinctively understand which plants to eat when they are ill, look at cats and dogs. We are animals but exchanging a nomadic life with agriculture, most people forgot, those who remembered were called shamans or yogis, now it's Chota Fools!" The yogi chuckled.

They had settled into a routine. Before dawn, a chilling splash beneath the waterfall, "Straight from Shiva's icy Trident." After drinking herbal tea beside their fire, they meditated, with Satya faithfully struggling with his base-sound mantra, but nothing ever happened, yet he loved the yoga sessions atop Flower Hill where the thick night frosts melted first. After a breakfast of parathas stuffed with legumes, they walked eastwards through the garden to where the yellow cliff curved down and died in six paces of scree which dripped into the abyss.

Upon extensive alps beyond their enclosed haven the view opened, revealing cold ridges and icy peaks rushing towards

Nepal. Satya felt like a bird. I'd prefer to be a snail. What if your feathers stopped holding air? At least the snail has its shell. They drank from the many springs upon the alps and cooked what they found back at the hut/cave where their afternoons were spent preparing the herbs for drying. Finally, they'd reward themselves with a cooling swim and lazing in the afternoon sunshine.

Satya loved painting the yellow marble cliff, it made the perfect backcloth to the blue boulders, vibrant plants and the stream which swelled when the noon sun melted the snows above. Sometimes he followed the stream to the haven's broad lip of worn blue rock to sketch water cascading into the sun shunned chasm whose far side was a stoney ridge hiding the world beyond. Hostile winds howled along this impenetrable canyon to be shot skywards by the perilously thin rocky bridge where it terminated, yet step back from the haven's screeching edge and it was mostly calm, warm, silent. Satya's fingers couldn't stop drawing. Detail fascinated him. Minute pink flowers, large blue ones; beetles whose backs flickered yellow, green and blue in the sunlight; the shape of an indigo rock curving from a tight pea-green shrub; falcons tumbling past.

Within their confined theatre, the outside world could be seen from nowhere but the top of Flower Hill, and only then Trishul's waves of ice and the canyon's far ridge which blocked everywhere. Perhaps the place had been chosen because it gave an impression of utter isolation - you, your cave, your haven, Shiva ice; air.

One cold morning Satya spotted a rat inside their hut, "Trap it before it eats our precious food!"

Chota Baba's shot back, "Feed it. It has as much right to live here as we do. We come and go, but this is his ancestral home."

"Des-res for rats!" Satya sniggered.

Late afternoons in the sunshine before their south facing hut, removing grain sized stones dishonest traders loaded to the rice and lentils. As their wild tuber and vegetable stews and fry-ups simmered, they performed yoga on the level grass by the pond and in the fading day they'd eat beneath a sun splashed juniper. They preferred to be late for Arti, racing up Flower Hill, biding goodnight to the setting orb, watching Trishul go pink, fade to apricot and as dark seeped across the garden they sometimes went to another cave twenty paces from their own. Erecting a notched tree trunk, "Our protection from snow leopard," they'd clamber up the smooth marble.

The small entrance quickly opened to a womblike space. "My first residence!" Chota Baba's voice rolled around the echo-chamber. "An ancestral guru found this in the pond, it's been worn smooth from centuries of prayer." The blue symbol of Shiva's virility balanced within Parvati's honey coloured vulva, long ago lovingly carved into solid marble. Using fresh water, Chota Baba washed the lingum with attention, chanting: "Aum, Namah Shiva."

When the man was done, Satya whispered, "Chota Baba, it is only stone."

Chota Baba laughed, "Ritual transforms it into something else."

"In your mind!"

"Ritual is a crutch which helps the lonely sadhu concentrate. Ritual is my theatre, it amuses me to sing these songs to the gods who probably don't exist - no worse than make-believing in TV soap characters. Mankind has always revelled in stories and such fantasies help me live this strange life I have chosen."

"Why this savage place? More accessible places must have the same herbs."

"Few dare visit here and being alone recharges me. The topography protects us, creating a warm haven. Rain is rare, the days are hot and sunny, the nights freezing so only specific herbs survive here."

Satya noticed the remoteness made him less rational, he came to wonder if there was a latent power in the second cave, or was it simply that the womb sensation returned you to your unstimulated self? Perhaps, lacking other stimuli, he felt charged by Chota Baba's tales of an ancient line of holy men who had sat there. He recalled a visit with Mater, a declared atheist, to Chartres Cathedral in France. Beneath the huge apex where they turned around and admired the entire building, Mater stood in silence for some ten minutes. It was the first time he'd seen her still. Later in a cafe he'd cautiously asked what had gone through her mind. Unusually, for she never revealed her thoughts, she'd spoken calmly, as if in a dream, "The symmetry, the perfect curves, the rainbows of light and the size which diminished the hubbub of human noise made time stand still. For a moment I could see why people came to believe in a God."

"Satya, you are a physical man, forget what you've learnt of meditation, mantras etc, simply do your postures with a soft awareness of the exercise." They stood and Chota Baba encouraged him into a deeper consciousness of his body's reactions to each pose. "Work as if it were Tai Chi, making each move a meditation. Exercising the body and the mind in synchronicity will lead you to a calm place."

Stretching his body-mind slowly, week by week, rather than as previously, second by second, moves previously done as exercises became a gentle expressions of his self. One late afternoon the herbalist explained the reason behind postures and what they did to the body. Satya asked questions, discouraged in the ashram and got an enlivened response, which enabled him to explore the discipline to his satisfaction at last. "Each posture stretches a specific set of tendons and muscles, pushing increased blood through chosen organs, refreshing them, slowing your heart beat. Adding breath control to the exercises makes yoga a powerful calming tool and a calm body heals better. Repeat a short routine - Sun-Worship, Triangle, Spinal-Twist, Seated Forward-Bend and the Plough, all with soft concentration. If you are sick or stiff, these postures can help."

Satya loved these elegant, interlinked postures and after thirty minutes he felt charged and relaxed. He then sat without aim, his mind content, at rest. He'd rise, wander about the amphitheatre, lingering to sketch something and he found his drawings took on a magical quality.

240

Satya realised he was experiencing something special, every moment with Chota Baba rang as if played out in a crystal bowl with the sadhu's gems suspended as glowing lanterns. His emotions were alive, almost the sensation of being in love but with both feet firmly planted amongst the herbs they gathered.

They were on Flower Hill, gazing at the three ice peaks making up Trishul's wavy ridge, watching the ice shift from pear, peach, apricot to orange. Satya felt overwhelmed by the task of attaining some sort of wisdom, freedom or enlightenment. "Chota Baba, life away from here is complicated," he waved his hand over the rocky lump which hid the steppes, the distant hills and the far-off craziness of The Plains. "In the material world you can't rest in the moment, you have to plan and work towards a better future."

"Planning makes humanity successful, but once work, shopping and chores are done, live for today, stop, enjoy little things like the sunlight on this tree. Doing this eventually makes each hour the one. The ever-shifting *Now* is the only reality we have, yet how little mental time we spend in it."

"Won't it get boring simply being?"

"Not if you are being simply!" The yogi giggled, "boring only if you 'think' yourself into doing so!"

"Thinking's the problem?"

"Thought is a vital tool, stopping it makes dams of stress, even mental problems. Play alongside thought, let it do its jobs but don't hang on to it."

Hey, creating comes from thought! "Humans need to be creative, otherwise we shrivel mentally."

"You can be creative when stimulated by this moment. Slow down, relish doing those little tasks, delight in each day of your incredibly short time on earth. Watch without getting egotistically involved and life will reveal its precious moments."

It was a balmy evening and a thin slice of moon hung above a time worn juniper. The old man said, "What peace under such a tree."

Hmm, from its girth, it could be over two thousands of years old. Things grow slowly up here. One hundred miles west, I know Pakistani scientists gave cooking gas containers to villagers to stop them chopping up a juniper forest with three thousand year old trees. Now that's old!

Chota Baba interrupted his musing. "Uncluttered, life's this simple."

"Is religion thus useless?"

"This moonlit branch becomes our holy image, the owl's hoot our prayer, time itself our meditation, empathy our creed, humility our character."

"Quite Zen, but vague."

Chortling, "See why they called you Satya!" Chota Baba continued, "there is something you can do whenever you have a spare moment. It will seep in to your day, gradually transforming the way you are. We live imprisoned in our minds." He hesitated, allowing Satya time to absorb the concept. "Lightly stepping aside from our thoughts and into our senses, transforms us."

"Tantra's sensuality nearly drowned me!"

"Forget all you've been taught and all you think you've learnt. Sit quietly, let your thoughts float away with their own energy, don't interfere. Casually watch your breath move through your body. Flit through the senses, not interpreting what you sense, but briefly looking, hearing, touching, tasting, smelling... without reaction. Do this 'Soft Awareness' and peace will arise."

"I prefer calling it 'Settling'. Eyes open or closed?"

Laughing, the sadhu said, "Either in both cases."

"So - feel, listen."

"We've forgotten how to settle naturally in to the moment."

Satya lay against the bark, who knows, Buddha may have settled into the moment against this very trunk. Tilting his head, peering through the branches, he let his mind roll past the Second World War in which his grandparents had fought, past the arrival of his British ancestors, before the Muslim invasions, beyond Alexander the Greek's intrusion into Afghanistan, beyond Buddha's birth. The tree might have been alive before Abraham lived, and even then one of Chota Baba's long line of teachers would have sat right here. Wow.

They watched night moths dart across the lake and migrant bats dash and dive in their hunting. Time passed without a click of thought disrupting Satya's head and he was surprised when the old man rose and walked towards the hut to sleep.

Enjoying the last of the sun by Buddha's juniper, their food cooking in the hut, Satya turned to the old yogi, "Chota Baba, what made you become a yogi?"

"Ho, ho," the sadhu chuckled. "It's a terrible tale which nobody knows. Why should I tell you?"

"It would be sad to die without anybody knowing the real you."

"Oh very well, so long as it remains with you. If Indians knew they would fear me."

"Naturally," Satya teased.

Chota Baba winked, "I hope you're ready!"

"It can't be as bad as my story."

"Ho, ho! I enjoyed hearing of your misdeed in London; I'm worse." He chuckled, untucking his tightly curled beard. "I grew up in a Gurkha family in Nepal and retired early from the British Army, having killed too many in undeclared skirmishes around the world. With the money I'd saved, I set up what became a successful import company in a North Indian city. When working late one evening, I was surprised by two figures entering my office brandishing cocked pistols. I attacked them with my khukuri, which, being a Gurkha, I always wore. Upset I'd killed, rather than injured them, I rang the police, who arrived promptly and agreed I had defended myself in all innocence. I'd killed a hit-man and the Indian partner tax laws insisted I have: with me dead, he'd have inherited the lot.

243

"Although not arrested, a trial was bought against me by his influential Indian family. The entire jury, corrupted by bribes, declared I was guilty and I was taken away to await execution. Gurkhas are not afraid of death, but we hate waiting for it!" Chota Baba chuckled.

"That first night I persuaded a greedy guard to let me escape, shamefully bribing him with the keys to my home where he could take what he wanted. When faced with unjust death you will do anything to escape its claws. I had no idea my young bride was there alone, having disobeyed my last minute instructions to go to her parents' house, she had stayed on alone to pack up and leave the next morning. Let out at midnight, in the street I gave the guard the address and ran to hide with relatives of a relative. In the morning I heard my wife had killed herself out of shame after her night with the unruly guard who told her I'd given him consent."

Satya was surprised to see the old man wipe his eyes. So, even yogi's harbour emotion.

"I now carried three unwanted deaths, and soon a fourth, for her brother killed the guard. Add on all those army killings and you can see what a monster I am. I apologised to her brother and family, instantly making a vow - they tried to stop me, but I ran like a madman and threw myself into the Ganga, knowing I would drown for I could not swim. Unfortunately, I was rescued by a boatman and an old herbalist traversing the river. That was the sadhu who transformed me."

Chota Baba gazed vaguely around their dimming haven. "It took weeks to walk up here. After a month of teaching me how to survive, he told me to stay alone in this desolate place for four winters to pay for the four souls I'd accidentally done away with. He didn't count the battle deaths, they'd been out of duty. With the knowledge of a mountain tribesman, I began my austerities expecting to die. How can you survive a high Himalayan winter alone in a cave? My guru briefly returned each autumn. It transformed me and, having no other reason to exist, I had to gain his passion for herbs!" Chota Baba laughed. "For years we moved from village to village all

244

spring and summer, we collected autumnal herbs and over-wintered here."

Satya sat in silence, chewing over the extraordinary tale. "I noticed the old you is still here."

Chota Baba's chortle went on for a long time. "Our old roots remain, but that's OK."

"Why?"

"They can inform us about others for we each have little Hitlers and Buddhas inside, what defines us is how we live with them and how we use them."

After they had eaten, standing upon the veranda wrapped in thick woollen blankets, Satya said, "Chota Baba, my family were in the Gurkhas."

"I can believe it. You are fearlessness but not aggressive because you have confidence in your physical abilities."

"Why are the Gurkhas like this?"

"For two hundred years we fought for our survival against Muslim invaders who wanted to convert or kill us. Exhausted, although fighting fit, we eventually retreated to the mountains, and still proud of who we are."

The full moon rose above the rim of their secret garden, transforming it in to a dreamland. In the womb cave the reflected light inspired the yogi to play hand-shadows across the inward curving entrance wall. "Satya, you are calmer these days. I notice your mind is leaving distracting thoughts of yogic achievements, Enlightenment and grandeur. Life's secret, when you eventually come upon it, is simple - a calm understanding of the way things are."

"How will I know my view is not an illusion?"

Chota Baba's laughter shook his body. When he calmed he said, "When you feel genuine compassion for living things."

"Compassion, caring?"

"We are playing with words and words will never convey it. When somebody attempts to, their words are written down and turned in to Bibles. Those who don't 'know', systemise the thoughts and examples of those who supposedly 'knew' and, to prove they are the inheritors of the Truth, they contest the systems others have constructed, whilst the original apparent 'knowers' accept one another's views." He laughed, "imagine me writing 'Chota's Thoughts!' What foolishness. Wrapping things up in complex words loses their direct simplicity."

"Ergo, 'Settling'. Practiced, not written, imparted as a practical activity, not debated, an exercise, not a ritual."

"Exactly."

"Baba, when a Zen master inherited an old temple filled with ancient Zen writings, he burnt the lot and smashed the archaic Buddha statue."

"A fine teaching! But unpopular with antique collectors, ha, ha, ha!"

I adore this haven! He though of Merricott's celebrated garden opened to the public twice a year: humble topiary leading to the formal entrance, yew hedges sheltering a variety of 'garden rooms' wrapping round the house, each favouring its own collection of insects and birds.... Blinking himself back, he listened to pipping mountain birds and humming autumnal insects. How boggling life! These creatures instinctively know what to do, their refined activities evolved over millennia; and these species are interlinked, creating this specific haven. Woof! This eco-system, like millions around the world, is unique. "And along comes modern humanity, destroying entire systems we don't understand, creating widespread environmental collapse. Why should I chose self-knowledge over environmental activity?"

Used to Satya's mumblings, Chota Baba chuckled. "Change will happen once people understand they will gain more from protecting the environment than exploiting it. This arises from empathy and this begins with amused self-mocking self-awareness."

That's a bit of a mouth-full. Gawd, I'm really worried ecological disaster looms beyond this haven. "We need a new economic order based less on profit, less on meat-eating, less on avid consumption."

"The environmental problems are enormous," Chota Baba twiddled his beard.

"Protecting nature is humanity's most important task. Each generation has its war, this is ours."

"But we must change ourselves first."

Satya sneered, "Back to ourselves...."

"You may snigger, but when we stop chasing satisfaction outside and realise it lingers inside, we'll do less, want less. Only then will nature get a chance to revive."

"The issue is complicated by neoliberalism and globalisation's greed."

"You need to be strong, calm and clear headed to fight for the natural world." Chota Baba nodded thoughtfully.

Cop-out, I'm not so sure. "Up here, aren't we avoiding the battle?"

"Show respect in your interactions with yourself, other creatures and plants and you'll see we are all interlocked in life's game."

Crickey, we're destroying so many evolutionary links! and here we are talking about self observation. "But things have already started to fall apart."

"....Yes. To understand this is to seek balance and to create a life which is just."

Blimey, I'm muddled. I want to do something, but maybe the old guy is right, maybe I need a bit more time sorting my head out?

Wow, November soon. Time in paradise passes quickly. Interesting. In the Zaminder's hell cell it clocked slowly. Dislike one and each hour drags, whereas the pleasant flashes past. How unfair. We'll have to leave the mountain soon. Have I found purpose? Possibly, for he was becoming a Yoga Zealot.

The two men were sat on their flat rock by the pond when Chota Baba lifted his hand. A single sound above the diminished waterfall, a breaking twig. Beside a rhododendron bush, green-yellow eyes, bright red tongue licking pale

247

cheeks, teeth glinting ivory, muscles rippling along a powerful back. The cat sauntered over, stopped within ten paces.

Satya trembled.

Chota Baba whispered, "It is seeking mountain goats driven downhill by the birth of winter above."

Terrified, Satya wished the man would shut up!

The forest leopard, huge, shook its head, looked at them. Satya's heart missed a beat, his body tensed in readiness for what instinct told was about to happen. A nervous swish of the tail, a ripple of flesh slipped along deep fur like water swelling across a pond's surface. The cat surveyed the two men it could kill without much effort. Satya's nerves were at breaking point.

Almost imperceptibly, Chota Baba rose. The leopard stretched its neck, yawned and as smoothly as it had arrived, it made an imperial exit, leaving large dimples in the grass. Satya's heart and body shook.

"Shiva! Jai Ho!" The yogi bellowed.

"Ssh!" What's he doing! The leopard will return!

"To see a leopard is a blessing."

"It could have eaten us."

"But it did not!" Chota Baba chuckled. "It came over the alps to our east, where Chandra's sister has her cave. A dangerous route, be warned. I once tried it after the rocky spine had iced over, but had to retreat badly bruised!"

Satya appreciated the power of the Himalayan sun. He was cold in the mornings as he crunched his frozen feet through the deep frost, yet upon sun splashed Flower Hill the rays warmed his body. He'd gape at Trishul with the improbable thought of Shiva and Julian dancing up there and peering down at him. "Chota Baba, why believe in reincarnation?"

"It is bred into us," Chota Baba chuckled. "But Trishul's trident isn't long enough to hold billions of us pining Hindus!"

Collecting dead wood for fires one afternoon, Chota Baba said, "It doesn't matter how and where you live your life, only that you do good and leave the world a slightly better place."

"That's the humanist's stance. Hence a punk can be a saint and a yogi a devil! But what is doing good?"

"For me it is being a herbalist, for you it might be creating inspiring art, Devi finds goodness in running her charity, Uma in being a mother and wife."

Hmm, how good to know a man who speaks from experience, rather than the illusive vagueness of No-Matter or the kind and knowledgeable Swami Prem who thinks from within the constraints of a traditional set of rules.

He said this and Chota Baba laughed heartily: "When we judge, it is an aspect of ourselves that we project. Listen with your heart to others, even those you consider idiots have their own knowledge. Never assume you know anything, be the wide eyed infant who is forever learning."

"Most Zen."

They laughed.

"We must shop," Chota Baba announced one morning. When the sun had melted the frosts they climbed Flower Hill, walked down its narrowing tail and faced the stone spine dividing their dark canyon from the one to the west. Satya edged his way forwards on his hands and knees, his fear a little less absorbing now he knew he could manage. They moved quickly down the grass steppes and reaching the three towering rocks, trotted along the drove track, greeting the last Tibetan traders returning north. They strode alongside wild Bhotia in woollen gowns on their way back from Tibet, their mules loaded with precious stones to sell in India's hill towns.

At the trading settlement a group of descending pastoralists were taking lunch whilst their huge herd of sheep, guarded by fierce mastiffs, swarmed the grasslands above the track. There was a group of pilgrims. Their long haired sadhu looked bloated with self-satisfaction, assuming the imagined airs and graces of an enlightened man, which made him appear untrustworthy. Satya was surprised to hear the group had walked to Shiva's holy Mount Kailash far off in Tibet.

Chota Baba advised Satya to maintain his distance, for people respected a sadhu's wish for silence. Satya was well used to being taken for an Indian... until he spoke. What did make him stand out, however, was his sketching. Having bought several plain paper schoolbooks, his fingers could not stop. He drew women bearing fresh vegetables and fruit from the village, they kicked off their sandals, washed one foot with the other at the spring, and he also traced their wet footprints across the busy plaza's flagstones.

In Chandra's shop he found a hand-coloured postcard from the mid 1940's of a flowery alp spread before Trishul. Few bought these cards hence the original stock was still being sold and on its yellowing back he wrote:

Dear Devi,

We are living in a lost garden with ancient junipers, a million flowers and a pool to swim in. So Zen, the Japanese would worship it. We've a comfortable hut set against a cave in which there's an underground spring. Looking today over the endless foothills and the distant plains, I think of you down there on your estate and wish we could have done this journey together.... *Love, Satya.*

Satya shoved his card in to the weather beaten post-box emblazoned with Queen Victoria's mark. Lone postmen still walked the remote mountain paths, delivering and collecting mail, tugging their pack horses through most weather.

Chota Baba left his dried herbs at Chandra's shop. After cups of tea and stuffed parathas, which Satya was glad to have, the two cave dwellers and Chandra walked back up the mountain bearing sisal sacks of provisions on their backs. Unlike Satya's and Chota Baba's thin robes, the gaunt Chandra wore suitable attire for those tempestuous mountains: homespun woollen jumper, Tweed waistcoat, jacket and trousers, each knitted and stitched by him and his family using cloth they'd spun from their own fleeces.

Satya walked ahead, letting the two men chat all the way along the horizontal track and up the long grassy slopes. They

250

arrived at the rocky chine an hour before the sun left it. With the sack in his hands, Satya was again terrified to cross. Noticing this, Chandra grabbed Satya's load and still bearing his own, walked over the spine as easily as Chota Baba had. Humbled, Satya edged forward on his knees. They washed under the waterfall, performed yoga on Flower Hill and sang Arti in the cave-hut as fresh village food warmed on the fire. Chota Baba chuckled, "Now I'm old, Chandra is my saviour. His shop supplies all I want and he refuses payment!"

"Baba, you pay me a thousand times over with your wisdom, and don't forget the time you saved my daughter. Satya, she was dying of pneumonia and Baba stopped the child killer."

"Chandra, you built this hut, without it, my days here would have ended years ago."

Chandra said, "Satya, I lived in this cave for three years before we built the hut. A winter gale once extinguished my fire and I moved to the depths beyond the spring."

"It's cramped in there, why not the Arti cave?"

"Our winter water's in here and it is also deliciously warm." All evening the two men shared memories.

When the morning sun had melted the frosts, with his empty sacks slung across his slender shoulders, Chandra strode back down the mountain with the look of a miserable child on the first day of the school year. Despite family, shop and village life, Satya perceived this was his haven.

They were resting on an elevated alp they'd not visited before, heavy bags of the last fresh herbs at their side. Satya watched the first vast bank of clouds in weeks drift from the faint smudge of the plains, roll across the forested ridges and stick between the peaks. Winter was approaching. They would be leaving soon. Would he be able to maintain his present calmness back in the real world? "From here the troubled world appears calm."

Chota Baba nodded, "The world will always be troubled. The trick is not to carry other people's weight on your

251

shoulders. Settle without effort in your inner silence and peace will be one thought away."

"I still can't see how in the midst of that chaos?" Satya waved at potential turmoil.

"Develop the sensuality habit. When stirring your tea, tug yourself from your thoughts by listening to the spoon-on-cup, watch the swirling liquid, smell the warm tea. Peppering each hour with such tiny moments eventually lets peace arise. Allow it to trickle into what you do or think. Rather than distracting you, it enhances your efficiency in each task you perform. Attention is the key to life!" the old man laughed. "When inattentive, we are shadows."

~~

With the first sprinkle of snow, Chota Baba took Satya down for another shopping trip. Bearing heavy sacks, they encouraged Chandra's loaded mule up hill. Fearful of a snow leopard or bear smelling the lone mule, the shopkeeper brought along three mastiffs and had to return quickly before nightfall. Satya and his teacher had spent weeks adding deadwood to older piles in a slit-cave used for timber storage. Satya asked why when there was already enough, Chota Baba replied: "It's an ancient tradition - help those who might over-winter here."

"Only you and Chandra would dare!"

"Others too, sometimes."

A snow peppered dawn, they quickly took their ritual wash beside the now ice-rimmed stream. They sang Arti and did yoga inside and ate breakfast. With his tongs, Chota Baba lifted a glowing ember, "You have learnt to calm your body and still your mind sufficiently to survive this hostile terrain. It will make you strong."

"Over-winter?"

With a tap of his tongs, Chota Baba split the large ember, placing one part in his lota, the other he symbolically lifted before Satya and sang, "May Agni illuminate your spirit and

252

take your thoughts to Truth!" He placed it carefully in the bright fire's centre.

Satya gawped in silence. The man's telling me to stay in the ice, yet I imagine walking with him through the chilling valleys, across the cooling plains. That's the sadhu's tradition. I dream of swimming in the Indian ocean. Lazing upon a beach with Devi, drinking coconut juice, doing yoga together as the sun settles over warm waves. I can't imagine surviving the intensity of a Himalayan winter, OK, Chandra did, but he's of this mountain, OK, Chota did, but he's a Gurkha. "Baba, I'll die!"

"Yes, if you're inattentive, but many have survived without this luxurious hut. With it, I have confidence you can."

"But...."

"Satya, we have played out our time together. Stay on for a while, to leave in haste will be to lose an opportunity."

"What opportunity? Truth, as you say, is simple, is everywhere, is not separate to ordinary life. Why stay?"

"To hone your mental blade."

"I'm hopeless at meditating!"

"Forget meditating! Being attentive is The Way. Forgetting this, people become fanatical about their system, their view. Draw, do yoga, cook, brush your teeth, keep your fire alive - all with attention. Make everything an artful activity. The market place will call you and it and it will teach you about real life. Discriminate, watch for each experience to reveal its own truth. Seek compassion in all situations. Knowing everyone is our teacher, try to understand and treasure all people, that is empathy. Develop empathy. It will stop you becoming harsh, fanatical. Love is not weak and floppy, that is sentimentalism. Compassion is calm, it listens, it finds a way forwards through common ground, it nourishes. Satya, may your future be bright!"

"No! I'll leave with you."

"We walk alone." Chota Baba stepped outside. A shaft of silver light illuminated Buddha's juniper. "Satya, if you are

253

stupid you will die here. Be attentive. Meet the many dangers of Himalayan winter-life without panic."

The speech's finality shocked Satya. There had been no inkling of this parting. Having boosted their over-night fire, they had laughed and bathed in the cold predawn light; over breakfast they had chatted, as they'd washed the dishes Chota Baba had played and sung and danced and nattered like a little boy. Such joviality was normal for the old yogi upon Trishul.

Satya walked through the snow splattered Zen garden with his strong old teacher. In the spotty snow at the crest of Flower Hill, the yogi looked more like a tatty slim Santa than ever. He stopped to give some practical instructions.

Satya wished to ignore the hint of parting forever. "We'll meet again."

"Satya my beloved, remember in your darkest hour this period is a treat, not torture. It is how we perceive things which matters, a rainy day is wonderful for farmers, but annoying for sunbathers. Jaia Shiva!" Chota Baba leaned into Satya and they hugged, father and son before a war. Stepping away, the old man looked up at Trishul's lashing ridge glowing in the silvery light. Minutes of silence. He raised his arms high and wide, bellowing, "Shiva!"

Satya watched the sadhu move downhill, along the widening blue tail, up the narrowing chine. At the summit Chota Baba turned, waved, disappeared.

Abandoned.

Nothing but sky.

Utter loneliness!

He began to weep silently. Why has my life come to this? Groomed to take over an ancient estate in gentle England and here I am facing a harsh winter with a rat in a Himalayan cave. It doesn't add up. What a stupid thing to be doing.

He rushed through the scatterings of snow, through the boulder-filled garden. At the cave-hut he quickly packed his things, put out the fire with water, secured the door, rushed up Flower Hill and down its far side. Leather bag tight to his chest, brushing aside falling snow, he edged his way along the

254

spine, glued to the cold rock. At the knoll, he stopped, regaining his breath with the world literally at his feet. I'm ready to return to life. And Devi. Yippie! The immensity of the scene awed him. Through the drifting snowflakes, Chota Baba, a dot in swathes of undulating grassland. The view made him hesitate, made something stir within. To leave is to fail.

Back at the hut, glad he had a lighter, he ignited the fire, chuckling at Chota Baba's Agni-tradition. Come evening, Satya felt a primitive fear. Winter was arriving. Alone, tucked into the side of one of the tallest peaks on Earth, he hardly slept, hearing the various noises as threats. Help, an avalanche! A hungry leopard! A starving bear bashing down the door? Oh Shiva! help me, a beast is on my roof! Inevitably when he checked, it was the wind. The tormenting wind.

In the morning, sunshine! He could escape! He ran to the chine, but snow coated the thin ledge. Help, I'll slip. Ha! by midday the sunshine will melt it. Nearing midday, from Flower Hill, he saw the sun just touched the chine which was coated in slippery snow. Help! It'll be spring before the sun warms it again. His escape impossible, he bellowed in fear, "I'm trapped!"

He sat down on Flower Hill's white summit and cried. Trembling with cold, he eventually rose and returned to his hut-cave. To get above self pity he read a passage from one of the diaries:

"It was mid winter and we were cornered by the Pathans, who are amongst the best fighting men in the world. They have no fear, believing death takes them to a heaven filled with virgins. You never know where they. Trapped, bitter in the Himalayan cold, we were in hell. Our rations were down and all we could find was a bag of mouldy grain in the half ruined barn we used as shelter from the bitting wind and bullets. Thank god there was a stream and a few dried branches which we used to cook the barley, our only food for a week. The tough Gurkhas never gave up, and each evening they sang their songs. When our food was gone we had no

option but to leave. We fought like scalded cats, khukuri's in
one hand, rifles in the other. Few survived."

Yes, many of my ancestors had it far worse and lived to
tell their tales. He started to relax. "Chota Baba's no fool and
he's confidence in me. I'm bound to be OK... he's shown me
how to cope. Ha, the devil! I have all those supplies. And a rat
as company!" He smiled at the sound of his own voice.

Drinking herb tea by his fire, he slowly faced his dilemma.
Others had survived. A winter is as nothing in the scheme of
things. If it grants me strength and contentment, it'll be worth
it. Contentment, after all, is accepting your situation. It could
be the most valuable thing I ever do. This's like entering
university, my subject - life in the cold and how it moves
around my mind.

ß

Noise within noise being swallowed by noise. The impression was total. The hut rumbled, the solid rock beneath shivered. The word *avalanche* locked in his mind. Which route would such a fury take? The echoing roar grew. An age of rumbling thunder. Total silence. Blinkin' heck!

Clutching his torch, he opened the door. Beyond the clear veranda, a wall of snow. Panic. I'll suffocate. How long till my fire dies out? Act fast. With a spade-cum-pickaxe and lit by the eerie glow, he dug for an hour before reaching the surface. When his head popped into the morning sunlight, he saw only a bit of backfill reached the veranda, leaving the hut and chimney free. The winter's first avalanche had created a long buff with a free zone running along the cliff, beyond this ridge the huge boulders and the pond had gone, leaving only one or two juniper with their verdant heads above the cover of white.

He worked hard to link his veranda to the cliff-walk, lastly he uncovered wood stacked on the veranda, some of which he took deep into his cave, beyond the burbling spring. It was late afternoon when, exhausted, hungry and thirsty, he sat with a mug of black tea and dipped into the barrel of emergency dried biscuits Chota Baba and he had made with nuts, dates, oats and honey. He made pan-fried barley cakes, smearing them with Chandra's jam.

Ignoring the sadhu's warnings, one morning Satya was clearing a route to Flower Hill when silent powder-snow gushed over the cliff, swept him off his feet. He flew with the flashing whites. It was quickly over. Instinctively, he gyrated, creating pockets of air, fighting snow crystals before they locked. Finding his legs, waist and lower back free, he struggled like a lizard, extracting himself backwards from his hole, his arms slipping through solid tunnels. His chin caught on a lip of ice. He was stuck. So this is it. An ignoble death frozen beneath Shiva's ice! Panic. No, it makes matters worse. His gasping lungs and pumping heart were trapping him and using up limited oxygen. Taking a deep Aikido breath, he relaxed, his head slipped sideways, his body slid out.

He stood up, but collapsed with his right knee burning. Humbled, humiliated, he looked around. Gosh, I've been carried across the haven, within four paces of the dramatic drop. Idiot! I could be a cold body deep in the gorge! Chota Baba had warned: "Straying beyond the cliff edge is dangerous."

He hobbled to the hut. From the safety of the cliff, he grew confident enough to sketch avalanches surging mid afternoon as the sun melted slopes far above. He had survived his worst nightmare. Life could continue, he had fire, water, food. With prudence I can cope. The simplicity - man working with nature, is thrilling, life is unreflected, there's no future - you take one hour at a time.

His open fire wasted energy, better build an efficient chai shop clay oven, with thick walls of stone and mud, placed central in the room to radiate stored heat. He was now able to cook without balancing pots on stones. He also made and hung a curtain with the sacking to keep the cooler cave-air from the hut-space. Satya craved the stash of dried dates and apricots secure behind the metal door, but following advice, kept them for weekly treats. He'd never paid much attention to taste, however, his simple meals became his entertainment and to enhance this he cooked three days without salt before adding it, on the last two days of the week he added another ingredient and the explosion of pepper or the burst of cumin turned his head. He taught himself to love the smell of tea and would linger, sniffing the steaming mug. When it was time for half an apricot on 'Seventh Day Heaven', he would sniff and nibble it and the sharp sweetness held him as he rolled each nip around his mouth.

The pond stone Chota Baba presented wasn't used for worship, rather, upon it Satya record the passage of days. Time, he discovered, is elastic. When he was busy chopping wood two hours would flit by, yet when he had nothing to do, each minute dragged. Hmm, absorption and emotion are the influencing factors.

Granting a touch of theatre to his peculiar existence, from deep within the cave every few days the field rat would emerge to restore its fat supplies. Following Hindu tradition, Satya left pinches of food from every meal when it emerged and Rattie would scuttle around without fear as he talked to it, its keen pink eyes and moving whiskers appearing to answer him.

The first section of cave behind the hut was big enough for Yoga, spot-jogging, Aikido training and there were periods when he could do nothing else, the outside being unapproachable for days. Changing space gave him a sense of freedom. During milder storms Satya walked the cliffside corridor to the womb cave. Lighting a second fire was wasteful, so he limited his time there, the fire quickly heated the small cave, although gusts invaded the narrow mouth. What primeval pleasure playing caveman, sitting on straw in a recess beside his fire, gazing out the entrance, imagining his flames keeping sabre-toothed tigers at bay. When sunny bouts arrived, attentive of the constant snow chutes and avalanches, he would run, walk and draw beside the towering cliff.

Leaving the womb cave for more firewood one afternoon, he spotted paw marks in the snow and froze. Being midwinter, this was the illusive snow leopard so perfectly camouflaged, almost impossible to spot, roaming frozen valleys faster than any other land animal, hungry, forever searching for small mammals and mountains goats. Or cave dwelling twits? A starving leopard with a body bigger than mine! Satya's pulse quickened. He retreated to the womb cave, lifted the pole-ladder and sat by his fire looking through the porthole at the white landscape devoid of leopard. Early one morning, with his head above the protective snow ridge, he saw a movement behind a sunken juniper. Two weeks later, again peering over the top, he watched the snow leopard stroll casually across the buried Zen garden, its big furry paws kicking up snow, strong head gazing over each rising and

260

falling shoulder. Caught outside, heart racing, Satya stood still as an icicle. The cat's lonesome yellow eyes took him in. Its twitching nostrils sniffed his meat. The soft thick fur of its body, cream dappled with honey, rippled in the breeze. Panting small puffs in the crystal air, it took several comfortable strides, and was gone. Perhaps the smell of woodsmoke on Satya's clothes warned of danger?

Though physically overcome with gladness, Satya was emotionally upset - few were the distractions in his white world and the cat's appearance had accentuated his loneliness. The vivid image of the majestic beast stayed in his mind for days, he woke thinking of it, wondering where it was, longing for, yet fearing its return. When they appeared out of nowhere, its fresh tracks always reminded him how isolated he was. The bounteous world was beyond his reach, depression gnawed at his mind. What a stupid place to be! It's the daftest of daft things to be doing! Oh to escape! Yet he couldn't. Not until the ice melted upon the rocky spine.

Gawd I'm bored. He had always been occupied: by Merricott's estate, at work, in the ashram; enjoying Devi's personality, stirred up by Tara, mulling over Julian's disturbing death and finally enjoying Chota Baba's charisma. Alone in the ice without even a leopard, only a damned rat, it dawned on him how little there was to do. What do you do when you have rekindled your fire, cooked your food, done your exercises and have no gaps left in your sketchbook? Hours, they turn, one after the other, each day a slow wheel with little change, week upon week. What good life alone in the world's highest mountains? The short days yawn in front of me. The long nights drag. The minutes crawl. Time is dull. He couldn't be bothered to always do his Yoga, exercises and 'Settling', but the emptiness their space left made him realise that in this mad existence he desperately needed them. Yet for days he couldn't lift himself. His 'Settling' sessions were mires of miserable negativity, even Yoga felt pointless, hence ineffective. What good 'Settling' when it does nothing to change my mood? Self-pity intensified. He had hut-fever. The cliff path was too limiting, he needed a walk. As if to further torture him, a tempestuous storm burst the sky apart, trapping him inside for days.

Reaching his limit one day, sure the darkness-within would kill him, he decided to go out whatever the consequences. Releasing the last of three catches, the door burst inwards, he was flung back by a storm streaming over the mountains. The fire's flame snuffed-out. Unable to stand, Satya clawed forwards, leaned against the door, pushing hard with his back. Slowly, slowly, it moved against the invisible giant, with a last shove the catch caught with a click unheard in the torrent of sound outside. He slid across the upper and lower bolts. How stupid - Chota Baba had warned him to listen out for the weather's tones.

Blowing the fire awake, he noticed the effort had invigorated him. Ha! happiness, depression, excitement, boredom - they are interchangeable mindsets. If you are healthy, you can move from one to the other, all it takes is wanting to. It was a Gestalt moment. His feet danced around his invigorated fire, his fists thrashed the iron-store-door, his body pranced into the cave, running deeper inside the mountain he drummed his flat hands on the spring-pool's surface.

"Eureka! I've survived!" Pouring with sweat, he sat down. But that's all I've achieved, I've not even touched my so-called soul.

ß

"I can't," Charles turned from Father. Damn it, he was only eight, why did the brute insist he strip off, run through the snow, swim across the lake and trot back barefoot?

"Stop being a wet. It'll toughen you up." Training his child Charles to be a soldier, Father used a calm, commanding tone, somehow intimate yet well projected, the confident voice of a man you dared not contest. Standing before the blazing kitchen range, a towel dressing gown draped over warm clothes, Charles' blue body would not stop shivering, despite Uncle Jack's constant rubbing.

Satya bit his lip. All his life he had blotted out his painful childhood, believing he had moved on from his past, so why did it pop up now? Would he go nuts? These visions were vivid and their unconscious power was frightening. In the isolating snows, without anyone to interact with, his inner life had become as real as his cave-world and he often had difficulty defining one from the other. With no warning the walls became the Zaminder's cell. The rapids pounded through the grill, the stink of his own faeces, the pain of the lathi, the welcome approach of death, were actual. His heart beat so fast he wondered if he would have a heart-attack.

"Don't be stupid, these are the devils the Buddha warned of!" he cackled to himself. He'd read an article explaining the mind is unable to distinguish between an imagined reality and the situation itself, the rope becomes the snake. He'd also read the gripping books of the Lebanese hostages, Terry Waite, John McCarthy and Brian Keenan, who'd been wracked by visions. Visions, the currency of the religiously inspired, no more than what those in solitary confinement experience. Chota Baba had said, "Visions are waking dreams, they're only your subconscious unravelling."

Satya knew tumbling thought is not to be shunned, as many meditators assume, but to be embraced. What we see as cascading thought is electrical charges flying along highways whose closeness enables them to spark with each other, generating interconnectedness. Its near-chaos enables us to instantly recall sunsets and people we shared them with. Oh Indra! To hear your talk!

Primal in his loneliness, he began to listen to the sounds reverberating around him: the crackling fire; the eddies of wind outside; his body: breath, heart-beat, grunts. But it was his voice which amazed him most. At first, to keep himself company, Satya chanted refrains. One of his London compatriots, an expert on the human brain, had explained certain sounds can affect the structure of cells in the mind and can change the pathways of thought. Inspired, he became absorbed in the swelling sound within his cavern. He experimented by rolling out consonants, vowels, guttural animal sounds and Vedic mantras, thankful nobody but the possibly worried rat could hear. The notes grasped and locked with thoughts, slowing them. He even saw Shiva surrounded by Himalayan sages. What fun! Lost in his cave, he began to understand the benefits of ritual. Chota Baba was right, ritual, even Shiva, were the yogi's friend, but nothing more.

In Chota Baba's company, celibacy had not been an issue. Alone with the snowstorms, Satya pined for Devi to warm his heart and he wished to feel her against his flesh. At night his sleeping mind conjured up a string of fantasies in which most women he'd met came to him. They began arriving in clutches when snowstorms pounded the mountain, perhaps the cleaner on one side and the woodchopper before him. Sometimes he'd relive that strange night with Tara, or the cleaner refused to leave him alone, or Uma would sweep his skin with her passing shape. In the daytime his women, including Devi, would talk about the rat, the snow, the ice, the weather, Chota Baba or the old man's 'Settling' technique.

He could clearly smell the cleaner's soaps, Tara's bhang, Uma's smoky coconut, Devi's freshness. Why, when smell is a sense I've ignored? The question opened a disturbing memory. Father gripped him by the hair, forcing his two year old nose into his own accidental puddle glistening on the kitchen's ancient slate flagstones. And, blast it! Father took

Satya's phantom women into the back of the cave, their lustful yelps drew Mother's anguished face close, reminding Satya how she bore the man's affairs. Charles shook his shoulders, attempting to rid himself of Father's steel-hard smell. The man used little soap - a military habit picked up in Afghanistan where Pashtun fighters could detect soap as you hid in ambush.

Day upon day these phantoms left their allure in the air. He drew in the cleaner's street-wise skin, Tara's sharpness, Uma's homeliness. Devi's assured aroma. He extricated his being from these wonderful wraiths, chastised himself, tried to 'Settle', but female smells and touches lingered upon his skin, making his tissue ache for more and some lovely form reappeared and played with his wakening body. They moved around the fire as he cooked, they sat in his lap, Parvati dancing Shiv alert. They laughed gaily in his satiated ear. Anguished, he rushed away bellowing abuse as he tried to push the still clinging forms from him.

The poor rat.

Panting, snarling, out of control, any 'thing' could rise and latch onto him. In despair, he sought tasks as distraction, but there was little to do. Satya tried to empty his mind with half an hour of Special-Forces speeded-up yoga until his body was wet from exertion. Yet Father glared at him when he sipped his tea too loudly, scalded him for speaking when the rat had not yet spoken to him, berated him for being lazy. Satya laughed when Father got twisted in knots trying to copy speed-yoga, in the old man's day yoga had been: "For wets", Father's stern, cold eyes burned Satya.

Quiet, stiff Mother, ever fearful of her husband, snapped at Satya who quickly recoiled from her sad visage. He tried talking with her, desperate to understand her, but she wasn't interested. Nothing new there. Why such coldness from your beloved mother? He spun in spiralling thought patterns, asking, asking, never getting an answer, erecting his SOS to protect his heart. One morning when a tempest threw snow about, he sat by the hut fire watching his cold parents bicker. And the rat? Yes, why didn't the rat defend Satya? He was going mad, he thought, then he remembered these hallucinations were usual in such situations.

Mother poked Satya's nose, exclaimed, "Ugh!" Father's dominance must have made her life difficult, even though they inhabited different wings of Merricott. Terrified of upsetting them, he had been a model son, an apology of himself. From them he learned few social skills and this awkwardness made him a loner. Perhaps driven me to become a fanatic up a frozen mountain seeking a weird mirage called Rat, oops, Truth? In his last moments, had Julian found Truth or oblivion? Poor Julian! Satya's mind kept reliving that last night. A life so spirited so easily snuffed out…. He cried.

Emotional moments at his boarding school consumed him and he relived being psychologically bullied for not being socially relaxed. Or for having a permanent Mediterranean suntan. He choked with anger at the injustices of the autocratic teachers who inhabited his cave. Disregarding Chota Baba's sound advice to 'Watch dispassionately', he'd shout, "Go Sir! I'm here to clear my head, not to dwell in my past." He'd quickly stand up, perform a few yogic postures and attempt to relax with slow, deep breathing. The teachers laughed.

One morning huddled by his glorious fire while ice pounded the slates above, Satya saw a hibernating wasp crawl from a hole in a warming log. Gosh, its perfect stripes are vulnerable by the blazing flames, its wings are as fine as gossamer, as fragile as the human heart. He sighed.

Backlit by lucent spring sunlight pouring through handsome Victorian sash-windows, a wasp seeking freedom. Charles reached forwards, but the phone on his desk rang, he skipped back. "Charles Merricott. Ha, Sir."

Scratching notes across the thirty handwritten pages of the report he had completed the day before, Charles' eyes flitted back and forth from the neatly written pages to the irritated wasp.

"The Chichi's seen a wasp!" guffawed a tight voice from a desk to his right. Choking on his aristocratic tongue, Dominic rose to mimic Charles' athletic prance, as he once used to do at their reputed school, and, as they too had done at school, the all-male audience cachinnated. Dominic rolled a newspaper as he moved theatrically towards the imposing windows, his puffy face full of self-satisfaction.

Charles mumbled into the phone, "But sir, the report is aimed at the public." Laying down his pencil, he opened a drawer, lifted a solidified rubber which must have lain there for fifty years. He had always wondered when he'd find a use for it.

"Merricott you've wandered off...."

Charles lifted his right hand, "Ruminating, sir."

All faces in the room were focused on Dominic, their hero for no other reason than being the son of an Earl. Charles, merely a Merricott, mocked for being of ancient Saxon lineage, not, as some of his tormentors, directly linked to Norman nobles who conquered England only a thousand years ago, snapped his wrist and his missile soared.

A shriek. The newspaper fell. "Who the heck?" Dominic rubbed his shoulder.

The phone demanded, "What's going on Merricott?"

"Sir, let's drop proposal 32a."

"Umm. Ha... wonderful! You do think out-of-the-box, Merricott, that's what we value you for - and of course your dedication and excellent work. Well done. Good chap!"

Dominic's gross frame loomed over Charles' desk. Fleshy fingers grabbed the obligatory fountain pen the department insisted on. Biros were banned, for the office rule was - first draft in ink, not typeface. Hayling argued it improved thinking to write long-hand. Charles quickly jabbed his pencil on the fat hand. "Next time it'll be the sharp end."

"Sorry, Merricott?"

"The sharp end is paragraph 46. Do excuse me, Sir, nature calls." Charles put the phone down and rose to face his assailant. "Dominic, insects have rights too."

Charles walked to the window, slid up the sash frame and guided the wasp into the fresh air and the creature flew towards the bright spring trees in St James's park. Turning

268

round, he saw Dominic undo an ink bottle and pour the contents over the handwritten report. Charles ran, leapt, crashing the portly bully to the ground. Dominic bellowed, writhing on his back, his flapping hand inadvertently sprinkling dark blue ink across his handmade rust-pink shirt and bespoke pin-striped grey suit, and splattering Charles' Savile Row trousers.

Utter silence. It was unthinkable that anybody, let alone the unpopular Chichi Charles, aristocratically endowed as he might be, should dare confront the son of an Earl. Even in twenty-first century London.

A door banged opened. Bearing the only photocopy of Charles' report, Hayling stopped. A pungent hesitation. "Merricott! My office, now."

"Only me, Sir?"

Hayling focused, neck forwards. "Merricott you upstart! I'm posting you to Lagos."

The public humiliation! Charles' social position was superior to Hayling's. Something inside snapped. "You forgot to chastise the office TWIT, Sir."

"Don't SIR me, Merricott! Follow me!" Hayling stormed stiffly out of the large office, snapping his heels over the parquet floor, copying the Prussian officer the man's great great grandfather had been. Marvelling at how quickly they had closed ranks, Charles acknowledged he'd always been the odd one out. He walked out to the chant of, "Chichi Saxon Charles! Chichi Saxon Charles!", which Hayling chose to ignore.

Hayling, sat behind an expanse of highly polished mahogany, laid the photocopied report squarely within the leather writing surface. He constantly aligned it as he spoke. "Surely after six years you should have settled in, Merricott ?"

For the first time in his life Charles was fired to speak for himself. It was a eureka moment. "In those six years this is my first reprimand. You have continually said my work is more than satisfactory, outstanding is the word you have sometimes used. Rebuke Dominic who makes all the mistakes the rest of us cover up, Sir."

Faced with reason, Hayling backed off momentarily. However, comprehending the weight of social pressure, he snapped himself Prussian straight. "Stop before you go too far, you whippersnapper."

"Insulting an innocent man twice, and once in public, is that not too far, Sir?"

"Beg your pardon?" Hayling spitting mad.

Nothing would stop Charles. "Rejecting one of your most loyal workers to side with a useless pedigree pup."

Hayling's face puffing red, "You're off to Lagos!"

Charles laughed, "Ho, Hayling, you are silly." Nobody ever called the man anything but Sir.

"That's it! Lagos!"

Charles spun round, paced his way down endless corridors, heading towards the back door. Outside, his leather soles cracked on gravel. He dodged the traffic, stepped into St James' park and followed a paved path to the duck pond where he slumped heavily on a bench, staring blankly at the water's surface for an hour. Without thinking, his eye followed a man he knew.

"Perfect morning, Charles. Not at work?"

"In need of fresh air, Julian. You?"

"Charles, I detect fury. Tell me."

Charles revealed all.

Julian's long Jewish nose pointed upwards. "Quit work. Your ancient farm alone is a great life-project! Peering at traffic from my bedroom above my parents' shop, I'd envy your life. Charles, you'll die one day and your part in humanity's self-absorbed machinery will be filled by equally able people, ad-infinitum."

Charles looked more closely at his friend. "Julian, your clothes..."

"Returning from court on Friday, I found a note. My wife's gone off with a flamenco guitarist. Gay as I am, I loved her. I was faithful too. Closing the door, I walked into the sunset wearing this suit. I soon discovered I'd left my wallet and keys on the kitchen table, stunned, confused, I slept on this park bench. The next morning, I thought what the heck, there was no more reason to be earning vast sums. I kept walking and over the past four days I've discovered Londoners help the destitute. It's been a liberating time. Charles, without the minuscule worries which infect our daily lives, LIFE is truly alive." Julian chuckled before continuing. "Remember our schoolboy discussions about humanity's occupation with trivia? How we laughed at the endless round of civilisations which rise, achieve great heights and decline into the dust? We laughed because they failed to learn from history! That's each person's failure too." The barrister summing up his case.

Charles looked at his childhood friend, reflecting on their differences. Julian's Jewish parents struggled, running a popular hardware shop to pay for an exceptional education, whereas his had hardly noticed the school fees. Julian had been one of the brightest lads in their world renowned school, but wasn't accepted because of his background. Charles was vaguely accepted because of his blood and land, yet even though he excelled at sport and was a determined, plodding scholar, his skin colour, acceptable in foreigners, shoved him, an Englishman with a difference, into the reject-group Julian dominated with his wit and charm.

Charles was unsure about quitting work, he never gave up and he had given himself to the Foreign Office. But Julian had given him an idea. He stood up, "Julian, I'd better go."

"Treat me to dinner."

"At eight?"

Charles sped across the park feeling lighter and plotting revenge. Quite unlike him. It was five-fifteen, most suited workers, including the blundering Hayling, would have left and within minutes cleaners would be moving down the long corridors. Charles dashed across the busy road. Looking over his shoulder at each turn, he scurried up a rear flight of stairs and through the labyrinthine passages. No one had seen him. Outside his batch of offices he checked none of the cleaners were about and slid through the door. He switched on

Hayling's and Dominic's computers. It made him nervous that they took forever to rev-up. When their screens arrived, running back and forth between the two offices, he tapped in the office's password for the day. Entering a secure site on each computer, he found a linked folder and flipped back through spreadsheets until he got to the date he wanted.

Charles whispered to himself. Keeping a tally on a sheet of A4 paper, navigating a host of sites, files and folders, he changed figures, fiddling several accounts, cleaning up balances, redistributing an ever increasing sum of money back and forth between accounts, masterfully masking his electronic passage by using a hidden holding post: one of the two Swiss accounts he'd inherited from each of his parents. Usual practice. Many official dealings abroad worked through anonymous numbered accounts to hide what the government of the day was up to on an international level.

Panting from shuttling between rooms, he whispered, "Hayling and Dominic are clots, they won't work this mess out." Charles was shifting extra mural expenditures, in other words entertainment bills, to him an abuse of tax payer's money. Amongst many extravagances, Dominic had hired a Michelin Star chef and lux-yacht on the Thames for a champagne and jazz party; Hayling had entertained his wife and four 'clients' (friends?) and their wives for a weekend 'conference' (fun?) at The Savoy Hotel. Honourable to the core, Charles intended to shift these sums to worthy causes, leaving Hayling and Dominic looking like fools for their mismanagement. Charles chuckled, "The 'Nairobi Harambee' project will be elated, that scheme in Palestine, the Romanian...."

His delightful cleaner's buckets clanged. "Oh no!" He couldn't be seen! Calm and masterly, he found rapid routes out of the many sites and securely switched off both computers. Gathering his notes, panting, he tiptoed rapidly to a back door. Closing it, he heard the enjoined-offices' main door open and the cleaner's trolley clank inside the cluster of rooms.

He leapt down the rear staircase. Casually walking to the darkening park, it struck him: "Damn! I forgot to move those vast sums from my Swiss account! I'll be imprisoned." He ran back and wove craftily through the corridors to his office. An alarm started ringing. Security began shouting, "Evacuate immediately!"

Soldiers at the main gate were used to him working late and hardly glanced up as he moved with the small group exiting. It was six-twenty. He must return before the office's daily passwords changed at eight o'clock. Thirty-five past, returning, he found the building surrounded by police, "A bomb threat, sir. The whole place's being searched."

They were still there at six-fifty. Seven-fifteen. Seven thirty-nine. Five to eight and he too late.

Panicking, he reached St James's park and ran like fury, yelling into his own wind, thumping the cast-iron lampposts, stumbling about like an angry fool. Panting, he sat on his favourite bench beside the pond, staring at the ducks. In the dimming light Charles didn't noticed his old friend arrive. Babbling, he told Julian everything, and questioned his acclaimed friend for legal advice. "How long till I'm found out?"

"Sounds like you've covered your tracks. Tricky one though, could go either way. To ensure your safety, flee Britain tonight. I'll post your letter of resignation, citing Dominic, Hayling, Lagos and all. Let's find Uncle Jack, he'll know how to arrange things."

Upon the train out of London, Julian said, "Charles, the world is now yours to explore. It will teach you," his soothing voice became sharp, "if you're willing to listen."

Charles was uneasy. Until this evening his life had been predictable: work, Aikido, rugby, reading the Indian diaries, galloping Flika with the dogs dashing alongside, Merricott's problems, and dear old Uncle Jack. He shivered, "But Julian, I wonder what life will show me."

Julian sparkled with mischief, "What you know and what you believe is merely your view of things, and this holds you from seeing clearly."

"Gosh." Charles recognised the quote, but couldn't place it.

Satya sat back with a start, blinking himself back to the cave. How extraordinary these visions. Julian's words kept rolling around the cave, echoing as if his dead pal was sat beside him. Dear Julian. Gawd, I miss you.

Visions! When the cover of rationality is drawn back and our undermind reveals itself with all of the complex fictions it has woven into truths. Although used to hallucinations, his old fear of being caught and imprisoned bounced back. But if they had been after him, surely he and Uncle Jack would have known by now. Furthermore, how could he repay his accidental crime? The sum stolen had started amazingly big for 'entertainment expenses'. With two years' compound interest, it's now huge. What can I do with this constantly increasing cash?

Tired of three months against the cliff, one calm and bright apres-dawn in February, wearing his warmest clothes Satya left his safety zone. He crunched past the tallest juniper heads rising from the encrusted snow, at the plunging lip of his bowl-like haven he took in the gorge's darkness and admired the frozen ridge which blocked out the mountains. He rose through the crispy snow to the top of Flower Hill and let himself be enthralled by Trishul's duvets of snow. Majestic waves, each line precise, each colour shift from white to blue, each sound lost in the enormity of space.

The air's warming! He did a skip. I've survived winter! Survived insanity! He yelled with joy. After this he could do almost anything, life itself did not appear too difficult. Truth was within his grasp. How powerful he felt!

ß

He woke shivering to his core. Disoriented, confused, he tried to work out where he was. It was dark, incredibly dark. His fire had gone out without a glint, which meant hours had passed since its last flicker. Why was he leaning against the wall wrapped in blankets? Ha, doing Chota Baba's 'Settling' I fell into a trance upon a tropical beach.

Where was the lighter he'd kept for such a moment? Scuffling around with his hands, wow they're cold, golly the wooden floor's cold, so what am I looking for? Ho yes, the lighter. Am I lighter? Ha, the fire's dead. Dead? No, I'm alive, well I think I am, therefore I'm not? Fire? Lighter! Ho yes, find it! How little he knew the layout when blind, ergo, why bother, easier to lay back and sleep. Ho, I'm sleepy, and he drifted back to his sunny beach.

Whoo, I'm cold. The fire, my fire! Light it! Fumbling in the dawn light, he found his mother's leather bag. Clumsily unzipping the front pocket with chilled fingers, he could hardly distinguish between the objects inside. What'm I seeking? Truth? The truth is I've no idea. Ho, fire, but it's gone somewhere, perhaps I could follow it and find a warm beach.

Golly gawd it *is* cold!

His fingers gripped a cylindrical object. Lighter? Heavier? Who cares. Let's try. Try what? Flick it. Solid fingers unable to spark it. He tried again and he tried once more, but failed. What a bother, why keep trying? Heck the cold! What a fool to have let my lifeline go out. How long will it take for the bitting air to kill me? Kill who? I'm disorientated, it's hypo-something, oh yes, thermia, yes, I'm suffering the initial stages. Weary, struggling to keep awake, unable to concentrate, hallucinating.

Bright sun slanted through the cracks around the window's shutter. There's no kindling! Lighting pages torn from his last sketchbook, he puffed and puffed, encouraging the flame to start. But failed; the paper hadn't enough body. This recent line of Agni totally dead.

It's warm outside. He dragged his stiff, complaining body out. Why bother? Surely the effort's damaging me? Better stay inside. Drift off. Woke, realised he needed the sun's warmth, got as far as the brightly lit porch and lay upon warming wood. What bliss the southern sun, even at altitude. He drifted in and out of sleep, woke in a sweat, threw off the duvet and was energetic enough to think of food. Easily moved inside, ate emergency biscuits, gobbling as if he had to eat fast before something stole his supply. Thirsty, he gulped down cups of water at the spring.

"I must get the fire going!" Stamping over the snow, he went to the firewood-cave and gathered chips, splinters, bark, dried moss, anything small enough to light the kindling. This time the fire lit easily. "My Lighter-Guru!" He mock-worshipped the plastic cylinder Chota Baba had laughed at, kissed it and chuckled, "Jai Ho! Plastic-Agni!"

Hypothermia had lowered his resistance. Streaming nose, non-stop coughing, headaches, sore eyes, weak as a squeak; crawling to fetch drinking water required will power although thirst itched his throat; feeding the fire was an equally difficult imperative. Days in bed, a zombie hardly able to think. Thank goodness he'd recently cooked emergency biscuits. Upon recovering from the virus, he noted he wasn't himself. Blast, torpor induced by illness has created depression.

He needed company, "Hello Rat, do you get depressed in winter?" The scuttling rodent hesitated, shivered its whiskers, ate the titbits, scurried off. Obviously!

Thoughts, he saw, clung together to form moods. When in tight enough clusters, their internal vortex created depression. By sidestepping these sinking whirlpools, he found they became less forceful. Whohoo! we can be masters of our mental worlds! Survivors of devastating destruction who'd lost all they knew after tsunamis, wars or hurricanes, were taught to rise from depression by stopping every few minutes

277

to look at, without interpreting, something's intrinsic beauty - the shape of a twig or, perhaps light falling on a wall. Hmm, drawing, you admire the object you capture on paper. I stopped drawing when space on my pages ran out, so I'll use charcoal on smooth yellow marble. Working hard, understanding the hand to eye co-ordination stimulates the mind, the images were pure, created by a mind able to be with things without distraction. It's so liberating wiping them clean each time.

Alert drawing, attentive yoga, trotting on the spot, all enhanced by Chota Baba's 'Settling', helped him rise from the dank mind spaces. All winter he had dipped into Devi's Zen text, the single book he had carried up. It claimed those who realise the Essential are alive to what happens, rather than existing within habitual responses, as most of us do. Religion bothered Satya, but Zen was practical, unencumbered by magical tales, yet it was austere, shunning the vast history of human thinking and culture. "Rat," he pondered, "where is Zen's music, fiction, adventure?" The mind thrives on imagination, OK, there has to be a balance - too much and you live within distorted mindsets, "Like some religious types, Rattie."

The rat peered back from the wisdom of nature, and Satya continued. "Rat, Chota's 'Settling' is flexible, can be done anywhere, at any time, it relies on no system, but it must be tempered with empathy for others, including rats!" He giggled and the rat twitched its nose.

"Rat, Uma knows this!" The rat's eyes glinted.

Inspired by Uma's grace, purposefully slowing his movements, he 'Settled' as he worked, encouraging himself to find contentment in small things. Yet it wasn't always easy. In difficult moments, weather permitting, he made snow sculptures. The first were crude people, animals, houses, things beyond the mountain haven, but as his expertise grew he created abstract forms. The sensuality of moulding snow helped him appreciate his hands. "Rattie," Satya chuckled when back by his fire, "I'm discovering a contentment-driven hedonism, rather than a novelty oriented one. Nor Tara's

278

philosophy-driven hyper-sensuality, but savouring the ordinary senses. What else is there but what we experience?"

Months of snowstorms and sunny spells ended with sleet. Freezing at first, but as the days turned it warmed to slush and finally rain. "Up here, early spring is dangerous," Chota Baba had warned.

Standing in the warming sun striking the protected path, Satya heard Shiva stirring upon Trishul's cyclopean slopes. Swathes of snow slid over the yellow cliff. The ground shuddered, his hut shivered and shook as all sound, all thought, all sensation froze within the great noise. He fled inside. One noon the iced-up waterfall melted trickle by trickle and early one evening the ice-dam above it cracked and grumbled. The following afternoon in a disarray of din, it burst, streaming a messy flash-flood of ice and snow over the cliff and this turbulent fury gushed between quivering junipers and sturdy boulders. Satya was thrown into the cold commotion by a splash from falling ice. Frozen, terrified he'd be taken over the edge, he clung to a clump of junipers. Scrabbling against the current, clutching and clawing, he moved through the shallows. Shivering, from a safe distance he watched the monster gush over the lip as a knotty torrent half as wide as the garden. Ha! That explains the stretch of bare rock!

The onslaught and the rain consumed the slumbering snow. Days later the waters became a manageable torrent. Within two weeks, almost everything was bared and after months in the white, Satya was in dreamland. On a boulder, he etched noble junipers, emerald shrubs, bulbous rocks and swathes of flattened flaxen grasses, in their centre, an ice-island baring a pebble moved about the revived pond. Delighted, he walked up Flower Hill, down the far side and along its blue tail. Before him lay the icy spine which the intense sunshine was melting. Thrilled, he pined for the world at the end of this deadly shaft. Four days later the spine was warm and dry. Ignobly shuffling along the dark arrette on his knees, he reached the gnarled knot and worked his way round

279

the slate. The dropping land rolled on and on, the countless crumpled hills stretched towards the faint hint of the northern plains, and held him captive for two hours.

Long entrapped within his haven's limits,
A babe emerging from the womb.
Free at last! He could leave.
Flee to Chandra's shop,
hear human voices.
Oddly, he felt
no urgency.

In those days of high altitude spring, Satya sat on a sunny rock beneath Buddha's ancient pool-side juniper watching life return. After his outstretched penalty of eye-blinding ice, leg-freezing air, mind-numbing inactivity and shrunken diet, he was a hippie tripped-out on sunshine, colour, movement, sound and taste. His mind could hardly keep up with uncurling ferns and sprouting shoots. Within days astonishingly bright shrubs carpeted Flower Hill. Rodents rose from hibernation, rushing through tunnels within the snow-yellowed grass, scurrying, creating nests, even the rat left the security of the cave-hut to find a mate. In response to this mammalian activity, raptors soared overhead, seeking, hovering, diving with deadly accuracy, flapping off in awkward horizontal flight from the dropping slopes, clutching pitiful creatures struggling in their claws.

Satya etched a snake wriggling mid-air, its mid-drift gripped by honed talons. Did it arrive recently from below, or do they hibernate at this altitude? Two minutes before he'd watched it strike and devour a large rodent, which had made it too slow to escape the eagle. It and its meal were now the feast. Smaller birds arrived and they darted here and there, snapping up innocent insects which had woken from winter to become food. Impossibly quick lizards were the insects' other demise.

Shocked but enthralled by the busting abundance and slaughter, he realised, not thought, that Darwin was right about the survival of the fittest - every beast eats something else. Life is harsh. Transfixed, any space in his previous paper sketches were splattered with flies, butterflies, voles, shrews and their various hunters. Chota Baba's face, for example, became a psychedelic mess. He'd drawn an ant, catching it's bright eyes, antennae and legs. So perfect a little creature!

And the noise! As with smell and taste, before his cave-life, he'd rarely been attentive to sound. After the silence of the snows where the wind was a novelty, Satya was in rapture. Each dawn he woke to cheerful songbirds unknown to him, all day their tunes played across the garden, rising over the buzzing of bees and the low hubbub of other beasts and all underwritten by the water's flow. This private concert was amplified by the curving yellow cliff. His diet exploded with nutty tubers, aromatic onion plants, and after a month, an abundance of legumes, including the wild spinaches, cresses and salads Chota Baba had pointed out.

The longer, warmer days steadily strengthened Satya's body and mind. He was on holiday in heaven with no desire to leave. He stopped washing in cold water at the back of the cave and with a pot of fire-warmed water he washed at the start and end of each day, enjoying the sensation upon his skin. The odd storm would sweep up, leaving powder snow which quickly melted. He understood why this natural bowl had been singled out: if you could survive the winter, (and I have!) almost all you needed was here: spectacular weather between occasional storms, an abundance of food, pure spring water, shelter, even a swimming pool... and in modern times, a shop nearby.

In an emotional moment Satya shook his head. Global Warming and habit destruction threaten and here I am lingering upon a mountain! Polar ice has never been so low, Polar winters are as warm as Polar springs used to be, yet humanity ignores this and carries on as normal! I'm part of this stupidity. I don't know what I can do. Is that a cop out?

Heralding summer's imminent arrival, the sky filled with migrating storks, eagles, geese which soared across the foothills as they headed for the enormity of Tibet, Mongolia, Siberia. Later, flocks of ducks were announced by rasping

281

calls, faint at first but gradually growing as arrows of the intrepid birds manifested in the sky.

Should he wait here until the birds' return in October? He longed for Chota Baba who over the winter had become his Buddha Myth. The weeks rolled on with him living in the moment, 'Settling' into himself. He watched shadows flow across the garden, the golden rock be tainted by the bounding waterfall. He sat, listening, watching, at one with nature. He stood with the Buddha juniper whose bark glowed dull red, whose branches were alive with green shoots, knowing it, rather than thinking about it.

One day a tingling spread from his chest to encompass his entire body.

My thoughts, moods, my traits, they drift past like clouds. Stuffy-old Charles, experience-driven Ewan and navel-gazing Satya still roam my mind, calling for attention, but no longer dominate. An immensity hangs between these personae I once created and yet I still exist. In this firmament, it's bliss! Contentment emanates from my pores. My body feels like a temple.

He treated it with detached care as if it were another being.

Without the usual distractions which plague humanity, he was able to retain this state of purity for weeks and what ever he did was done with grace. Was this a result of the burst of spring or the inner growth he'd attained over-winter? Who cares. Things are as they are, and they're truly stunning.

He had little urge to draw, but did so to keep his self-imposed routine running. One evening in a small gap between drawings he wrote: *'Rattie has fled and I share my thoughts with no one. Not even the smallest desire taunts me, my attention is here, I am calm.'*

After breakfast one morning, Satya noticed his supplies were dangerously low. He had no interest to visit the shop, but before a rogue snowstorm blocked him in, more than herbs were needed to stave off starvation. Carrying two hessian sacks and his wallet, he skipped down the reviving grassland, loving the exercise, singing to the sky, blissful in

282

his new state of mind. Meeting Tibetan traders and their line of loaded yaks upon the horizontal trail rendered him speechless; respectful of hermits, they bowed reverentially. Legging his way jauntily round the enormous bluff, lost in his peace, the eventual sight of the bustling trading hamlet awed him. Dumfounded, inside the shop he nodded at Chandra, who quietly filled the sacks with the usual supply of dried goods. Having taken the requisite sum Satya insisted on paying, Chandra bade him sit outside the nearest restaurant. Satya quietly enjoyed the luxury of a bench and table, how easy and practical after the floor. With his taste buds in overdrive after months of black tea, he mindfully consumed a cup of milky ginger-tinged tea and three honey sweetmeats.

Chandra came out, sat down, stared purposefully at Satya. "This afternoon I was to walk up and tell you bad news which arrived yesterday evening," the man looked beaten.

"Yes?" The World with its troubles seemed irrelevant.

"A trader from the market town said two weeks ago at Yat Tal, Chota Baba was killed by a leopard."

Satya gawped at Chandra. In an instant, his peace fled. He rose, moved absently from the busy plaza and along the trading track. Stepping down into the forest, he sat upon a fallen tree and wept uncontrollably. I've lost my father, brother and friend. Eventually, he realised Chota Baba would have been unimpressed by tears.

It was a long, heavy journey back to his mountain haven. In amongst a dense thicket of juniper there was a sound in the undergrowth. Satya stopped dead. Has Chota's killer-cat returned to higher hunting grounds with the taste of human flesh? Chota Baba felt no fear when the leopard came to our haven, yet, regardless, the Yat Tal leopard killed him. To it, to the python, we are easy meat.

Fear coursed through Satya. He dropped his shopping, climbed a tree to its top, aware leopard slept in trees, and sat there for half an hour, listening, listening. No sound but the faint breeze. Feeling foolish, he clambered down. Damn it, facing death, three years of yogic training honed by winter in

283

a cave have come to this - fear! Yow, if you are not insane, instinct over-rides discipline.

He continued the weary task of moving up the mountain slopes with his heavy goods and heavy heart. Had the old man been able to maintain Swami Prem's supposed peace in the midst of pain?

Knees on the rock spine, he gingerly pushed one sack across the gap, repeated the manoeuvre for the second load. He looked across the haven. How harsh, remote, dangerous it now seems. Chota Baba's distant presence had made this mountain bearable; without the wise and cheerful old herbalist, there was loneliness. His reaction, immensely human, was ego-driven. Thought I'd gained some sort of freedom from my ego, it was obviously based on the presence of one man.

Dear Chota Baba. What a horrific death; more fitting to have fallen off the rock-spine at the end of his last visit. How unfair. Life is made up of random events that we try to make sense of. A Hindu might say it was karma, the ex-Gurkha paid for those four deaths. Rubbish, that's warped logic propping up belief. A hungry cat ate meat - the Law of the Jungle! People suffer; somebody dies each minute of each day, they're young, old, sick, healthy.

Conflicting thoughts rampaged, tearing apart his emotion, shivering his chest, shaking his muscles. The depression he'd known earlier returned and struck hard. Devastation gripped him, numbed his mind. My extraordinary peace and joy have fled; emotion rampages. I'm so, so angry!! Schiezer! I've everyone I've loved - Julian, my parents, now Chota Baba.

All the pent-up hostility he had purposefully buried the morning after Julian's burial exploded. He yelled, he hollered, he screeched, he blew every nerve, allowing the immense sound of emotion to echo about the haven and drift into the vastness around it. He threw stones at the rock face, he lifted and shoved an immense boulder into the pond. He kicked Buddha's old tree until his foot hurt. Broken, he sank to its base.

Gradually, over two hours, his temper cooled. The storm was over. Weak, empty, a wreck, he slumped against Buddha's tree and slept. With sunset, Chandra arrived. Having warmed the curry the shopkeeper had brought, they sat talking about Chota Baba without sleep until dawn. From the top of Flower Hill Chandra proclaimed to the rising sun, "Chota Baba always acted with compassion. That alone makes a person great."

Gripping the rocky knot at the far end of the spine, Satya said, "I hope people aren't going to turn Chota Baba into a mini god."

Chandra said, "His legacy is in the people he stirred from sleep, not memories of him."

Satya watched Chandra scramble down the steep slope and stride over the grassy slopes. This easy, strong man certainly was one of those Chota Baba had animated.

"Life's cruel!" A terrified shrew sped from Satya's pile of set-aside food. "That's all there is to it!" His voice echoed back and forth, To it, tort, taught, twit, ttt....

He strode around the pond. What use meekness? It holds you in your own little puddle. Rather - assertive interaction makes things happen. He yelled at the yellow cliff, "Lost in your head meditating gets you nowhere but the tip of your blinking nose!" He touched the protrusion Mother had made him dislike. "Nose, noose more like. She's trapped me into disliking myself." Self, elf, fff.

Bellowing into his echoing voice, "What am I doing ALONE upon a remote mountain?" Mountain, taint, ai, nnn.

Verbalising this made his current life bonkers. Must reclaim myself. I'm not a nameless hermit seeking the indefinable nothingness, but a person with a history, with desires and something to offer. But what? I'm currently a waster! Fluffing about doing nothing while the Earth suffers.

A day gathering fresh firewood. The next morning he put out his fire, laid a fresh one, cleaned up, left a wad of cash in the pantry, suspended his boots, winter gear and duvet from hooks in the rafters for whoever might need them. At the top of Flower Hill he shouted farewell to Julian and Chota Baba and imagined them snowboarding Trishuls' gargantuan waves. With his mother's leather bag secure over his shoulders, he bumped his bottom across the dangerous spine for the last time.

He spent two nights in Chandra's village. The two men required few words, which was handy because Satya had forgotten the art of casual chatter. On a postcard, he scribbled:

Dear Devi,

Dreadful news. Chota Baba was eaten by a leopard at Yat Tal. It has turned my head. I wish to discover what real LIFE is rather than contemplating nothingness. With no news from you, I assume you are fine? How long since we heard one another's voices. I'll ring when I get to a phone.

Love Satya.

Upon another card tucked into a pacakage, he wrote:

Dearest Uncle Jack,

Autumn, winter and spring turning to summer in a high Himalayan cave have shown me Fate means nothing, that Truth, an empty quest, is life as it unfolds around us, no more. I'm on my way downhill to rediscover real life. Here are my cave-drawings.

Love, Satya/Ewan/Charles (See! Even my name confuses me.).

On Chandra's advice, he began a walkabout designed to let himself slowly into the affairs of mankind, moving for weeks through the villages Chota Baba had worked. People everywhere respected his wish for silence. Sadhus were the linchpin connecting people's difficult lives to the hope of the eternal. Yet Satya's mind was not holy, nor was his silence filled with peace. Everything he saw made him quarrel with himself, every thought made him ache, each emotion was a spade digging him deeper into madness' yawning chasm.

ß

Uma led him down the steep bridle path to the village. Passing through the neat lines of houses, they wove through fields of ripening rice and summer wheat and nearing the end of the hanging valley, they crossed the river's ford. They lingered, admiring the large pond where Julian's worries once drifted across the surface, soared over the waterfall, flitted above the market town and flew to the distant line of peaks where he now skied with Chota Baba. Satya tried to find poetry in the wind twisted oaks, but his mind was incapable of positivity.

Sounds out of place made him peer through the gnarled trees. He gulped. Covering the once flower-abundant grass, men shovelled gravel from piles higher than themselves. The ancient walls which once contained the bridle path had been knocked down and the old stone paving overlaid with tar, creating a road linking what appeared to be a building site to a new government road above. At this fresh junction, an old chai wallah's was painted bright yellow and boasted the name: 'Lingum Stop'.

As if on cue, Andhaka manifested. "Lingum Stop! My new brand name! I'm gradually taking over and modernising all local chai wallahs."

Uma sniggered, "Andhaka is becoming rapidly rich."

"Andhaka, what are you doing?"

Andhaka smiled broadly, wagging his head from side to side, waving his arms widely, "We buried Chota Maharaj's remains. See!!"

In the centre of mounds of sand, Satya noticed a crisp cement tomb resting on a plinth hemmed-in by a metal railing painted gold. "You've done all this in a few weeks!"

"Money works fast in India," Uma stated.

Andhaka bowed before the tomb, "Chota Maharaj is very, very happy. His temple will beat Nachi's in splendour!"

"Plain Chota Baba" Satya heard himself snarl.

288

Ignoring the admonishment, Andhaka pointed at the grove of twisted oaks. "Those trees will shade the paved terrace of a twenty-bedroom hotel, eventually expanding to fifty. Westerns and Indian pilgrims will relax by the lake within hearing of Chota Maharaj's holy bells! Look, I hired a local company to make a feature about Chota Maharaj." Pointing at two men filming and sound-recording, he smiled, "Filming my project! I will sell it to TV channels. Satya Baba, tell your story, be our international star! We will film you at Chota Maharaj's Trishul cave." Andhaka scratched his brow, "I have never been there, but you can lead tours - luxury bus from the market town up to this hotel, a day's relaxation, onwards with pack horses to Trishul. One day I will build a hotel up there and arrange Holy Treks on mules around Holy Trishul. Everyone will admire Lord Shiva's Holy Trident from all angles, knowing Chota Maharaj saw Lord Shiva daily. I will organise the gathering of herbs and build a factory to make Chota-Baba-Chawanprash! This is the start of a big business venture. This is showing the world Chota Maharaj is Great and is still working his magic from heaven."

"Andhaka, Chota Baba is dead. You're showing you're a businessman. No more." Wow, Andhaka's seen his chance and is going for it. But such people mess up the world. Everywhere becomes the same as local quirks, customs and individuals are homogenised by economic forces. He shook his hurting head.

Uma, normally ironic, clucked. She led Satya to what was Chota Baba's rock. The attractive moss had been scraped off, the granite polished with a grinder, a brass plaque explained: "Chota Maharaj meditated upon this holy rock."

"Uma, we must stop Andhaka. He will ruin Trishul."

Uma sighed. "He bought this land for nothing. We didn't see it coming. Once we realised what the man is capable of, our village head wrote to Chandra and everyone is working on ways to block him." They sat on the now smooth rock and gazed at Trishul's reflection floating on the pond, ignoring Andhaka's strident voice ordering his labourers to work harder. After a while, unusually for a rural woman, Uma stood close by him. In her intimacy there was friendship, a spaciousness. "Satya, you will not grow here. Go."

Did she mean London? Nowhere but India existed for him now. Because of his hopes for Devi?

"Find your way by understanding your past, see how it brought you to your present."

He looked at her. Tears wet their cheeks. Satya was surprised at the emotion flooding through him.

"Uma!" Andhaka's harsh voice dragged them apart.

"Namaste, Uma. Namaste, Andhaka." Satya laid his palms together. He lifted his leather bag, the bag Tara made snide remarks about but which Chota Baba advised he keep because it had been his mother's. Uma stood dutifully by her husband's side as Satya walked away.

ß

Drowned in an afternoon storm, Satya pounded muddy paths for several hours. Arriving at the Yat Tal, he was lead along the lake's turbulent edge. By an erect stone marking the precise spot, the Major said, "Blood-curdling screams. Saw old fellow defending himself. What suffering! Used to it old chap, but when it's somebody you admire...." The Major wiped a tear from his wrinkled eyes, smoothed his heavy moustache. "By time we got there, only an arm, the gnawed head.... Sepoys hunted down the leopard. Can't have a man-eater loose."

So, poor Chota Baba didn't experienced Swami Prem's sadhu-peace in the face of death. Bang goes another theory. Few of mankind's beliefs can be trusted. Did the old man live a deluded life? Were his spoken gems a fool's wisdom? Does it matter?

Half crazy, Satya kept walking and the further he went the more unhinged he became as he surfed the void's edge where nothing human was of consequence. The universe sneered at his desire for contentment and this turned him cold. To those along the way his dispassion was familiar and taken as saintly. He shrugged. Let the fools think what they might of my faux-sadhu's cant.

Seeking solid ground, Existentialism's escapism became attractive - invent a meaning for your insignificant life, although it may be absurd, and live by it. It'll give you purpose. Although he knew to temper this with empathy, he couldn't. His being, he decided, belonged not to him but to the Existential flow of life - his awareness but a cracked window the universe briefly opened upon itself. And it worked - with his mind passively part of a machine called Life, he ignored his woes.

He met Devi in their favourite Haridwar cafe. Detached, disinterested, he found talking difficult, words couldn't portray what he'd experienced. What Devi had to say about her life felt insubstantial, the problems she outlined, unimportant. It hadn't helped that the monsoon pounded the foothills and soaked the Northern Plains. Devi said she found him dispassionate, cold. Her parting shot was: "Go see Tara, she'll suck you back to earth."

Maybe. Maybe not. What else to do? Walking to Varanasi will give me direction, if only for a couple of weeks.

A thousand temple bells echoed through the twisting alleys; he increased his pace. Arti faded as darkness descended and he arrived at Varanasi University's lodge. The old gatekeeper phoned Tara. Satya paced the illuminated semicircle of tree-lined avenues. Piercing the jacaranda leaves, "IVAN! Oh... tattered robes..." her voice trailed off, she stopped running.

"Namaste Tara." Satya nodded.

Reading her repulsion, he thought, We want others to conform to our expectations. However, he said, "They call me Satya now."

"Come Ivan," she lead him to her ground-floor apartment and offered lemonade. In the balmy heat their conversation faltered.

After a while, Tara said she'd had a dreadful eighteen months. "My bad experiences with gurus...."

"The Major told me you'd looked rough when he handed me your address."

She flushed. "Nachi made me pregnant and threw me out, accusing me of sleeping with the sweeper! Flaring liar! The abortion went badly wrong."

"Abortion." Death. Julian. Chota Baba. Blinked.

"Depressed, struggling for a way out, I came here. In ten months I completed my thesis as a book linking Western philosophy and Hinduism. The University asked me to lecture on it."

Frozen in his own abstracted mind, he was untouched by her troubles. They are as nothing compared to the suffering in India.

"Ivan, you've not noticed I'm no longer a happy-go-lucky slick hippie."

He peered at her. Yes, she looks sophisticated, urbane. Yet another trivial human disguise. Oh how we adorn fashions to avoid being who we are.

She explained her thesis, trying to engage him in debate, but he felt no wish to work his mind into her new way of seeing things. Her energy's wasted on obscure discourse over irrelevant minutiae, argument for argument's sake. "Life's for living, not discussing," though he himself couldn't 'live-it'

"Rubbish, such an attitude got me into trouble."

Missing the cue, he tried to lighten up, "Flaunting Tantra now Faking Teacher."

She screeched, "Fiddling with my 'F' words!"

He surprised himself by laughing. She hollered and they squealed together. He hadn't laughed since his last morning with Chota Baba. But this was different, not light hearted but emotional. There's something about this woman which draws me out. She's attractive because she loves living and wants more. They settled to the food Tara's maid served. Chewing a samosa, she asked, "Ivan, what'll you do now?"

"What use are most human endeavours?"

"Advances in medicine have saved countless lives."

"And swelled populations so we threaten every one of the Planet's ecosystems." Satya's gaze became steadfast. "We chase careers, money, gadgets, but we miss out on being alive." Noticing he was losing her, why did he care?... he tried for that laugh again, "True contentment lies beneath the Fizzling intellect and the Flapping senses." Words, ideas I no longer hold - what's happening? I want her, she's sizzling, sharp, alive, everything I'm not.

She scoffed. "Your selfish peace?"

"For you peace is selfish because you want verbal interaction, but the Indian farmer understands it as familiar territory and respects those who have it." Blast, more empty words.

"Farmers!" Tara snarled. "You fizz in your head several steps back from life. You've lost it. Come, recover Ivan with me - I'm off to London next week to promote my book."

294

"London!" Umph, fearful. The next course was brought in and they ate in silence.

"Ivan, show me your mountain drawings."

"Art is ego-driven, it takes you nowhere."

"The arts are our greatest expression. And what's wrong with ego, tempered of course." Tara looked at him quizzically. She asked what his cave-diet had been, peered into his eyes, looked at his fingernails. "You're half starved. Eat this." She shoved a bit of lamb in his mouth.

"I don't eat meat." He spat it out.

"Humanity evolved to."

"Hindus don't."

"Their genes have adjusted over thousands of years. Being of Western stock, you need it, you twit."

"I'm strong enough to have survived a Himalayan winter."

"A winter on stale white rice, dried beans and lentils with minute treats of dried fruit and nuts lacked protein and amino acids. OK, in the summer you had more vitamins, but few essential minerals, your body wasn't able to recover without meat's complexity. You're spaced out on malnutrition! That's what gave you your visions and stultifying calmness! It's a well researched phenomena: those who suffer poor diets space-out."

"Whatever." Yet he did think back to the hostages' diets in Lebanon.

She leaned over, nuzzled into his neck. "Ivan, it's good to see you."

This first lingering touch in ages shivered his detachment. How often he'd woken in the night wanting to slip back to her. He pulled from Tara, "I'm avoiding my desire-led persona." But am I? I want her.

"You're still an animal," she, stunningly female, glowing with passion, licked his lips.

The impact of moist hunger on a body ignored was enormous. Deep within a surge; his veins tingled; his body leapt for joy. How stupid I've been! How can you expect to know life when denying a basic instinct? Without sex there's no life, ergo, to know life you ought to know sex? The deaths, the harsh winter, the austerity, loneliness, diet, these numbed me. Society with its rules fears freedom but Tara doesn't. Oh! Her traveling fingers. Every pore wants more. This is real, unlike all that meditating. This... this is what I want, need, should relish. Aah.

Hang on, there's more to this: pursuing Truth, I've shunned emotion. I need companionship and commitment. Tara isn't offering closeness, her tenderness is physical, I pine for security and warmth, not greed. Hang on, why judge another? Tara's simply being sensual - just as I tried in my simple cave-fashion. He gently pushed her away - frightened of getting hurt again. "Sex is fleeting."

"So's ice cream, doesn't mean its bad." She blew softly across his eyelids, "Himalayan Satya's learnt about being a Fuzzed-up demigod and little about being a Fertile human. Satya is screwing up Ivan. Ivan, abandon Satya, screw me."

Yes, austerity encouraged my colder side to dominate. Yet raw sex, even ritualised, once drained this heart. "Sex without context is empty."

"So's the void where our rotting bones will spend eternity."

He wanted to run from the chasm opening inside, to dive into her, to let her being fill him.

She continued, "You're a body with needs, a mind with desires. That's context. Desire fuels our lives, drives civilisation, inspires technology. Our desires form our characters, pave our paths. Evolution's gas is desire."

"Sex has meaning as an expression of love." Yet wasn't love desire? Desire to weave your heart around another's so they feel inclined to stay with you? Damn, she's right!

"Flapdoodle!"

Her 'F' anger released him. "You've dragged me from my cave-mind."

"Get real!" Her tongue stroked his under-chin.

"Your touch revives Ewan."

"So Ivan, fill me or fuck-off."

Panicking, wanting more, but confused about nestling into her personality before he was strong enough to cope, he said, "How about lunch above the ghats tomorrow?"

"What?"

"I'm not sure I'm ready…."

She hissed, "Get thee from me Satya!"

ß

Satya drifted aimlessly about the dark city unpicking the dynamics of his evening with Tara. Why Tara? Because Devi's out of reach. So why reject Tara? Fear. Yet the energy beyond words ripped off what little remained of my yogic veil. After being with her, my seeking days appear empty, my desire for Truth hollow, my Peace an escape. This wish for physical comfort is an ego-need. I neglected this entity called 'ego-self', taking on Father's cold discipline and pursuing Truth fitted that. Discipline's an escape. It flawed my character, created my Stiff Outer Self, which others shunned, hence my loneliness. Tara said I was a loner, kept my distance, was attracted by Aikido, Yoga's isolation, Chota Baba's solitary lifestyle, chose lonely friends like Julian. Why didn't I realise this myself? Because I was too wrapped up maintaining inner discipline! Swami Prem was right, I must unravel my chilling upbringing, not turn from it as always.

The lonely, he'd read in one of Chandra's New Scientist magazines, were more prone to obsessive behaviour. Yes! Yes and yes! A cruel cycle I've not been able to escape. He was now obsessed with thinking about his inner state! Satya bellowed at the dark Ganga, "HELP! I'm lost!"

The thought of renting a room locally gripped him. Tara'll drag me out of this thought-spiral, stimulate my emotions, teach me to live honestly with my shunned ego.

Varanasi would help too. Varanasi, the 'City of Learning', 'City of Lights', the city of music and art, where tradition meets austerity meets the Market and Hedonism. He could not imagine tiring of Varanasi's blinding theatre. Everything from the crumbling ancient to the garishly modern, the suave to the ragged to the flashing jet-setter, bombed-out hippies and learned pundits. Yes, Tara and the city will devour and spit out SOS-me.

Oh, Mark Twain wrote, Varanasi, "Older than history, legend, tradition...." Even this'll become dust. Satya couldn't escape such negate thoughts. Yet with Tara, I'd felt positive.

Yes! Varanasi, also called Kashi; two names like India-Bharat, one temporal, the other spiritual, a city so holy. Varanasi, a reflection of Trishul, so venerable Hindus aim to visit her before death. Along with Haridwar, one of three holy jewels along Ganga Ma's eternal route. "Kashi," referred to in the ancient Vedas as old. So important that waves of invaders tried to snuff out her flame - in 1194, 1376, 1496 and 1656 mosques were erected on destroyed Hindu temples and inhabitants were forced to convert or die. Yet undaunted, Hinduism continues to thrive.

Dawn tinted the dark. He stepped from the soothing peace of a temple's inner courtyard to be confronted by the bustling bounce and mayhem of banging, bulging, modern India. Yet look! beyond the Ganga, humpbacked oxen, expansive fields. The Ghats were coming alive. The stone steps, old as legends when Buddha stood right there, having attained Enlightenment an hour's walk away. Gosh.

Worshipers crowded the ghats, vying for space, shoving even the frail and elderly who came to die with Shiva. Curled tight snoring beneath blankets, sadhu pretenders. One of my ancestors meditated his days away upon these very ghats.

Serious seekers bolt upright watching the fading night, rising, walking to the Ganga's edge, dunking three times, turning full circle, facing the sun rising over crops upon the far shore. Lifting Ganga in their folded palms, they let Her trickle over their heads. These waters drift to the sea, evaporate, form clouds, some fall as snow on Trishul. I might have washed in this handful. Life is a cycle, but what's it turning for? Such internal mumblings kept him from the terrifying canyon within.

He sat with his feet in the Ganga. A swirl of current brought a human nose to the surface. Ugh, urrr! He jumped up the ghats, leaping over slumbering faux-sadhus. At a tap, with great care he washed his legs using soap from his wash bag, ridding himself of the rancid river's germs and he hurled the soap into the gangrenous Ganga. People worship this putrid soup! They believed it kills all suspended nasties.

Clinging to hope, they take the liquid home in bottles to bless their newborn. I'm as lost as them.

He opened the old family folder. Flipping through the pages he found grandpa Hugh Merricott's 1946 letter: *'India's rivers need attention. Take the Ganges whose pristine waters are polluted from the moment they pass the first Himalayan villager evacuating his bowels directly into them. Add together the myriad villages, towns and cities which offload unprocessed sewage filled with microbes and who toss body parts into the Ganges' many tributaries, and as she flows past Varanasi she is arguably the most spoiled river on Earth. This fouled water seeps into the North Indian water-table.'*

Yuugh. No more lassi. Tea, boiled, is safer. Grandpa's words disturb me. And today, with chemical waste, they're ruining their own environment! To think like this feels like a betrayal. India is now my arcane home, England is faint, even Merricott, the library, Uncle Jack. I realised this when Tara suggested I travel with her to London.

He ploughed against fussing worshippers dressed in white. So many people! Like me, everyone thinks the universe revolves around their own life. And we are unaware of the next person's inner story or agony. In truth, how lonely we are. This spun him to the edge of the abyss, "I must do!"

At a busy chai wallah's atop the heaving ghats, he drew the orange sun skulking above the far bank, taking care to capture its serpentine reflection on the pale river. Chewing a meat samosa, Satya strolled aimlessly along the line of steps which plunged to the Ganga. Tara's right, eating meat doesn't make you any worse a person. Our English butcher is compassionate. More than he could say for a meditating, self-absorbed vegan, friend of the delightful office cleaner. It's not what you eat but what you think. He took another bite.

He drew boats taking people midstream to collect the holy voodoo waters in plastic bottles or to sprinkle their deceased relative's ashes over the choppy Ganga. Drawing the crazed crowd annoyed him. His pen an irate line swirling upon itself inscribed these ten thousand figures swimming over a double-page spread. A parting in his wiggles defined a serene woman gliding through this agitated human torrent. Did the gap around her show that her tranquillity slowed some of those hectic pilgrims she passed? Ho! Stop thinking! SOS was back as a defence against the void. I'm void of love!

The following morning, he lingered by riverside hostels built centuries ago by wealthy philanthropists to house those awaiting death. They arrived from all over India, convinced that only in Varanasi would Shiva haul them off to Mount Kailash, but only if you thought of him in your last moments. Half-starved, driving themselves to fanaticism, had these thin bodies in white cotton chased, as he had, the intelligence of emotion and empathy from their sunken chests? Desperate, exhausted, mustering up faith, intoning a worldly king who built Varanasi over three thousand years ago, they align their minds to a myth by reading texts older than the Old Testament. Andhaka was turning Chota Baba into a god. Buddha, Jesus, exemplary individuals like Socrates, no more. We create legends to inspire our empty lives.

Smoke from funeral pyres beneath the hostels curled around the stark rooms. Like the pensioners in white in the hostels above, black-robed Tantric yogis watched the process of death, letting their minds wander over life's impermanence whilst contemplating Shiva meditating on the void. Satya looked at the multiple burnings with great attention, not for the sake of Tara or Shiva, but because he, like those dying, was lost. The repulsive smell filled his lungs. He retched. Julian's dying face rolled about with Chota Baba's head. Life is a moment. We are alive; sooner than we realise our bones will be rotting beneath the moist soil. The fleeting generations roll on. Each creature, each species merely trying to better its finite existence.

A young woman's tenor chant to her dead husband cut through his thoughts. This plaintive voice lilting over the flames emitted love, conveyed her pain. Listening to her, he felt more isolated than high up his mountain. I want somebody to want me as this woman wants her husband. Tara! No. She doesn't want me. His struggling mind filled

301

with Tara's alluring lips, her desire to draw him in. Why are men allured by the Taras, not the Devis? It's biological, our seed seeks physical perfection... but I'm better than that. I seek love.

Is love delusional? Do people manipulate each other with fondness and fidelity, tying one another in webs of silver, simply to have company? Were 'love's' attributes of concern, understanding, empathy and assistance social necessities which enabled children to grow protected by stable parental relationships? Relationships, as basic to human continuity as reproduction? If so, by rejecting them how can we understand who we are?

The ghat-meditation was designed to detach the Tantric sadhu from life - the effect on him was the opposite. Death inspired him to want the intimacy that woman's voice clearly portrayed. He pined for somebody who wanted him. Devi! Tara offers a pleasurable gallop, Devi a walking relationship, challenging in a manageable way, compassionate, inspirational, a fun, evolving friendship. Oh, for Devi's spontaneous laughter, the delicate smell of her skin. Devi and I suit each other. Why does she never reveal her heart? Perhaps she's waiting for her Indian paramour. But is she really beyond me?

Dizzy, he leaned against a wall and began to sweat. Had he ignored Devi because of his drive for Truth? Had he missed his moment? How cold he'd recently been with her in Haridwar! An emotional surge went through his sombre mind. I must show her what I feel before she commits to another.

In a shop he found a large postcard of the sun rising over the Ganga, and wrote:

Dearest Devi,

Forgive frozen Satya in Haridwar. Tara pointed out Satya was barmy on malnutrition. You were right - her passion for life woke me from Satya's zombie walk. Nothing physical happened. Watching the burning ghats, I realised life is about properly RELATING - to our own selves, to others, to all of life. Devi, I need to learn that and intimacy and empathy. Your society imposes rules on you which affect how you and I

302

should behave, what we must expect. Perhaps you share some of my sentiments, perhaps not... do tell me.

Love, Satya/Ewan/Charles, oh who knows what to call me now....

It was far too open to be read along the route and so he bought an envelope before posting it express-recorded-mail.

Plastic bottles bobbed down the Ganga, plastic film caught by the breeze stuck like alien roses in the trees, in the gutter lay plastic cups, plastic bags, plastic boxes. He sighed. For countless millennia waste has disintegrated to become fuel within life's cycle. Yet in less than fifty years we've despoiled the land, the oceans, the air with chemicals, plastics and tat. OK, our grandparents acted in good faith, thinking they were improving things, but today this is our battle.

We must save the world. We are each responsible. We must each live as lightly as possible, do what we can, time is very short! Oh dear, what can I, a wraith swept up from a Himalayan cave, do?

Satya sat watching birds flit across the fouled waters. Then he saw. I'm responsible for an enclosed valley three miles long and one wide. That might seem an insignificant area, but I CAN do something meaningful with it. He allowed his mind to wander across Merricott Vale.

After some time, he rose and sought out an internet cafe. Inside, he sent a handsome sum from his estate-fed bank account to Uncle Jack's private one. He then wrote a lengthy letter to Uncle Jack, part of which called for change on the farm:

"5,000 years of weather on tracks spreading from Merrie-Hill's bronze age hill-settlement have cut deep holloways into the slopes, one holloway ten metres deep ends by the remains of a small Roman barn at Merricott Vale's entrance. These things illustrate thousand of years of agricultural activity on our land. The vale is big enough to be generous to nature and my intention is to return it to a more natural balance whilst undertaking profitable farming. Ask the staff to work

alongside the local wildlife society so they both take ownership of the project.

Water meadows must only be used only for grazing, not hay, to assist natural flora and fauna. Leave bands of wilderness each side of the brooks, stream and around the western half of the lake and let coppices and hedgerows grow twice their width. Allow all these to link-up, creating an untouched network of wildlife corridors.

Aim to increasingly sell our produce locally. Build a small farm-shop inside the gates. Inspire staff families to sell their jams, garden plants and crafts there. Attach a cafe-resto using Merricott produce and create a lake-side beach by the cafe, with a shower block for swimmers (Paul is already a part-time lifeguard).

Make a website promoting Merricott's change from modern farm to a profitable organic haven for nature which grants a good income to those who live there. Explain such things as - environmentally sensitive farming replaces chemical repellants with 'companion planting'. Use my wing of Merricott for courses to inspire other local farmers, showing nature-sensitive organic farming is profitable. Merricott Estate makes sufficient money to underwrite all this."

Satya/Charles wanted all of his estate's profits reinvested in the land and property, not to be his any more. Uncle Jack was fine, he had his own income, but how to give me one? The subsequent email was long, for he asked Jack to buy a London house and arrange for it to be divided it into four flats, renting our three. This'll give me a bolt-hole and an independent income.

Once he had sent the emails, he stood up and walked along the Ghats. At last I've done something worthwhile in my life! This makes me feel alive, inspired. For the first time in my life I have purpose. Chota Baba said purpose would arise when I found myself through 'Settling' and watching my mind. But purpose has come from observing how Himalayan farmers live in harmony with nature. Ah, another saint tumbles off his pedestal!

That evening, sipping spiced tea above the Ganga, he thought, I must call Devi, a postcard isn't enough. He found a phone in a nearby hotel. "Hello Devi."

"Satya," Devi was cautious.

"How long will you be home?"

Her voice cool, "Until February."

Thwarted, "Is it OK to visit?"

"That would be fine."

Gabbling to fill the frozen gorge between them, "I need to walk to sort my head out before we meet. I'll take roughly ten days."

Relenting, "The TV says it's getting colder. Autumn's here."

Baffled, "See you soonish then?"

"Bye."

ß

The heavy door swung open and ebony eyes took him in. "Satya!"

He hesitated, hardly recognising Devi in a crimson silk sari. *The lively ring in her voice makes me dizzy.* He found himself saying, "I'm not so sure about Satya."

Devi waved at the avenue of mulberry trees he had enjoyed walking beneath and following her hands, he noticed a stream gushing from the hillside, feeding a pond with an ancient stone shrine upon a small island. "Indra's in Haridwar. He'll feel cheated not to have welcomed you to our home."

"Perhaps not now I'm a fallen yogi bear."

"That's twice you've doubted yourself."

His weak smile showed his confusion, "I used to be so definite...."

"What's changed you?"

"You haven't received my card? Hmm, I'll tell you all later. How are you?"

"You've noticed me!"

He blinked, "Sorry about our last meeting, Devi."

"Not just then - you've always been self-obsessed."

He hung his head. "Few people really listen to others."

"You've not been one of them."

Why's she never said this before? Or has she and I didn't notice? Highly possible. He rubbed his eyes, "And now I'm hopelessly out of my depth."

"You always were but never knew it." Her gaze candid, though not unfriendly. "Since we first met I've watched you peeping over the SOS shield that hides your emotions, straying outside for a while, but frightened, jumping back behind the insecurity of your lonely barricade."

"Yes, how little I know about relating. Even after three years of self-watching."

"That's typically fanatical! You were the Aikido fanatic, work fanatic, Yoga fanatic! We grow by stepping beyond our desires to understand ourselves and others by watching the way we relate." She stepped inside and he followed her across a spacious hall laid with marble flooring.

Devi spun round. "Satya, I'm sure I've found the temple town."

"Temple town?"

"Your Mughal miniature - you scanned a copy ages ago, asked me to find it."

He looked at her and remembered, but what use his family quest now? However, to please her he said, "Where?"

Mimicking his fragile voice, "I'll tell you later. By the way, this came today." She handed him an envelope. "Jack enclosed it in a charming letter to me. He said he has to speak to you."

"It must be about my note on organic farming." They continued to a door framed within stone lilies.

"Organic's a Western word for what we've always done here."

"I know. Himalayan farming taught me a lot."

She stepped into an inner courtyard. Sunlight trickled through an open cupola of interlinked floating arches carved as towering lilies, delicate patterns of shade fell upon a series of half-hidden marble benches. They sat down. Without words, the strung atmosphere between them settled and a stillness grew. Gradually it became a knowing silence and he eased into her company. I love the way her subtle emotions flick across her face, the way her body gently shifts. I feel alive in her presence. Gone was his nervousness.

A man with a saffron turban and cream robes set spiced tea and sweetmeats on an inlaid Kashmiri table. Satya watched her tongue lick crumbs from a corner of her mouth and come to rest. Why, when my truth is her, did I shun her to seek Truth? Although perhaps a little unremarkable when her face was at rest, Devi, he noticed, shone with Uma's rural grace, she pulsed subtly with Sati's femininity and she glowed with the purity uncomplicated emotions produce. Yet she was more - a vibrant woman, a sophisticated urbanite, even a princess, and most of all, she was herself. Devi's undoubtably Devi, clear, strong, unafraid of playing the fool, yet gentle, caring,

307

attentive. How can one person manifest so many attributes? Because she's at ease with herself. Did that arise from love received in childhood? Did this create a stable basis from which to evolve into a balanced person? It must, for all hinges on relationships. Could I learn to relate? Yes! He had seen we can always change, all that's needed is the knowledge that we can and the desire. Tara was right, desire wasn't necessarily bad.

A fountain, simple, elegant, delicate, against the back wall. They watched fish in its pool and listened to soft birdsong rippling off the curves of pale honey-stone. He noticed curved balconies, lilies opening to rooms above. When their eyes locked, he felt himself open to her and saw it was reciprocated. But he closed up. They'd not stand a chance. She was high caste and a Hindu; he was a foreign agnostic. Nervous, he asked, "Devi, have they found you a husband?"

Blinking rapidly, "Ugh? Oh. Yes and no. Several, but I prefer another."

"Who?"

"You know him."

He panicked, his eyes darting around, searching his memory. Oh no, not the Zaminder! Stop thinking like this. We were never to be. His eyes grew wet. To take attention from the intensity of feelings, he asked, "Devi, what good is religion?"

She shook her head. "When not dogmatic but tolerant, it gives people a vision bigger than themselves and also purpose." She again offered the silver platter of sweetmeats.

Yes, fearing the void we construct castles in the sky and live our lives admiring them. How he wanted to touch the hand which held the dented silver tray. I'm floundering. He gazed at the play of water, listened to the tune it made within the tranquil space.

"I sense you've gone full circle," Devi tilted her head.

Oh god, how poetic her poise. "From English prat to yogic fool and now who knows where."

She giggled and the tinkle stirred his soul. "We evolve in spirals, rising a little each circuit. What has it all taught you?"

308

"Ideals and reason created most of our problems because we ignore empathy."

Devi clapped and bowed. "Great oration garrulous guru! Oh Satya Sadhu, what of greed?"

Pretending to ignore her teasing, how playful he felt, Tara goaded the burly beast from him, but this was lighter, unencumbered by desire's fizz, undisturbed by adolescent interplay. "Greed," he hesitated, caught by her Orphic gaze. Apart from Chota Baba, nobody else has stilled my mind with a single look. A flock of green parrots swept through the arches to settle and squabble by the pond as they scooped up water in their beaks. Devi smiled at old friends. Satya sighed, This is heaven. Alarmed by a darting shadow, the parrots fled in a fuss of feathers. They laughed. Satya sought words to hide his emotion. "Greed," he continued, "arises from dissatisfaction, which comes from forgetting life's simple things satisfy most." He stopped, "Oh Devi, I'm no longer sure what I think because I am just discovering who my ego is."

"To truly live, we must always be beginners." She smiled, continuing the game, "and, Great Master Satya, what of ego?"

"Ego, the devil shunned by religion, yet ego must be understood before we can be ourselves...."

"... and be able to help others.... So what of art?"

Still lingering on what 'ego' was, his reply was far too serious, "Art? Hmm, animals appreciate beauty. Look at birds' mating displays. Chimps dance when they come across waterfalls. Cavemen painted great works, they danced, played music, sang and told stories. Art is our natural expression."

"Himalayan sage," she tilted her chin in mock annoyance, "what of friendship?"

His voice wavering, "All my life I've avoided closeness because I was afraid of being hurt, which is what my parents constantly did to me." Tara flipped through his thoughts.

Devi fiddled with the hem of her sari, asked, "And emotion?"

He sighed, "Yet another thing I've ignored." How I wish to merge my life with hers. She's intelligent, fun, stable, she's tough, yet delicate. And not predictable. Ho! Stop, she's taken.

"Satya, emotion rather than reason drives our clumsy passage through time. We only grow by watching our emotions as we interact with people and events. By escaping our feelings we cannot fundamentally change the way we behave."

"Yes. Psychopaths lack emotional reactions... and psychopaths control our world - top businessmen, politicians, religious leaders, great artists and entertainers, entrepreneurs...."

She cut him short, "If emotion is properly understood it leads us to empathy - to relating properly."

Ho, I wish we were suitable in the eyes of her society. Anxiety rushed through him. Must say something. Anything. "Why do you visit the ashram?"

"Satya!" Frustration loud in her voice. "To see friends. To hang out with my brother." She tugged a long tress of hair.

He'd been so preoccupied with himself that he'd not noticed her hair had grown... even on their scrambled morning in Haridwar. He looked with guilt and intent. Oh how the black locks spilling over her slender shoulders soften her! Oh Devi.

ß

Satya settled into a soft chair in his allotted bedroom. It had been ages since his body had been in such a comfortable seat and he relished the moment. What an evening. They had eaten delicately spiced dishes in a cosy dining room lit with candles. He had smiled when Devi said her family disliked their formal banqueting hall when it was empty of a crowd. She had been shocked when he revealed his parents ate alone, each in their own wing, that he ate in the kitchen with Uncle Jack, the cleaner and the cook. They revealed the mad things they had each done or thought since Julian's demise. Satya had been fascinated to hear Sati was travelling Europe for the estate's charity and that Devi didn't miss roaming about, her first exit from the estate had been their Haridwar meeting.

He rose from the chair and slowly moved about his spacious bedroom. He opened a door to his private balcony looking over the inner courtyard, the fountain's tinkle reminded him of how they had laughed at the parrots. Through an arch, he saw the hanging landing where he'd last seen Devi - the stairs separated, one set flying to the family rooms, the other floating to the guest quarters.

Satya closed the inner door and crossed his room to arched French windows, opening them he stepped onto a suspended external veranda which bowed outwards with subtle lily curves of floating stone. His balcony rippled into those either side and those to others until they merged with rounded pavilions at the four corners of the mansion, adding a touch of magic to the simple honey-stone structure. Aah, the night air's refreshing. He gazed at flat-pruned mulberry trees shading the paved space before Devi's elegant home. The small palace wasn't much bigger than Merricott, however, with its inspiring spaces, it felt larger. It was older too. That afternoon Devi had shown him where the Buddha had given a sermon twenty-five centuries before - on an island one of her distant relatives had created within a pond to encapsulate the spot forever.

312

Typical of her, Devi had revealed nothing. Did tradition thwart her? Was it her own disinterest? Or was she muddled? Distracted by such thoughts, he went inside and found himself accidentally doing what he had wished to put off, not wishing the world he had left a lifetime ago to intrude. Uncle Jack's letter opened easily and moving closer to a standard lamp, he held its many pages. Might as well read it, it'll take me from these confusions, allow me to get some decent sleep.

It was strange to see his uncle's familiar handwriting. Although Charles/Ewan/Satya had turned from one man into another and was turning again into he knew not what, the letter showed Uncle Jack was the same as he had been when they parted in Paris over three and a half years ago.

'I am behind you on the organic-environmental issue, as are the staff who love Merricott as much as we do. Everyone is excited, well done.'

Satya/Ewan looked out the window. So my purpose is to assist Merricott's evolution from afar. How easy is that!

'What an artist you are and the scribblings beside your drawings are evocative. Before your lengthy email from Varanasi, I had longed to go to Shiva's City, but your descriptions made me rethink!!! Tara, what a woman. I've read reviews of her book and emailed an invite for a rest here during her UK book-tour. It's a visit I look forward to!

Poor Julian.... How I loved his spirit.... What can one say.'

Charles/Satya read on, turning the pages filled with news until one in particular held him:

'On their last day my brother was furious with your mother for issuing divorce papers.'

Divorce? This was news! Why? And why so late in life? Had mother met another man?

'In his cool temper, Roland forced her into his 1960s Jaguar. At your mother's insistence, I drove after them through the estate. Whilst I was closing the cast-iron gates, Roland, impatient to get to the solicitors without me, shot across the public road. As you know, a huge grain truck swerved. Unfortunately my brother mimicked it's adjustment.

313

As your train sped towards us from London, your mother held Ronald's bleeding head in her lap until he died thirty paces from our gates, apologising to her, to me and wishing that you Charles were there. Why only in death?

With no airbag to protect her, doctors suspected her liver and kidneys had been crushed. I recall your mother looking up through the wreckage gasping, "Oh dear, Jack, why me? Why now?"

Tears flooded down Charle's face, he laid down the letter and rose. Upon his balcony he peered into the impenetrable Indian night. Poor Mother. Dry as baking paper against stacked hospital pillows. Intense blue eyes shining with suffering attempted to reach over the glacial years of our shared lives. She tried to move a hand towards me. One huge tear burst over her bloodless cheek. She sagged. Was gone.

Blubbering like an infant left on a winter step, he fell against Devi's stone doorframe. Within his Himalayan cave he had purposefully recreated this scene and had assumed he'd mentally burned these inner seeds by 'Settling'. Yet here again proof that contemplation was no substitute for facing real, rather than manufactured, emotion as it arose.

The clear stars shifted across the intense sky.

Acute restlessness made him constantly rise and walk about, but he'd slump against the balcony's stone banister, mentally revisiting a host of passages from the letter. Where was his peace? Damn it, why, after his insight at the ghats, did he still want peace? Because it was better than this inner ranting! You needed a degree of detached calm to think objectively, to see the wider picture and form sound conclusions. But how to attain that now? How many hours have I paced back and forth across these slabs? All night.

Another paragraph in the letter popped open in his head:

'Satya, there is much to be repaired. I have had troubled nights.... Clearing up your mother's suite some weeks ago, assuming you'd never return, I came across a diary covering her first week of marriage. Do forgive me, but I could not put it down. I have scanned the relevant pages for you, I trust you will be able to take it squarely.'

314

Faint blues tinted the eastern horizon. He looked at the dim gardens. Uncle Jack talked about the need to resolve things. Although Devi had found the temple, going to the place he had dreamed of finding all his life had unexpectedly become less appealing.

The bells of Arti tinkled somewhere in the mansion. He felt an urge to rise and stand at Devi's side on this first morning in her home, but emotion bound him.

Delicate peach reached over the gardens, smearing the pale building. Fussing parakeets flew across the rising orb. He yearned to paint them - pea-green wings, keen yellow eyes, laughing ruby beaks set upon a scarlet sun within a grey-blue mauve sky.

The final crescendo of bells, Arti's end.

In a fluster, the parakeets landed on his and other balconies, their chatter and restlessness lifting him from his waking dream. A loud knock. They fled in a flurry. His door creaked open. Tea was left on his bedside table. Immobile upon the balcony, he closed his eyes.

His door opened cautiously, Devi's voice dragged at his thoughts, announcing she was peering in. "Hello? Hello? Ah, yes, yes Pratab, the bed hasn't been slept in." She told the man to leave. He heard the door close, listened to the patter of feet across the broad floorboards, felt the swish of a sari against his shoulder. "Satya, you're still wearing last evening's clothes. Are you all right?"

Wanting to reveal all, he heard himself sob. He turned. Her ebony eyes perfectly reflected the bright sky. Dropping beside him on the slabs, Devi touched his cheek; it pulled him from the depths. How he had longed for this moment, yet now it had come he was in tumult.

"Satya?" Absence from Arti, unheard of for a guest, not attending breakfast, extreme rudeness.

"Devi," he stumbled through his mind, seeking a way to reveal the complexity of his night, but words fled. He tugged the pages from under him, "This...."

She read.

315

Drinking in her strength, he realised his instincts had been right, he ought to have left the letter sealed. It would have given Devi and me time to adjust to each other. Now raging emotion dominates. Why is life such a jester?

ß

The temple stood where the first Himalayan hill touched the broad river whose flat surface created the illusion of supporting the distant snow peaks. Devi and he surveyed the red sandstone arches holding up the double white cupola. Perfect craftsmanship, but laced with cracks and creeping ivy. They ignored the fetid stench of an open sewer slurping through the surrounding shanty town. This, my Mughal miniature's truth. The delicate building had fired his imagination, had helped him escape his dismal childhood, but Jack's letter had burst his dream, as other dreams had crumbled these past three years. Hmm, run from your dreams, more like!

Making their obeisance to a crude statue of Kali, they laid roses from Devi's garden beside marigolds set down by three chanting women in worn saris. This crumbling structure not abandoned, but part of everyday life. Reeling from his shattered fantasy, he felt an urge to replace it with something. A local project! "Devi, let's make amends for Merricott history here. Start with sewage. Create an example, showing how to deal with it, you know, reed beds, sand...."

"You are obsessed with sewage!"

"It is a major Indian problem. Look at the Ganga!" He was on the defensive, "it'll clean up the environment and improve health. I wonder if the Maharani and Maharaja will be interested."

Devi hit him playfully, "Jack showed us that the family have good reason to send you running." Beyond the cramped slums, they hesitated in a bustling market place. "Wait here. I'll go and introduce myself."

He walked about, fingering Mother's trusty leather bag. He had once spotted it in a honeymoon photo beside the temple. Had Mother bought it in this very market as retail therapy during her dreadful week here? A tear spilled down his left cheek as more lines from Jack's letter jumped into his mind:

'Satya, to explain why we must meet the Maharaja, here is a copy of your mother's diary entry written two and a half hours before the accident:

'7am. Tuesday, 4th May. I have always wished to be honest with Charles, but convinced it would destroy the boy, I never could and consequently struggling with myself to find the perfect words, I have appeared to be a cold fish all his life. Will he forgive me? Perhaps yes, because he is softer than me. What love I could reach was bled out of me by Roland. The divorce proceedings start today. Tonight I will go to London and tell Charles why I am finally taking this route. I will read him parts of my honeymoon diary. Yes, that's how to do it.'

He sighed heavily, recalling those included pages she mentioned. No! No! I mustn't go over that again. Distract thyself.

Blinkin bongles, worldwide environmental destruction for this! He waved his arms at the quantity of tat on sale. Plastic this, plastic that, plastic everything. Eventually, it'll break down into pellets so small they'll become part of the water system. What to do? I know! A website-hub linking sites actively helping the planet, providing examples to inspire individuals, ways to get involved, local contacts, the best forums. Hmm, I'll need to employ a good web-builder, maintenance master and others to sift the websites. Well, income could come from green-businesses advertising and I've the *stolen* money to kick it off.

He stopped. A woman stirring a pot over an open fire. Wisps of smoke curled around her babe greedily suckling her breast. Before her, two infants played in an oily puddle. Behind her, her cardboard home. He bent. Her smile so sure. The back of her right wrist, not to defile what she assumed was his higher caste, gently pushed his hand away, showing no surprise at the high value notes furtively offered. Regardless of her dire situation, she appeared content. Dropping the money in her lap, he moved away.

It's me who needs help.

Have I learnt anything?

Perhaps.

Each day is ephemeral. Longed for experiences take ages to arrive; before you properly register them, they're memories. Savour each hour, however odd. Discover 'me' in your senses, emotional reactions, patterns of habitual thought. As the ego relates to other egos, creating multiple 'egos' to deal with each relationship, make empathy the inspiring force, not desire. It does not matter if you believe in a supreme being, existence itself is supreme if it is lived with sensitivity to all of life.

"Whoo hoo! Satya's Truths! - the thoughts of a lost man, how vain is that."

His chortling startled some children. Apologising, he moved on. Ho, ho! Sophisticated, rugby playing, aikido me became a long-haired sadhu in robes and yesterday, shorn at the barber's, a sedate twit in smart chinos. Devi! She eased my way through these past days as we strolled through her gardens unpicking my life. Her face! when she asked, "Do you want another name?"

"Perhaps I've had enough!"

Standing before Buddha's island she'd sung: "Chewing, U-Thong a flash-in-a-pan! Satya-Ewan, de crazy coot; Charles-de-snooty, hey what a hoot!"

Her playfulness spellbound him.

"And now I'll, name him Charlie." She'd tweaked his nose.

Gazing across the market, touching his nose, he looked up at the imposing fort. On the phone she had not wished to warn the Maharaja and Maharani that a Merricott wanted an audience. And she would be calling him Charlie.

Changing names has been fun, but Ewan, so flexible, is no longer needed, Uncle Jack made this clear in a footnote:

'Cuts at the Foreign Office have masked your fiddling. Your old boss Hayling was rewarded for 'mismanagement' (your crime), by being posted to ... guess where... Lagos! Hayling did not demand an investigation, perhaps the stupid man had no inkling of what had really happened. Good riddance. You are safe.'

"Charlie! Charlie!"

Heart in a twiddle, he stepped up the grassy slope soaring from the busy market. Within a towering entrance designed to take battle elephants, Devi, beside an elegant young couple. Humbled, Charlie raised his hands in namaste.

"Maharani, Maharaja, I present Charlie." A gust lifted Devi's long hair from her shocking pink sari.

"Namaste," Charlie bowed. Whee, the parents must be dead, pressure's off.

"My wife Shakti, call me Rudra," the Maharaja barked, his pale Nehru jacket flapping open in the breeze.

"Devi tells us you became a Himalayan yogi," Shakti's voice as terse as her husband's. Smoothing down her wind lifted green sari she stepped into a grand courtyard once used to the activity of battle.

Accustomed to stiff jousting in British aristocratic circles, Charlie smirked, "I think one learns more in the marketplace."

Trying to ease the atmosphere, Devi teased, "Tantra of the Fruit Stalls?"

Charlie tittered, "Tantra! It's in relating that I lack skill."

Rudra was brusque, "The Merricotts were no good at intimacy."

Gawd, what antagonism. Oh, of course! this is India. Family is central to everything and grievances pass down from one generation to the next. He smiled broadly, attempting to relax the man, "I fully agree."

"Come, let's take tea," Shakti invited, her voice eased slightly.

"We have much to discuss," Rudra, a mite more approachable.

Rising from the wide slabs of red sandstone, they moved up an outside staircase and onto a terrace bound by crenelated walls which once protected archers. Charlie and Devi peered at the impressive river far below, over the other side blue hills shivered in the afternoon heat, a cooling wind falling from the remote mountains rippled the water.

Seeing Trishul, "I could walk this valley to my cave!" How poetic. Ha! the Mughal painting defined my Indian circle.

They sat at a linen covered table. "Magnificent," Charlie said after swallowing a bite of sweetmeat.

Rudra coughed. "The castle was enlarged in the late 1300s when our family married a Gurkha Rajput who stayed behind as her tribe moved up the valley to Nepal. Ironically, five hundred years later, Gerald Merricott employed Gurkhas to crush us."

"I am so sorry," Charlie said. "I'm uncomfortable with much British history."

"It is time the truth came out," Rudra emptied quarter of a glass of water in one gulp.

"Before we begin, I have a peace-offering." Charlie announced strategically. All eyes turned to him. "Maharaja, Maharani, I wish to return what is yours as an apology." Charlie handed the rosewood box to the Maharaja.

Raising the lid, Rudra opened the silk envelope, revealing the valuable Mughal picture. He looked at it for a moment before saying, "The temple was built in the early 1400s to house an image of Kali the Gurkhas had brought west from their Rajasthani temple which was destroyed by invading Afghans. In the 1640s it was doubled with the second dome to include a shrine to Parvati, Kali's sister form." Rudra handed the picture to Shakti.

She exclaimed, "We have three equally fine paintings by the same artist, done to celebrate the second dome."

Devi looked at Charlie and smiled encouragingly. His nervousness amazed him, making him wonder how little he had achieved on his accidental 'quest'; down here in the marketplace his reactions were laden with old complexities and emotions. Chota Baba was right, detached meditation was a blind alley, tempered with the practical art of 'Settling', the 'market place' was where to gain empathy and compassion.

Charlie was dragged back as Rudra read a paragraph from Gerald Merricott' note of the 15th May 1857: *"After the dreadful event I found this picture in the blood-splattered dust. I looked up and beheld this exquisite temple resting on these rounded rocks above the swathe of river. What shame I felt to have defiled this ancient ground for nothing more than East India Company profit. Bharat, forgive me. Today I have debased you and I will never forgive myself. Will you ever forgive my thus tainted family? On second thoughts, I will keep this painting to remind me of our shame."*

Charlie sighed. The Merricotts! We're named after Merrie, a jovial but cruel Saxon invader who, in about 460AD, settled what became known as Merricott Vale. Six hundred years later, to retain our valley, we sided with the invading Norman. We Merricotts first came to India as proud Elizabethan envoys, only to discover Europe's best was dwarfed by India's brilliance. We grew wealthy from trading with India from the 1580s onwards. In the 1750s we aligned ourselves with the East Indian Company, which gradually depleted a once mighty land. Charlie knew most Merricotts had admired and loved India's timeless culture and its ebullient people. In 1932, Daphne Merricott had written: *"Mother India, you are more than a country, you are vaster than a mere landmass. I sense you are indeed the enchanted territory called Bharat, a realm where magic and mystery charge the air. Your worldly streets are hung with invisible portals which warp material existence with baffling ease."* But still, a mighty Maharaja had been brought to his knees in 1857 by a red faced Merricott.

Replacing the note, Rudra was solemn. "My predecessor evaded the Salt Tax levied by the East India Company because it crippled our people. The Indian Mutiny against The Company was ripping through northern towns, Lucknow's beautiful centre was levelled as The Company met every show of dissent. Our Maharaja fought well, but his men couldn't match battle hardened Gurkha soldiers wielding superior weapons."

Devi said, "A little good came from it. Appalled by the Company's brutality, the British government took over responsibility for the country."

"They were fairer, although sometimes as unyielding," Rudra groused.

"Not as corrupt as some of our current government ministers," Shakti snorted.

"We tricked you, cajoled you, stole your wealth," Charlie said.

Rudra told the attendant staff to leave. "Charlie, I've long feared our meeting."

Charlie blurted, "I came to make peace."

As if Charlie had not spoken, Rudra stammered, "After my father's funeral, my…"

Charlie interrupted, "Rudra…." but was cut short as his emotions made him splutter. Embarrassed, he stood, gazed across the river and found himself reliving more lines from Uncle Jack's letter:

'Your father insisted they spend the first week of their honeymoon with the Maharaja. Fatigued, your mother could hardly stay awake at dinner and your father began flirting with an attractive maid. The flirting continued and the busy family didn't notice. On the third afternoon your father and the maid were finally caught by the Maharaja's brother in what had become their habitual bed.

It was a terrible stain on the respectable family's reputation. Carrying a bottle of malt whiskey, the brother went to console your distraught mother and they drank the lot. Her final diary pages state your mother only tasted sex once (poor woman!!!) because she never let my brother Roland take her. This explains why 'your parents' slept in different wings. And why 'your father' continued to be a renowned philanderer, (as you were to discover). You must have wondered about your skin colour. I had always assumed it was an Indian affair within our family lines, rather than your mother's.'

Charlie looked at the distant mountains. Imagine Mother's torture, a painful time from which she never recovered. For days this scene had afflicted his mind, as had the thought that this is what she was going to tell me the night of her death. Father, an Adonis, thought little of his wife, and later, of me.

Mind you, Mother was from the same mould - stiff, aristocratic, little external sign of emotion. It had been bred out of them centuries ago: they had been moulded for leadership. Yet I too am capable of being detached, but immoral like Father? Maybe. Absorbed in Tara's succulent lips recently, to run from my inner void I'd almost gone with anything she desired. Thankfully, like Mother, my vision's broader than pleasure.

In Mother's moral make-up, I was baseborn, fatherless and illegitimate, misbegotten and adulterine! Worthless too in Father's eyes. Yet they played the game of my authenticity to save face; not mine, but theirs. More of Jack's words entered his mind:

'Agitated, ridden with guilt, your mother never gave you love. With all of my own daft love, I tried to be your parent and even the sibling you never had.'

Charlie smiled. I *AM* a chichi! It explains my nose, golden-brown skin and why Mother placed the Mughal miniature above my cot and later over my bed.

Rudra came over, set his hands on the battlements. "My mother revealed your father's antics and said that my uncle, who was a playboy type, spent the night with your mother. Hearing later of your mother's pregnancy, they were uncertain of your parentage. As you can imagine, in our family, Merricott does not make a pleasant sound."

"You have stolen my thunder…." I can't tell if the man is angry or not. He moved off, thinking the worst and laid a hand on Devi's shoulder. "Maharaja, Maharani, thank you for your hospitality."

Devi and Shakti didn't stir.

The two men looked across the river.

A vulture swept over the gardens to land on a dead dog stranded upon a beach, the sky soon filled with spiralling wings. Charlie watched two gardeners walk to the river. The birds took off in a confusion of feathers, flapping low over the wide flow until they gained height. The men used poles to push the carcass into the rushing waters.

Rudra croaked, "What a skeleton we have."

"Hmm," Charlie locked on to Trishul's distant shape.

Devi stood up, "Rudra, we always have choice: to close doors or to open them. Difficulties can be resolved with a meeting of flexible minds."

"Humph." Rudra turned his face back towards the river.

Charlie said tentatively, "What's important is how we deal with events, not always the events themselves."

Rudra snapped, "So your cave has shown you something."

Ignoring the slight, Charlie nodded, "That I know very little."

Seeking to ease the atmosphere, Shakti set her elbows on the table and with her chin resting on her interlinked fingers, asked Charlie which creed he adhered to.

He pondered, "Oh gosh, how to put it. Um, the scientific explanation of the interconnectedness of all things. I hope my actions will be in harmony with nature and arise from a pliant intelligence born of experience and empathy, not dogma."

"That too could sound dogmatic," Rudra scolded.

"Charlie put it well." Shakti stood, went over and curled an arm round her husband's waist. Devi moved closer to Charlie and the four of them watched the vultures follow the half sunken dog downstream. Other scavengers soared over from the distant hills and when the dog was tossed ashore by shallow rapids, the now tiny figures landed and tussled for a place at the meal.

Was the Maharaja's brother arrogant, gentle, wise, cruel? "Rudra," Charlie asked quietly, "what was your uncle like?"

Relieved to break the silence, Shakti gushed, "An intelligent playboy who loved playing pranks. He used to creep down to the twin-domed temple late in the night and make ghostly noises, putting fear into the people - until the temple sadhu caught him!"

Charlie laughed. "I'm afraid I'm rather dull."

Devi shot out, "Our past gives us a basis from which we create our characters."

"How right you are, Devi," Shakti took her hand.

Struggling, Charlie stepped along the crenelated wall, letting his heaving emotions clear. *What a roller coaster life, and since my very inception! I've so often been turned upside down and every major disturbance created new beings: the hurt child, introverted ardent student, determined sportsman, disciplined worker; calculating criminal, cautious fugitive; the bemused seeker and finally now, somebody actually discovering himself. This unstable mass is my ego!*

Tapping his nose, Devi said, "We ought to leave, it's a long drive home."

They were led to a stairwell which landed in a formal reception space. Devi froze before an oil painting. "Who is that?"

"My playboy uncle, Narada," Rudra said.

"Charlie, it's you! Look, your nose!" Devi laughed.

"Humph," burst simultaneously from Charlie's and Rudra's mouths. And they both felt their prominent noses.

Shakti quickly opened a small portal within heavy doors and ushered them out to the courtyard. Making well-mannered comments to meet some vague moment in the future, the two couples said farewell. Devi's car, tiny before the elephant stables, rolled through the time-gnarled portcullis, past the battle-dented red-stone walls and down the grassy defensive slope.

Devi asked the driver to stop upon a rise overlooking the twon. She tugged Charlie outside, "Well?"

Covering his eyes, he blinked, "Before I could even think, this view grew inside me. It epitomised hope ... and Bharat. India, like me, would do well without these two conflicting identities."

Devi ran her forefinger down his hooked nose, "Your temple-dream has withered."

Her delicate touch excited him. "Another expectation dashed."

"Hope, which is what the Western outlook is based upon, is a dangerous thing."

327

"Indians hope for a better rebirth. Hoping to link my past and present, I thought I'd find myself."

"You have! Charlie with a noble nose." She tweaked it.

Bloody Father! Poor Mother. "I must purge this place from me."

"Draw it." She handed him a sketchbook she had bought in the market.

How thoughtful.

He studied her. Relationships *are* more important than ideals. They delve into the world of emotion, which offers up its riches when empathy controls activated thinking. Ideals, so frequently based on suspect logic, or even false notions, often mislead, whereas empathy reaches out to the real world, encouraging us in to sharing life.

"Drifting off again?" Devi tapped the point from which his nose grew.

He found 'Settling' difficult nowadays, however, drawing 'Settled' him so he sat on a rock and studied the view. A stillness soon arose from within, an uncomplicated, clear awareness. His skin tingling with the sun's warmth, Charlie smelt the hot earth, listened to bustling sounds rising from the voluptuous town. His still mind observant, he weighed up the location's values. A heavy pen defined the horizontal Plains. Flowing lines recreated the layered Himalayan foothills; deft flicks caught the river's serpentine passage; angular scrapes set down the town, the fort. A fine pen traced the temple, at this distance sublime upon those rounded rocks. Satiated, his fingers flew to the deceptively delicate peaks.

Watching his final mark, Devi whispered, "Trishul's waves."

What a time he'd had up there chasing visions. And oh! the joy of spring. "This traces my journey from No-Matter to Chota Baba and back to the Mughal miniature."

Her glittering eyes drilled his. "That temple - your lifelong obsession, has it gone?"

Yanked to her presence, he mumbled, "I hope so."

"How easily you let go."

"I've had to, to survive."

328

"Will you turn from the one you love one day?" Those inky pupils expanding.

Hesitating, wanting confirmation but getting only her well defined eyebrows raised, he plunged onwards, "Each of us must work out what makes life worth living." He admired her face, so serene, shining with vibrancy, exquisite in her various moods. "You are right Devi, we are at our best within an empathetic relationship. For me, that is with you."

Pushing him playfully, "For how long Charles/Ewan/Satya/Charlie?"

"You stirred my heart that first day we walked along the Ganga, but I was afraid of being hurt. You have your destiny after all. And I knew I had to change; like my parents I was not bred to properly relate."

Devi exhaled, "Charlie, you're starting to see others as they are, rather than as projections of your own complexes."

"Ouch." Still she isn't revealing how she feels.

Hands on hips, legs astride, she shot, "You know Charlie, the problem with you is you live inside your own life. Me, Indra, the rest of the world, are faint impression you peer at outside the lining of your bubble. Let me tell you, we are different to what you see!"

"Ouch, ouch!" He drank in her spirited eyes, their lucidity zinged his brain, tingled his chest. Oh, HELP! Have I lost her?

"Relationships are about being interested in the other, not assuming the other is there for you!"

"Ouch and more ouch!"

"OK, I'll be kinder." She laughed - a confusing a mix of excitement, trepidation… and more? "Your body language has altered. Ewan was athletically tense, Satya intense, but Charlie is tensile."

He shrugged, "With my conflicting selves grappling to make sense of new truths."

"We shift between one guise and another, rarely settling into who we are. That is humanity's folly."

She's giving nothing away. How do I regain ground lost between us? "Devi, with you I feel alive."

He followed an eagle whose wings appeared to sweep Trishul's distant glaciers. Twenty-million years old those mountains. When they stop rising, the emotions which bind me to Devi will have been lost in the dust of time. Will there even be people left on Earth?

Devi flicked the tip of his nose, "Come out of your cave-mind!"

"Hey!"

She trilled, "Fallen hermits feel pain?"

"If they've a bit of Indian-blue blood," his voice heavily Bollywood.

"Assume your mother's royal fling makes up for your dodgy yogic attainments?"

He wobbled his head comically, "Hopefully it make me a suitable boy?"

Her accent perfectly cut-glass English, "Cheeky Chichi quoting an Indian author."

Catching her waist, he tickled her, "Will you ever stop teasing me?"

Rolling her mesmeric eyes, "Maybe, maybe not," she twisted his nose.

"Ow!"

THE END.

names in the novel explained overleaf....

331

names in the novel explained overleaf....

The Indian reader will realise most personal names in 'Satya's Truths' were not chosen randomly. In common with certain European languages, many Hindu names reflect a particular god's properties. To maintain consistency, most names here-in are related to the god Shiva, who was selected as the god through which Hinduism's structure could best be understood.

EWAN. A Gallic name meaning 'the good, the well born, the youthful'. I chose Ewan because it can easily be mispronounced and also shows how we are made up of multiple personalities to suit each encounter.

SATI. Shiva's first wife who burnt herself because her father didn't respect her husband. She was later to be reborn as Parvati. This myth has inspired the illegal practice of 'Sati' - wives throwing themselves upon their husbands' funeral pyres.

DAKSHA. Sati's father who insults Shiva, but later repents and is forgiven by Shiva.

KAITABHA. A demon at the start of creation, who, fearful of Shiva's wrath, hid in the Creator Brahman's ear.

INDRA. Leader of the minor gods. God of thunderstorms, protector of morality and ethics. He is brave, lovable and seeks Truth.

DEVI. Goddess of light, representing consciousness and discrimination. She represents all women and is the female counterpart to male energy.

TARA. She represents the Tantric Arts. Tara and protects cremation grounds. She is fierce but approachable.

UMA. Another name for Parvati.Parvati, peaceful aspect of Kali. Kali, warrior manifestation of Devi, The Goddess.

GOWRI. The silent power of Shiva. The strong one, the perfectionist who aims to serve those around her.

ANDHAKA. The blind one. A man who tries to abduct Parvati and is killed by Shiva.

CHOTA (Baba). A term of endearment for a child. The delightfully childish one.

SATYA. Truth. (a name rarely used in Hindu families).

SAMBHU. An alternative name for Shiva. He aims to spread happiness.

SHAKTI. The dynamic force of life.

RUDRA. The archer, the wild one, but he is kind and protects against forces of darkness.

NARADA. A playful saint who is continually distracted by life's joys.

The author has asserted his moral right under the Copyright, Designs and Patents Act, 1988, to be identified as the author of this work. Copyright © 2014 Iain Dryden - Original Copyright reference - 284681635 on 3rd June 2014.
A CIP catalogue record for this title is available from the British Library.
Published by Beret Books iaindryden.com
Contacting author - iaindryden.com
Font - Times New Roman / 12
98,713 words
Published in 2018 by FeedARead.com Publishing
First printing (as Indie writer) - November 2014.
2nd reprinting & 2nd edit - April 2018.

Other works by Iain Dryden - @
iaindryden.com/books

Lightning Source UK Ltd.
Milton Keynes UK
UKHW041507230420
362144UK00001B/103